PROTECTOR OF CONVENIENCE

VICTORIA PAIGE

Edited by: edit LLC
Content Editor: Edit Sober
Proofreaders: A Book Nerd Edits & Penelope Croci

Photography by: Wander Aguiar

1

ARIANA DIDN'T MEAN to be a stalker.

She was not this person—a person who couldn't take a hint when several of her calls went unreturned. But the thought of losing her business and letting her employees down had her swallowing her pride. So here she was, stepping out of her vehicle and approaching the woman with the high ponytail.

"Candy?" At the sound of her name, the blonde spun around, face grimacing at the sight of her. Ariana's feet compelled her to run back to her SUV, but she resisted, the faces of her employees flashing before her.

"Ari? What are you doing here?" Candy's smile was brittle, forced. Without waiting for Ariana to answer, she continued walking up the path toward her house.

"I left you messages."

Candy stopped and rummaged through her bag, presumably for her keys. "And I didn't return your calls for a reason." Finding them, she resumed walking toward the door. At least the other woman didn't say she was busy because that would be a lie, judging from the tennis outfit she was sporting.

"Have you talked to the board at least?" Ariana asked.

Candy was on the corporate board that managed the building where Ariana leased space for her business. The two women had standing spa dates every two weeks. She thought if they'd spent time together, naked, and caked with either mud or seaweed, they were considered intimate friends, right?

But at this moment, Ariana felt she was seeing the woman for the first time.

Releasing an impatient breath, Candy finally leveled her with a stare. Ariana's heart sunk at the blast of disdain from the woman's eyes. "The board agrees with building management that having you as a tenant is no longer in its best interest." After delivering that statement devoid of any emotional inflection, Candy started for her house again. Upon reaching her door, the blonde fumbled with the locks before pushing it open. She was in the act of closing it when Ariana tried one more time to plead her case, putting her palm on the wooden panel to prevent it from shutting.

"Candy, please——"

The woman peeked at her from between the crack of the door and its frame and Ariana had never felt more unwanted in her life.

"Don't show up here again, Ari. Otherwise, I'll be forced to call the cops on you for harassment."

And with that ultimatum, the third door that day closed on her. At least this one eased shut and was not slammed on her face like the previous two, but Candy Lovell had been her final hope.

Backing away, Ariana pivoted on a spindly heel and strutted back to her Audi SUV, gathering the last shreds of her dignity along the way and praying she wouldn't face-plant in front of the house.

After getting into a vehicle with a price tag incongruent with her current situation, Ariana drove to her business in Beverly Hills——or should she say, her soon-to-be former place of business. The gnawing pit in her gut rankled and she simply could not comprehend how her life had imploded in the past year. What started as a pissing contest between her brother Raul and Hollywood Mogul Peter Woodward was the stuff of movies. Life imitating art couldn't have been more accurate.

When she entered the lobby of the Wescott building, the front desk guard glanced away upon seeing her, as if a blinding giant scarlet letter was imprinted on her forehead. Paranoia coupled with her frayed nerves made it difficult to discern between normal interaction and being treated like a pariah. So when the elevator opened and it was empty, she breathed a sigh of relief. Ariana needed the respite from judging eyes.

Rejuvenating Vital Infusions occupied a prime location on the fourth floor. Its frosted floor-to-ceiling glass was emblazoned on one side with the name of her company. But instead of the blazing warmth of interior lighting, what greeted her was darkness. A somber reminder that not two weeks ago, she furloughed her employees after building management refused to renew her lease. Citing disruption of peace and danger to the other tenants, they invoked a clause in their lease agreement that allowed the termination of their contract.

She'd been given three weeks to vacate the premises.

A bitter smile etched her features because she had no defense against this. In the days leading up to her brother's death, Ariana was kept in helpless seclusion. Cartel men staked out the building, some of their henchmen even caused a scene in the lobby demanding her whereabouts.

No blood was spilled, but the damage to her reputation was absolute.

She unlocked the door to her clinic and switched on the lights, illuminating the boxes stacked against the wall. The etched grooves in the deep purple and ochre swirls on the carpet hinted that they were once furnished with white leather sofas.

Pain tore through the center of her chest, and her hand flew to her mouth as a sob snagged at her throat. Shaking her head from side to side, trying to rein in the gravity of her loss, her knees buckled.

Ariana sank to the floor beside the reception desk, leaning her back against it for support, and slowly unhooked the straps of her thousand-dollar stilettos, tossing away the shoes.

As the sister of fallen crime lord Raul Ortega, she'd always lived under the shadow of her brother's infamy, but she had been protected.

Before Raul's death, she had a business. People would bend over backwards to do her favors. She was welcome in every social strata, be it the grandeur of a Hollywood star's home or the humble dwellings of an immigrant day worker.

After Raul, she had nothing.

She was shunned by everyone. By the wealthy because she'd become more of a liability than an asset, and as for the rest of them? Who knows?

Fear maybe.

Ariana couldn't blame the people around her. Once a person was marked by a cartel, the stigma was perpetual. Even when Migs—

No. She would not think of him.

He left her.

She was just a job to him.

The pain in her chest rooted deeper, intensified. What this experience taught her was that friends and money were temporary. Ariana had to rely on herself to survive. Her shoulders pulled back and her chin inched up.

She was an Ortega.

She had the blood of a Sinaloan.

They were survivors.

Getting to her feet, she padded to her office. Her desk was the only remaining furniture in this space. Most of the drawers had been emptied. Her business was computerized and left little paper trail by using a cloud service. Pulling open the bottom drawer, a brief smile touched the corners of her lips as she lifted the comfortable flats she kept there.

Putting them on, she walked back to the reception area and took one last look at the surroundings. The movers would come tomorrow and transfer the rest to storage as Ariana figured out how to rebuild her life.

For now, she was leaving the old one behind.

She walked out the door and left the stilettos where they lay.

A LONE FIGURE sat on her front steps.

Ariana lived in an affluent neighborhood in the Brentwood zip code, but her Mediterranean-style house didn't have a gate or a fence. She didn't like them. Having spent much of her childhood wondering what was on the other side of the intimidating walls of mansions, she balked at the idea. Now that the security of Raul's protection was ripped away, she wondered if it was time to get over that hang up.

It was after eight at night, and her foyer lights illuminated her unexpected guest. She recognized Connie—the head nurse at her clinic who held the fort when the CIA had taken Ariana into hiding. The nurse also held things together when Ariana fell ill soon after Raul died. When she recovered and was strong enough to take back the reins of RVI, Ariana was shocked at how bad business had gotten. They'd steadily lost customers since the first fentanyl attack—a casualty of the vendetta between her brother and Woodward. But still, she and Connie tried to regroup and get RVI back in the black until Wescott gave them notice that they were terminating the lease. That destroyed all hope that her clinic could bounce back. Ariana gave her employees a generous payout plus health insurance until the end of this year while she debated restructuring. She wondered if Connie needed more.

Pulling up beside the walkway, she got out of the Audi and rounded the vehicle to meet the nurse. Her smile faded when Connie's angry expression blasted through her.

"Connie?" Ariana approached the other woman warily. "Is everything all right?"

She wasn't prepared when Connie rushed her.

A stinging slap sent her head jerking to the right and a woman's keening wail rang in her ears.

Shock and confusion gripped Ariana, and she barely understood the words of Connie's rapid-fire speech.

"The cartel took Leah! It's your fault! You put us all in danger," the other woman cried. "Why? Why did I ever stay with you when everything was going to hell?"

Ariana raised her arms to ward off another blow, but it never came. She lowered them and saw the horror on Connie's countenance as if she'd realized that she'd attacked her boss.

Connie buried her face in her hands and started to sob. Leah was her fifteen-year-old daughter. A child on the cusp of womanhood. A block of ice settled in Ariana's gut as the implication of what could happen to her at the hands of the cartel.

"Let's go inside," Ariana said gently. "Tell me everything."

"SHE WAS WALKING home from the mall this afternoon when they grabbed her," Connie said when she calmed down. It was unsettling for Ariana to see her head nurse distraught this way. Connie Roque had been with her since the beginning of Rejuvenating Vitamin Infusions five years ago. Ariana had seen Leah grow from a chatterbox child with glasses and pigtails into a beautiful, precocious teen. There were many times she'd seen her friend clash with her headstrong child. As a single parent, Connie had a lot on her plate, but she somehow managed to run RVI with efficiency as well as being on top of her own personal life.

"How sure are you it's the cartel?"

"I'm sure!" Torment glazed Connie's eyes. "Leah's friend was with her and described the tattoo. A bird in flames holding a sword."

Ariana stilled. She'd seen those tattoos on one of the groups who supported Raul. *Águila y Fuego*—Eagle and Fire. "That's a gang tattoo, Connie, not cartel."

"You weren't there!" Connie turned from her and stared out the window, fidgeting with her fingers in a sure sign of anxiety.

Ariana didn't point out that she wasn't making sense, but waited for her to say more. She did.

"When you ran away ..." There was an accusing tone in Connie's voice.

"I was taken into hiding by force."

Her friend's mouth twitched in disdain. "Must be nice."

Ariana sighed. "We talked about it, remember? I gave you a chance to close RVI while I was gone."

"I was trying to keep your business running for you!"

"And I appreciated that. Even when I fell sick, you continued to do so, and you even took care of me. I owe you a lot, Connie."

Her friend seemed mollified to a certain degree. "Anyway, I recognized that tattoo from the guys who were hanging around the clinic when you weren't around. One of them probably saw Leah when she came by after school. That's how they marked her."

"You reported this to the LAPD?"

"Of course! But Leah's friend didn't want to talk. She's scared and she told a different story. Said Leah went willingly into the van. So they're classifying this case as a runaway."

Ariana had heard that the business of human trafficking

had escalated in the Valley ever since Raul died. It was one business her brother did not condone and was one reason he never saw eye-to-eye with the cartel from Tamaulipas—a cartel that until last year wasn't a major player. But it seemed Raul's death triggered its rise to power. Since then, there were rumors that it had acquired the loyalty of the gangs in the Valley.

"Have they made any demands?"

Connie emitted a derisive laugh, but her eyes were close to tears again. "You know this is not kidnap for ransom. It's not something we can pay off."

Both women stared at each other. The fear in their eyes was palpable and having worked with the immigrant population, they were no strangers to the toll of human trafficking.

"What do you want me to do?" Ariana raised her arms up and down helplessly. "If you know someone, I have the financial resources—"

Connie was already shaking her head. "Money won't help. It's who you know. Please, Ari, is there someone who is still loyal to Raul you can ask? The window of opportunity might close very soon and we'll lose track of Leah forever."

Her plea strangled her heart since Ariana didn't have many influential friends left except one. Someone who was in a position to help her with this. The question was if she was willing to pay the price for Leah's freedom.

2

A DESK JOB.

This was essentially what it amounted to as Migs glowered at the spreadsheets on the screen. He was not a damned analyst. Going through the financial statements of a company rumored to be involved in arms dealing in the Pacific Northwest was not the job description he signed up for when he joined the agency.

Granted they did have a reason for sticking him in a corner office in Bellingham, Washington. The agency was not too happy with the very public coverage of the Ortega incident, and if Migs had a doubt how the CIA tortured their operatives who'd gone rogue, that doubt was gone now. He should be grateful they didn't kick him out of the agency or send him to Alaska.

"Waaaaalker." The annoying voice of the resident analyst chimed behind him.

Maybe Alaska was better.

Getting stuck in a cramped office with Bob Taylor could be the worst punishment inflicted on anyone in his opinion. The man in question appeared by his desk and perched at its corner, a bag of chips in one hand, with the other shoving those crunchy bits into his mouth.

The crunchiness was annoyingly loud because Bob was chewing with his mouth open.

Migs ground his molars as a stray piece fell from the man's mouth and landed on his table. How he knew this without looking at Bob, Migs wasn't sure. What he did know was he'd find crumbs on his desk when the man left. It also seemed the analyst was looking to stay and chat.

Fuck.

"So about happy hour—"

"Working—" Migs clipped.

"Aw, come on, man," Bob whined. "You need a break."

"I'm good."

"Look. The spreadsheets will still be there tomorrow, and there's no rush on this. All the focus on this coast is finding that doctor." Bob caught himself. At least the analyst wasn't too dense to know that was a sore subject with Migs.

Charles Bennett was the virologist who sprung Ortega from the CDC's station in LA and disappeared. With the CIA intent on covering their asses in DC, they muzzled the people who could have gone after Bennett—namely Migs and Garrison. The ones currently in charge didn't know shit on how to sort out the conflicting intel. And here they were, eight months later no closer to finding Bennett.

Migs was banished to Bellingham and put on desk duty.

God knew where the fuck Garrison was.

He leaned against the back of his chair, hoping the expression on his face was enough to silence Bob. He didn't have a lot of patience nowadays and his temper had gotten him into trouble before. The last thing he needed was another mark on his record for decking an analyst who wouldn't shut up.

"Guess you're really busy," Bob said in disappointment as he straightened from the table.

Hallelujah.

Migs dipped his chin.

"I'll leave you alone then."

"Appreciate it."

"You don't talk too much, do—" Bob raised his arms in surrender as Migs narrowed his eyes. "I'm going. I'm going. Just saying. You're gonna miss all the fun and cheap beer…" The analyst's voice faded as he walked away.

When the door to the office closed, a strong urge to bang his head on the table overcame him. Migs counted to ten instead, although when it came to Bob, twenty was a more realistic number. His eyes landed on the crumbs on the table, and, letting out a resigned breath, grabbed the folder beside him and swept the particles into the trash bin beside his desk.

His eyes returned to the screen, but he wasn't seeing the numbers. The reminder of Charles Bennett only exposed the raw nerve that had the power to pull his thoughts to the fiery Ariana. She was never far from his mind. He stalked her online, but that only made him feel like shit because he'd witnessed the implosion of her business on social media and there was fuck all he could do about it.

The agency had him on a very tight leash.

He hadn't wanted to leave her, but the alternative was getting charged with insubordination, and he wouldn't put it past the agency to throw him into the brig with a bogus charge like treason. And if he tried to contact her in any way? They'd pull her surveillance which is something Migs wouldn't put past them to keep him in line. If that didn't suck enough, they revoked his level-three security access and left him to request information from Bob when his basic one wasn't sufficient. But despite the gravity of what Migs had done, he knew the CIA valued his skills and connections in Mexico. He just had to be patient, but he was the first to admit that it was wearing thin.

It was almost midnight when he finished his report. He thought about stopping at a bar on the way back to his apartment, but he was brain dead. Doing a job he hated and being forced to do it was a sure fire way to give a person a migraine. As he turned off the office lights, his phone rang with an unknown number.

Staring at it for a beat, he swiped the screen. "Walker."

"Done for the night?"

"Garrison?"

"Miss me?"

Migs sidled up to the window, peeked between the blinds and down the street. That might be a silhouette of a man under a tree away from the street light, but it was hard to tell for sure. The spook was too smart to expose his presence like that.

"I thought they'd sent you to Antarctica."

There was a brief chuckle. "Close enough."

"Does that mean I'm getting out of this town?"

"Meet me at Oxford."

FIFTEEN MINUTES LATER, Migs was striding toward the bench at Oxford Park which was technically closed to the public by nine and made it the best place to meet John Garrison.

Garrison had been his handler in the Ortega op and instead of letting the FBI take over the case when teen stars Theo Cole and Emma Haller got kidnapped, everyone agreed to go rogue to save them.

John was already waiting for him at their rendezvous point, sitting back, an ankle crossed over a knee with both arms over the back of the bench. When Migs sat beside him, Garrison straightened his posture and leaned forward.

"Tell me good news, John."

"Antonio Andrade is on his way to LA."

Migs stiffened. He certainly wasn't expecting that news. "Brave move. Are you going to arrest him?"

"He hasn't done anything wrong."

"You're certain beyond reasonable doubt?"

"According to my sources, he's as hell bent as we are in finding the culprit who'd used one of his labs to manufacture the Z-91."

The Z-91 virus was a weaponized version of Ebola.

There could be only one reason why Andrade was heading to LA. "He's going after Ariana." It took all his self-control to remain seated. There was no way he was staying in Washington now. "Get me out of here."

"Ariana called him."

"What?" Migs couldn't believe his ears. "She hates him."

"Hate is a strong word," Garrison said carefully. "Maybe she wanted to defy her brother's wishes in marrying her off to Andrade."

He didn't like where Garrison was going with this. "What are you implying?"

"Could be she's seeing Andrade in a different light."

"He wants her as a trophy wife," Migs sneered. "Ariana is better than that."

"Would that be so bad given her dicey situation?"

Migs jumped to his feet and glared at the other man. "What the fuck? I thought Andrade forbade the cartel to touch Ariana after they killed Ortega."

"You're talking about the PNO. I'm talking about Carillo."

He froze at the name of a supposedly dormant organization that left John's lips. "So the rumors are true? They're back?"

John nodded. "They've gained the loyalty of major gangs in LA."

Migs scrubbed his face. This was bad news. Eight months not being able to do shit in this hellhole and the cartel he'd paid a high price to put away was back. "They're bad fucking news."

"Don't need to tell me that. Human trafficking has gone up in the Valley."

"Why the fuck am I only finding out about this now?" It sucked to be stuck in *Nowhere*, Washington, stripped of level-three access.

"Your cousin should know."

"You know more than anyone that we don't talk like we used to." Emotion lodged in his throat.

"It wasn't your fault, Walker. Your uncle shouldn't have trusted the Carillos."

Migs looked away. "We should never have used him."

"He was the best asset we had."

He glanced back at Garrison. "Is that what this is all about? My connections to the Alcantara family?" He laughed derisively. "You think they don't suspect?"

Garrison regarded him carefully. Under the glow of the streetlamp it was hard to tell what the spook was thinking. "It's been four years, Walker. It wasn't your place to tell them what happened." He leaned back against the bench again and resumed his initial posture when Migs arrived. "But we're talking about Ariana and Andrade."

Hearing Ariana's name linked with that motherfucker's grated on his nerves. "There's no Ariana and Andrade."

Even in the dim light the arching of Garrison's brow was evident. "There might be. Unless we can find her an alternative solution."

"Solution to what?"

"Let's just say our girl is in a bind."

"Is she in danger?" He was fast losing his cool with the spook's obvious hedging.

"That depends."

"Goddammit, Garrison. Get to the point."

"She wants Andrade to arrange a meeting with one of Carillo's lieutenants—"

"For God's sake, why?"

"Negotiate the release of a friend's daughter, but I believe it's a setup. The man who took over for Carillo had a strong beef with Ortega. He wasn't satisfied with his death and sees an opportunity for revenge."

"I still don't understand." Migs started pacing the short width of the bench when all he wanted to do was drive straight to LA. "Besides, would Andrade be willing to talk to Carillo? Would the PNO even accept this?"

Garrison shrugged. "You know the history of the Mexican cartels. Allies today, mortal enemies tomorrow."

Didn't he know it. He started walking away.

"Where the hell are you going?" Garrison demanded.

Migs turned around but was walking backwards. "Los Angeles. Not wasting time hashing this out. I know you'll send me what I need to know."

He spun on his heel and headed toward the parking lot, knowing more intel was forthcoming from Garrison. He wasn't a fan of wasting time, and he couldn't wait a second longer to get back to Ariana.

3

WHAT POSSESSED her to ask Antonio Andrade for help?

Desperation. He was the only powerful friend she had left. Hell, he was the only friend she had left, and he wasn't even that. More like an acquaintance. An acquaintance who desired her.

Contrary to what was widely believed in their social circles, Andrade had not offered to marry her, but it was certainly the way Raul wanted to spin it. It was for her protection, he said. As for Antonio, she had no doubt he was eyeing her like another of his acquisitions. In what capacity, she wasn't sure.

Standing in front of Spinelli restaurant, she inhaled a fortifying breath. Antonio wanted to pick her up, but she wasn't sure she wanted to give him the opportunity to get inside her house. There was a darkness around him, a ruthlessness she didn't quite trust. A public place with a private room was the best option for this meeting.

Jen, the Maître D, recognized her and smiled. It pained Ariana that, because of the last few weeks, she had to wonder if that smile was genuine or not.

"Thanks for coming back to see us, Miss Ortega." Jen

extended her arm, leading the way. "Mr. Andrade is in the green room waiting for you."

Ariana thanked her and followed the slender woman past the main dining room into a hallway flanked with private chambers. Jen slid the door open to one, and the man waiting inside stood, saturating the room with his presence.

"Ariana, it's been a while." Antonio moved from behind the table and greeted her as Jen discreetly slid the door closed and left. He kissed her on both cheeks before leaning back to survey her. "Beautiful as usual, but you look tired."

She laughed lightly. "Didn't your mother teach you what to never say to a woman?"

"I'm honest." He helped her to a chair before taking the one across from her. "I know you have a lot on your mind."

"And direct to the point."

He waved his hand in a careless gesture. "I don't like to … how do you say it … beat around the bush." He picked up the bottle of wine on the table and started to pour her a glass. Ariana noticed it was from her favorite winery in Napa. An uneasy feeling settled in her chest. As the ruby liquid filled her goblet, she wondered what happened to the initial attraction she felt for Antonio when she first met him at a party all those years ago.

Their server came into the room and started reciting the specials for the evening. Letting Antonio ask the questions, Ariana picked up her glass, taking a sip while stealing a surreptitious glance at her dinner companion.

A man of polish and sophistication, his dark suit clung to his body in a way that left no doubt that it was tailored to his exact specifications. His dark hair was slicked away from his face, highlighting his broad forehead, the sharp angles of his jaw, and the white jagged scar at his temple. It was in stark relief to his tanned face, but it gave him an edginess. His rough upbringing on the streets of Rio was frequently refer-enced in articles about the billionaire. Was this why Ariana shied away from a possible relationship with him? Antonio hid a brutality beneath fine wine and threads.

Unlike Migs, of whom she had an opposite opinion. On the outside, he bore the appearance of a rough and gruff biker thug, but she'd caught glimpses of the tender man beneath his tattooed skin.

Migs appealed to her very much and she entertained fanciful notions about him, until his betrayal left a hollow feeling inside her. An emptiness she still couldn't shake, blaming it on the loss of her brother and not the man she thought lit a fire in her heart.

Antonio's deep blue eyes turned to her. "Are you okay with the prix fixe, Ariana?"

She winced apologetically because she hadn't glanced at the menu yet. Her childhood years taught her not to be picky with food and she ate everything except tomatillo. Giving the set course a once over, she nodded. "That sounds good."

They exchanged small talk about the future of her vitamin infusion clinic, but Antonio wasn't one for idle chitchat as he had warned. He went straight for the jugular.

"The tattoo you described does belong to Águila y Fuego, a gang now affiliated with the Carillo cartel," he confirmed. "You were right that they were loyal to your brother before."

She blew out a breath. "Okay."

"So you want me to mediate between you and Carillo?"

"Yes."

Antonio circled the rim of his glass with his finger. The expression on his face was grave, far from promising.

"You understand that my alliance is with their rival, the PNO ... the Pon—"

"I know who PNO is—" Ariana cut in with some impatience. She was the sister of a crime lord, for heaven's sake, not some spoiled debutante who needed to be shielded from the wolves. "The Ponce-Neto Organization." She was also sure they killed her brother, but Leah's life was more important at the moment. "But as history shows, cartels break up and form new alliances—"

"There's a reason I steer clear of the Carillos."

Ariana might have an idea why, but she waited for him to elaborate.

"Human trafficking is an area I don't want anywhere near my business," Antonio said.

"That's exactly why you should help me. Connie's daughter ... she's only fifteen."

"How do you know she's not already in Tampico."

"Tampico? That's where they take them?"

Antonio nodded, a hint of disgust twisting his mouth. "That's where the buyers come to look at the girls."

"Connie said she was taken three days ago."

"PNO has control of the routes I need for my shipment. I'm not willing to break with them." He paused. "Even for you."

She sat back in her chair and glared. "Then what's the purpose of this dinner? Why even come to LA if you're only going to turn me down?"

"I have an alternative. A proposal."

A wariness stole over her. "I'm listening."

"I can hire people to rescue your friend's daughter, but I need to let the PNO know what I'm doing. This will escalate tensions between them and though they have no problem thwarting the Carillos, they will see this as a favor to me."

"So it's going to cost you," Ariana said. "I have money, but I doubt it'll be enough—"

Antonio's smile sent a shiver up her spine. "I don't need your money."

"I can't be your mistress either." She meant it as a joke, but her voice came out strangled and she grabbed her wine to hide her consternation, but only managed to cough when it caught in her throat.

"Not mistress. My wife."

Her gaze snapped to his and she had to look away at the chilling intensity in them. It didn't make her warm all over. It didn't creep her out either.

It elicited a kind of guardedness she couldn't explain.

An aversion to being drawn back into the world that stole her brothers. She had no doubt Andrade still lived in that world despite the urban facade he projected.

"What? Come on, Antonio." She attempted levity. "We both know you're not the marrying type."

He shrugged. "I'm forty-two. It's time I took a wife."

"But—"

"This would solve both our problems. I need a hostess for my dinner parties. I don't want a socialite or one of those anorexic supermodels." There was a brief flash of heat in his eyes, but it made her want to flee, as if she was prey getting sized up for the kill. "We also come from the same background."

"What about love?"

"What about it?"

"It's important. Don't you think?"

Antonio exhaled a resigned breath. "That is something I cannot give you because I don't know how to love." He spread his hands. "Isn't it more important to be practical? I'm offering you a safe haven from your problems."

"But then you'll be indebted in a way to the PNO." Ariana shook her head. "I'm done with that life and I can't allow you to make such a sacrifice."

He smiled. "I'd say it's a worthy sacrifice."

"Antonio, I just can't. All my life, I refused to follow Raul's path and, deep inside, I know he didn't want it for me either."

Something akin to pity crossed his face. "We can't escape what we are, you know." He nodded at her, then touched the cuff of his suit. "These expensive clothes, they do not change us integrally. That's why I think we'd make a good partnership. We don't forget where we came from."

Ari gave a short disbelieving laugh. "We've only met a handful of times at gatherings. How can you make a life-altering conclusion like that?"

"Gut instinct," he said. He was interrupted from saying more when the server came in with their first course.

An appetizer of a single scallop on its shell covered with a layer of cheese was set in front of them. Their waiter asked if they needed anything else and when both of them said no, he withdrew from the room.

"Where were we?" Antonio picked up his fork and plunged it into the creamy dish releasing its aroma. "Ah yes, I was making my case for why we make the perfect match." For the first time that night, he flashed her a charming smile. It was easy to see how he controlled an empire. He was charismatic and commanding. Fortunately for Ariana, she grew up around men like him. Unfortunately for Antonio, she knew how dangerous it could be to fall for the silver tongue of powerful men.

"I know about your charitable work," he continued. "You give back to those in need. Even when you've attained your dream of having a business in one of the most recognizable zip codes in the world, you never forgot your roots."

"That dream crashed and burned."

"It doesn't need to remain in ruins," he insisted. "I have the resources to help you rebuild elsewhere. Bigger. Better."

"See that's one point where we are so different. Bigger isn't always better."

Antonio forked the creamy scallop into his mouth, a ghost of a smile touched its corners, but he chewed carefully, leaving her statement hanging between them. Ariana sighed and dug into her own dish.

"That's true," he said finally.

"How are we going to make it work? I'm not leaving LA."

"I'm not asking you to. I travel frequently. I can make LA

my home base." He smiled again. "Does that mean you're considering my offer?"

"I don't know, Antonio." There were merits to his offer, but there was a question she couldn't bring herself to ask.

As if reading her mind, he said, "It's a marriage of convenience, but it will be consummated."

A piece of scallop stuck in her throat and she grabbed her goblet to wash it down, resisting a cough, her eyes watering. She glanced at Antonio and he quickly disguised the laughter in his eyes.

"That was blunt ..." she mumbled under her breath. When he was about to say something, she held up a hand, not sure if she could take more of his candor. "I know ... I know ... you get straight to the point. I'll consider your proposal, but right now, it's a lot for me to absorb."

He seemed pleased. "I'll have my lawyer draft a contract."

"A what?" Ariana laughed, nearly spitting out the wine.

"An agreement."

"Oh, the prenup... uhm, I think that's getting too far ahead."

His brows furrowed. "You said you would think about it."

"Yes, but I imagine a prenup happens when I've agreed to your crazy idea."

His frown deepened. "You know, Ariana, many women would consider me a great catch."

"I'm sorry, it's just ..." she pursed her lips, unsure of what to say. What was wrong with her? She had a billionaire proposing marriage except ... it wasn't how she envisioned a proposal of marriage. It was so ... cold and business-like. "I need time to think about it."

"You realize I can't do anything to help your friend until I'm sure."

That almost sounded like blackmail and maybe it was. She stared at Antonio and held his eyes to see if she could bear to be married to a man like him. Including sex in the arrangement might be more of a danger to her than to him. Specifically to her heart, because she could not separate the act from her emotions. But if marriage to him meant saving a young girl from the trenches of human trafficking, then maybe she could redirect her love to something else if he could not give it to her. With his money and influence, she might be able to do more and make a difference. Not just with Leah.

"I understand."

At her clipped response, his nostrils flared and jaw clenched and she spied a glimpse of the ruthless man he was rumored to be.

To her relief, two waitstaff came in. One of them cleared the dishes and reset their place settings, while the other laid down their second course.

As the server explained the wine sauce glazing the braised pork belly dish, Ariana could sense Antonio re-strategizing. With street smarts honed into her at a very young age, Ariana knew this was not a man to be trifled with, nor was he a man she could marry.

So, where did that leave her?

When the two servers left them, Antonio seemed to have regrouped and had slid into the role of charming dinner companion.

Ariana gave him her full attention and as they bantered over dinner, cartels and marriage proposals were never mentioned again, but they weighed heavily in the back of her mind.

"Run it by me one more time," Garrison said from the driver's seat. Their black Suburban was parked on the street across from the Spinelli restaurant. "You're just going to ambush Ariana at the entrance?"

"Yup," Migs replied.

"With Andrade standing right there?"

"I don't see a problem."

John snorted. "That's why you suggested I come along. So I can run interference with his bodyguard."

"What's the matter, Garrison?" Migs mocked. "Task beneath you?"

"I wouldn't miss that meeting for the world."

Migs didn't reply as he received a text from inside the restaurant that Ariana and Andrade were leaving. With his restored access to high-level agency data crunchers and analysts, it was simple to find where Andrade made reservations for dinner. Using its employee roster for a background check made it easy to pinpoint which one to bribe with three hundred bucks. Even by LA standards that was nothing to sneeze at for the little bit of information required in return.

"I mean you're the last person on earth Ariana wants to see," Garrison added.

"Thanks for the heads up, Captain Obvious." Was he worried Ariana wouldn't talk to him? Not really. Migs admitted his knuckle-dragging bullheadedness had its merits. It was a frustration Ariana had with him, but he wondered if she secretly enjoyed their clash of wills. It was a look in her eyes, a look that almost made him forget his job. He lost track of the number of times he wanted to grab her and kiss her. That Latina temper of hers …

"Christ, you better wipe off that dopey grin," Garrison muttered. "They're coming out."

Migs realized he was indeed smiling. He cleared his throat and straightened in his seat, watching a full-figured woman exit the restaurant ushered by a tall distinguished gentleman who had a hand on the small of her back.

"Easy there, tiger."

Ignoring Garrison's quip, he unclenched his fists and grabbed the handle of the door, surprised he didn't crack it, and shoved out of the SUV. He stalked toward the restaurant.

He was halfway across the street when Ariana's mouth gaped open when she recognized him. Andrade, who was at her side, stepped in front of her as if to protect her.

The gesture incensed him, but he had to play this smart and not let his hot-headedness get in the way of Ariana speaking to him.

That, plus he didn't want to be the sputtering idiot in this scene that would contrast him with the calm and collected way the other man was eyeing him.

"Step out of the way, Andrade," Migs said softly when he reached them.

"Ariana doesn't want you here," Antonio replied.

The woman in question went around Andrade, glaring briefly at the businessman before concentrating her furious gaze on Migs. "What are you doing here?"

"Heard you need help."

"Oh, let me guess, your employer is still keeping tabs on me," she fumed.

"Employer?" Andrade said, a derisive smile curling his mouth. "Interesting."

"Stay out of this," Migs stated more forcefully.

"Problem here, *chefe*?" A stacked man who was a head shorter than Migs appeared beside them.

Migs glanced behind the newcomer and watched Garrison lean back against a Mercedes sedan.

"Nothing I can't handle," Andrade told his bodyguard. "Maybe you want to keep our friend company." He nodded toward Garrison. "Make sure he doesn't steal anything from our car ... hmm?" The billionaire's eyes connected back with Migs. "Your employer, I presume—Miguel Alcantara Walker."

They stared at each other, nose to nose, both men matching up at six-three, their builds similar, but hard to tell for sure in case Antonio was hiding some padding beneath his stuffy suits.

"See. I know about you too," Andrade said. "You're not the only one with resources."

"If they're any good, then you know you shouldn't be in the U.S." Migs shot back. He was bluffing of course. Garrison confirmed the Brazilian was clean but judging by the narrowing of the other man's eyes, Migs hit his mark.

"I haven't broken any laws," Andrade said.

"Doesn't matter." The smile Migs gave him was shark-like. "If you did your research right, you know we can make up shit."

"Excuse me," Ariana interrupted. "I don't have time for this cockfight. I'm going home." Without waiting for their reply, she spun on her heel and strutted away from them.

"Ariana," Migs growled and made to go after her.

Andrade grabbed his arm and Migs finally lost his temper and pulled back to punch him, but Garrison was there, yanking him off the Brazilian and pointed a warning finger at the bodyguard who hurried back to help his boss.

Suddenly, Ariana was in his face. "Oh my God. Were you going to hit him?" she yelled, her body inches from his.

His own came alive. "Ari—"

"You left!"

"I had no choice." Why did it sound lame this time? Seeing the hurt in her eyes made him bleed, made him feel lower than a sewer rat. He betrayed her when he'd promised to keep her safe, and now she was in danger from the cartel. He needed to make this right.

"And you have such nerve simply showing up here, ambushing my date."

His jaw clenched. "A date?"

"I've asked Ariana to be my wife," Andrade said as if he was talking about the weather.

Ariana turned her displeasure on the other man. "Not helping, Antonio."

A boulder dropped in Migs' gut and grew into his lungs. It

took every effort not to snap at Ariana. "What. Is. He talking about?"

"Fuck," Garrison muttered as his grip tightened on Migs' arm.

Ariana averted her gaze. "Can we not talk about it here?"

"Agreed," he clipped and extended his hand. "Keys."

Her eyes flew to his. "What?"

"I'm driving you home."

"Not happening," Andrade snarled. "You don't owe him anything, Ariana."

"Listen, motherfucker—"

"Stop!" Ariana got between them again but was addressing the Brazilian. "I need to talk to him."

"You don't owe him an explanation."

"He saved me from the cartel. Give me time to think, okay?" Ariana pleaded.

Think about what? His proposal? If Migs wasn't in such a precarious position with Ariana, he'd drag her away right this fucking second.

Andrade's eyes flicked over her head to his. Ice-cold blue. This man would smother her spirit. No way was Migs allowing that to happen.

"Okay, Ariana." Antonio lowered his head to kiss her on the forehead.

Forget dragging Ari away, Migs was this close to throwing her over his shoulder and carrying her off like a caveman.

When she turned to him, the exasperated look she cast him didn't help the surge of possessiveness he had to contain, so he clenched his fingers. She fished out her keys from her purse and held them out to him. Migs grabbed them as she stalked off.

Garrison's hold eased on his arm and they exchanged looks, an understanding.

John was going to keep an eye on Andrade while he made his case with Ariana.

4

ARIANA WAS SEETHING.

Her nerves, already frayed under Antonio's scrutiny, were lit up like a Christmas tree. Her skin prickled, feeling every movement, every hungry look he shot her way. There was an overwhelming urge to scream at Miguel, but she didn't want him to know how much his leaving hurt her.

She did not trust him. She had to remind herself of that.

But it wasn't just Migs. She had little faith in people nowadays.

But that didn't lessen her awareness of him. The way his gaze devoured her when he opened the door of the SUV for her to get in. The way he rounded the vehicle, eyes always watching the surroundings, always vigilant. Familiar actions giving Ariana a sense of déjà vu to the time he'd spent as her bodyguard. A time when she fancied being receptive to the attraction between them.

Until his betrayal.

A reminder of that betrayal plunged sharp pain straight into her heart. It made it difficult to breathe.

He got into the driver's seat and started the vehicle. She didn't bother telling him where to go because she didn't trust herself to speak. He knew where she lived anyway. She was sure that even if she changed residences, he had ways of finding out. They certainly knew about her predicament. She was relieved as well as bitter about it, and she was annoyed at herself for the conflicting emotions this man invoked in her.

Migs pulled the Audi into traffic. "Is it true he asked you to marry him?"

She bristled, but why deny it? "Yes."

"And?"

"And nothing. I said I would think about it," she tossed back.

"Why?"

"Why not?" She knew she was mocking him, but she couldn't help it. The complicated feelings between them needed an outlet. What they shared wasn't a mere bodyguard-protectee relationship. She understood the difference because Raul had assigned her bodyguards over the years, especially when he was in a power play with other criminal organizations. None of those came close to what blossomed between Migs and herself. In the beginning it was business as usual. Migs kept a watchful distance, but all that changed during the charity drive at the clinic, when he insisted on getting her out and took her into a safehouse. For three days, they existed in a bubble where both their walls came down. Nothing happened, not even a kiss, but their friendship became intimate. There was a promise of something more until Garrison showed up and it was revealed that Migs worked for the CIA.

The CIA.

Ariana knew there was more to Migs than her brother's hired thug. She'd asked him about the tattoos on his arms because that had been her first suspicion that there was more to him. There was ink, and there was expensive ink. Having been around the Hollywood elite herself she could spot exceptional body art.

"You deserve better than Andrade," he growled.

Ari couldn't help raising a brow. "You know he's a billionaire, right?"

He cast her a sharp glance before returning his eyes on the road. "You never cared about money, so that's not it. And you don't want to be a trophy wife either. That's not the life you're meant to have."

"What is this, Miguel? You've known me for what, six weeks? And the first four you kept your distance, barely speaking to me, and now, suddenly you're an expert on Ariana Ortega's dreams and aspirations."

"I know you," he said roughly.

"No, you don't."

"I know you," he repeated, more insistently. "More than you realize. I kept my distance, but I watched you. I studied you. I know how you care about the immigrants who come into this country. It doesn't matter if they are from Mexico or Ukraine. If they've been abused, if they are being kept here by force, you want to find ways to help them."

"It's been eight months since you've seen me. A lot has happened. I'm not that person anymore. I'm powerless," her words ended on a barely audible whisper.

"But the heart to help is still inside you," he said just as quietly. "You were one of the reasons why Raul never condoned human trafficking and why the Carillo cartel wanted him gone."

She stiffened when he mentioned the Carillo organization. "Can you offer an alternative?"

"What's he offering you?"

"He's going to get Connie's daughter back."

She watched his knuckles whiten over the steering wheel. "And the answer is marriage to him? Bullshit."

"He said he's going to have to solidify his alliances in order to make this happen."

"What alliances and what's going to happen?"

"I don't feel comfortable telling you these things," Ariana

said. "I know who you work for, remember? I don't want him to get in trouble because he wants to help me."

"Fair enough," Migs gritted. "What if I tell you we have eyes on your friend's daughter?"

"What?" she whispered.

"Unlike Andrade, we have no patience for human traffickers."

"She's still here? Where?" Ariana and Connie were so scared that they'd already taken her out of the U.S.

"In the Valley. We have people positioned to move in, but Garrison isn't clear if it's just a bait."

"I'm not following you, Migs."

"Did Raul leave you anything to safeguard?"

"There were a couple of documents in his safe, but I had to surrender them to the LAPD."

"Then they're in the evidence locker," Migs muttered as though he was talking to himself, then glancing over to her again, he said, "We have reason to believe that Carillo has Doctor Bennett—the virologist who helped your brother escape."

"And it has some connection to me?"

"That's what Garrison and I are trying to figure out." The corner of his mouth twisted into a sneer. "Andrade's offer to help isn't all that benevolent, Ari. Carillo has something he wants, too."

"The virologist?"

"Yes. This has something to do with the experiments done in the CDC lab while your brother was there."

"Well, if this person helped my brother escape, then wouldn't he know where it is or have it?"

"I don't have all the intel yet, but Garrison and I are back on the case and we're thinking your brother had custody of some of the research and stashed it somewhere."

Even though she was sitting in the car, a lightheadedness gripped her. "What? Where?"

"Where are all your things from Vitamin Infusion?"

"In storage. Some are in my house."

"Good. Let's go there first."

WHEN THEY ARRIVED at her house, Ariana was appalled to see the front door open. Another vehicle was in her driveway, and the red-haired guy she knew as Hank Bristow approached their vehicle.

Migs barely stopped the car when she got down from the Audi. "What's going on?"

Hank nodded to her in greeting, but didn't answer her, his eyes riveted on Migs. The two men met up in front of the Audi and engaged in hushed conversation, leaving Ariana fuming. She turned away from them and hurried to her front door, anxious at what could be awaiting her inside. A giant of a man emerged from her house, one she wouldn't want to meet in a dark alley if he was a stranger.

But she did know Levi James—another associate of Migs.

"Miss Ortega." The way the Irish-Samoan man said her name, with pity and regret, tightened the bow-string tension holding her emotions together.

She entered her house and that tension broke.

Drawers on the floor, cabinet doors flung open. Her lungs expanded as she struggled to contain the sob rising up her throat.

The gilded antique sofa set she'd won at a charity auction was torn into shreds, its upholstery and pillows ripped open, feathers and foam scattered on the accent rug. She walked over to the bureau, her eyes taking in the overturned oriental jar at the corner.

Everything that could be torn was shredded. And anything that could be broken was smashed, including her photo with Raul and Jose. The last photo taken when Jose was alive.

"Fuck." Miguel's curse vaguely registered in her ears.

The world receded and a tunnel engulfed her. All she could see was the faded photograph that lay among the shards of glass. She bent over and reached for it, shaking the chips off, and then straightened.

A finger traced the outline of Jose and then Raul. She was fifteen in the photo. Jose was twenty and Raul was twenty-six, already a second-in-command of the cartel in Tijuana.

"Ari ..."

"I know you guys didn't do this," she whispered, still staring at the photo. "Will this ever end? Is it my life they want?"

"Don't say that!" Migs said fiercely. She could feel the heat of his body against her back, but her body shuddered with a chill radiating deep within her. It was as if she was standing on a precipice of a cliff, waiting for someone to push her over and end her misery.

She was raised Catholic. It had been ingrained in her that suicide would lead her straight to hell, but there were times she believed that getting hunted down by the cartel was even worse. Their brutality was legendary and falling into their hands would indeed be the worst kind of hell.

Ariana turned and faced Migs and was taken aback by his feral eyes, the hard set of his jaw. If Ariana wasn't able to express anger, he was doing it double-time on her behalf.

"Can you honestly say, Leah wouldn't be in this predicament if I'd died with my brother?" she asked.

Migs flinched at the mention of her dying. Ariana admitted she could be dramatic. It had been the story of her life from the start—full of drama. She didn't know how to live without the chaos. She tried, even shunning Raul after Jose died. But her surviving brother worried about her and reeled Ariana back into his world, whether unwittingly or not, in his attempt to shield her.

Resentment bubbled up inside her. If Raul took a different path and didn't get caught up with the gangs, where would she be now? Ariana shook her head in self-deprecation. "I'm blaming Raul. See what a bad sister I am? He's dead and here I am wishing he was alive so I could yell at him for days."

"You're very forgiving," Migs clipped.

She canted her head in question.

"I'd be wishing he were alive so I could kill him all over again."

"Oh," Ariana said. "But why do you hate him? He was just a job for you."

"Why do I hate him?" His hands grabbed her shoulders, giving her a slight shake. "You have to ask?"

"Migs—"

"Because of his selfish ambition, he put you in danger! Because of his greed, he put you in the cartel's crosshairs," he gritted. "Now even in death, you're still a target because of him. And you ask me why?"

"But—"

"No buts. I'd drag your fucking brother from his damned grave, just to kill him again. And fuckin-again."

Ariana crossed her forehead and chest. "It's bad to speak ill of the dead."

His eyes lightened and a slight smile curved his mouth. "You started it."

"Not to the extent you did. I just wanted to scream at him."

The back of his hand caressed her face. She didn't shy away. In fact, she wanted to lean into the comfort of it, but she remembered she wasn't supposed to trust him. Migs came back because his people needed something from her. As if deciphering the conflict in her features, he lowered both arms and took a step back. Just then, movement from the door drew their attention.

Ariana could feel the waves of displeasure roll off Miguel as she lifted her gaze and was shocked to see Garrison and Antonio. Migs invaded her personal space again, and she felt like a lone fire hydrant in the dog park, judging by how the man beside her and Antonio traded scathing looks across the room.

Then Antonio turned his attention on her wrecked house and fury darkened the businessman's usual stoic face.

"Did Carillo do this?" Antonio was looking at Migs.

"You don't know?" Migs replied. "Didn't you tip them off that you were coming into the country?"

The other man's jaw tightened. "I didn't expect them to do this." He walked into the house as Garrison followed behind him.

"You told me you wouldn't negotiate with them until you had my answer," Ariana said.

"It's not unusual to make exploratory talks."

"Do your friends at the Ponce-Neto cartel know this, Andrade?" Migs asked. "Or did Carillo do a pre-emptive strike because they know you're just stringing them along and planned to double-cross them in the future?"

"They would be suspicious anyway. Once they heard that I was in LA," Antonio said.

"But you tipped them off," Migs insisted. "You did that because you knew how they would react. If Ari came home to this, she would have no choice but to accept your fucking proposal. For protection."

Feeling left out, and especially since it had everything to do with her, she glared at Migs. "You don't know that." Then she turned her glare on Antonio. "Is this true? Did you bait them?"

The businessman pressed his mouth together and glowered at Migs.

"Oh my God. All the while that you were indulging me in expensive food and my favorite wine, you were stabbing me in the back."

"That was not my intent," Antonio objected. "I did not

know they would have the audacity to carry out such a provocative response. Not while we were at dinner."

"Sure… " her ex-bodyguard taunted.

"I've had enough of your side-comments, Walker." Antonio slitted his gaze.

"Wanna take this outside, Andrade? Heard you were quite the scrapper back in the day."

"Again, with this cockfight." Ariana stomped a foot. "Enough. Both of you are like boys fighting over a toy, and I am sick of being everyone's punching bag. Tell me what you all are after. I will tell you what I know, so you can all leave me the hell alone."

"Can't do that, Ari," Migs said. "From what's gone down here, I'd say Leah was just a diversion. The new cartel capo wants two things, revenge against your brother, but they're also looking for something."

A knot formed in her throat. "Who did you say it was?"

"Benito. He ousted his cousins and now has control of the organization."

John Garrison who had been quietly—or rather blatantly enjoying this exchange—straightened from his lean near the door and approached their circle. "Has Migs informed you of the missing virologist?"

"The one who helped my brother escape? Yes," Ari responded.

"Your brother was smart. He knew he could be betrayed. Prior to infecting himself with Ebola, he'd prepared himself to survive it." Garrison looked at Antonio. "Care to elaborate?"

"My company was one of the frontrunners in producing a vaccine," Antonio said. "Unbeknownst to me, another lab was weaponizing the virus. Long and short is, the Z-91 and the modified vaccine can be used to produce the ultimate antiserum."

"So whoever has the virus and the cure …" Ariana started.

"Has a very valuable weapon on his hands," Antonio finished.

"Valuable," Ariana scoffed. "How can you let this happen?"

A muscle ticked at Andrade's jaw. "I'm not shirking responsibility. That is why I need to fix this."

"In short, you fucked up," Migs said. "But you're not using Ari as a pawn."

"Do you enjoy twisting my words, Walker? You want me to look like the villain of this piece?" Antonio fixed his gaze on her. "Walker wants to turn you against me, but we need to fix this together."

"Because my brother started this ..." she whispered in defeat.

Miguel's massive body shifted in front of her, blocking her view of Antonio.

"You. Are. Not. Using her." If Miguel's fury was an eddy before, it was a tsunami now.

"You have a better answer? The cartel won't leave her alone."

"We already know that," Migs snarled. "We can protect her."

Ariana laid a placating hand on his arm. Her emotions were as confused as ever, and she was no stranger to manipulation.

"Oh, and after you get what you want, you'll leave her to the wolves, just like you did when Raul died," Antonio taunted.

"That's not gonna happen," Migs snapped. "I have a plan."

"The best thing for her is to come with me to Brazil," Antonio said. "Wait for things to calm down. Think, Ariana. I'll have a security team to protect you. You want to open a beauty business, Brazil is the place to do it. People from all over the world flock there to have world-class plastic surgery."

Ariana couldn't argue with him there, thinking of the words 'Brazilian butt lift.' Not that she needed assistance with her posterior. A corner of her mouth lifted.

"You're not seriously thinking about this, are you?" Migs exploded, clasping her arm and spinning her around to face him, the thundercloud in his face immediately chased away all thoughts of frolicking in skimpy bikinis on the beaches of Rio de Janeiro.

"Calm down, Walker," Garrison warned.

"Of course not," she snapped.

"Unhand her," Antonio snarled.

"Ari …" With his face backlit, Migs eyes were dark and more sinister, and yet she wasn't afraid of him. She was, however, infuriated at his bossiness.

"Stop, Miguel. Just stop! Can't a woman just stop and think?"

"You can't stay here," Antonio said. "I have the penthouse at the Westin. It has several—"

"I don't think so, pal. Who do you have with you? Quasimodo?" Migs said.

"I have contacts in security companies. I can hire more to protect her. They can have men for me within the hour."

"Don't waste your time. I've got her."

The scream inside her was growing louder and louder. She had to pick one of them. As it was, she was a sitting duck, and she changed her mind about being better off dead. This whole deal with the cartel was pissing her off. But in order to thwart those *pendejos*, she needed to survive first. And she knew her chances were better with Migs. She didn't know Antonio that well, and she still wasn't sure if he deliberately set her up.

"Migs is right. I'm going with him," she said.

"Ariana …" Antonio's jaw slackened, and for the first time, vulnerability flashed in his eyes.

"I can't marry you, Antonio."

The man's mouth flattened. "Don't make rash decisions. I can still make you untouchable from Carillo."

"How about—" the tattooed biker started.

Ariana planted herself in front of Migs, glaring up at him. "Enough. I'm handling this."

She grabbed Antonio by his arm and led him to a corner, all too aware of Miguel's eyes on them. Fuck that bossy man. He could give her this.

When she was sure they were out of earshot, she tilted her chin up to Antonio. "I don't think we're right for each other."

"I see," he said, before flicking his eyes over her shoulder. "And this has nothing to do with Walker showing up?"

"No." That was the truth. Well, partly.

Antonio's eyes narrowed. "There's something between the two of you. I'm not blind, Ariana."

"He was my bodyguard …"

"And nothing else?"

"I'm more comfortable with him. This is such a confusing time for me. I don't want to regret marrying you."

"If you don't want marriage, would you agree to be my mistress?"

Ariana had to laugh at that. His bluntness. "No."

"I don't give up easily," he said. "You don't see our union the way I do. We'll be good for each other. We understand how the world works behind the walls of the perfect Latino family."

He raised his hand and brushed her cheek the way Migs did earlier, but although he didn't make her flinch, she didn't want to lean into him. How interesting. Two attractive men and yet totally different responses.

"No, we don't. You don't require love—I do."

His face shuttered. "And you think you'll find that with Walker?"

"Migs is just a friend. I'm not sure we're even that right now." Ariana didn't know if she could ever trust him with her emotions, but deep inside, she knew she could trust him with her life. "I have no expectations of him. I have no expectations of my life except to survive this mess my brother left me."

Antonio nodded. "Don't forget, I'm a phone call away. Anything you need, Ariana." He stepped back and, without saying another word, turned around and headed for the door.

"I'll keep in touch," Garrison called as the businessman passed him.

Ariana only released a sigh of relief when Antonio was out the door. Now they had to focus on getting Leah back, and then as though the universe heard her, Bristow appeared at the entrance with Connie.

Ariana rushed over to her friend, anxiety surging at the look on the woman's face. "What's wrong?"

Connie handed her a scrap of bloodied fabric. "This was in a package delivered to my apartment. That piece of cloth is from Leah's blouse." Her voice trembled. "There's a note. A demand."

"What do they want?"

Her friend's eyes pleaded with hers. "You."

5

"I'm not liking this."

Miguel's voice came into the earpiece they'd outfitted on her. She parked in front of a house in San Fernando Valley. The note with Connie had a phone number instructing Ariana to call. She was given directions to this address that, thankfully, was the same one Miguel's team was staking out.

"It's me they want, and they said to come alone."

"You could've bargained."

"You know they won't fall for a bodyguard coming with me. They're going to make you. If Antonio did, then they probably have a file on you already," she said. "And you have the thermal signatures, you know where everyone is."

A frustrated breath came out loud and clear in her ear.

"I'll be careful," she added. "Besides, Garrison said it'd be good to get a feel for what they want from me."

"And Garrison also said we're not sure if the blood on that fabric belongs to Leah." There wasn't enough time to run DNA and Ariana wasn't willing to wait.

"You've been overruled, Walker," the man they were discussing came over the line. "Now stick to the plan. Connie has received proof of life. You can step out of the car, Ariana."

Showtime.

This wasn't her first rodeo and, as she opened the SUV door and stepped down, she recalled the time she offered herself in a swap for the teen stars Raul had kidnapped. But this case was different. Back then, she knew her brother would never harm her. She didn't have those reassurances from the men in the house.

The CIA didn't know who they were with certainty. The ransacking of her house didn't prove they were looking for something, it could also be their way of tormenting her. A way to make her life miserable. As if kidnapping Leah wasn't punishment enough. She could see the fear in Miguel's eyes, fear he attempted to hide with his grumblings about being a bad idea, but his unspoken words were clear.

What if they shot her on sight?

She'd changed out of her dinner clothes and wore jeans and a loose blouse. She'd layered a camisole underneath to hold in the wire and wore sneakers. Better to run with just in case. She should be baking in this warm weather, but her fingers were like ice.

"No sniper in sight," Bristow reported. "She should be fine. Go ahead, Ariana."

Gulping back the rising nausea in her throat, she made her way to the house. The men were talking in her ear, and as much as she wanted to listen, all she knew was Leah was in the back of the house and Levi was leading a team to get her out. Migs and Garrison were hiding in the shadows, ready to swoop in and grab her in case things went wrong. Nadia Powell, a woman she'd never met but was familiar with, was handling surveillance. Powell also planted an insect drone inside the house.

When Ariana reached the door, it opened without her knocking. They must have been watching her on a camera because Bristow or Powell would have alerted them if someone was at the window.

She didn't recognize the man before her. He was not that much taller than Ariana with a thick mustache over his mouth. His hand clamped over her biceps and yanked her in, slamming the door.

She could hear Migs cursing in her ear.

"Miss Ortega."

"Where's Leah?" she asked.

The man's fingers squeezed her arm. "You don't ask the questions. We do." The man felt her up for weapons or a wire. The one they put on her was like tape and could be hardly sussed out. She still held her breath when Mustache Man paused around her torso and then she gritted her teeth as he squeezed her breasts lingering there, the lecherous look in his eyes made her skin crawl. But she was doing this for Leah. Poor Leah.

"I want to see her. Make sure she's okay." They sent Connie a video of her daughter in front of the TV switched to the ZNN news channel to show proof that she was alive and okay. At the man's glare, she insisted. "Or I'm not saying anything. Your choice."

"*Perra,*" the man spat. He dragged her along a narrow hallway, and she noted the number of men with guns in tow. There were four. Ariana wasn't familiar with the type of weapons but they looked like the high-powered ones that the military used. The cartel was better equipped than most military or police in Mexico.

She was hoping Powell's drone was getting all this even if Garrison's team already had an idea of what they were up against.

They arrived at the last room and Mustache Man opened the door and that was when she caught sight of his tattoo, but Ariana's attention was quickly drawn to the girl in the room sitting on the bed watching TV. It looked like any other young girl's room complete with frilly bed sheets.

"*Tia* Ari," Leah exclaimed and flew off the bed, but her captor pushed her back and shut the door and locked it from the outside.

Reeling from what she saw, not able to reconcile Leah's better-than-expected condition to the bloodied scrap of fabric Connie had shown them, a niggle of doubt took root in her gut. It sprouted like a weed and wrapped around her lungs, squeezing it tight.

The smirk on Mustache Man fed that doubt, and the cursing over her earpiece escalated her flight response.

"What the fuck," Migs muttered. "Did you get that Powell?"

"Roger that."

"Who's with Miss Roque?"

Connie. Did she set her up? That wasn't possible.

As she walked back with her host to the living room, she glanced at the door.

"Can you tell me what you need, so we can get this done?" she asked.

"What's the matter, somewhere you need to be?" The smirk turned into a malicious leer.

"Let Leah go. You have me."

"Not yet."

"You were the ones who broke into my house."

The man didn't admit anything, but Ariana noted two of his men gathering around her.

She swallowed hard. "I don't know what you were expecting to find."

"We don't know either," the man answered and then everyone burst out into raucous laughter. Then Mustache Man turned serious and whipped out a knife, holding it up.

Ariana stepped back, but the other two grabbed her from behind and forced her into a chair.

She gave a frightened yip but tried not to scream. "Why don't you just tell me what you want?"

"Your brother—"

"He's dead."

The tip of the knife touched her chin, then the cold blade flattened against her cheek. "Your brother Raul had mine killed."

"Because of him we lost our other brother," Ariana said bitterly. The voices in her earpiece had grown eerily silent. Did it fall out? It was a transparent filament that was hard to feel or see.

"So get in line," she added bitterly. "I know what my brother was, what he did. So if killing me will give you peace, go ahead." Her chin inched up even as she gnashed her teeth to prevent them from chattering.

The glint of the knife caught her eyes as the man sat on the coffee table in front of her, and that was when she noticed a tray of buccal swabs in a test tube. She'd seen those before for DNA test kits, the ones that tested your ancestry and biological predispositions. Beside it was a row of syringes.

"What's that?" she whispered.

The words barely left her mouth when the lights went out, windows exploded, and the door flew inward. There was a loud bang, and the room filled with smoke, and somewhere around the house she heard more crashing sounds, shouting and screaming, rounds of gun shots that went suddenly silent.

Crying.

"Leah!"

Someone grabbed her under the arms and lifted her. She bounced on a hard shoulder and then they were moving. The muffled pops of silenced weapons sounded in her ear. Her eyes watered with the smoke and then suddenly there was fresh air and she inhaled much needed oxygen.

"I have her," Migs yelled.

"Leah is secure," a man who sounded like Levi said.

"Migs, put me down!" Ariana managed to sputter despite the jarring ride on his shoulder.

"Not yet," he muttered, and she wasn't sure if he was talking to her. Her head spun as she was set upright and bundled into an SUV. She rubbed her eyes as the driver door opened and Migs got in beside her. A water bottle appeared beneath her nose. "Use this."

"EXFIL now, guys," Powell's voice came over the wire telling them to get out of there. "The other two groups I've been watching have mobilized."

"ETA?" Garrison demanded.

"Three minutes."

Migs started the engine and the vehicle slowly started rolling forward.

"You okay?" he asked, voice rough.

Ariana finished dousing her eyes and blinked a couple of times, finally able to focus on him. "Yes."

"I'll get you out of here, okay?"

"Where are we going?"

"Not sure yet."

Migs pulled the vehicle forward from the narrow alleyway between two houses and carefully eased onto the road, presumably not to draw attention.

Garrison's voice came over the wire. "Head to Assassin's Hill."

THEY WERE ON THE 101, but they were not clear of the cartel yet. Valley PD had swarmed the house according to Nadia, so whatever evidence had been there was toast. Bristow was hanging two cars behind with Garrison further out.

"Any sign we're being followed?" Migs asked.

"I thought we had a tail earlier, but it took the exit," Bristow said.

"Fuck. Should we go to a different safe house?"

"Dammit. Let's head to the one in Burbank," Garrison ordered. "Stay on this secure line."

Normally, Migs would be all gung-ho about confrontation, but he had Ariana with him and that made a huge difference. It always had. He didn't want a single hair on her head harmed. And after the jaw-breaking danger she found herself in tonight, he wanted to take her far, far away from this. Her immediate safety was priority, but he needed a long-term solution to make her off limits to the narcos. Migs was no stranger to cartel brutality, and he still couldn't wrap his mind around what could have happened if they hadn't rushed that house when they did. The moment Ariana's captor pulled out a knife, Garrison called the raid. Forget what other information they could've gotten. Migs wasn't about to stand by and have Ariana lose a finger and John knew that.

Five minutes into their journey on the freeway, Bristow's voice crackled on their secure channel.

"You have a tail. The one that just joined us from the last exit. Follows your lane changes. Explorer."

"Dammit," Migs muttered.

"I think there's another one behind me too," Bristow said. "Confirm, Garrison?"

"Dark Nissan Sentra?" John asked.

"Yes."

"Have my eyes on it. If you noticed, then it's possible."

"BOLO on relays," Migs said. "These guys are notorious for it."

"Roger that," both men confirmed.

He hoped Carillo was treading carefully because Garrison was doing it as well. The agency was known for indirect action, preferring to let the cartels get rid of each other. The last incarnation of the Carillo was squashed four years ago. Benito wasn't even a prime player then. The CIA and DEA thought they'd gotten rid of every head of the hydra. But as the history of the narcos went, you could never get rid of them completely.

As long as there was a demand for drugs, there would always be greedy people willing to provide them. There would always be a struggle for power, control of the *plazas*—turf wars that controlled the drug routes—were never ending. One could say the U.S. was responsible for causing the ongoing bloody cartel war when they pitted one turf against the other and weakened the position of the godfather who united the *plazas* under one organization. That started the cartel wars, and no one—not the Mexican government nor the United States—knew how to fix the mess.

Migs eyes narrowed as the vehicle in question sped up.

"Explorer is pulling up on Ariana's side," Bristow said.

"I see that." Migs wasn't going to let that happen. He cut into the right lane, close to the bumper of a Corvette. The Explorer slowed but kept on their ass.

The driver of the sports car rolled down his window and gave him the middle finger before accelerating but freed enough space for them to maneuver.

Ariana, who'd been quiet since Bristow told them they had a tail, gave a nervous laugh. "At least he doesn't seem to be one of them."

"Nope." Migs already clocked the Corvette and driver earlier. He glanced at the rear-view mirror again. "Brace."

"What?"

The word barely left Ariana's lips when a thump jarred their vehicle.

"Are they forcing us off the road?"

"No. They're just intimidating us."

Another thump. This time stronger. Ariana didn't say another word, but he felt her rigidness beside him, and he imagined she was white knuckling the door handle and the console.

"Are you guys all right?" Bristow asked.

"Call this in," Migs said. "Have highway patrol take care of this fucker."

"No," Garrison countered. "Let it play out. They don't seem intent on driving you off the road. Benito is probably pissed we fucked up his plans for Ariana."

But Migs knew better. If this was a Carillo soldier, they'd be only too eager to prove themselves, and he wasn't about to serve up Ariana for their egos. "Where's the other one?"

"Sentra is tailing Bristow," Garrison said.

"The exit to Burbank is coming up. I'm not liking this. Get him off my tail."

"Copy that."

Bristow pulled up beside the Explorer. The three vehicles were driving in a tight formation and if a patrol saw them now, they would all be flagged.

"Speed up and cut in front of me," Bristow said. "I'll block him."

"Copy that."

Migs floored the gas and swerved in front of Bristow and continued on. He had to chuckle when his friend thwarted the Explorer from following them.

"You've got another one on you, Bristow." Garrison's voice came over his phone in a way too calm manner.

"You sure?" Bristow asked.

"Not a hundred percent. But must have seen the Explorer blocked and is rolling up to help."

"Why are they so persistent?" Ariana whispered.

"It's in their nature," Migs gritted. There was only one way to change the game, and he was willing to accept its consequences.

"Time to show your cards, Garrison. Get them off my back," Migs said. "Get the cops on them. I don't care if you and Bristow get thrown in with them."

They'd be freed in no time, but that would give Migs a chance to get Ariana away from this stalemate. An idea that he'd been toying around with finally found clarity. She needed more than a safe house. She needed the protection of the Alcantaras. Four years of skeletons in his past were about to get rattled.

"Copy that," Garrison said. "Will see you in Burbank?"

"Yeah." No.

He heard Garrison radio the highway patrol for dangerous activity on the freeway. Migs turned off his phone just as he saw Bristow force the Explorer to the shoulder.

"What are you doing?" Ariana asked, twisting in her seat to check their tail.

Migs didn't say anything.

"I thought we were going to Burbank." She twisted again in her seat to look out the window just as they passed their exit.

"We're heading to Vegas," he replied.

THERE WERE things he'd learned working as a CIA operative and one was to have a backup—several actually—for everything. His main vehicle and motorcycle were in Assassin's Hill, but he had an apartment in Victorville before the 15 to Las Vegas. He took the cover off his Jeep Wrangler. He kept the vehicle here just in case he had to venture into the desert. It wasn't the most comfortable ride, far from the smooth one offered by Ariana's Audi, but he couldn't risk Garrison tracking them down yet. Not until he was done.

He ignored Ariana's twenty questions as he transferred whatever was needed to the Jeep. He changed license plates and checked the overall health of the vehicle. It was only when they were back on the 15 and he'd made sure that they weren't being followed that he spoke.

"I have a cousin in Vegas," he said.

"Why are you breaking away from Garrison now?"

"He's not the one who can help us." The spook had his

own agenda, and Migs wasn't willing to risk Ariana without a safety net.

"What about Connie and Leah?" she asked.

"Levi took them to a safe house. They're fine."

"You took my phone and smashed it. You did the same with yours." She was talking to him as if he'd lost his mind. He probably had. "You don't want John to find us? Migs, what's your plan?"

"You have to trust me."

Her laugh was brittle, incredulous. "That's expecting too much, don't you think? Especially after how you left me the last time."

"It was for your own good. Can you deny that everything I've done is to protect you?"

She faced away from him to look out the window.

"Can you, Ari?"

No response.

"There's your answer," he said. "I didn't want to leave you, but in protecting you and helping in the rogue op to rescue Theo and Emma from your brother, Garrison and I were forced out of LA or we could be charged with treason."

Her head whipped around. "You didn't betray your country. Surely you could have defended yourself."

"At that time, someone else was in charge of the agency. I was warned not to contact you in any way. The CIA was still keeping an eye on you and I didn't want them to pull surveillance in case I defied them."

Ariana wasn't surprised. She always felt she was being watched. "And now?"

"That person is out. He fucked up by letting Carillo bounce back with a vengeance, but also because after so many months, efforts to find the weaponized Ebola and the virologist had led to dead ends."

"The person in charge now … you and Garrison can trust him to have your back?"

Migs gave a puff of laughter. "He's a rule breaker just like us. He'll get it."

"I'm not sure I'm very comforted by that thought. I don't want you in trouble because of me."

"It's my choice. It's the CIA's misstep for letting the Carillo bounce back."

"Who killed my brother?"

"The cartel."

"Which one?"

"That's what Garrison was trying to get Andrade to admit."

"Wait. You mean the man who proposed marriage to me is the man who had my brother killed?"

As much as Migs wanted to throw Andrade under a bus, he couldn't lie to Ariana. Not about this.

He checked their rear-view mirror and the open road ahead to give him some time to answer.

"Migs?"

"Are you familiar with the Ponce-Neto organization?"

"I know Antonio does business with them."

Migs chuckled darkly. "Is that what he's calling it nowadays?"

"He said they have his routes."

"Precisely. Your brother was withholding the money for the XZite pills."

"How much?"

"Ten mil."

"Ten? Oh my God. But why?"

"Cash flow issues I believe. It's nothing compared to the hundreds of millions in revenue they make from moving XZite for Andrade, but you also know narcos don't forgive those who cheat them."

"But why would Raul do that?"

"He was erratic in the end, wasn't he?"

"The PNO killed him?"

"Ariana, they wanted to kill you too, but Andrade forbade it." Saying that was like pulling a string of tacks from his throat, but he felt it was the right thing to say.

"So both cartels are after me," Ariana whispered.

"Yup." And that was just the beginning.

THEY'D BEEN on the road for approximately four hours when they reached the Strip. It was almost three in the morning and people in flashy clothes were on the streets as if they were just starting their evening.

Ariana was asleep beside him, her head lolling from one side to another. He cursed the unsteadiness of their ride, but he could trade for a better one today.

He picked up his burner and swiped a number. It rang seven times before it went to voicemail.

"Hector. It's Migs. Call me on this number." He repeated for good measure. He passed the Mirage and the Cosmopolitan hotel before he arrived at the Michoacán. It was a luxury hotel with a casino for high rollers and was one of the business holdings of the Alcantaras. Before he left Washington state, he made sure his cousin was there just in case he needed another form of backup. He wasn't expecting to rely on Hector less than twenty-four hours after seeing Ariana.

The lady in question stirred beside him and made a moaning sound that held a direct line to his dick.

Down boy.

He needed to keep his attraction to the gorgeous woman beside him under control. He still needed to debrief her and find out what happened during those few minutes she was inside the house. Her life was at stake and he didn't have Garrison to back him up. The spook must be cussing him to hell and back right now.

New phone, no cards. Cash only at the gas station. Migs wasn't planning on staying off the grid for long, but he needed enough time to execute his plan without interference from John. But it would only work if he could convince Ariana it was the best solution out of the mess she was in.

"We're here?" She straightened in her seat.

"Yes. Are you hungry?"

She uncapped a bottled water and took a sip. "I could eat."

"Good." Because Migs was starving and he could think better on a full stomach anyway. "They serve a twenty-four-hour breakfast here."

"Why here?"

"Wanted to avoid the more popular places."

"But wouldn't it be harder to find us in a crowded area?"

Migs chuckled. "Now you're thinking like a woman on the run."

She huffed. "It's too soon to make those kinds of jokes."

"I'm sorry." But his mouth was still pulled into a grin.

Ariana looked away from him, but not before he saw the flash of her teeth, that smile he'd been dying to see since he'd come back. Too bad she turned away, but he promised himself he'd put that smile back on her face.

He avoided valet and went straight to the underground parking, still a bit antsy that his cousin hadn't returned his call.

They left their things in the vehicle, although Migs tucked his gun in the back of his jeans.

"Are you supposed to be carrying that?" Ariana raised a brow.

He didn't want to tell her that in this hotel, most of the people did. They'd just gotten off the elevators on the first floor when his burner rang.

Fucking finally.

"Hector?"

6

ARIANA'S EYES bugged out when a giant platter of pancakes landed in front of Migs.

"Do you know how much sugar and gluten are in that?" She couldn't help pointing out as she dug a spoon into her yogurt and fresh berry parfait.

Migs rolled his eyes and grumbled. "Haven't eaten since lunch yesterday."

She arched a brow. "You had beef jerky in the car."

"Ariana," he growled. "Let a man eat."

Their server came back with an assortment of bacon, sausage, and eggs. The aroma of the smoked meats tickled her nose and her mouth watered. Ariana was all about balance in her diet and, after indulging in a decadent flourless chocolate cake last night, she needed to make healthier choices today. Still, with the Carillo organization after her, it was silly to think about the width of her butt when this could be her last meal on earth.

"Woman, just eat the bacon. You need some meat on you."

"I look thinner to you?"

Migs took a healthy gulp of coffee, poured more from the

carafe and then lowered his fork. "We're not doing this. You're not going to ask me if you look fat."

"That's not what I asked you."

"There's a catch there somewhere," he muttered as he resumed attacking his pancakes. Then she thought she heard him mumble that she was gorgeous.

She bit back a smile and picked up a slice of bacon, her lids fluttering close as she enjoyed the crunch.

"*Cabrón!*"

Her eyes flew open and her body turned rigid when a tall, fair-skinned Latino with dark eyes and a narrow nose approached their table. Four men flanked him. They were dressed like her brother's former lieutenants, in slacks and open neck long-sleeved shirts. Some of them sported gold chains.

Had the cartel found them?

The newcomer's face was angry. This couldn't be Miguel's cousin who he was talking to on the phone, right?

"Migs," she whispered, panicking. Ariana prayed that these men had more sense than to simply spill blood in this hotel. In Mexico, it was not unheard of for them to simply walk up to an enemy in a restaurant and shoot him while he was eating dinner. Such were the ways of these outlaws … they had the law in their pockets, but not here.

Hopefully.

"I got this." His voice was low, but it didn't reveal his mood. He picked up the napkin on the table, taking his time wiping the corners of his mouth and stood. "Hector."

His cousin stopped short of their table. Twin slashes of brows drawn into a scowl. "You have a lot of nerve showing up in my town after shunning the family for four fucking years."

"I had my reasons."

"So you say. And now you want me to help you?"

"That's what family is for."

Hector took another step closer. This time, Migs rounded the table and blocked Ariana from the other man's view. But she instinctively leaned sideways, fascinated by the exchange. She should have noticed that they were the only ones in the cafe. Was that on purpose? No one to film this exchange and post it on YouTube?

No witnesses.

She gulped.

"Family?" The man sneered. "You talk about family. When was the last time you saw *Abbi* Mena?"

"Last Christmas actually."

"Bullshit." The man moved closer, and Ariana started sweating, her heartbeat skipping at the base of her throat.

"You know what we do to men who disappoint their *abuelas*?"

"No, Hector, why don't you show me?"

The two men stood nose to nose, glaring at each other, and then very slowly, Hector's scowl relaxed, and his mouth split into a smile. "Fuck, cuz! Where the hell have you been?"

It was as if a balloon of tension was popped by a pin.

The two men embraced and thumped each other's backs. "Glad to see you're still a motherfucker," Migs chuckled. "I was afraid Joaquín had rubbed off on you."

Hector grimaced. "Please, don't compare me to my stuck-up brother. I'm still your lovable cousin. You forget how we loved Han and Lando?"

They were referring to Star Wars? Growing up with Raul and Jose, this sounded familiar.

"Are you going to introduce me to the lovely lady?"

A slight hesitancy on Migs part had Ariana frowning. "Ari, my cousin Hector Alcantara." He pointed at her. "Ari Ortega."

Hector's smile faltered, and when it returned, there was a tightness at the corners of his mouth. "Not *the* Ariana Ortega."

"The one and only," she confirmed, her chin lifting in defiance.

Miguel's cousin gestured for him to sit and joined them at the table. He sent his bodyguards away, telling one of them to tell the server to bring more coffee and Irish whiskey.

"A bit too early for that." Migs observed.

"I think I'll need it." His cousin laughed. "You come back to the family, you like to do it with a bang."

"You make it sound like we're the mafia."

"Aren't we?"

"And I never left."

"No, you just do a fly-by at the family gatherings. Never stay more than thirty minutes and call it done and dusted."

Ariana was putting the pieces together in her head. Michoacán, Alcantara. "Are you the Alcantaras of the Michoacán state?"

"The one and only." Hector grinned, tossing her statement back at her. "You mean, my cousin didn't tell you?"

"He never tells me anything." She turned to him. "What are you up to?"

Migs was saved from answering when their waiter returned with a fresh carafe of coffee and a bottle of Bailey's Irish cream.

"I'll tell you what will happen," Hector said as if relishing what he was about to say. "Tia Delia and Abbi Mena, not to mention all of your sisters, are going to be heartbroken."

This was confusing her. Shaking her head, she turned to Migs. "What is he talking about?"

Hector glanced between them, while Miguel's annoyance with his cousin became a palpable beat beside her. If she hadn't witnessed the warm reunion earlier, she could have sworn Migs was ready to murder the other man.

Then his cousin burst out laughing. "*Dios mio*, Miguel. You haven't told her, have you?"

"No, you dipshit," Migs growled. "I was going to ease her into the idea."

"Tell me what?" Ariana asked. "Ease me into what?"

Migs turned in his seat. The determination in his eyes sent anxiety up her spine.

"Marrying me."

Ariana lost the ability to speak. No words would come out of her mouth. Her eyes darted to Hector who was sitting back like a spectator about to witness a train wreck.

"Look at me, Ari," Migs ordered, and she did. "It's the right thing to do."

Her mouth opened, and then shut, too stunned to say anything. Why couldn't she say anything? She was composed when Andrade made the same proposition.

"Say something, Ari." His eyes searched hers.

"Are you out of your damned mind?" she yelled. Her hands flew to her mouth. "Migs, that's crazy."

"That's what I told him and that was before I knew who you were," Hector chortled. "Although I relish breaking the news to Elena." He glanced at Ariana. "That's my brother's wife and she's more stuck up than he is."

"Hector." Migs speared his cousin with a silencing glare. His cousin must have gotten the message and held his hands up in surrender.

"We're not doing this." She cut her hand in a firm negative sign. She dug a spoon into her yogurt and took a bite, and it immediately backed up her throat. She grabbed her coffee cup, her hand shaking. "This is crazy," she repeated.

"There you go," Hector said, and she could have sworn there was a slight disappointment on his face. As if he was denied entertainment. *Well, fuck him.* Not at her and Migs' expense.

"This isn't the place to talk about this," Migs said.

"There's no place to talk about this. Period. Is this some sort of competition between you and Antonio?" she asked.

She should be flattered, but she couldn't understand his benefit in all this. Ariana already felt bad that she could have ruined his career. She didn't know what kind of family Migs had. She vaguely remembered the Alcantaras as rich landowners—*hacienderos*.

She wouldn't feel bad about not wanting to marry into such a family, and if she read the situation right, he was estranged from them. Maybe because they were a snobby lot. She couldn't imagine him growing up behind the opulent walls of the McMansions in Mexico anyway. Migs was down to earth. His cousin was the exact opposite and epitomized the spoiled scions of these *hacienderos*.

Hector couldn't be more than thirty and he had four bodyguards and God knew who else was at his beck and call.

Prejudiced much, Ari?

Instant shame hit her, and she could feel the heat rise up her cheeks. Suddenly aware of the silence in the midst of her mental diatribe, she glanced up and realized Migs had not answered her question. He was waiting for her to give him eye contact.

"No. This is not me taking a page out of Andrade's book," he said coolly. "That's insulting. Eat. We'll talk about this later in the privacy of our room." He turned to his cousin and ignored her, leaving her reeling from his last statement.

Wait. What?

Our room?

AFTER BREAKFAST and after getting his go-bag from the Jeep, Migs led her to the elevators. With the keycard Ariana saw Hector give him, Migs swiped the reader on the panel and then punched a blue button for one of the top floors. There were four, all marked differently. Crowns of different designs and an ace, probably alluding to a card deck.

"We have the King suite," he said as the elevators slid open and they stepped out. "We should be secure here. This floor is card-access only and Hector assured me only his trusted staff has access to this level."

"When you said room, you meant the entire floor."

Migs smiled sheepishly. "Hector insisted. He said I needed the ambience to convince you."

"I thought we were done with this nonsense." She should've known better though. If there was one thing she knew about Migs, it was his persistence.

"You need sleep," he said. "We'll talk—"

"Miguel!"

"Sleep," he repeated. "I want to kick Hector for springing this on you."

"Shouldn't you have talked to me about it first?" she asked. "And what's with this bossiness? First it's 'eat' and now it's 'sleep'! You think I can sleep after finding out about your crazy idea?"

"It's not crazy."

"It's more than crazy. It's insane!"

His jaw flexed. "You want to talk about this now?"

"The best thing would be to never talk about it again," she said. When he only regarded her with unwavering intensity, she glanced to her left to the wide expanse of windows that swept around their suites where the glittering lights of Vegas gave her something to look at besides the intimidating presence of Migs in front of her. "You expect me to marry you after you disappeared for eight months?"

She felt him invade her space.

"Is this about trusting me?" A pause. "Look at me and tell me you don't trust me."

She inhaled a shaky breath, and slowly exhaled before bringing her face forward to stare up at him. It was a mistake. His eyes were dark pools that could easily suck her in and make her do anything. "I trust you with my life."

A muscle twitched in his jaw. "Then what's the problem?"

Their faces were too close, and when his eyes fell on her mouth, she involuntarily bit on her lower lip. One of them gave an audible hitch of breath. Probably her. "The problem is marriage. It's not something I take lightly."

"You considered one with Andrade."

"And I turned him down." She backed up a step because she couldn't think straight when he was this close to her. "And I am turning you down, too."

"Without hearing me out?"

"How would marrying me add more protection than what you are providing now? You are only going to put your family in danger. Why can't you see this?"

Migs sighed. "If you're not willing to hear me out now, I'm only going to ask you again later."

"Is that a threat?"

"Take it any way you please. So, you can forget sleeping peacefully, because I'm not abandoning the idea. I've already crossed so many lines, I'm not about to go about this half-cocked."

"You are talking about defying Garrison."

"Among other things." He squared his stance and crossed his arms. A sure sign he wasn't budging from his harebrained idea. "Okay. I'll hear you out."

"Then take a seat."

She sat, figuring the sooner she complied, the sooner she could hammer some sense into this man. The man who was currently pacing in front of her, running his finger under his chin as if he was choosing the words to say to her with care.

Seconds passed.

"You haven't thought this through, have you?" she asked dryly. Ariana had the oddest urge to laugh. Maybe it was nerves.

"I have." Migs scowled at her. "But I don't know where to start and explain why marrying me is the best solution." He stopped burning a hole in the carpet. "My family name will protect you. The Alcantara name, but it's not that simple right now."

"Because you're not on good terms with your family?"

"Because I haven't been fully honest with them with what I do."

"That you work for the CIA?"

"Yes."

"What do they think you do?"

"Freelance mechanic."

"And they have no clue?"

"My dad suspects, but he never outright asks."

"And now?"

"I'm taking you to my family's ranch in San Diego."

"What?" Ariana didn't need more people's lives on her conscience. What the hell was wrong with him? "You're going to put your family in danger!"

"The cartel wouldn't dare cause any trouble while you're there." There was a satisfied smile on Miguel's face.

"Does your family have an army protecting it?"

His face transformed, softened into an expression that could only be described as fondness. It made her heart jump.

"No. It's because my grandmother lives there," he said. "My *abuelo*, Amado Alcantara, was well-respected in all of Mexico. He was generous to everyone—the farmers who worked the land. Some of them have ended up becoming narcos, but they never forgot his kindness. As his widow, Abbi Mena—that's what everyone calls my *abuelita*—is off limits to any cartel. No one will dare go against the matriarch of the Alcantaras."

"Then why do you need Hector?"

"If you want news to spread from Sonora to Oaxaca, you tell my cousin."

Ariana chewed on her bottom lip. "So, as your wife ..."

"They would think twice about coming after you. But

Benito Carillo is a wild card. Our marriage would make him take a pause and figure out what he wants from you. Will make him reconsider if hurting you is worth the wrath of those who respect the Alcantara name."

Her mind suddenly remembered the contents of the tray on the coffee table. "I'm not sure what he really wanted. That wasn't Benito in that house, right?"

"No. Garrison said he'd identified one of his *sicarios*, the hitman they called Mamba." His face hardened. "The one who held a knife to your face."

"I don't think he was planning to cut me, but I remember syringes on the table."

"They were planning to drug you?" Migs eyes turned scarily dark.

"You think they plan to get me hooked on drugs as their way of revenge?" She shook her head trying to make sense of it. "There were other things like ... do you know what DNA sampling kits look like?"

Miguel's body froze. "Yes."

Ariana thought back to what she remembered. "There were three of those. That didn't make sense."

"I'll get this info to Garrison. See what he can find out."

"But you're off the grid, right?"

"Until we marry."

"Why? Because he'll think it's a bad idea?"

"Yes, but not for the reasons you think. It'll mess with his plans."

"Migs ..." she sighed. "I haven't agreed to marry you yet."

"It's the best solution to your problem right now," he insisted with increased urgency. "We can keep moving you to different safe houses, but they have connections everywhere. And is that really the life you want to lead? They need to know you're untouchable."

"But you're hinging my protection on their honoring the Alcantara name."

"Right now, you're only as safe as how well we can hide you. It'll also give us an idea of how badly they want you. How much they're willing to sacrifice to get to you. We need to get you to San Diego."

"San Diego?"

"Yes, my father's business is imports. One of them is green gold."

Ariana smiled. "Avocado." Of course. Michoacán was famous for it.

"You can have all the guacamole you want," Migs deadpanned as his long strides closed the distance between them and he crouched in front of her. "So what do you say?"

"Marriage seems like an excessive solution for endless guac," she laughed.

"My grandmother is a good cook." His eyes were nostalgic. "I'm sure I could entice you with her tacos al pastor."

This was a Migs she'd never seen before, and her heart ached for him knowing that choosing his job over his family must have been difficult. His cousin said four years. What happened four years ago? Ariana was sure he'd been in the CIA already by then, but that would be a question for another day.

"I still don't know, Migs," she said honestly, trying to fight the urge to jump into this, the promise of a home, of a grandmother's cooking. But more than anything else, and if she was honest with herself, it was the promise of finding out the layers beneath this man in front of her. "What will your family say when you suddenly show up with a wife?"

"They'll be horrified." He chuckled as he got up and sat beside her and then nudged her shoulder. "Just kidding."

She probably looked horrified herself. "No, you're not." She blew out a breath. "Weddings and *quinceañeras*, those are big affairs in our culture. I should know, even if I haven't been back to Mexico in a long time, I have friends in the Latino community. Well, at least I used to."

"I'm sorry, Ari."

Leaning back against the couch, she shook her head. "I don't know where I belong anymore."

She took that moment to lift her gaze straight to his eyes and was smacked by the fierceness in them and she couldn't look away.

"Migs," she whispered.

"I want to kiss you so badly," he murmured. His face grew closer and she stared at his mouth, but before their lips could touch, she pulled back.

"We shouldn't complicate things."

His brows furrowed. "What?"

"If we are to do this, it has to be in name only." She buried her face in her hands. What the hell was she doing? *Was she agreeing to this?* "Oh my God, this is going to be so bad when we divorce."

She felt his gaze singe the top of her head and when she looked up, there was an amused yet irritated gleam in his eyes.

"You have us divorcing before we're even married?"

"Miguel, we need to set expectations so no one gets hurt."

He stared at her for a long time as if he was studying her, as if he was figuring out what made her tick. She squirmed under his scrutiny.

"Stop doing that," she mumbled.

His mouth quirked at the corner. "Stop doing what?"

"Making me feel like I'm under a microscope."

Finally, he scooted back into the arm of the couch, spreading his arms and cocked his ankle over the knee, giving her space and yet holding her captive with his gaze. "So I'll give you my name, but no sex?" He grinned. "Are you sure? That's the best part of marriage I hear."

Her cheeks flamed. "Miguel!"

"That's the truth."

"What if we aren't compatible?"

His eyes grew heated. "There's one way to find out."

She huffed. "No. We're doing this the wrong way."

"All right, babe. How about this? Nothing physical until you ask for it, but I am fucking kissing you when Elvis says, 'kiss the bride'."

She squinted. "You're certain I'm going to say yes."

"Ariana, you like cutting a man's ego into pieces, don't you?" he sighed.

Her heart leapt. What the hell was he talking about? "I don't know what you mean."

"What I mean, Miss Oblivious, is I've listed all the reasons why it's a good idea to marry me—to protect you and in name only if that's what will make you comfortable with this arrangement. I can even have Hector's legal team draw up a contract that you can divorce my ass at any time. You have nothing to lose, while I have everything on the line. So it leads me to believe that you find me so ugly you can't stand the idea of being married to me even if it's in name only."

"Is this a form of reverse psychology?" she demanded, because that was exactly the opposite of what she was feeling. Any physical intimacy between them would put her heart in danger. She just knew it. This charming, brusque rascal would be easy to fall in love with. If she allowed herself.

His brows shot to his hairline. "No."

Her own brow arched. "A form of misplaced chivalry?"

And yet his grin nearly displaced her heart in its chest cavity. "You can say that."

Her tattooed knight riding to the rescue.

"So what's it gonna be?"

She exhaled in resignation. "Okay."

7

"You may now kiss the bride."

All thoughts of how he wanted to throttle his cousin for arranging a gangster-themed wedding for him and Ariana disappeared when the Al Pacino lookalike, channeling Tony Montana from *Scarface*, spoke the words he'd been waiting for.

He turned to his bride, radiant in a simple white dress, and lowered his head to capture her lips while drawing her in. Ariana's hands clasped his biceps. He felt rather than heard her gasp as his tongue invaded her lips and he tasted her for the first fucking time.

Migs deepened the kiss and did the whole dipping-her-body move. He could hear Hector heckling them, but he didn't care. Her fingers tightened, clung to him as if for dear life.

Ariana was in his arms and he was relishing this moment because she became his.

Even if it was in name only.

He could work with that.

He reeled her back to her feet, and her eyes flashed at him in annoyance. He winked at her. A reluctant smile curved her lips and her thumb came up to rub at the corners of his mouth.

"You've got lipstick on you," she chided.

He slowly wiped it off with the back of his hand. "It was worth it."

Her brows furrowed and what she was about to say was cut off by Al Pacino's twin.

"May I present, Mr. And Mrs. Miguel Alcantara Walker!"

They turned to face Hector and his secretary who acted as witnesses. Two of his cousin's bodyguards were also in attendance.

"Congrats, cuz," Hector said, walking up to them and shaking his hand, before clasping his jaw and giving him a kiss on the cheek. Then Hector turned to Ariana and did the same. "Welcome to the family." As his new bride accepted the well wishes from the others, his cousin leaned into his ear. "Have you thought about how you're going to break it to Tia Delia?"

"No."

"The five Marias?"

Shit.

Seeing his face, Hector burst out laughing. "Now this I don't want to miss."

AFTER A QUICK DINNER WITH HECTOR, Migs took Ariana back to their suite, declining his cousin's invitation for a night on the town.

"My wife needs her rest." He had his arm around Ariana and her body froze at the word 'wife.' That only made him tug her closer possessively.

Hector smacked his forehead. "Of course! How insensitive of me. I've been single too long."

"You're barely thirty. I'm thirty-six, so …"

"Still, I should know it's your wedding night, huh?" He

waggled his brows and if Migs wanted to throttle his cousin earlier, he wanted to string him up by his balls now.

"Hector," he said quietly, glancing down at his bride who had taken on the color of the wine she drank at dinner.

So HERE THEY WERE, back in the opulence of the sweeping King suite.

They stood just inside of the foyer where the things they'd purchased this afternoon were still in shopping bags. Ariana needed a whole new wardrobe following their mad dash to Vegas.

They stared at each other, awkward as you please.

Ariana broke the lock of their gazes first and went straight to the kitchen. "I'm thirsty. Do you want anything?" she called over her shoulder.

Migs followed her leisurely, enjoying how her ass shook as she walked. Sexy as fuck. He wanted to sink his fingers into that pillowy flesh, lift her against him, and rub her luscious form against his. He flexed his hands. They were itching to grab her.

"Migs?"

His gaze lifted, and he smirked as she rolled her eyes.

She leaned a hip against the counter. "Staring at my ass again?"

When he'd been her bodyguard, she caught him several times watching that particular part of her anatomy. At that time, he'd been embarrassed at being caught. He fought hard not to stare, but sometimes with Ariana's penchant for body-hugging dresses, it was a futile endeavor. And he was a hypocrite for cutting other men off with his death glare whenever *he* caught them ogling her ass. "It's perfect. Can't help it."

"So my husband is an ass man, huh?"

"Yeah."

Her smile was almost a shy one, the one she gave whenever he complimented her, and she couldn't quite accept it. She gave an amused shake of her head and resumed her initial quest for water. "Want a beer?"

"No. I'm switching to Scotch." Migs went to the drink cart, and sure enough it was laden with expensive liquor and a gift from his cousin.

"Hector left us a bottle of Dom Pérignon."

Ariana walked over, taking a sip of her water. She'd kicked off her shoes and padded barefoot. Migs loved her toes. She hated them for being square, indelicate and fat she'd said, but he found them adorable to look at.

He was more than an ass man—he was more like an Ariana man.

His wife.

Fuck. Now that they were married, he didn't quite know what to do with her. His throat went dry at the thought.

"We haven't talked about sleeping arrangements," he said.

She looked at him, puzzled. "I can stay in the same room I slept in this morning."

They had exactly four hours of sleep before he'd whisked her off to shop for her wedding attire and his, and he remembered her quip from this morning.

"You want me to marry you, we're going to appear properly before the officiant," Ariana had said. "You're not wearing faded jeans with holes in them."

Most of his jeans were threadbare and ripped around his thighs. Hours riding the Harley would do that. Though shopping wasn't his favorite sport, he'd been trained well by the women in his family. And it was all worth it in the end. He watched her now, her cream dress with that dangerously low neckline that teased the valley of her generous tits while the rest of the fabric draped sexily into her tiny waist and flared to hug the rest of her hips.

"Miguel?" She called him by his full name when she wanted his attention.

What was she asking? Oh, yeah, right. "We need to get used to staying in the same room."

She stared at a spot on his chest. "So soon?"

"We're driving down to see my family tomorrow. Might as well get used to it."

He stepped into her and as she tried to step back, he grabbed one of her hands. "You can't flinch when I come close to you. We need to start practicing this now."

She took a healthy gulp from her bottled water and set it down. "You're right."

"Maybe we should break out the champagne?"

She looked at him dubiously.

Migs didn't know whether to get ticked or amused. "Ari, I'm not going to take advantage of you. I promise. Even if you beg me to fuck you—"

She gasped.

"I won't. Not tonight." He pressed closer until her tits brushed against his torso.

Fuck this was torture. His head lowered by her ear. "Get used to me talking dirty to you." He trailed the fingers of one hand up and down her bare arm. "Get used to me touching you like this." Migs leaned back and noticed she was panting in sharp bursts. "When I kiss you, kiss me back like you can't breathe without me."

Then he fastened his mouth to hers, moving her arms to wind around his neck and his hands slipped down her sides, tentative at first, until her rigid body relaxed against his and she started kissing him back. Their tongues dueled and twisted wildly and without rhythm. Ari pressed closer and he couldn't concentrate keeping his erection down and keep this whole practice session under control.

Because that was what it was.

Practice.

He tore his lips away, groaning. "Wait … wait…"

Her eyes glazed with her own want, and he wished he hadn't promised not to fuck her.

"What?" she asked.

Migs gave a puff of laughter. "I guess we'll pass the family."

A wry smile formed on her lips. "It wasn't too hard." She turned from him and walked away.

"Where are you going?"

She swung back around with a teasing smile on her face. "I'm going to change into pajamas. The ones with little sheep on them. The ones that a woman would never wear on her wedding night."

"We need to share——"

"Then I'll come back, and we can sip champagne," Ariana paused. "Then we have to make sure we get our story straight."

"Then?" His voice lowered.

"Then we're going to sleep in the same room." She smiled teasingly. "But you're sleeping on the floor."

LATE THAT NIGHT, with Ariana a little buzzed from the champagne, she stared at the glass ceiling, watching their reflection lit by the fractured beams of moonlight.

She was on the bed. Migs was on the carpeted floor beside her. The couch in the room was too small for his frame. He could have picked one of the four bedrooms in this suite, but *no*, he said, they had to get used to sleeping in the same room. He could have requested a cot, but according to Migs, the floor was more comfortable. He folded a comforter in half and grabbed one of the pillows on the bed.

"Run it by me again," Migs said below her, his voice thick with sleep.

Ariana groaned and rolled to her side and looked at him. "You've asked me several times."

"If you can say it in your sleep, that means we're good."

She laughed lightly. "I met you when I was having my car serviced. Your schedule was full for the day but you said you would work overtime to fix it if I agreed to a date. Our first date was a street corner taqueria. You wanted to find out if I was as high-maintenance as my car."

"Why do you keep on inserting that high-maintenance part? And it was your idea to have the taqueria as our first date. Do you know my sisters will be horrified?"

"You did take me to a taqueria the first time I asked you to surprise me with lunch."

Migs chuckled, that brief chuckle of his that vibrated deep in his chest and made her feel doubly warm. "I was tired of you torturing yourself with that vegan place that thought it could make tofu taste like chicken. Just no, babe."

She smiled in remembrance. "You made me cheat so much."

"That ass of yours was wasting away—"

"Again, enough with my ass. You're obsessed with it."

"What's the first movie we watched?"

"Avengers. Not exactly a romantic one."

"But it's a safe one, even my sisters love it."

"You really have five of them?"

"Yes. Although sometimes I wonder if I'm adopted," Migs deadpanned.

"I can't imagine you with five sisters, but I guess that explains why you were very patient on our shopping trip. I can tell they have you well-trained."

He grunted. Then they both rehearsed the basic favorites: color, food, first vacation together, both of them loved tacos—she loved fish tacos, he loved carnitas and al pastor, and cars. Of course Migs would make cars as a necessary knowledge. Ariana just wanted a car that wouldn't break, and he was hoping to restore a sixty-four Shelby.

They agreed to be honest about her relationship to Raul. There was no hiding it anyway since the manner of his death was still being discussed in online chatrooms. The public had no idea how close the conspiracy theorists were to the truth of CIA involvement.

"Would they think I married you just for the protection of your name?"

"That's an insulting question, Ari." There was laughter in his voice, so she knew she hadn't offended him.

"I'm sure they consider you a good catch. *El único hijo*," she teased.

Migs grunted again. She could only imagine the pressure as being the only son of a rich landowner and belonging to a prominent family.

"Are your parents disappointed that you didn't get into the family business?"

Migs didn't answer for a while and she thought he'd fallen asleep. Ariana flopped on her back and saw that he had his arms crossed under his head and his eyelids fluttered.

"I was not meant to work the land," he said after a while. "I'd rather be a part of policing the cartels."

"But you joined the Army."

"The Army has a way of making a man out of a boy," Migs laughed. "You saw Hector, right? I could be an older version of him if I hadn't signed up for the military. The plan was always to get into the DEA. I did that for a couple of years and then the CIA picked me up."

"Is that all I need to know because my memory recall with the nitty gritty might be a problem. You've led a colorful life."

"So did you, my Sinaloan princess," he said.

"Opposite sides of the law," she murmured. "And here we are."

Ariana didn't know how long they chatted. Her eyes got

heavier and heavier and Migs' voice grew thicker. She just fell asleep.

THEY LEFT Las Vegas before noon and were approaching San Diego before evening. A trip that normally would have taken Migs five hours took almost seven with Ariana as a passenger. Every time he asked if she wanted to stop, she said yes. Not that he didn't enjoy their road trip.

He did.

Immensely.

He couldn't believe this woman beside him was his.

Migs couldn't remember a time he'd been committed to exploring a relationship with another woman. Apparently when he did, he did it without any brakes and went full throttle.

Married.

It didn't make sense, and he should be terrified, but he was strangely looking forward to what their life together would bring.

The I-5 exit came up and he guided the Escalade Hector lent them toward the off-ramp.

"Thank God we're almost there," Ariana said with relief.

"You don't need to pee again, do you?"

"Not really, but my butt really hurts." She shifted uncomfortably.

His glance slid to her before returning to the road. "I can give it a massage."

"Oh, you give good butt massages, do you?"

"I give good massages. Period," he said.

A frown crossed Ariana's face. "Have we discussed your past girlfriends?"

"You don't need to know about them because the last steady girl I had was in high school. See right there. I said *steady*. Gives you an idea how long it's been since I've been in a relationship."

He could feel her gaze burn down the side of his face. "But why?"

Migs took his time to answer and concentrated on merging their SUV in I-5 traffic.

"Numerous deployments in special forces isn't exactly conducive to building a relationship. And when I joined the DEA? Forget it. I was undercover in a world of crime and drugs. I didn't want it to touch my family. I had to stay away from the one I already had because I was at an age where they'd push every proper Mexican girl at me."

This time it was Ariana who grew quiet. He slowed down behind a car, noted that they were going to move five yards for every five minutes and glanced at his passenger. "I don't like that look on your face."

"I'm not proper or a high-bred Mexican *elitista*. I'm the sister of a crime lord who wreaked havoc in LA." Her voice pitched higher. "Maybe we should call this off."

Hell no. "I get it. You're nervous about meeting my family."

"Yes! You're bringing a mongrel into your home."

Migs chuckled. *The drama.*

"It's not funny."

"What do you think I am? I'm more of a mixed breed than you are."

"That's not what I meant, and you know it. Your blood is practically blue."

Her statement pissed him off. "Fuck that."

Her eyes widened at the sharpness of his tone. A car honked behind them as the traffic started to move. It also gave Migs a chance to get over his annoyance with Ari for suggesting he was some kind of royal blood. Far from it. He hated that she was seeing this as an issue, but he had to look at where she was coming from.

He knew her history before she even told him about it. CIA and DEA had a file on her. Orphan from the age of seven, she had two brothers—Raul and Jose. They lived with an aunt for a while but that didn't last. Raul, who was already nineteen at that time, took his siblings to Tijuana and raised them. Raul got recruited by a *plaza* boss. Jose wanted to follow in his footsteps and got killed in a botched border-crossing shootout with the Mexican Federalists.

Raul uprooted Ariana from Tijuana and joined a rival cartel with connections to a dominant gang in LA and the rest was the crime lord's colorful history. There wasn't much about Ariana during her growing-up years, but she said her brother sent her abroad to live in Switzerland for a while. It was probably there that she got immersed in all the vitamin nutrition shit. While she was learning to preserve beauty and life, her brother was its destroyer and wreaked havoc in the LA criminal underworld.

"Look at me. See this?" He pointed to his earring. "And my tattoos? My grandmother barely lifted a brow when she saw my first sleeve. You're basing your opinion of my family on Hector. I'll admit his side of the family is more snobbish, but they sure as hell didn't get it from the Alcantara side. My dad is a gringo, and yet my Abbi Mena chose to live with us." He gave her another brief glance as the I-5 traffic slowed to a crawl again. "I can assure you until I'm blue in the face, but I'd rather let you find out for yourself. And I can promise you this—I won't throw you to the wolves. Got me?"

"Okay," she whispered.

"Now, I can't say the same about my sisters." He felt her freeze, but he let loose a brief chuckle. "Hell, even as their brother I don't understand their moods. Tessa is two years older than I am—she's thirty-eight. Youngest are the twins and they're twenty-two. You don't have to deal with anyone going through puberty. The twins are in college right now, so you're not getting the full force of the five Marias on day one."

"Thank God," Ariana said, and he was sure she wasn't saying that out of sarcasm or jest. It was relief. Not that he'd blame her.

He picked up her left hand, felt her stiffen, and cast her a warning look. She relaxed her arm. He knew it would take her some time to adjust to his affectionate gestures, but he had to prime her for his family because they were an affectionate bunch. He ran a finger over the wedding ring he put on her yesterday.

They both wore plain bands. He fibbed that he didn't get her a diamond because they were keeping the cover that he was a mechanic and he was being practical and saving for their house instead, but in reality, he had something else in mind. His family would be horrified because Migs did have a share in the family business even while he wasn't a part of its running.

He brought her hand to his lips and kissed the back of her fingers. "Sorry I didn't get you a diamond."

"What you said made sense for your cover to them," Ariana said. "I don't think I could look them in the eye if your family gushed over it. It's for the best."

"But you like diamonds?"

"I do," she said. "I like well-made jewelry and I certainly wouldn't buy from a designer store in Las Vegas. I know many artisan jewelers in San Francisco. I'd rather buy from them." She grinned. "We did good, Miguel."

"Just know that my family is going to gripe at me for not getting you a proper ring," Migs said. Or giving her a proper wedding for that matter. "You're going to back me up on this, right?"

"I will." She glanced out the window. "How much longer until we get there?"

Migs checked ahead at the flow of cars and then at the clock. "Another twenty minutes."

"Okay."

He squeezed her hand. Words weren't needed to show her that he had her.

She gave his own a squeeze too, telling him she had him.

Yup, they were in this together.

8

FROM I-5, Migs drove them past his family's avocado warehouse, showing Ariana the massive facility that spanned an entire block. From there, they took the same road to the ranch, which was a mere five miles out. Turning from the main road into its entrance, the person manning the guard-house waved them past while giving Migs a friendly salute.

It was a stretch of a driveway, it could even be classified as a private road.

"Wow." Ariana leaned forward in her seat to take in the tree-lined drive of the Alcantara estate. "It's beautiful." She marveled at the gently sloping hills as the sunset brushed the color of gold on the green of the landscape, mixing in with the encroaching shadows of the evening. At the end of a driveway was a sprawling Spanish-style one-story structure, which was a cross between a Mediterranean villa and a ranch house. Wrought iron lamps hung on the outside stucco walls and illuminated the entrance.

Three people stood in front of the house. One, Ariana presumed was Migs' dad. She knew he had called his father when they exited the interstate.

"I guess that's your dad?" she asked about the lone male in the trio that awaited them.

"Yes. And that's Mamá and my sister, Bella." It was hard to discern their features with the lighting and the distance, but she could tell Migs got his height from his dad and his coloring from his mother. Before she could draw any more conclusions, the Escalade stopped next to them.

They were all smiles, and Ariana couldn't help returning one of her own.

When she stepped out, the older of the women embraced her as if she was a long lost daughter. "I couldn't believe it when my son said he had found the one!" Ariana was kissed on a cheek and then was turned over to Bella. Miguel's sister was a beauty. Almost as tall as Ariana, she had the dark eyes, delicate nose, and perfectly formed lips of a true Spanish mestiza highlighting the attractive combination of American and Spanish heritage. After giving her a hug, Bella immediately picked up her left hand, her mouth falling open.

"Miguel! Where is the ring?" Bella exclaimed.

Migs disengaged from his mother's hug and walked to them. "Mind your own business, Bella," he growled. "C'mere and give your bro a hug."

The affection was obvious between the two siblings as Bella squealed and launched herself into Migs' arms, peppering his cheeks with kisses. "I can't believe you're married!" she shouted. "How could you deprive me of my bridesmaid's dress?"

"Jesus," Migs muttered as he set his sister down. "You could deafen a man's ear. No wonder you're not married yet."

"Don't say the Lord's name in vain, Miguelito," his mother interjected.

As the two women and Migs traded barbs, his dad came up to her, extending his arm. "I'm the sane one in the family. Drew Walker." He nodded to his wife and daughter. "And since Migs is slow in introductions, that's my wife Delia and our daughter Maria Isabel. She also goes by Maribel but decided to change it to Bella after that vampire movie came out."

Ariana burst out laughing.

"Your abuelita and your sisters are busy in the kitchen," Delia told her son. She turned to Ariana and grabbed her arm. "I hope you're hungry." As his mother swept her into the house, Ariana looked back helplessly at Migs who had an amused look on his face and was following at a leisurely pace. *Traitor.*

"You can call me Mamá," Delia said, their feet hustled over red floor tiles. Ariana's eyes took in the dizzying display of Southwest charm and Mexican architecture as Delia continued. "We're a mixed-tradition household. The kids call Drew, *Pops,* while they call me Mamá." She paused and must have noticed her interest in the interior. "I'll show you around later. Abbi Mena doesn't like food getting cold." They exited into a portico that led into another part of the house. The scent of turned earth filled her nose and her eyes took in the vegetation silhouetted in the fading light.

"That's our vegetable garden. Migs or Abbi Mena can show that to you in the morning, too."

Migs did say his grandmother was a farm-to-table cook. One of her conditions in moving in with her oldest daughter was that she would be provided an expansive vegetable garden.

Soon, the most delicious aroma hit her nose and made her mouth water. "Oh my god, what is that?" she couldn't help saying.

"I hope you're hungry." Delia repeated her earlier statement.

And from the darkened portico, they walked into the biggest kitchen Ariana had ever seen in a home. High ceilings, wrought-iron light fixtures and a long heavy dark wood table sat in the opposite side of the kitchen in an alcove similar to those chef tables in exclusive restaurants. A farm table stood in front of granite kitchen counters. Between the counters and the stove were three women. The first one had a toddler hanging off her hip and was tasting out of a stock pot almost as big as the child she was carrying. Another woman was making tortillas on a griddle. The third and oldest of them was checking on their work as she wiped her hands on a towel. Over at the farm table a man with salt and pepper hair and mustache over a weather-beaten face was talking to a younger guy with tanned skin and threadbare shirt.

"Everyone," Delia addressed the room. Five pairs of eyes shifted to them and Ariana wanted to retreat. "They're here!"

From behind her, reassuring hands clamped down on her shoulders, and she instinctively knew it was Migs. He nudged her ahead.

"Miguelito!" The older woman came forward. Silver hair with a few streaks of black was pulled back loosely into a bun. Spectacles rested on a strong nose, but Ariana was in awe of the serene beauty of Miguel's eighty-year old grandmother. Very few lines marked her face, even as the light olive skin hinted of time under the sun.

"Abbi Mena," Migs said with affection, leaning in and kissing his grandmother on the cheek. Freckled, gnarled hands grasped his jaw, squeezing it. "*Mijo*, you break this old woman's heart getting married without my blessing." The Spanish accent was thick. Those sharp whiskey-colored eyes landed on Ariana. "Introduce me to your bride."

"Ariana, my grandmother—Filomena Alcantara. Everyone calls her Abbi Mena."

"Nice to meet you," she squeaked.

"Mami, *no la asustes*," Delia admonished.

"I'm not scaring her off, but I need to see who has captured my favorite grandson's heart."

Ariana glanced at Migs, the guilt of this fake marriage was weighing heavily on her chest, strangling her throat.

"She's joking," Migs told her. "She says that to all her grandsons."

"Bah! You are the most handsome one and strong as an ox," his grandmother was telling Ariana like she was selling a bull in the market. "You're very beautiful. You're Mexican?"

"I am."

"From where?"

"Sinaloa."

"Ah, that would explain your coloring, your eyes. Sinaloans are known for their beauty. It's the Lebanese blood. You have it, *sí?*"

"I think so."

The older woman smiled, a satisfied glint reflected in her eyes. "I forgive my grandson for getting married without family around him. You and he will give me beautiful great-grandbabies."

Ariana's cheeks flushed as she kissed her in greeting.

"Mami, dinner is ready, and you don't like it when it gets cold." Delia winked at Ariana, coming to her rescue.

As Abbi Mena got distracted by her daughter, Migs introduced her to his two sisters and the two other men at the table, but Ariana was already in overload, not sure she remembered their names.

A flurry of activity ensued as she was led to the dining area in the alcove.

The table was set, but there was hardly any food yet on its dark walnut-colored surface.

"Christ, I'm hungry," Migs growled. "Where's the food?"

"Ah ...ah ... brother," Bella said as she laid a glazed cast-iron pot on the trivet. "Abbi Mena hears you cursing, she's going to pinch your ears."

"And you wonder why I don't come home often?" he asked.

"We know that's not it." Bella eyed him slyly and flounced away.

"I think your family is more astute than you give them credit for."

"Jesus, I hope not."

"Stop taking the Lord's name in vain."

Migs shook his head and flashed her a charming smile. "*Sí, querida.*"

As THE FAMILY sat down to dinner, more people came in to join them. Ariana tried her best to remember their names and was developing a headache in the process. She wasn't new to Latino family gatherings. She'd been to many and had seen both sides of the spectrum and the ones in-between. The gangster-style ones had the men wearing wife beaters under long sleeve plaid shirts while the women either wore baggy pants or butt-baring shorts. Heavily kohled eyes were also favored. As for the families on the right side of the law, you had men and women respectably dressed who went to church regularly—their moral values heavily influenced by Catholicism and traditional values of home. And then there were the elitistas.

Migs family crossed all levels of the spectrum, with Migs of course providing the gangster vibe. There was something to be said about a rough and gruff tattooed guy going all marshmallow sweet—okay, that might be an exaggeration—when interacting with his grandmother.

"Want me to make you another taco?" Migs asked her.

Ariana already had two, and judging from the spread on the table, tacos were just an appetizer. "Another carnitas?"

As Migs prepared her another taco, she asked, "Do you always eat this way?"

It was his married sister Tessa who answered, "No. This is more than a usual evening dinner, but less than a true feast because my little brother here sprung a surprise on us, and we didn't have time to prepare." Tessa was the one with the toddler—Gigi. The man beside her was her husband Cesar who was the operations manager of their avocado warehouse. "No, Miguel, you're preparing it wrong, don't forget to put the tomatillo."

"She doesn't like tomatillo salsa."

"She will like mine," Abbi Mena said without looking at them, apparently keeping track of several conversations at once. "Put it on the side. If she does not like it, you can eat it for her." She resumed her conversation with Delia.

"What am I, the garbage disposal?" Migs muttered.

"Stop complaining and do it." His grandmother interjected without missing a beat in her discussion with her daughter.

"When did I say I hated tomatillo?" Ariana asked.

"When I took you to the taqueria on our first date, remember?"

"You took her to a taqueria on your first date!" Bella yelled and all conversation at the dinner table ceased as all pairs of eyes glared at Migs.

"It was my favorite one." He transferred a prepared taco on her plate. "And what's wrong? We're having tacos tonight, right?"

"Yes, but we also have roasted snapper," Lettie, Miguel's third sister, who was seated beside Bella, said. "And *camarones*."

"Please tell me it was one of those fancy taquerias that use shaved truffles on their tacos." Tessa turned to Ariana, not willing to let it go.

"Why the hell would you put truffles in a taco?" Migs grumbled.

"Hah! I'm surprised you know what a truffle is, gringo."

"You're half-white too. And who wouldn't know what a truffle is? It's chocolate," Migs declared.

All his sisters' faces looked horrified and then they realized their brother was teasing.

"Jes—" Migs caught himself and grinned. "I'm not that much of a hick you know. I do live in LA. Still, if you ask me, that stupid fungus is overpriced."

"You're just not very cultured. Maybe in Ariana's company your palate will become more sophisticated." Tessa returned her attention to Ariana. "I'll settle for a celebrity restaurant chain. Please tell me that's where he took you."

"Uh … no. It had those $3 tacos … a step above a food truck."

Everyone turned and gasped their displeasure at her newly minted husband. "Miguel!"

Migs rolled his eyes and slanted his gaze at her. "Throw me under the bus, would you?"

"I don't want to lie," Ariana stated primly. "But," she paused, making sure she had everyone's attention. "Save for the tomatillo salsa, everything in that place was delicious. Though it doesn't hold a candle to the food on this table."

Everyone nodded their approval and chatter resumed.

Migs leaned in and whispered, "Thanks. Now give me a kiss."

"What? Now?" she mumbled through a corner of her mouth.

"Perfect timing."

Her chin inched up, and his head lowered as he gave her a sweet lingering kiss.

"Oh my goodness, you two, get a room!" Bella teased.

"What?" Migs fired back at his sister. "I'm on my honeymoon and I have to spend it with you guys."

"Better than getting disowned, sí ?" Delia scolded her son. "Imagine when Hector told us the news." There was more than simple displeasure on his mother's face. There was despair and disappointment. Ariana's guilt was doubling with every bite. Unfortunately, she ate when she was guilty. She also wondered if her drive to do charitable work was driven by her desire to atone for Raul's crimes.

"You're not really married until you get married in a church. We shall plan a wedding. I can get it ready in two months," his mother said. "I'll talk to Father Tomas and see if he has an opening."

Ariana kicked Migs under the table, urging him to say something.

"Isn't Abbi Mena's eightieth birthday coming up?" Migs said. "We can make it a double-celebration?"

That was not what she expected him to say and kicked him under the table again. The corners of his mouth lifted. What was he finding so funny?

"That's in less than a month. No time to prepare and all the invitations have been sent," his eldest sister said.

Bless you, Tessa.

"Yes, it might be too soon," Bella added. "It'll take me more time than that to find a dress."

Tessa stared at her sister across the table. "You realize Ariana is the bride, right?"

Bella shrugged her shoulders. "Just saying. In case someone wants my input."

Ariana cleared her throat. "There's no rush, really. We're already married anyway." She smiled at everyone, but more than one person was shaking their head.

"How do you like my tomatillo salsa, Ariana?" Abbi Mena asked.

"It complements the carnitas very well," Ari said, welcoming the older woman's pointed change of topic. "I've always had bitter or extremely spicy ones."

"Larger tomatillos are bitter and never make this salsa from canned tomatillos. Their acidity doesn't preserve well unlike the red tomatoes."

Ariana didn't add that her aunt made the most horrible salsas, often too spicy for her young taste buds, but she was forced to eat them as a child because there was nothing else for food. So by the time Raul moved them to Tijuana and was making good money as a lieutenant for a plaza boss, she had developed an aversion to the condiment.

Eating and conversation resumed at the table. It was a mixture of Spanish and English popularly known as Spanglish. Migs told her his dad was useless at picking up language and there was a running joke in the family that he married Delia so she could be the interpreter in the business. His sisters spoke mostly English because of this. As for Abbi Mena, she had traveled extensively and could speak many languages. In the seventies, she lived in Berkeley, California to study advances in agricultural practices so they could update their farm industry in Michoacán. But when his grandmother and Delia conversed, they fell back naturally to speaking Spanish.

Soon it was dessert time, and frankly, Ariana couldn't eat another bite, but when the first churros came out of the deep fryer, she quickly changed her mind.

"Remind me to work out tomorrow," Ariana groaned.

"I can think of another kind of workout." Migs waggled his brows.

"You're seriously enjoying this, aren't you?"

"Every second of it."

9

How COULD he tell Ariana how he simply loved watching her interact with his family? Except for the awkward moments in the beginning, somehow he knew she would fit right in.

When Ariana offered to help them clean up, his sisters all but shooed them out of the kitchen. After they said goodnight to everyone, his mother led them to their bedroom. Leon, who was the security chief at the warehouse and had been a part of his family since he was a kid, oversaw the transfer of their belongings to their room while they were having dinner. He caught the look in Ariana's eyes questioning having someone else moving their belongings to the room given Migs worked for the CIA. He had three reasons: everything that was classified was in his head, his gun was locked in the glove compartment, and lastly, he trusted Leon with his life.

His mother led them to the corner bedroom located in the left wing of the house. As Migs opened the door to let them in, she said, "Leon had the *muchachas* air out the room yesterday." He happened to glance at Mamá, spying the gleam of tears in her eyes. His chest contracted with the guilt he'd lived with these past four years when he limited his time with the family.

"I'm glad you came home," she whispered.

"I was here last Christmas," he reminded her.

"You know what I mean. It was always so quick and this last time something was bothering you deeply," his mother said.

Had he been that transparent? Migs thought with guilt. He wasn't mentally present then, his mind occupied by Ariana at the time when he'd been ordered to stay away from LA.

Delia turned to his wife. "Thank you for bringing him back to us."

Ariana nodded mutely.

His mother reached up and squeezed the left side of Migs' jaw to emphasize her previous statement and then left the room.

After he shut the door, Ariana erupted like a pressure cooker that had blown a gasket.

"*Ay Dios mio!*" Her voice was hushed, but full of panic, her arms gesturing wildly. "What are we doing? Your wonderful family! We're deceiving them."

Migs crossed his arms, expecting this drama. "What are we doing?" he regarded her calmly. "We're newlyweds."

"In name only!"

"That's where you're wrong."

"What?"

"You refused any stupid contract I willingly offered. I'm not hiding the fact that I'm attracted to you, and sex isn't off the table. You just have to ask for it."

"That will compli—" her words cut off when he narrowed his gaze at her. With Ariana, he had trouble keeping his face blank. His training and years as an undercover operative were rendered useless.

He prowled toward her and clasped her shoulders. "I swear, woman. If you say one more time that it will complicate things, I'll throw you on that bed and show you complicated."

Her breath caught. "You wouldn't."

"Test me." He lowered his head, and she stared at him with wide-saucer eyes, lips parted. His gaze dropped to her full mouth and his whole body flooded with the urge to fuck the stubbornness out of this infuriating woman.

Not just any woman.

His wife.

"Test me," he repeated, his erection pressing against his zipper. Fuck, that wasn't helping.

They were both breathing heavily and, if he didn't pull away, he'd be on her in the next second. "You can freshen up first."

He dropped his arms and forced himself to move to the nearby couch. He sat and began to unlace his boots, doing his best to act as if he didn't just threaten to fuck her, trying not to watch her walk away, yet fully aware of that sexy body leaving his peripheral vision.

The one thing he'd always loved about her, she was aware she was beautiful—Sinaloa was known for their beautiful women. It was very likely she had Lebanese blood in her as that part of the country had the most Arab-Mexicans in the nation. He smiled to himself. No wonder Abbi Mena was already thinking of grandchildren. At that thought an uneasiness swirled in his gut. Was it fear? Excitement? Or the uncertainty of it all?

What the fuck was he thinking about? He wasn't some damned teenager panting after a high school beauty queen, though he certainly felt like he was.

Pulling off his boots, he stood and unbuttoned his jeans and tossed his shirt on the couch, walking over to his duffle where he had a few days change of clothes. Both he and Ariana needed to buy more basics as he doubted they'd be able to get out of here for a few weeks.

Shit, he needed to call Garrison and tell him the *happy*

news. The spook hadn't crossed his mind since they arrived at his family home.

Fishing out the burner, he thumbed the number he knew by heart. It wasn't a direct line to John, but more of a call-in service. He followed the instructions and ended the call. Garrison should call him back. He was about to check if Ariana needed anything in the bathroom when his phone rang.

Huh, that was quick.

"Walker."

"Where the fuck are you?"

"San Diego."

"With Ms. Ortega?"

"She's Mrs. Walker now." Man, he relished saying that to Garrison.

Dead silence followed, and a niggle of doubt about fucking up rooted in his gut. "You there?"

"What happened?"

It was more rhetoric than a question, but Migs answered him anyway. "I married her Vegas style."

"Is there something going on between you two?"

"Not really."

"Dammit. I told you I didn't want a repeat of Yemen."

"I wasn't in on that op and I'm not one to gossip, so I don't know what the fuck you mean."

Garrison kept on cursing and muttering about his assets falling like flies.

"Are you in love with her?"

"Ah ... we're working things out."

"Then why marry her ... Why—wait a minute. Shit, something about your family name, am I right?"

"It was worth a shot."

"And Miss Ortega is on board with this?"

Migs gritted his teeth. "Mrs. Walker. And do you think I held a gun to her head?"

"Know what I think, Walker? You're in deeper than you're letting on."

"You think my plan was a bad idea? They were about to hurt her—"

"About that—" Garrison started.

"They were going to shoot her up with drugs."

"That's not confirmed."

Migs paused. "But Ariana said—"

"I checked with Nadia, the CSI team retrieved a set of vials similar to the ones used for buccal swabs. The syringes at the scene weren't loaded with any toxin."

"What were they for?"

"Can't determine at this point. From the looks of it they were going to draw Ariana's blood."

His thoughts raced. "The virologist. You think they want to duplicate what they did to Raul? The buccal swabs were to check for DNA compatibility."

"That theory crossed my mind, but there were no viral agents found in the house."

A chill skittered down his spine. "I fucked up."

"Explain."

"I told my cousin to spread the word that Ariana is my wife. Shit. If the cartel wanted her bad enough—"

"I still don't get it."

Migs repeated the explanation that made Abbi Mena untouchable. "Though I wonder if the newer narcos would respect the code."

"Your plan has merit. Culture-wise, the matriarch of a dynasty is sacred, especially given the age of your grandmother and how respected your grandfather was—she would be off limits." Garrison blew out a breath. "I'm waiting to hear back from my contact at the DEA regarding the state of the cartels. Heard something is brewing."

"Keep me posted."

Protracted silence hung between them, and Migs thought

he'd lost connection until the other man spoke, "You threw a wrench into my plans."

"You'll adapt," Migs said automatically, then paused. "What plans?"

"Andrade's cooperation. Remember him? You married his presumptive bride."

"I did, didn't I?" he thought smugly. "What else would you need from him?"

"In case you've forgotten, we still don't know the culprit in his organization who fabricated the Z-91."

"I didn't forget," Migs said. "That's your problem. Mine is the LA and Carillo link."

"Fucker," Garrison muttered. "I'm sending you an encrypted phone. Don't wreck it this time. Oh, and congratulations."

The line went dead.

Migs continued chuckling long after the phone call. He was sprawled on a chair, but as he replayed the information Garrison had given him, his humor faded. That was how Ariana found him when she emerged from the bathroom, dressed in a shiny pajama set instead of the ones with the silly print she wore yesterday. No matter how she tried to downplay her curves, clothes clung to her the way Migs envisioned getting wrapped around her.

The way her gaze meandered to his torso heated his blood until it felt too hot for his skin to contain. His muscles contracted when her eyes swept briefly to the exposed trail below the unbuttoned jeans with the zipper partially lowered. Did he do that on purpose?

Maybe? Christ. Sleeping in the same room with her would be torture. Keeping from tasting every luscious inch of her would be agony. But he promised.

As though Ariana awoke from a trance, her eyes flickered away, and she started drying her hair with a towel. "Were you on the phone?"

"Garrison."

"Oh." She lowered her arms. "Did you tell him?"

He grinned. "I did."

"And?"

"And he extends his congratulations."

Her short burst of laughter was a magnet that pulled him to his feet, and he walked to her to get behind her, taking the towel from her hands. "Let me."

"Miguel ..."

"Shh ... let me do this."

She relented, and he massaged her scalp as she leaned into him, the coolness of the satin giving momentary relief to the fire on his skin. She moaned in pleasure.

"Fuck, Ari," he muttered, dropping the towel, clasping her shoulders and turning her around to face him. His fingers combed her wet hair over and over and she closed her eyes, unabashedly pressing her soft tits against his chest and she swayed from side to side.

Unable to help himself, he cradled her head and he kissed her, slowly at first. Tentative. And then his tongue pushed between her lips and tangled with her own. He explored her in air-stealing gulps, sucking her tongue as his hands traveled down, molding her curves, before sweeping up to cup the fullness of her tits.

Tearing his mouth away, he sought her eyes. "I want to give you more." Her slight nod was all the encouragement Migs needed. He scooped her up and laid her gently on the bed. He climbed on, keeping his eyes on hers for any sign of panic or rejection, but all he witnessed was acceptance. He pushed her legs apart and wedged his hips between them. "Beautiful," he whispered as he resumed kissing her. He plundered the sweetness of her lips for a while, letting his fingers explore, paying attention to what she liked even as his own need rose in painful hardness at his pelvis.

Her moan only fueled his arousal and he stroked his erection against her core, the friction driving them both wild, the searing heat of her pussy was like a brand on his cock. Yes, she owned him now.

Migs moved lower to her neck, unbuttoned her pajama top, and his breath hitched when he saw her tits bared to his eyes for the first time. He'd dreamed about them, how they'd feel against his palms. He cupped each and splayed his hand over them before mouthing a nipple, flicking the tip with his tongue while his hand moved lower. It slipped beneath the elastic of the pajamas and sought her slick hot center. He found her tiny bud and used his thumb to rub circles against it, then he dipped a finger into her entrance. Fucking wet. Adding a second finger, her pussy sucked that right in, too. His brain short-circuited.

But Miguel wasn't the only one close to being mindless. Ariana's back arched and her fingers clawed into his hair. "Migs ..." she breathed.

He released the nipple he was teasing, and he wished he could delay the gratification of tasting her arousal, but he was blinded with need. As he scooted down her body, his fingers caught the waistband of her pajamas and slid them over her hips, revealing her naked pussy, her scent making his nostrils flare.

Dispensing of the pajama bottoms, he settled his shoulders between her thighs, taking in her shadowed cleft that he couldn't wait to devour. "I knew I skipped dessert for a reason." His tongue gave her a lick.

"You're killing me." She squirmed as her legs tried to clamp together.

He shoved them apart. "Careful, babe. Don't want to suffocate me before I give you that tongue-fucking."

She puffed a short laugh as her legs fell open. Now that was a damned sexy sight to see.

Ariana Walker all laid out for him to eat.

Her juices glistened between pinkish lips. He couldn't

resist any longer. He dove right in and groaned at the immense pleasure of his first taste.

Mine. Fucking mine. His brain roared with that possessive mantra while he continued to attack her pussy with abandon. His tongue stroking up and down, swirling, savoring and then his mouth returned to that core of sensitive flesh. Ariana cried out, and he nearly came in his pants. He continued to draw out her orgasms, could feel her flesh swell beneath his tongue, and he knew she was primed and ready to take him. All he had to do was shove down his jeans and slide right in.

But something stopped him.

A little voice telling him to tread carefully.

He kissed his way up her body and then captured her lips again, giving her a taste of herself. She wrenched her lips away. "Migs ... Migs ..." Her neediness clawed at him, her legs rounding him and keeping him pinned to her. His cock at her entrance ready to take possession.

"Ari," he murmured.

Her eyes opened fully, glazed with the same heat he was feeling.

"I want this to mean something," he said quietly. "So, I'm not going to fuck you right now."

"What?"

His forehead dropped to hers as his body sagged. A rumble of a chuckle vibrated in his chest. "Funny, isn't it?" The way they were positioned in bed was too provocative for him to state what he wanted to say with conviction. So, Migs levered away from her and sat on the side of the bed. "I want to make you mine in every way, Ariana Walker. I had full intention of leaving you alone until we got to know each other more, but you walked out of that bathroom and I lost control."

Ariana sat on the bed and placed the pajama bottoms over her pelvis, covering the temptation between her legs. "So the shirtless look and the unbuttoned jeans weren't your intent to seduce me?"

Migs bowed his head, and gave her a look, catching his bottom lip with his teeth as he tried to deny it, but he couldn't. "Not starting this marriage on a lie, so yes, I fully intended to seduce you."

"And now you're getting cold feet." A delicate brow arched.

"Damn, babe, you're making me sound like the frightened virgin."

She laughed and then caught herself. "I'm sorry, I didn't mean to rain on your machismo."

"Stop that."

"But why? You may be half-American but your other half is pure Mexican machismo. That's why you're so bossy."

"When have I ever been that?"

"Hmm… let me see. The time you forced me into hiding? Then when you came back you wouldn't take no for an answer until I got into the car with you."

"I wouldn't have forced things if I didn't know you secretly enjoyed it when I get all bossy and shit."

"Are you saying I'm playing hard to get?"

"No, I'm saying I like your drama."

Her eyes slitted. "Be careful what you wish for." Ariana's expression grew thoughtful. "Before you effectively seduced me with that hair massage, you never told me what Garrison said."

Migs debated how much to tell her. "They did find those syringes that you mentioned but getting you hooked on drugs didn't seem to be the objective."

"Doesn't make sense, does it?"

"Nope. Garrison's digging deeper." Migs stood and walked over to his duffle, slinging it over his shoulder. "Make a list of what you need and we can either go to a shop tomorrow or get what we need online."

"Are we supposed to use credit cards?"

"You forget I have five sisters."

The way Ariana was looking at him made him shift on his feet and made the wall suddenly interesting.

"Before I met your family, I couldn't imagine you with five sisters," she said huskily.

His attention returned to her and their gazes locked. "And now?"

"Now I understand where that marshmallow part of you comes from."

He scowled. "Marshmallow? That's insulting."

"Migs, I find it very endearing." Those words and the dazzling smile she shot him became his undoing. He needed space from this woman who had the ability to spin his emotions on a dime.

He was falling for his wife.

Fast.

10

Ariana came awake to a kiss on her brow, her eyes opening to a blurry image of Migs leaning over her. His hair was wet and stuck out in short tousled spikes. The woodsy notes of cedar and leather tickled her nose. The familiar scent of Migs was a welcome comfort while she took in her unfamiliar surroundings. It was morning, the rays of the sun peeking through the slats of the blinds behind him. The unexpected crow of a rooster added to her disorientation which, thankfully, was temporary as she swam past the surface of sleep-hazed consciousness and remembered the night before. Miguel's family, dinner in an expansive kitchen, but her thoughts were dominated by what followed after.

"Hi," she whispered.

"Good morning, babe. Sleep okay?"

"Like a baby. You?"

He shrugged. "All right."

He slept beside her on the floor again, but unlike the hotel's carpet, hardwood was not as forgiving. The couch in the room was longer than the one in Vegas, but with the width of his shoulders, it wouldn't be comfortable either.

"Migs, it's ridiculous for you to sleep on the floor. This bed is big enough for both of us." He backed up a bit as she sat up and leaned against the headboard, rubbing her eyes to erase the last remnants of sleep.

"Are you sure that's going to be okay with you?" His head dipped slightly as he peered up at her.

"After what happened between us last night? It'll be silly for you to torture yourself. And don't lie about sleeping, okay? Those dark circles under your eyes say otherwise."

"Sure you can resist me, babe?" He smirked.

Her brow arched. "Seems you're the one who can't resist keeping his hands to himself." Her mouth curved into an impish smile. "I bet your shower this morning was because you couldn't forget about last night either. What you did to me down there?" She dipped her chin.

His eyes widened and his throat bobbed.

What are you doing, Ariana? She was careful about flirting. She wouldn't say she was a beauty queen, but she'd gotten into awkward situations in her teenage and young adult years with men. She'd been called a tease. A *puta.* And the worst part was when Raul got wind of it and made that offender disappear. She carried guilt from that too. But with Migs, she was discovering an inner siren, and she reveled in it. He was her husband after all, she thought possessively.

"What's the matter, Miguel?" she asked. "Cat got your tongue?"

A slow smile chased away the shadows under his eyes, and he leaned forward to kiss her.

"No!" She put a hand to his mouth. "We need to establish ground rules!"

He reared back, brows knitting together. "Ground rules?"

"One, no kissing upon waking up. Both of us need to rinse our mouths."

"Wow, that's—"

Ariana shot out of bed. A pet peeve of hers coming to the fore. "I know we see it in movies all the time … they wake up, they kiss. I'm like ewww ... brush your teeth or use mouth-wash. You will say that I smell heavenly." She waved her arm with flourish. "Or I smell like roses. You'll say anything so you can have morning sex—"

She stopped because Migs was cracking up, and he was actually swiping at the corners of his eyes.

"Are you okay?"

"Yes," he said, still choking with laughter. "Go on—"

"I don't know if I should. What are you finding so funny?"

He cleared his throat even when his eyes still danced with mirth. "Nothing, babe. It's just ... you're very particular about morning breath." His face turned serious, but the twitches of his lips gave him away. "What if I want to wake you up with my mouth?"

Heat pulsed between her legs, the little bud of her woman-hood awakened to his lusty proposition, and she had to squeeze her thighs. "What? Like kiss me all over?" Her voice turned husky.

He stood and moved closer; she stepped back, mouth dry.

"Waking you up with an orgasm. I'm going straight for the prize between your legs, babe."

"Oh." It was her turn to swallow. "You're still not kissing me on the mouth, right?"

"I don't know, that might follow."

"Hmm ..."

"So what's the second rule?"

"I haven't gotten that far yet. I'll think of something." She spun around and padded barefoot to the bathroom to freshen up, just in case he had the crazy idea to steal a kiss. She wouldn't put it past him. With four younger sisters, she could imagine him as a merciless jokester, and yet she could see him as a staunch protector, too.

That was Raul and Jose. Tears brimmed her eyes as she stood in front of the mirror. They were both gone. How was it she had two brothers and she lost them both to the narcos. Jose—she could have prevented.

Migs appeared in the reflection of the mirror, leaning against the doorframe. His smile faded as he took in her expression. "What's wrong?"

She shook her head, grabbed her toothbrush, and started her morning ritual. Migs waited patiently for her to finish. He wasn't going anywhere until she answered him. Her husband was that stubborn.

"I thought about you with your sisters, and I remembered my brothers, okay?"

"Ariana ..."

She couldn't stand the pity on his face. There was no question Raul may have deserved his violent end, but every time she thought of Jose, her heart couldn't help aching at the thought of a wasted life. A life of promise.

"I'm okay." She walked to the door and gripped its edge. "Now scoot. I need to pee."

Ten minutes later, they both headed to the kitchen for breakfast. Coffee was already brewing and Leon, who Ariana realized was the man talking to Tessa's husband yesterday, was instructing one of the girls to fetch Abbi Mena.

Unlike the night before where they had dinner at the table in the alcove, the farm table directly in front of the kitchen counters was set for breakfast. Platters of sunny-side-up eggs, sausages, and other breakfast meats were covered with wire mesh domes similar to the ones used for a picnic. Leon handed them each a mug of coffee.

"Gracias, Leon," Migs said and immediately took a sip.

Ariana thanked the older man as well.

"Your Pops wants to see you in the office after breakfast," Leon said.

"His office here?"

"Yes."

They exchanged a bit of small talk before Leon left the kitchen through the door leading to the patio.

"Your father works early," Ariana commented.

"Michoacán is two hours ahead." Migs peeked under the wire-mesh dome at the food and scrunched up his nose. "I don't know about you, but I'm ready for old-fashioned cereal and milk."

He stood and disappeared into a pantry or what amounted to a whole room. Curious, Ariana followed him and lounged against the frame of the open door, marveling at the shelving made of roughened wood, giving the space a rustic and frontier-like flare. In front of the shelving were sacks of heirloom corn of different colors, a good variety of beans, coffee, and crates of avocado. Off to one corner a leg of ham hung from the ceiling. Meanwhile Migs approached holding a box of Wheaties.

He laughed at the disapproval in her eyes as he passed her back into the kitchen. "What?"

"There's so much food and that's what you're going to eat?"

"Don't worry. Food won't go to waste. That's also for the workers in Abbi Mena's garden."

"Workers? How big is her garden?"

"She has a field of different heirloom corns, so yeah, it's big."

"How about your sisters?"

"Tessa doesn't live here. They have a house a block away, but they usually come for dinner after working at the warehouse."

"She works there too?"

"Yes."

"And Bella?"

"All three of my sisters work there, but Bella usually goes in late. Lettie not so much, only when they need an extra hand. She prefers working in the field with abuelita."

"Huh," Ariana said as she sat down and sipped her coffee. While Migs rummaged through the fridge for milk, she mulled over her impression of his sisters.

Tessa seemed as bossy as Migs and had expensive taste in food. Bella seemed to be the fun-loving one. Ariana couldn't make up her mind about Lettie yet, she seemed like the quiet one who thought before she spoke. And if she was out with Abbie Mena, maybe Lettie was the one following her grandmother's philosophy of farm-to-table.

Just as Migs came back with two types of milk, a loaf, and white queso, his grandmother and Lettie entered the kitchen.

Each was wearing a wide-brimmed straw hat and long-sleeved shirt, both toting a shallow basket laden with ears of corn.

"We're going to have a good harvest," Abbie Mena declared.

"Is that so?" Migs quipped.

His grandmother lowered the basket on the kitchen counter and picked up an ear, peeling back the husk and exposing the kernel. "Firm and plump, right, Lettie?"

His sister nodded.

"The peppers are coming along well too."

"Don't make them too spicy, Mamá." Drew strode into the kitchen.

Abbi Mena glanced over at Ariana. "I need to have different sections for peppers. Everyone in this family wants different heat levels."

"I like them hot," Migs said, without skipping a beat. "So dry them up for me."

"I'm with your Pops," Ariana said. "I don't like it too spicy either."

"Drew likes mild." Abbi Mena headed over to the sink to wash her hands. "He only likes jalapeños very watered down."

"No, he'll eat a Chipotle," Lettie corrected. "That's as far as he would go."

"Lettie, go wash your hands so we can start eating," Abbi Mena said as she dried her own with the kitchen towel and sat at the table.

"Where's Mamá?" Migs asked.

Drew removed the cover from the platters and glanced at his son. "You've been gone a long time. You forget Delia's ritual on Friday mornings?"

"Ah, Market Fridays," Migs explained to Ariana. "She visits the wet market and stops by the Farmer's one too."

"I told her I could send a *muchacho* to get what she needed." Drew took his seat at the head of the table. "And sometimes she's okay with that, but you're here with a new wife and the twins are coming home from Berkeley this weekend, too."

"You'll meet double-trouble," Lettie said.

"Don't go scaring my new bride away."

"She's not a bride yet because you didn't have a wedding," a voice from the entrance joined the conversation. Bella shuffled into the kitchen wearing fluffy slippers and matching designer sweatpants and hoodie. She kissed Drew on the cheek and did the same to her grandmother.

"Yes, we did," Migs shot back.

"Having Elvis declare you man and wife does not count as a wedding." Bella plopped down in the chair to the left of Ariana, and beside her dad.

"Tell that to the thousands of brides and grooms for whom he did," Migs countered and Ariana's head swung back to him. "And just to be clear. It was Tony Montana who married us."

Bella rolled her eyes. "That's even worse."

"You both know arguing about this won't get anywhere." Drew pointedly looked at his son, an amused glint in his eyes.

Like a tennis match, Ariana's head swung back to the left.

"Just teasing Bella, Pops."

"*Your* just teasing could send her into tears."

Bella rolled her eyes again. "Pops, that was four years ago. I'm not eighteen anymore."

"Yes, but it was like World War III exploded," Lettie piped in and swallowed a giggle, nudging Abbi Mena on her left, who gave a shake of her head.

Curious, Ariana asked Bella. "What happened four years ago?"

"I dyed my hair pink to impress a guy in a rock band." Migs' sister picked up a tortilla from a warming basket and handed the container to Ariana. "He was having a party at his house and it was an eighties theme, so big hair, right? Migs comes home after four months of absence. I was excited to see him, too. You know the first thing he said when he saw me?"

Everyone was quiet at the table as Bella paused dramatically. "'Damn, sis, did a cotton candy factory explode on your head?'"

Ariana's mouth fell open as she twisted her head disbelievingly at her husband who was quietly shaking with laughter, his face turning red.

"Miguel!" she admonished.

"What?" Migs said in a defensive voice. "I didn't know she was going out on a date."

"Well, guess what, jerk-face? You ruined the evening." Bella leaned forward and glared at her brother.

"She wouldn't stop crying and her eyes got all swollen," Lettie supplied.

"But months later you said that the gringo was not a good man, right, *mi amor?*" This from Abbi Mena. Ariana was starting to see her role in the family. She was the equalizer, the referee, the person who knew when to steer the subject back to even ground.

"He turned out to be a player," Bella admitted grudgingly. "Got two girls pregnant."

"Oh boy," Ariana said.

"You just saved your brother from doing time, because I sure as hell would've put him in the ground," Migs growled.

Bella cocked her head in her brother's direction. "Love you, big brother."

The affection passing between brother and sister was palpable. It made Ariana's heart clench with a yearning for a relationship she would never have again. As the Alcantara-Walker family broke their fast, she wondered if being around them was a good idea or if it would end in heartbreak once her marriage to Migs was over.

11

"COCAINE IN THE AVOCADO TRUCKS?"

After breakfast, Miguel's father asked him to step into his office for a chat. He thought Pops was going to grill him about Ariana, but he didn't expect the bomb Drew Walker dropped on him.

"Yes, I don't know how long this has been going on under our noses. My meeting with Joaquín this morning yielded no answers either. He's adamant the coke didn't originate in Michoacán."

"Agreed. The people of Cayetano fought too hard to let the cartels back in."

Years before, when Americans started falling in love with the green fruit, the avocado business boomed, and the cartels took notice. It wasn't called green gold for nothing. Farmers were harassed, lands were usurped, and those who resisted were killed—their bodies hung along the road as a warning. But where the Alcantara family ruled in the town of Cayetano, the residents were loyal and quickly rose up and formed a private army. Mexico's government was fighting its own drug war and left them alone. The narcos who went after the Michoacán agricultural business were splinter groups from the larger cartels and newer blood. Migs wondered if the remaining leaders would honor the unspoken code not to touch the Alcantara family.

His uncle Don Pepito—Joaquín and Hector's father— hired mercenaries to fight against the splinter group and train the Cayetano private army. Four years had passed since his uncle's death—a death that riddled Migs with guilt and made him stay away from his family.

"The truck broke down in Sinaloa," Drew said. "Driver called Joaquín and said he was staying overnight. Your cousin got suspicious and sent one of his men to inspect the truck while it sat in one of the truck depots. Sure enough, fucking coke was mounted in the wheelbase."

His father rarely cursed and was a very chill businessman, so this gave Migs an idea how this turn of events had shaken him.

"So the driver is a suspect. How many truck drivers do you have?"

"We have one hundred and twenty who are full-time. Same number part-time."

"Shit."

"The farm employs over five hundred workers and we have around a hundred in our warehouse. Cesar has six supervisors under him."

"Is Tessa aware of this problem?"

"I haven't told her because ..." Drew let the statement hang and Migs sucked in a breath.

"No way is Cesar in on it, Pops," he growled. "Did Joaquín suggest that?" He never liked that particular cousin of his even when they were kids. Joaquín was the same age as Tessa, his sister being older by a few months, and Migs recalled the ongoing competition between the families about who was the first grandchild. And Tio Pepito's wife had the audacity to say that it was the first male grandchild who mattered. Avoiding Joaquín would be impossible at Abbi

Mena's eightieth. He might as well prepare for the inevitability of veiled looks and clipped conversation.

A nagging suspicion persisted that Joaquín knew of Migs' involvement in Tio Pepito's demise.

"He did not," Drew paused. "Not directly. He pointed out that someone would be on the receiving end here."

"You have a hundred other possibilities."

"Look, I didn't bring you in here to get you involved. Just wanted to give you a heads up why I'm distracted. It's not because I'm ignoring you or Ariana while you're visiting." Drew smiled, his face relaxing. "I'd say that's the single best news I've received in weeks."

"Thanks," Migs acknowledged. "But fuck keeping me out of this, Pops. I'm here. Make me useful."

Drew's brow arched. "I thought you were a disenfranchised ex-soldier."

"I'm still an Alcantara," he said roughly. "The livelihood that supports you, Mamá, abuelita, and the five Marias— everyone in this house is important to me."

Drew leaned back in his chair and regarded him thoughtfully. "What are you suggesting?"

"Is the truck still at the truck stop?"

"Yes. The mechanic was returning with the parts this morning to do the repairs. Should take a few hours. Joaquín is debating whether to call it back to Michoacán."

"Why did he get suspicious?" Migs' brain bounced around the information in his head. "There's nothing unusual with transport breaking down. Happens all the time."

"Let me back up a bit." His father hinged forward in his seat. "A week ago, a business rival made a snide comment at a society party. High-ranking government officials overheard the statement about the cartels getting their piece of Michoacán gold and said your cousin was too naïve to take over the business."

"Ouch."

"The man suggested that maybe the wrong heir was put in charge."

"Did he mean Hector?" Migs said incredulously. "I'm surprised he's going to make it to his thirties with the way he's partying it up in Vegas." And using the excuse that he was running the hotel. Everyone knew the Alcantaras had capable staff managing that part of their business.

"You, Migs."

"Me?" His brows drew together. "Does that man even know I work as a mechanic in LA?"

"After you left the army, the Mexican government was very interested in you."

Migs was aware of this. He'd been approached a couple of times by agents of the CNI—Mexico's intelligence agency. His handlers at the DEA and later at the agency had to make sure his cover was airtight as a former spec ops guy disillusioned with Uncle Sam who joined a biker gang and had become a mechanic. Migs also made sure he built enough street cred in LA as a bruiser-for-hire.

"Thought they'd be over that myth by now."

"You weren't a myth. You never talked about it, but I knew you believed in what you were fighting for." A sad look came over his father's eyes. "I'm sorry our government let you down."

Migs held his father's gaze as much as he could. The lies he'd told his family had been weighing heavy on his shoulders for a while, but he reminded himself it was for their own good. They would be horrified if they found out he was in the thick in the fight against the cartels, especially with what happened to Tio Pepito.

"That's in the past. I'm happier now...although you know who Ariana's brother was, right?"

A pained expression crossed his father's face. "If I hadn't, you can be sure your sisters gave me the scoop. Tessa wasn't very sure but looked up Ariana online." His dad paused. "What the hell is a vitamin infusion spa?"

Migs chuckled. "I'll fill you in on that later. Now tell me what else you know about the cocaine in our trucks?"

"I DON'T UNDERSTAND why we need vitamins injected into us." Abbi Mena invited Ariana to tour her sprawling garden. Different heirloom corns, a variety of peppers, vegetables, and other herbs like cilantro were in full growth.

Ariana laughed, not offended at all. "You know how fast-paced LA is. The stress. The nightlife. Stars with hangovers need a quick fix to be up and looking vibrant in front of the camera within a few hours."

"Your vitamin infusion does that?"

"Yes, I see immediate benefits in our clients."

"Maybe it's just dehydration?" the older woman looked skeptical.

Ariana laughed again. "That too. When people are fatigued, they need vitamins and nutrients. You've heard about the banana bag that they use to cure hangovers? The vitamin infusion we use is from Switzerland."

"Miguel said you lived there for a while." Abbi Mena bent over to inspect a squash. Even if she was schooled in modern farming the older woman explained, she still followed the ancient tradition of Tres Hermanas—three sisters—corn, beans and squash. Corn was a nutrient hungry plant and the beans enriched the soil with nitrogen. The corn provided the bean with a pole to climb, and lastly the squash crept along the ground and blocked sunlight, becoming a natural weed killer.

"Yes, I lived there for three years and made frequent trips back." With Switzerland on the forefront of advanced medical technology and Ariana making LA her home, she knew skin care and anything as elusive as the fountain of youth would be a hit in the city of angels, but she believed no amount of topical cream was enough if the internal health was not in sync. "Many of our clients are too busy. They may even have a personal chef or a food service which provides them a balanced meal, but many times they are stressed. And stress depletes essential vitamins and nutrients. That's why they need an infusion. A percentage of them have stomach issues and with my methods what they need is delivered straight into the bloodstream."

"All right, I won't argue with you," Abbi Mena said. "I still think real food is better." She waved at her corn stalks. "The American diet has made corn the enemy. It's because most of the corn is GMO. In Mexico, the farmers put a lot of pressure on our government to outlaw this because it is contaminating our heritage crops." Fierce conviction framed her face. "Corn is deeply intertwined in our culture. People think corn is just carbs—starch. It's not. Take the masa for example."

"The nixtamalization process releases the B vitamins," Ariana said.

Miguel's grandmother nodded—a pleasantly surprised look flashed across her face. "Very good."

"I will do a disservice to my clients and my own culture if I don't know this."

"Abuelitaaa!"

They both turned to see Lettie calling from the kitchen entrance that fronted the garden.

"Mamá is back from the market."

The older woman gave her a sideways glance as if sizing her up. "There's a lot to prepare for the weekend." A smile tugged at the corners of Abbi Mena's mouth. "Let's have some fun."

· · ·

THE ENTIRE FARMER'S table was covered with assorted plastic and paper bags. Migs walked in, carrying more, a fistful in each hand. Bella followed him holding an armload of bottles. They were arguing as usual.

"I would think living in LA would've sucked that machismo out of you."

"It was one bag, Bella."

"You could have broken the olive oil! Tessa would be pissed. That's her special request from Mamá." Migs' sister turned to Ariana. "Why do men insist on carrying the bags in all at once?"

"It was three trips, and this was the last one." Realizing there was no more room on the table, Migs rounded by Ariana on his way to the kitchen counter. "Give me a kiss, woman."

A gleam in his eyes caused a flutter low in her belly. "So bossy," she murmured before doing as he ordered.

"You like it when I boss you around." He smirked and passed her.

"I think, Bella, it's because our brother couldn't wait to see his wife," Lettie said sagely.

"They just had breakfast together not two-hours ago," Bella said.

"They're on their honeymoon." Delia walked in. A towel was draped around her neck and she was fanning herself. "Hooh, the market was hot, but I think I got everything you want, Mami."

Abbi Mena was at the sink, already preparing the market haul. "This fish is very fresh. We can bake it in the outdoor oven or marinate the other one in lime. Leticia!"

Migs' sister walked over to their grandmother who gave her instructions on what to do with the fish.

"Friday is usually fish and leftover day," Bella explained, walking to stand beside Ariana. "But I heard we're having *lechón* on Sunday."

"Roast suckling pig?"

"Yes. Mamá told Migs to check the outdoor fire pit."

"Wow."

"And that's not even considering tomorrow." Bella grinned at her.

Migs came back around and grabbed Ariana by the waist, tugging her close while addressing his mother. "*Sí*, Mamá. What's for tomorrow?"

"Ask your abuelita. I bought too many things, I don't remember anything," Delia answered without looking up from sorting the bags. "Some of these are Tessa's. That daughter of mine has expensive taste. Where's the olive oil?"

Bella nodded to a corner of the kitchen. "There. Migs nearly broke it."

"Aren't you supposed to go to the warehouse?" Her brother shot back.

"I don't feel like going in today. Tessa can handle the guys. It's Friday."

"She has to do payroll. Why don't you help her out," Delia said. "That way I don't have to listen to you and your brother argue all day. You'll make Ariana think that's all you two ever do."

"That's probably fifty percent true," Migs muttered under his breath.

"All right," Bella said grudgingly. "I know when I'm not wanted." With that, she flounced out of the kitchen.

"Do you really fight all the time?" Ariana asked her husband.

It was Delia who answered. "Typical sibling fights. For some reason Miguel and Bella like to get into it. No harm," she paused. "Most of the time. I only said that so Bella would go help her sister. She's been lazy lately."

"She's moping about her breakup with Carl," Lettie announced.

"Still?" Delia said, surprised. "That was six months ago."

"What did Carl do?" Migs growled.

"Miguel, go check the fire pit," Abbi Mena interjected.

"You aren't roasting the pig until Sunday," her grandson countered.

"Do your abuelita a favor and go check. *Sí*, Miguelito? So I can put that one thing out of my mind?"

He exhaled heavily as if chastised. "All right." He stalked out of the kitchen.

After he left, Abbi Mena turned to her daughter and Lettie. "You two should know better than to mention Carl in front of Migs. You know how he'll react." The older woman looked at Ariana. "My grandchildren. They argue all the time. Sometimes it's their way of showing affection. Sometimes they are mortal enemies. But when one of them is hurt by someone outside the family, you can be sure they will be the first to protect each other."

A warm ache settled on her chest. "I got that feeling about Migs yesterday. It's the same with my brothers. When we were children, they teased me mercilessly, but if someone at school made me cry, they'd be the first to beat the guys up." She didn't add when Raul got older, the retribution he meted out was much worse.

The older woman's eyes grew soft. "You miss them."

She teared up, feeling so alone, and yet Abbi Mena's words brought her comfort. "Yes."

A look passed between them and Miguel's grandmother came over and took her hand, squeezing it. "One day you can tell me the story."

MIGS WIPED the sweat off his brow as he excavated the debris that had accumulated in the fire pit. Unlike the *Cochinillo* of Spain, the Latin American version was called lechón and could be heavier than twelve pounds. They would need a bigger pig to feed the entire Alcantara household and that also depended where the twins were on their diet. Were they vegetarian this month?

He chuckled as he thought about Maripat—Maria Patrice, and Maricor—Maria Corazon. They also went by Pat or Cora. Both were in their third year of Environmental Science in UC Berkeley and from what he'd gleaned from Pops, they were thinking of a master's degree in Agriculture and Natural Resources. His family had a strong affinity with the land, and Migs was determined to protect their dreams.

Burying the pole deeper into the ground to make it steadier, he nearly didn't feel the phone vibrate in his pocket. Fishing it out, he answered the call.

"I've instructed my contact at border patrol to let the truck through," Garrison said.

"Thanks."

"Sure you don't need my help?"

"No. At this point it's a family matter."

"They *are* bringing coke onto American soil."

"Still not our purview. It might not even figure on the DEA radar with the amount of cocaine being brought in. But I'd appreciate intel on the splinter groups that are terrorizing the Michoacán province." Migs walked under the shade of a peach tree. The noon sun was a killer.

"I left word with my DEA contact. I'll let you know."

"Have you gotten anywhere with Connie Roque?"

"She insists she wasn't involved."

"Right. Do you believe her?"

"No. But she hasn't had direct contact with any Carillo lieutenants. She was in a relationship with one of the Águilas. She could have been targeted for her access to Ariana. It'll take me some time to find out information on both fronts, but until we know more, we're keeping Connie and her daughter in a safehouse."

"Good." That was what Ariana would have wanted.

"I'll call you when I have more."

Ending the call with Garrison, Migs turned to see Ariana approaching with a beer in her hand.

"That for me?" he called.

"I was instructed by your abuelita to bring my man a cold one."

Migs chuckled. "She probably waited until she was certain I'd fixed the fire pit."

Ariana handed him a Miller Light. He hated these watered-down beers, but his sisters and father liked them. He'd probably do a beer run with Cesar and catch up. Thinking of his brother-in-law brought a frown to his face. He took a pull of his beer to hide his reaction.

"What's wrong?"

"This is like water," he said.

"Maybe that's what you need. If you're done here, lunch is almost ready."

"You mean they cleared that pile on the table?"

"No, we're eating by the alcove."

"Great, as long as it's not out here. I'm roasting. Come on, wife."

FRIDAY LUNCH at the Alcantara household was an informal affair. As everyone worked in the kitchen, finger food was laid on the table along with baskets of warm tortillas and salsas at each end. Leftover meat from the previous night was reworked with some sauce to provide a filling for tacos.

Bella walked in freshly showered and appeared to be dressed for work. She picked up a tortilla and slathered it with red salsa.

"You and Ari should come with me. Show her the warehouse."

Migs swallowed the bite he had in his mouth. That was

actually not a bad idea. Gave him a chance to suss around the place.

"Or not," Bella said.

"I was thinking it was the best idea you had today."

His sister rolled her eyes.

"No, really. I'm sure Ari would love to see it, but I promised to take her shopping …" Migs let that hang.

And his sister walked right into his trap. "Duh, do it online. I'll help. I have nothing to do in the office anyway except answer phones or emails."

"Oh, great, can you all drop off the corn at the Pateros grocery?" Lettie called from across the kitchen. "That would save me a trip."

"What happened to the corn grinder?"

"It broke. We need new lava rocks," Abbi Mena said. She was frying empanadas at the stove. Lettie, Mamá, and Ariana were filling and shaping the half-moon shaped snack.

"Make sure it's tortilla grind not tamale, okay?" Lettie said.

Migs chuckled. "Ah, Maria Leticia. How does she do that?"

"What? Keep track and listen to several conversations? I think she's learning that from Abbi Mena," Bella grumbled.

"I heard that!" Lettie laughed. "And these empanadas are for the workers at the warehouse. Why don't you wait a bit so you can bring them along?"

"Anything else, *mi hermana y señora*?" Bella sighed.

"What are you complaining about? Migs is right there with the muscle."

"She's becoming as bossy as Tessa," Migs muttered.

Everyone laughed.

12

"Do you know where the word avocado comes from?"

Ariana barely heard Bella's question as she stood in awe of the enormous facility. Forklifts were removing pallets from trucks and moving them to their assigned location. Different sized boxes and crates stood in columns and rows.

Turning to the other woman, she smiled. "No, but I'm sure you're about to tell me."

Bella's eyes twinkled. "The Aztecs discovered the fruit in 500 BC, they called it *āhuacatl*."

"Bella," Migs grumbled.

The teasing on his sister's face intensified, and it spiked Ariana's curiosity past the typical small talk. "And?"

"Well," Bella paused for dramatic effect. "It means testicles."

Ariana snorted a laugh. "Seriously?"

"Yes. Haven't you noticed they mostly grow in pairs and their shape and texture resembles that part of the male anatomy?"

Ariana's smile widened as she looked at Migs. "How about that? I learned something new today."

Grinning while shaking his head in amusement, Migs led

them around the perimeter of the warehouse. "The main packaging facility is in Michoacán. We handle almost thirty truckloads a day. This facility is mostly storage and distribution, but there's a section in the building used for repackaging."

Ariana rubbed her biceps. It was freezing inside where they were. Migs replaced her hands with his and gave her a rub-down.

"They need to keep the fruit cold," he explained.

Cesar and Tessa met them at the bottom of a flight of steps. Ariana glanced up where it led and saw an overhang structure—an office with sweeping windows that overlooked the entire facility.

The two men shook hands and embraced. Tessa hugged her brother and Ariana. "He's introducing you to the family business, I see." Pulling back, she eyed Bella. "Glad you're here. I need to do payroll."

"We dropped off some empanadas at the sales office," Bella said. She turned to Ariana. "After you're done with the tour, meet us back there and we can do some shopping." Tessa shook her head and walked ahead. "Later, guys. Busy day."

"Whelp, I better help her," Bella announced. "Enjoy the tour."

The sales marketing office was an outbuilding attached to the warehouse and it was their first stop when Migs pulled the Escalade into the parking lot where three trucks were waiting to be unloaded. As popular as avocado had gotten in the States, Ariana wasn't surprised, but her brain couldn't wrap around the sheer volume that was coming in, considering the Alcantaras were only one of the many distributors.

Cesar looked at Ariana. He was a few inches shorter than Migs and leaner. Everyone was leaner than Migs. The sisters made a joke that he was adopted, because none of the males in the family were bulky. The women were more on the stocky side as well. All boobs and hips, just like Ariana. Migs was a hybrid of gringo and Mexicano, Bella said.

Migs was perfect the way he was, Ariana thought wistfully of her husband.

"Ready for the tour?" Cesar asked.

"I hope it's not too much bother," Ariana said.

"Not at all. The workers are on their lunch break."

Most of the facility was indeed for storage, but Ariana was most impressed with the repackaging section of the plant. She was amazed at the automation. Conveyor belts and high-resolution optical grading facilitated the sorting of good and bad avocados, offering different levels of quality to the customer. Cesar said it was the same equipment they had at the main packing plant in Michoacán on a larger scale. He explained the cooling process started upon harvest, and the cooling chain was maintained until it was delivered to the customer to ensure quality.

"That would be a problem when the truck breaks down," Migs interjected. "Heard one of them was stalled in Sinaloa."

Cesar frowned. "Yes, but the cooling system was still working, so we're good."

"Have you ever lost an entire truck load?" Ariana asked.

"I can only think of two instances," Cesar replied, his eyes darting to Migs. "First was our truck breaking down far from town. The refrigeration unit was faulty, too. Driver didn't recharge his satellite phone. Drew and Joaquín were not happy. The other was a roadside wreck."

"How far will that set you back?" she asked.

Cesar shrugged. "We have a few days of stock, so it's not bad." He grinned uneasily. "Insurance covers such cases." He looked ahead at the contraption that was lowering boxes. "Here we have our box formation."

Ariana went along as Cesar droned on. She understood the basics of the assembly line and this was basically the same, but she was more curious at the uneasiness that bloomed between Migs and his brother-in-law.

"Is something the matter?" The tour didn't take long, maybe all of twenty minutes. Cesar excused himself, citing work he'd forgotten to do and left them to go up to his office, remarking that he would see them that night for dinner.

Migs held open the side door that led from the warehouse to the sales office. "I don't know what you mean."

"There was a tone between you two. Like the truck breaking down in Sinaloa was Cesar's fault."

"You're imagining things."

Ariana grew quiet. Maybe she was, but maybe she wasn't because Migs' face shut down. "It's okay if it's a family matter. Just say it's none of my business."

Migs head whipped to hers, jaw slackening. "You're family now."

"Not really, remember?" And she was glad when Bella met them near the entrance.

"Finally. I was getting bored out of my mind."

Her husband scowled at his sister. "It wasn't even twenty damned minutes."

"What's up his ass?" Bella cocked her head at her. "Did you two have a fight already?"

Ariana stared at Migs, making sure she communicated *I'm not imagining things* clearly with her eyes. Migs returned the irritation in her stare with interest.

Whatever.

Shaking her head, she stepped forward and tucked her arm into Bella's. "Don't mind him, we've got some shopping to do."

Ariana was dragging Bella away even if she didn't know where to go. There was a pinch in her heart, a pinch that reminded her that this was temporary no matter how believable their situation seemed at times. Getting attached was bad. Her arm on Bella loosened as she dropped her limb back to her side.

No. She shouldn't get attached.

MIGS WAS in a black mood as he waited for the corn to be turned into masa at the Pateros Latino Market. He left Ariana at the sales office so she could order what she needed with Bella at the helm. After a glorious forty-eight hours of married life where he figured everything was smooth sailing, reality smacked him right in the face. And it was all his fault. The half-truths he carried as an undercover agent were catching up with him, and he had no clue how to navigate that path while he was married to Ariana—who was herself a mark. Or used to be one.

One he was trying to protect, but his business with the avocado cocaine truck was a family matter and he was confused as shit what to do. His father confided in him alone, not even his sisters knew or his mother or even Abbi Mena. At least that was his gut feel.

His burner vibrated. There were only two people with his number. Garrison and Ariana. It was the latter, but the message was from Tessa.

More requests from the grocery.

Migs sighed in a mixture of mild irritation and fondness, which was his default reaction when dealing with the different personalities of his sisters. He walked over and scooped up a shopping basket and moved down the list Tessa had given him.

When the masa was ready, and he'd paid for the groceries, he drove back to the warehouse, nodding to the guards at the gate and Leon. Drew hired nothing but the best and that was why Migs was comfortable leaving Ariana in the sales office with another guard outside the door.

He parked right outside the entrance when Tessa, Bella, and Ariana emerged.

"You never responded to the text," Tessa said, getting into the back of the vehicle. "Did you get everything on my list?"

"Look behind you," Migs replied, his eyes on his wife climbing in beside him. "Were you able to order what you needed?"

"Yes."

"You owe me three thou, bro," Bella chortled behind him.

"That's it?" he deadpanned.

"See. I told you you should have ordered more."

Ariana shrugged. "I have enough for now. My things are in LA."

"How long are you planning to stay?" Tessa asked, followed by, "Thanks, Migs. What do I owe you?"

He made a tsk sound. "Just make me your tres leches cake and I'm good."

"That's it? I should ask you to shop more."

His two sisters carried the conversation and Ariana smiled at the appropriate times, but something was missing from earlier. A light had died in her eyes, and he didn't know how the fuck he was going to bring it back.

DURING THE SHORT drive to the house, his plans of cornering his wife and making her feel better about the situation were thwarted by the arrival of trouble.

Well, double trouble.

"Miguelitoooo!"

Pat and Cora.

He barely got out from the SUV when he was tackled by shrieking girls. They were the shortest in the family barely clearing five feet. Migs suspected they were four-eleven, but they insisted they were five one.

They also had a habit of pinching his cheeks.

"Hey, hey ... you're gonna ruin my pretty face," he winced. He was immediately dragged around the vehicle as Ariana also stepped out, but if her face was anything to go by, it was as if she wanted to climb back into the Escalade.

"Introduce us!" Pat ordered.

"Ariana, my crazy sisters Pat and Cora."

They smiled big.

"They're adopted," he deadpanned.

Cora elbowed him, her bony joint actually caught him unaware and he coughed.

"Don't believe him!" Pat yelled.

"Maripat, Maricor." Tessa shot the twins a sharp look. "Inside voices, *por favor*."

They hugged and kissed Tessa.

"Where's Gigi?" The twins looked for Tessa's two-year old.

"With Cesar's mom. He's going to pick her up on the way here."

"I can't wait to eat," Cora announced. "I'm starved. Pat and I wanted to wait for you."

Migs was about to point out that it was only four in the afternoon and then remembered it was Friday.

And they ate all day.

His sisters chatted up his new bride and, like his mother yesterday, they ushered her into the house with Bella following them. That left him and Tessa to unload the vehicle.

As he picked up the container of masa and some of the shopping bags, Tessa said, "I like your wife."

Migs grinned. "In case you haven't noticed, I like her too."

"Marriage is not easy, little brother. Don't mess up this one."

His head reared back. "It's my only one."

"Good." And with a cryptic smile, Tessa picked up a grocery bag in each hand and left him to carry the rest.

———————

THE HEAT of the day retreated with the setting sun and a mild breeze moved the family gathering to the slate patio. Latin dance music blared from the outdoor speakers as they settled in groups and chatted.

Pat, Cora, and Abbi Mena had Ariana's undivided attention as they debated agricultural practices, environmental economics, and the nutrition of the typical American diet versus a Mexican one.

Migs was staying out of that.

Tessa was rocking Gigi to sleep, standing over Cesar who was talking to Leon and his father.

He kicked back on a wooden bench, feet propped up on a coffee table constructed out of reclaimed pine, welcoming the peaceful company of Lettie while watching over his family. Bella was on her phone inside the house and he hoped to hell it wasn't with that Carl guy.

Delia appeared beside them, holding a tray of *paletas*—Mexican popsicles and a favorite in his youth. His eyes lit up, lowering his boots from the table. "Ah, *mi Mamá* ... what do we have here?"

"Peach and *horchata*. The peach is from Mami's fruit tree. You can have two."

Migs lowered his beer and picked an *horchata* one, eyes seeking Ariana. "Babe, you gotta try one of these," he called out.

Delia handed the tray to Lettie. "Why don't you bring this over to the others. I haven't got a chance to talk to Miguel all day."

"You and abuelita were busy prepping for the weekend," Migs said, sucking on the ice pop made of rice milk and cinnamon. His mother occupied the space Lettie vacated. "This is so good."

"It's rare we get the family all together like this." Delia reached over to his forehead and pushed back the hair that had fallen over. "You need a haircut."

Migs chuckled and dragged his fingers to comb his hair away from his face.

"I'm really happy for you, Miguel. Ariana seems to have hit it off with Mami. That's a good sign."

"There's a but there somewhere ..."

"Just a bit worried."

"Because of who her brother is——"

His mother studied her spread fingers. "Did you marry her to protect her from Raul Ortega's enemies?"

Should he deny it? It was the main reason he acted so quickly.

When he didn't answer, his mother added. "Do you love her, Miguel?"

At his continued silence, Delia sighed.

The *paleta* in his hand started to melt, the sticky liquid dripping to his jeans.

"You better eat that." His mother started to get up, a resigned look on her face.

"I care for her. A lot."

She angled toward him and settled back on the bench. "That's good."

"I'm attracted to her." A smile played at the corners of his mouth. "A lot." He emphasized again and took that time to swipe at the *paleta*, catching his wife's eyes on them. Sitting beside his mother kept the filthy thoughts at bay, but he kept a lock on Ariana's gaze until she was forced to look away.

A brief laugh broke from his mother's lips. "Oof, what am I worried about? The heat between you two is enough to melt that *paleta* in your hand."

"You think abuelita suspects?"

"Maybe. She's of a different generation. Hers was an arranged marriage, but I can tell you she and Papá had a good marriage. One with lots of love and respect. I believe she came to love him very much. As for Papá, he adored your abuelita. Maybe that's why Mami has taken to Ariana so quickly. She sees a part of her as a new bride."

Migs set aside the popsicle stick and picked up his beer. "That explains a lot."

And it gave him hope that the marriage between them would work. Now if only he could convince his bride of the same.

13

ARIANA WOKE up to a splitting headache. She was face down on the pillow, her mouth dry as cotton. Prying her eyes open took sheer willpower. The room was dark save for the bright sunlight peeking through the slits of the blinds. Somehow, she knew it was late in the day.

She also knew she drank too much the night before. Migs' sister, Pat was the resident bartender and shoved her one flavor of mojito after another. It also didn't help that she and Migs were in a weird place yesterday, and it appeared he was giving her space or maybe he knew that keeping Ariana away from his sisters was a futile endeavor. She didn't feel abandoned. In fact, she felt a form of respite to be away from him if even for the evening. Letting herself float in the craziness of his family.

She groaned and fell on her back. Canting her head to the right, there was a body pillow beside her, and it did seem Miguel slept in the bed last night. She just couldn't remember.

Wait. She did.

He was holding her hair while she was throwing up in the toilet.

Mortified, she gave a little whimper. She shouldn't have

drank that much, and should have told Pat not to ply her with liquid fortitude. But seeing Migs and Delia in a very serious conversation made her nervous, and the way Migs stared at her from across the yard made her stomach do a couple of salsa jigs.

She recalled Migs coming over to their huddle, telling his sister that Ariana was cut off. She tried to stand and tell him otherwise but ended up falling into him. He probably kept her upright so she wouldn't make a fool of herself.

Oh my God.

How could she show her face downstairs?

She glanced at her watch. Ten a.m.

Ten!

She bolted up on the bed and regretted it. Her brain bounced around her skull. A glass of water sat on her nightstand with a note.

ABBI MENA HAS a hangover cure for you, but you'll have to get out of bed and come to the kitchen. No hiding in the bedroom, babe.

M

Despite the thousand little men chipping away at her head, she had to smile. She had a feeling Migs' abuelita was going to prove to her that indeed food worked better than an infusion.

IT WAS the first time Ariana had seen the kitchen devoid of the hum of activity. At the farm table was Abbi Mena, Delia, and Migs. None of Migs' sisters were around. When she walked into the kitchen, her husband looked up from shoveling food from a bowl, and the way his expression softened at the sight of her made her heart skip.

Goodness, Ari. It was just a look.

It wasn't even his heated look; it was more of an affectionate one… one could even say there was love.

"Where's ev..everyone?" she stammered.

"What? You haven't had enough of the five Marias?" Abbi Mena smiled. She pushed back from the table and headed to the refrigerator.

"Twins and Bella are still asleep. Apparently, you're not the only one who had one too many mojitos." Migs took a sip of his coffee. "How's the head?"

"It's making me pay for last night," she said sheepishly.

"You have to forgive my twins. They turned twenty-one and they couldn't wait to try all kinds of cocktails," Delia said.

"That was over a year ago," Migs reminded her.

"Is it?" Delia said in wonder, taking a sip from her cup. "It feels like yesterday."

"They say they are model students when they are at Berkeley." Abbi Mena walked back and handed her a glass of pale-yellow liquid. "Drink this."

"What is it?"

She smiled mysteriously. "Figure it out."

Ariana gave a puff of laughter and lowered herself to the chair Migs slid back for her. Taking a tentative taste, she knew immediately what was in it. Jose gave her a similar concoction when she snuck out to party when she was fourteen. "Sugar-cane juice and ginger?" She smacked her lips a couple of times. "Lime?"

Abbi Mena smiled serenely at Migs. "You picked well. Your wife fits right in with our family."

"Oh, Mami, don't pressure them about the need to fit in," Delia chided. "As long as Migs and Ariana are happy together, we're happy for them, right?"

"Were you not happier when you had children?"

"It was a different kind of happiness," Delia said, her gaze softening, and then she reached out and covered abuelita's hand. "And then you came to stay with us. Made us more complete."

"You're just happy you have someone to cook for your big family." She turned to look at Migs and her. "And I hope I'll live to cook for your little ones, too. Like I said the first day, your children will be strong and beautiful. Good hips, your Ariana."

She felt heat creep up her cheeks.

"Mami, leave them alone. You sound like a horse breeder."

"Nonsense." Abbi Mena gave a wave of her hand.

"You two need to spend some time away from family," Delia said.

Migs chuckled. "We just got here."

"I mean lunch. It's going to be a cloudy day, not too hot. Rare in July. It won't rain," Delia said. "Go to the stream, hmm? There's a good picnic spot."

"Where the Ficus tree is?"

Delia nodded. "You won't miss it."

IT WAS A SETUP. Although Ariana was ready to be alone with her husband again, she had an inkling that Delia knew more about their arrangement than what they presented to his family. Ariana thought she was doing her part well. She wasn't flinching anymore when Migs put his hand on her waist and tugged her close.

It felt … natural.

Their situation was confusing her, but maybe it was her fault by going along with Migs when he hinted he wanted to make this real and not asking him how *real* he wanted this to be.

As Delia sent them off with a basket of food, and with the family standing in a line at the back of the patio as if seeing them off, it was almost comical … like "Shoo …Go be alone and have your honeymoon."

They walked silently along a path that rimmed the corn

fields, Migs helping her over uneven terrain. Sneakers were becoming her favorite footwear.

"Sorry about that," he muttered when they disappeared from his family's line of sight.

She laughed lightly. "Your mom doesn't do subtle, does she?"

Migs didn't reply, just continued to walk.

"Does she know?"

He stopped moving and faced her. "She knows I married you to protect you."

"Oh." She stared off in the distance. "I guess it's not so hard to figure that out."

"Never had a serious girl. Never brought home a girl-friend." He grinned wryly. "Guess I didn't prepare them for anything."

"Wow! Go big or go home, huh? You surprised them with a wife."

The sun escaped the clouds and blistered them with its heat. "Come on." His hand on her waist was firmer now and lost its earlier tentativeness.

"Do the rest of your family know?"

"What do you bet they're making speculations now?"

"Well, if your mom is pushing you to spend time with me—"

"I care about you, Ariana. I care about you enough to give you my name to protect you."

"Is that what you told your mother?"

"Yes."

"She was okay with that?"

Migs exhaled in frustration. "She is. Everyone likes you. Everyone told me not to fuck this up."

Conversation momentarily ceased when they arrived at the tree line and he had to help her down a steep bank. At the bottom of the mound, her eyes widened as she took in the beauty of their surroundings.

"This is still your property?"

"Yup. Don't worry. Our land extends past the stream, but it's more valley and not as flat. Need an all-terrain vehicle to explore. It's fun. I'll take you around some time."

"This offers a lot of privacy."

A teasing tone entered his voice. "Why? What did you have in mind?"

She gave him the side-eye. "Food. I hardly ate this morning."

Concern furrowed his brows. "How's your hangover?"

"Cured within an hour of taking that sugarcane brew. Ariana-zero, Abbi Mena-one."

Migs burst out laughing. "Is there a competition between you and abuelita?"

She smiled. "Not really. You can call it a difference of opinion."

"You're both opinionated."

"I'm a very agreeable person."

The look Migs shot her gave her a clear idea what he thought about that statement.

Ariana bit back a smile.

They continued plodding along until they reached the Ficus tree Delia described to them. It was over forty feet tall, maybe more and almost as wide.

"It's kind of bumpy over here but there's enough space between the roots to have a picnic." Migs set aside the basket and spread a colorful Aztec printed blanket over the ground. He flipped open the lid of the basket and showed Ariana its contents—bread, cheese and lunch meat items, including a bottle of wine.

"Mamá said you've had enough Mexican food coming out of your ears since we arrived. Time for a break." He smiled when her face lit up. "Missed bread, did you?"

"And butter." She could feel the saliva pooling at the underside of her tongue as he set the crusty round boule on the small cutting board. When he cut a piece and handed her one, she held it to her nose and inhaled. There was nothing like the aroma of fresh bread.

She realized her eyes were closed, because when she blinked hers open, Migs was staring at her with that familiar heat in his eyes. Like she was the meal and not what was in the picnic basket.

"What?" she challenged.

"I thought you were about to have an orgasm." He returned his attention to the task at hand. "You know you ruined my plans last night," he added conversationally.

"What plans?" she asked, slathering a generous amount of butter on the bread.

"I was saving a popsicle to use on you."

Her heart started to race. "What did you have in mind?"

Her voice was breathless, and warmth bloomed between her thighs. Done with cutting the loaf, Migs set the knife aside, reached into the basket again and unearthed a blocky kitchen towel. Unwrapping that, he revealed two *paletas* between reusable ice packs. He confused her when he stashed it back into the basket.

"Those are going to melt."

"That'll depend on you."

"Me?"

All humor and heat disappeared from his face, replaced by an expression akin to resoluteness. His eyes held hers prisoner like an interrogator about to ask the most difficult question. From a kneeling position, he leaned forward, caging her in, his face inches away.

"You."

She swallowed, cursing the bite of bread she'd eaten for stealing the moisture in her mouth, or maybe it was Migs and his very dark, determined eyes.

"I don't like this state of limbo in our marriage," he said.

"I—"

"Circling around each other. Like we're always waiting for the other shoe to drop."

"But it's true," she argued. "We're waiting for Carillo to make a move."

"And then what, Ari? After you're safe, we divorce?"

"Migs, that was the plan. You laid it out like that. Why are you—" she caught herself. He hated the word 'complicated' to describe them and judging from the narrowing of his eyes, he knew she was about to say that. "And you reminded me yesterday that I was not family. Not really."

"Ah, so we're getting to the root of why you froze me out yesterday." He moved from in front of her and sat beside her. "But if you remember, I said the opposite. You are family, Ari, but somehow you managed to twist it in your head."

"Why is it always me?" She angled her gaze at him.

"Remember the first night we were here? I told you I wanted to make you my wife in every way. That was why I was taking this slow."

"I don't think you understand the word *slow*."

He grunted. "It's hard when we share the same bedroom and, before you banish me back to the floor, I refuse to go about this the wrong way."

"We did start this the wrong way."

"My grandparents' marriage was an arranged one."

This surprised her, but then again, arranged marriages weren't uncommon in Mexico.

"And it worked," Migs stressed. "And we are way ahead of them at this point if we're doing comparisons."

She could feel herself turn red.

"I'm not talking about the sex," he said.

"We haven't had sex."

"Stop reminding me. You made me sleep on the floor on our wedding night." An aggrieved expression appeared on his face.

Ariana slapped a hand to her mouth to keep from

laughing aloud, but she ended up snorting one out anyway.

"I'll never live that down. It's an affront to the Alcantara pride."

"You mean the macho image."

He scowled. "We're getting off topic. Again. You seem to have a way of making me forget why I wanted to clear things up."

"The status quo is fine."

"Is it? Admit it. You were pissed yesterday when I couldn't tell you my problem with Cesar."

"All you had to say was it was family business."

"And you keep insisting you're not family and it's annoying as hell."

"I'm annoying?"

"It's a slap to my face, Ari. Think about it. I gave you my name, and you're throwing it back at me. My family has taken you in as their own. I'm not expecting gratitude. It was no hardship marrying you. I know I let you think it was just temporary, but I'm realizing this charade we thought we're going to keep up? I can't do it. I can't pretend to be your husband and not show you what it means to be one. It's fucking with my head. It's fucking with my family. I was an idiot to think it was easy to pretend."

His eyes singed into hers as she realized her lungs had not expunged air the whole time he was speaking.

"I'm starting to care for you something deep." He took her hand and placed it palm down over his chest. "In here. And before we fuck this all up, we need to make a decision. If you think you can't feel something for me in return, I'll continue to give you the protection of the Alcantara name, but we can't lie to my immediate family. I need to move out of our bedroom, and we certainly cannot sleep in the same bed because I can't promise I wouldn't be balls deep inside you if you make the mistake of draping yourself all over me and humping that pussy on my hand when you're having a sexy dream."

Her cheeks were flaming now. "Is that what happened?"

"Last night." He clipped, his breathing turning rough. "Yes. Why did you think I put a pillow between us? You can't seem to stay on your side of the bed. Don't get me wrong. It was the sweetest torture, but know there will be consequences, and I don't want to be accused of taking advantage of my wife."

He dropped her hand and she noticed how his own shook until he clenched them into fists. She knew Migs was attracted to her, but she thought it was a natural attraction of a man to a woman, but now it seemed so much more. Like he was a powder keg about to explode. Did she do this to him?

The word *tease* reared its ugly head.

She reminded herself that he was her husband and if the constriction of her clothes was anything to go by, her attraction to him was as combustible as his was.

The idea of what she did last night in the throes of a wet dream she didn't remember, rubbing herself on him ... made her incredibly hot. An unfulfilled arousal pulsed between her legs. A heat that needed to be cooled.

By his tongue.

The popsicle.

Oh, God, she was in danger of bursting into flames.

Why was she so scared to make the jump? He was right. They were awful actors. Their interaction since the beginning had been real. Feelings were getting muddled and their relationship needed to get out of limbo.

Migs had been staring at the stream as her mind battled against itself, but now he glanced at her, eyes guarded. He appeared in control of himself again. "So, what is it gonna be, babe? In. Or out."

It was an ultimatum.

But it was also a survival.

Of her life.

Of her emotions.

Because she couldn't deny that her heart was falling fast for the man before her.

Not just any man.

Her husband.

"Miguel," she whispered, shifting to her knees, she leaned over and extracted an ice pop from the basket.

His eyes flared with heat as the implication of her actions left nothing to interpretation.

She was in.

"Come here," he invited, guiding her to straddle his lap. A pained look flashed across his face, but with it was measured control. Her slacks were made of linen. They were flimsy and she felt the roughness of his jeans beneath her crotch. She held the popsicle right in front of his face and gave a slow lick from the underside of it where it was starting to melt, and all the way to the top.

"You're killing me, babe," he groaned as he shifted her closer. She put the tip of the popsicle to his mouth and he took it, taking off the edge, he played with the chunk in his mouth. She rocked gently against him as she licked and sucked the popsicle.

A growl vibrated deep in his chest as his fingers deftly unbuttoned her blouse. She gasped as his palm slipped into her bra and cupped a breast, flicking a nipple with his thumb. Then his other hand brought the cold dessert back to his lips giving it another swipe before he filled his mouth with her breast. She shuddered as his cold tongue swirled around her nipple. Goosebumps raised on her skin, but her body was ablaze with need.

The popsicle was dissolving rapidly into her fingers as Miguel plundered each breast and then her back was on the blanket, the *paleta* gone from her hand.

"Don't want to waste this," he murmured as he hovered above her, licking her hand where the sweetness dripped.

Ariana was panting. The core of her throbbed with a need for release. "Miguel."

"Ah, babe…. The way you say my name …"

He trailed the cold treat down her body, following with his icy kisses that made her hot all over. When he dipped it into her belly button, she almost came, her back arching with such force, she thought she'd cramp. Her sneakers were gone and, before she knew it, she was naked from the waist down, her legs were over his shoulders and he was licking her with ferocity. He swirled his tongue before spearing her entrance. All frozenness gone as the friction from their flesh chased away the chill. She writhed on the blanket, her fingers gripping the fabric as Miguel ate her pussy like it was his last meal on earth. Her orgasm crashed into her in one gigantic wave. She tried to muffle her cry with the back of her hand, but she moaned as the ripple of endless pulses quaked through her core. Over and over she came until Migs took one final swipe and climbed up her body.

"Delicious," he muttered, lowering his head to capture her mouth in a long, languid kiss. He eased back, leaving her puzzled when he didn't do anything else. She arched into his erection that was as hard as an iron rod and he grunted, moving it out of reach.

"Are you stopping again?"

He nodded, the clenching of his jaw worried her. Did she do something wrong?

"Did I scream too loud?"

A choked laugh gusted past his lips. "No, you didn't. I love the sounds you make when you come." His eyes searched her face, his fingers combing strands from her forehead. "I love making you come."

"And I've yet to hold you at my mercy," she grinned as she playfully slid her hand between them to touch the hardness he'd been keeping from her. She frowned when he snagged both her wrists and held them on either side of her head.

Her smile faded, confusion taking over. "What's going on? Are you practicing some kind of abstinence? It's not lent."

He laughed again. "Even if it was, I'm a non-practicing Catholic."

"Then what?" Releasing her wrists, he pushed away from her and picked up her slacks and panties, sliding them up her legs. Then he buttoned her blouse, patted it as though making sure she was neat and tidy.

"It's some misplaced sense of chivalry." He dropped beside her, propping on an elbow. "I deliberately didn't bring a condom so I wouldn't be tempted to fuck you."

"Miguel, I hope you know I'm not a virgin. You don't have to prepare me for a wedding night."

His eyes flashed. "I hope you're joking."

"Uhm, okay, but I don't understand. You're being so vague.."

His eyes darkened. "I don't fucking care if you're a virgin or not. But I don't want to discuss the men you've been with either."

She sighed, trying not to get aggravated with her husband. "Then …"

"If I had a condom, I'd be fucking you now and wouldn't have cleared the air between us."

Ariana reared back. "You have that little self-control?"

"Where you're concerned—yes." He glanced at her ruefully. "My control is hanging by a very thin thread. A frayed fucking thread. You're not the one with images of us this morning in bed."

She giggled. She rarely giggled. "I'm sorry."

"But …" he caught his lower lip between his teeth as his eyes roamed her body. "Tonight. You better be ready for tonight." He glanced at the food spread that had been knocked almost past the borders of the blanket. "You better eat a lot. You'll be needing it."

14

"Joaquín should give a speech."

"What about Miguel?"

"Let all the grandchildren give speeches."

"I don't like sitting in the center spotlight for too long," Abbi Mena said, looking up briefly from crocheting.

The Alcantara-Walker family was gathered in the family room. Joaquín and several of his other relatives were in a web-session on the TV screen, finalizing the program for Abbi Mena's eightieth birthday. Hector wasn't on, which wasn't surprising, as he was probably partying it up somewhere in Vegas.

Migs sat on a couch with Ariana tucked into his side. After their hot encounter by the stream this afternoon, they couldn't seem to keep their hands off each other. As it was, he was playing with a curl of her hair, and he couldn't resist kissing the top of her head randomly. He and Ariana hadn't been contributing much to the flurry of conversation bouncing around the room. He felt as much like an outsider as his wife right now. His mind was occupied with filthy things he wanted to do to her after this meeting was over, and he didn't give a flying fuck whether Joaquín wanted to make the speech. Migs would rather honor abuelita in private, not show off in front of a crowd.

His older cousin didn't acknowledge him or his marriage either, unlike his other relatives who immediately welcomed Ariana to the family. He knew Tessa wanted to call out their cousin on this blatant snub. His sister was always ready to fight for her younger brother, but it also wasn't unusual to ignore the elephant in the room when the whole clan was involved. Abbi Mena had six children. Many of them had formed their own families, drifted away, and only gatherings such as this brought them together.

"Okay, not everyone will give speeches," Tessa said. "I say we give them before dinner. If we give them after, some will leave."

"They won't leave," Joaquín scoffed. "Who wouldn't take advantage of an open bar?"

If it wasn't for the family's avocado business, he doubted Joaquín would be a constant in his parents' everyday lives. Migs and Hector, though, were as thick as thieves. Or they used to be. Hector was the little brother he never had, and, apparently, his younger cousin shared his lack of enthusiasm for these clan meetings. Observing his older cousin now, Migs derided that Joaquín had never changed much since he was a boy. Hair slicked back, button-down shirts always starched, and Migs would bet they were spotless. It must be Tío Pepito's influence—the desire to mold his son into the head of the clan. At the thought of his uncle, the familiar guilt pinched his chest.

"Our guests are not like that," Tessa shot back.

"You make it sound like your friends are better than mine?" Joaquín said. "It would have made more sense to have this gathering in Michoacán."

"She had her seventy-fifth there and invited the whole town of Cayetano," Delia interceded because Tessa looked as if she was about to reach through the screen and tear Joaquín a new one. "She wants a cozier gathering now. Not a thousand, but two hundred. Friends and family, of which the majority is living in the U.S. and Canada anyway. No politicians."

"She has many close friends from the UC-Berkeley," Pat added. "My professor knows the great Filomena Alcantara."

Abuelita put down the crochet piece she was working on. "All right. Enough." She turned to her daughter. "Reservations have been finalized, *sí?*"

"*Sí*, Mamá." Delia said. "We already paid."

"Why are we wasting time arguing about the venue and speeches. It's my birthday. There are appetizers, right?"

"Yes, there's a cocktail hour."

"Have the speeches before dinner. I care more about my grandchildren being nervous about giving speeches and not being able to eat, than people who just come to eat and can't wait fifteen minutes for their food." She glanced at Tessa. "Is the menu finalized?"

"Yes, we just need a final headcount."

Transferring her gaze to Bella, she asked. "After the food, there'll be dancing, *sí?*"

"*Sí*, Abbi Mena."

"Then we talk about entertainment. Who will be dancing?" Abbi Mena glanced over at Migs.

He froze.

"You danced the tango with me before. You did it very well."

Ariana pulled away from him, an impish grin on her face. "You dance?"

"Last time was at your birthday five years ago," he reminded his grandmother.

"You have three weeks to prepare. I see no problem." Abuelita tipped her chin at Ariana. "You know how to dance?"

"I do," Ariana replied instantly and Migs would even say … eagerly.

"Dance with Miguel." Her gaze swept across the room. "I want everyone to dance. No excuses."

"Migs and Ari should dance the Cubana Salsa," Bella declared.

"Hell, no," he muttered at the sister who seemed to be the bane of his existence.

That same sister now plopped down beside them. "Convince him, Ari. He's really good at it too. He used to make the girls swoon in high school."

"Seriously, how would you know this?" Migs shot back. "You were what? Five?"

"Six," Bella said. "I used to answer the phone all the time"

"He really did," Tessa laughed. "Mamá would be so annoyed with all the girls calling the house—"

"I'm sorry. Are we done now?" Joaquín cut through their conversation and stared at his watch. "Because I have to wake up early tomorrow."

"We're done," Tessa clipped. "I'll just send your part of the bill. How about that?"

"See you in a few weeks." Joaquín signed off.

When the last of the relatives clicked off, Tessa threw up her hands. "What's his problem?"

"I knew having a big celebration would be a problem," Abbi Mena sighed.

"Don't say that, Mamá," Drew, who'd been quiet through the whole meeting, said. "Joaquín is just stressed, Tessa." He addressed his oldest daughter. "You shouldn't be too hard on him. He handles the day-to-day operations of our farms and there are slight problems." Pops' eyes cut briefly to Migs, pulling him out of his Ari haze and smacking him with the problem his father brought up yesterday.

Tessa turned to Cesar, who'd been holding their daughter.

"Is that why you've been distracted these past few weeks? Is my cousin giving you grief?

"No, he's not. There are problems, but it's nothing new."

"Problems like what?"

"One of the trucks broke down." Cesar stood and handed Gigi to her. "Which is why I said I might be working late tonight." He slipped out his phone and looked at it. "Yeah, truck driver is saying he's almost at the warehouse. I'm going to go let him in."

Miguel's focus sharpened, watching his brother-in-law's actions and words carefully. Ari's hand trailed on his thigh and he grabbed it to stop its upward path.

"Why do you have to be the one?" Tessa asked. "You have several supervisors under you?"

Cesar's jaw tightened. "It's the weekend, Tessa."

Drew stood. "I'll go with you."

Migs kissed the top of Ari's head in resignation and stood as well. "No. I'll go, Pops."

"You?" Delia asked. "Why you? You have a wife to take care of."

His conscience wrestled inside him. His father's face was neutral, and Cesar seemed like he couldn't get out of the room fast enough.

A calming hand interlaced with his fingers as he felt Ariana stand up beside him.

"It's okay," Ariana said, with teasing in her voice. "Maybe it'll give me a chance to catch up on my sleep."

Everyone laughed, his younger sisters making gagging noises. He turned his head to Ariana, the understanding in her eyes made his heart lurch, and he couldn't resist grabbing her face and planting a deep searing kiss.

More gagging noises from the peanut gallery, but he didn't care.

"I'll wait for you in the driveway, bro," Cesar said.

Migs waved him off without breaking his kiss, but when he finally did, he was staring deeply into her eyes, searching.

"Wait for me?" he murmured.

"I'll try." Her lips—swollen from all their kisses during the day—tipped up at the corners.

He planted another kiss on her forehead before following Cesar.

CESAR WAS WAITING for him in an old Bronco. Migs knew his brother-in-law loved the pickup his old man had left him. Tessa's husband was half-Mexican, half-American like the Alcantara-Walker children. His mother was the daughter of a rancher near Laredo on the Texas-Mexico border and his father was the foreman at the ranch. After their ranch had been overtaken by the cartel and his father was killed, Cesar's mother took him to San Diego. Tessa's husband was no stranger to the violence south of the border, which was why Migs couldn't believe he'd be involved in cocaine smuggling.

Unless someone was threatening Tessa or Cesar's mother.

Or even the Alcantara-Walker family.

Migs was here now. He'd be damned before he let his family handle this mess alone.

"So, how's it been going?" Migs probed. "We haven't had time to catch up."

Cesar started the Bronco and pulled away from the driveway. "Been busy. Business is good. Pain in the ass. Gigi keeps us awake at night, but I can't complain." He glanced at Migs briefly before returning his eyes to the road. "Between my mom and the Alcantara-Walker family, I have it really good."

There was silence for a few minutes, then Cesar said, "I know Drew suspects something. I have a feeling he pulled you into this." The Bronco decelerated, and Migs stiffened.

Despite his trust in his brother-in-law, he was still thankful he'd grabbed the Beretta from his room.

Cesar parked on the street, three blocks before the warehouse and turned to him. "The truck may be carrying cocaine. Leon and I will be interrogating the driver when he comes in." He exhaled a frustrated breath. "I hoped I'd have more information before I broke it to Drew. How did he find out?"

"Joaquín knew. He suspected when someone at a party tipped him off about it."

Cesar cursed and punched the steering wheel.

"How long has this been going on?" Migs asked.

"Two months. I don't know if it's been going on longer than that. The shipment with the cocaine happens every other week. This is the first time the truck broke down."

"How did you find out the first time?"

"A worker noticed the avocados in one of the boxes seemed off and called my attention to it."

"Avocados?" Migs was confused. "What are you talking about? The cocaine was in a modified wheel well."

In the darkness of the Bronco cab, he could see the flash of Cesar's smile. "No, my brother. That's too amateur for whoever's running this operation. If the custom's officer or dogs didn't find it, Leon certainly would have."

"But that's where Joaquín's man found the cocaine."

Cesar shrugged. "Then we'll check there too." He glanced at the dashboard clock. "We need to get moving. Leon should already be there."

RAMON WAS TIED to a chair in the office overlooking the warehouse. He was the driver of the tractor-trailer.

He denied knowledge of the mastermind of the cocaine shipment in the Alcantara truck. He could be telling the truth as drug mules were frequently kept in the dark as to who hired them. There was always a middleman, and the mules were a conduit, bringing the goods through the border, no questions asked. They were paid handsomely, too. Leon found ten thousand dollars in the driver's overnight bag.

They were speaking in Spanish.

"I'll ask you one more time, Ramon," Leon asked. "Who hired you?"

Finally, Ramon said he didn't know, but his contact was a man only known as *El Silbador*—*the whistler*—because that was how he made himself known as he emerged from the darkness with his cohorts hauling boxes of the drug.

As Leon continued to try different tactics to extract information, Migs picked up the fake avocado. The skin appeared to be made from truck bed liner and the cocaine was in a condom coated with paraffin and shaped into the seed. It weighed twenty-eight grams. Street price of each avocado was twenty-eight hundred dollars. Twenty-four avocados in each box and fifty boxes?

Over three point three million dollars.

Was he surprised? No. This was one reason why cocaine was big business.

"What were you planning to do, Cesar?" Migs asked.

"This is the biggest shipment yet, and I'm thinking about not letting this through, except ..." Cesar's exhaled deeply. "I don't want to start shit, brother, when Abbi Mena's birthday is coming up."

Migs would agree. Without knowing who hired Ramon, it was risky to throw a gauntlet when a gathering was planned by the family in a public place—the San Diego Country Club to be precise.

"So, in answer to your question ..." Cesar paused as if still figuring out what to do. "We're replacing the avocado box we muddled with a real one. It's what we did before when we first discovered it."

"They won't suspect?"

"They might, but it would be better than no shipment."

"Where is this batch going to?"

"Las Vegas," Leon answered.

"Always?"

"No. Most of the time it's LA."

"Do you know if—" Migs canted his head, hearing scraping on the roof, creaking.

Cesar and Leon glanced up too.

"Who's guarding the gate?" Migs demanded.

"Per—" Leon started.

A blast rocked the entrance of the warehouse.

"Fuck!" Migs hastened to the window overlooking the facility. Figures in black assault gear emerged from a cloud of smoke and were moving toward the stairs. He glanced at Cesar and Leon, who'd drawn their guns. "Don't."

"Get the hell behind us, Migs," Leon growled.

The words barely left the older man's mouth when two dark figures crashed through the office windows, knocking Cesar and Leon down.

Migs had his arms up when he saw the patches on the men's uniform.

"DEA! Don't move."

It was a raid.

15

"On your knees!" A DEA agent barked. The newcomers' faces were streaked with camouflage paint.

Migs complied while keeping his arms raised and his mouth shut.

Cesar and Leon were shoved to their knees. Ramon, who was still tied to the chair, was so close to tears that Migs felt a twinge of pity in his chest because he knew without a doubt that the man's life was screwed.

The second agent walked over to Migs, checked him for weapons, and found his Beretta. Cesar's eyes widened when it was held up, but Migs kept an impassive face.

Footsteps stormed up the staircase and, with a show of force, the rest of the DEA team flooded into the room.

One of them broke away and stalked over to the mess of avocados on the table.

"Fuck me," he said. "These traffickers are getting more creative by the day."

"We were handling it," Cesar gritted out. "We were questioning our truck driver when you guys swooped in."

Don't antagonize the man, Cesar, he thought. Migs didn't want to blow his cover if he didn't have to.

"Yeah. So you knew he was muling the drugs in." The agent who inspected the fake avocados said.

Cesar clamped his mouth shut.

"Not talking, huh?" The agent taunted. "Guess you'll need a lawyer." He turned to Migs "And who are you?"

"Miguel Walker."

"You're Drew Walker's son." The whites of the man's eyes all but disappeared as he approached him. "I've heard all about you. Aren't you supposed to be in LA?"

"Visiting my parents."

"And you just happened to be on this drug bust?"

Silence.

The man brought his nose within inches of Miguel's. "What exactly are you doing here, Walker? Heard you've been thuggin' it out on the streets of LA."

Fuck. Maybe his reputation wasn't helping him at the moment, and he'd be needing his get-out-of-jail free card sooner, except he doubted he'd be able to use his phone any time soon.

The agent gave him a smug smile before glancing over to the man who'd confiscated Migs' weapon. "I hope you guys have licenses to carry those weapons."

Addressing the room at large, the presumptive lead DEA agent said. "Cuff them and get them to the station. Let's see how they get out of this mess."

———

Ariana heard voices. She'd been trying to stay awake, waiting for her husband, but she'd dozed off a couple of times. A fitful sleep. A restless one. At first, she attributed it to the anticipation of finally consummating their marriage. Migs left at around nine with Cesar. She figured they would take an hour or two round trip, so at around ten she soaked in the tub, hoping her husband would walk in any moment.

He didn't.

Deciding against turning into a prune, she'd glumly gotten out of the tub and went through the motions of getting ready for bed.

Her anticipation slowly devolved into worry, remembering how Migs didn't want to tell her about the tension between him and Cesar. She'd also convinced herself that Migs was fully capable of taking care of himself in case his brother-in-law wanted to hurt him.

Por Dios, Ariana. She berated herself. She wasn't living in her brother's world anymore. The Alcantaras were normal people. A family she wanted to have, a place to belong.

A home.

Siblings.

A grandmother she could talk to.

This was her chance.

The voices grew louder, and she heard a door close. She glanced at the clock. It was three in the morning. All the warm fuzzies she was feeling disappeared as an icy fist wrapped around her heart and strangled her lungs. She grabbed a robe and put it on, hurrying toward the door.

In the hallway was Drew, and he was arguing with Delia.

"You better be honest with me," Miguel's mother whisper-yelled. "Why are the cops here? Tessa just called me. Cesar hasn't come home." She looked at Ariana. "And it appears neither did Miguel."

"Delia, hon," Drew attempted to put his hands on her mother-in-law's shoulders, but she warded him off.

"Where's Migs?" Ari's voice was a level above a whisper as anxiety exploded in her chest. "Is he okay?"

"He's okay," Drew said. "No one is hurt, they just want me to go into the station."

"I don't understand. They've been arrested?"

"There was a raid at the warehouse. I'm sure I can clear this up."

"You're going to the station?" Ariana asked.

"Yes, but I need to get dressed now."

"I'm coming with you—"

"Ari, my dear …"

"Because if you can't clear his name." Her voice was firm. "I know someone who can."

Drew regarded her intently, seeing determination in her eyes. "Okay. But hurry up and change."

As Ariana turned back to her room, she heard one of Migs' sisters call out.

"Mamá? Pops?"

The house was awake.

IT TOOK Ariana less than five minutes to get ready. She tied her hair in a ponytail because her curls were driving her crazy. She put on jeans, a t-shirt, and nearly left the room with a different shoe on each foot. She had to double-check that her shirt was not inside out, but that was the least of her worries. The most important piece was the phone in her hand. The one Migs had given her in Vegas and pre-programmed with a number to call Garrison. It wasn't a direct line he said, but she would get through to him.

After leaving a message for Migs' handler, Ariana called Tessa while Drew made his own calls, one to his lawyers and another to Joaquín.

Their Expedition followed the patrol car that visited them in the wee hours of Sunday morning.

"I'll meet you guys at the station," Tessa said, her voice panicky. "I can drop Gigi off at Cesar's mom … or—"

"Tessa," she cut her off. Her sister-in-law was not in the right frame of mind to drive anywhere. "Stay put, okay? Listen to me. Pops and I have this."

"But—"

"Call Mamá. She'll need your help to keep the other

Marias calm. Also, Abbi Mena." Although Ari would bet their grandmother was the lake in all this. Ariana was surprisingly calm after she realized she had to step up. She was the one with experience dealing with visits from the police, especially after Drew told her what the situation was all about.

The narcos were smuggling cocaine in avocados? Would wonders never cease?

The cartels hired the best chemists. One would be surprised at the level of ingenuity that cocaine traffickers would come up with to circumvent the law.

Now they had a virologist, too. Her train of thought cut off when Drew cursed.

"Joaquín denies he did this," he growled. "But I'm sure it's him."

"Why would he call the DEA on his own truck?"

"First, my nephew never saw eye-to-eye with Cesar. He'd always wanted me to hire someone from Michoacán to take care of the San Diego warehouse. And second, to show us who is in control of the business."

"Which explains why he wants Cesar out."

"Yes."

"Will Cesar be okay?"

"My lawyer is on his way. He's calling some contacts as well. This has all been a mix-up." Drew cut her a brief glance. "Thanks for talking Delia out of coming along. The Marias need her. How's Tessa?"

"I told her not to drive. Just call Mamá if she wanted."

"How about the man you said can help?"

"I left him a message." And fingers crossed, he would call back.

"THAT'S MORE than three million dollars of coke in that shipment."

Ariana was reeling at the amount estimated by the DEA agent in charge at the San Diego police station.

"We had a warrant to search the premises and we're holding them for possible possession." The man in black who still had on face paint told them. His mouth tightened. "They're not talking."

"Didn't you hear my father-in-law?" Ariana fumed. "This has all been a mix-up."

"Just be glad we're not arresting your father-in-law, too." The man's eyes narrowed. "Wait a minute. You're that Ortega's sister, aren't you?"

Uh-oh. Maybe it was a bad idea to come here.

"Yes. And Miguel Walker is my husband. Have you given him his phone call?"

When the DEA agent didn't answer, she added, "You're in violation of his rights."

"Listen, lady." The man stepped closer, his lips curled in a snarl. "He's not under arrest. Yet. They didn't ask for that phone call. And don't think you can just come in here and make demands. I know exactly what your brother did and the many lives he ruined." His eyes flashed to Drew's and back to hers. "Maybe you have an outstanding warrant on you somewhere. And I'll arrest you as well."

"Don't you dare," Drew growled.

A similarly geared officer came up to them. "Call for you, Lenox. A Richard Grayson."

Lenox smirked at Ari and Migs' Dad. "That's our DEA Division head honcho. Probably congratulating us on our haul." He turned away from them and spoke into the phone the other man handed him.

"Sorry about this, Mr. Walker," the officer said. "I'm sure we'll have this sorted in no time."

"Not a problem, officer."

The man nodded and turned away.

"You know him?" Ariana asked.

"He's the one who called me first. He's a lieutenant with the SDPD and has been deputized into the DEA task force."

Her phone buzzed.

She checked it.

Unknown number.

"I need to take this." She hurried to the sliding doors. "Hello?"

"Ariana?"

"John! Thank, God!"

"Walker got into a bind didn't he?" There was amusement in the other man's tone. "Serves him right."

"How can you say that?" How could he make a joke at a time like this. Migs' family was worried!

"Maybe a night or two in jail would serve him right for stealing Andrade's bride."

"No stealing has been done," she argued. "Can you do something? And ... quick-like?"

"So demanding ..."

"John!"

"I do miss your fiery attitude. Hope Walker is treating you right."

"Can you do something?" She repeated, her patience running out.

"Already done."

Click.

"John?"

He hung up. Arggh. When she turned around, Lenox was walking toward them, the face paint couldn't disguise that he was pissed or ready to kill someone. He marched right up to Drew.

"Your son could have said he was working for the DEA."

Drew's pallor turned sickly white. "What?"

Lenox frown eased into a grin. "You didn't know? Well, I'll be damned. They're processing him, your son-in-law, and the old guy. The driver will remain in our custody." He checked his watch. "Guess it's a good morning."

Without another word, the DEA agent spun on his heel and left a stunned Drew staring into nothing.

Ariana didn't know what to say, but her lack of reaction soon gained her father-in-law's attention.

He exhaled in a resigned breath. "Did you know?"

"You need to hear it from him."

"He's been a federal agent all this time?"

"Drew ..."

"DEA. God ..." Drew pinched his brows. "I think I felt better when he was a mechanic."

Ariana suddenly wanted the ground to swallow her up. Movement in the hallway caught her eyes, the purposeful strides of her husband heading their way gave her relief on so many levels.

That relief propelled her forward, partly because she wanted to get away from Drew, but mostly because she couldn't wait to touch Migs again.

"Miguel," she breathed.

She barely registered Cesar and Leon behind him as her husband swept her into his arms and kissed her deeply, ignoring the heckling at the reception area. The people around at four a.m. weren't exactly the kind outraged by public displays of affection.

Tearing his mouth away, he growled, "Why are you here?"

"Where else should I be?"

"I left you safe in the house." His jawline was taut, expression frustrated.

"I am not a damsel in distress." She held up her phone. "You gave me this for a reason."

His mouth twisted wryly. "So you saved our asses?"

"Damn right." She was getting annoyed. She shouldn't be annoyed. She just got him back! But husbands, apparently, could be infuriating.

"Son," Drew called and Migs' eyes shifted to his father. "Is there something you wanna tell me?"

———————

"I DON'T KNOW how I can keep this from Delia."

"Lenox has a big mouth. He shouldn't have said anything to you." Migs was driving them home. His father was in the passenger seat while Ariana and Cesar were behind them. Leon was sprawled in the third row. "You need to keep this from Mamá. Just a little while longer."

"And the cartels?" Cesar asked. "How involved are you in monitoring them?"

Shit, he was so not ready for this. For one thing. He didn't work for the DEA. Maintaining two covers was going to be a problem with his inquisitive family.

"I can't talk about it. I won't talk about it."

"That tells me you're in deep," Drew said. "Can you at least tell me why? Is it worth it, son? Your mother sacrificed leaving her homeland for fear of her children getting embroiled in cartel BS, and yet here you are, eyeballs deep in that shit. At least, I think you are." He paused. "Guess you know that, Ari. Is your marriage a sham?"

"Careful, Pops." Migs voice was sharp. "My marriage to Ari is nobody's business."

"I beg your pardon," Drew replied, tone just as sharp. "If any of the cartels find out you're in league with the DEA—" his voice died and then, "Jesus Christ. Tell me you had nothing to do with Pepito's death."

Migs' mouth flattened.

"Oh, Christ, son," Drew whispered. "Jesus. That's why …"

"This is not the time nor the place to discuss this," he clipped.

A dead silence descended in the confines of the SUV.

White knuckling the steering wheel, jaws clenched tight, Migs could sense his years of respite was at an end. His secrets. His guilt. After long moments of non-conversation, he said, "I think we need to focus on who's trying to frame the Alcantaras for smuggling cocaine."

"Joaquín denies calling this in," Drew said.

"*Pendejo*," Cesar spat. "He can deny all he wants. He wants me out."

"I know you all think otherwise," Leon said. "But it doesn't make sense to me that it was him."

"My take? It's political," Drew said. "The U.S. is cracking down on the cartels again, especially after that incident with Raul Ortega—no offense, Ariana—"

"None taken," his wife replied dryly.

Leon was still playing devil's advocate. "Your cousin has always played straight and maybe with the U.S. cracking down on the cartels, he wants to show the corporation's commitment to fighting drugs."

"Bullshit," Migs growled. He was trying to look good in front of Mexico's elite. "After you told me about his embarrassment at the society party, of course he had to save face. But throwing Cesar under the bus? Not cool."

"Tessa is going to be pissed," Cesar sighed. "She's going to ask questions."

"She can be pissed all she wants," Migs said. "As long as she doesn't get in the way of us finding out who's using our trucks to move cocaine."

"This is going to hit the news," Ariana said. "Your company needs to release a statement."

"Fuck, you're right," Drew groaned. "We have a good public relations firm."

"I'm sure Joaquín can spin this to our advantage," Cesar replied sarcastically.

"He said he'll take full responsibility," Drew said.

"I'm sure," Migs muttered.

"I'm going to reassess security at the ranch and the warehouse," Leon said. "I would appreciate some input, Miguel."

"Sure." They just passed the guard gate at the ranch. The villa was unusually lit with outdoor lights at five in the morning. The horizon was still a line of yellow over a dark blue sky. Tessa's car was parked at the driveway and all the women were waiting for them.

"Not a word," Migs reminded them. "I'll tell them when the time is right."

"Don't wait too long," Drew said quietly.

As they got out of the vehicle, Tessa went directly to Cesar, while Delia and the rest of his sisters came to him first. He didn't answer their questions about what happened. He was itching to wash away the stench of that drunk tank the DEA stashed them in. When the women moved to Cesar and Leon, Abbi Mena was the last to greet him.

"We were worried," she stated simply.

"I know. I'm sorry, abuelita."

It must have been in his tone, the way he said the words, the way they meant more than the current situation that etched a sadness in his grandmother's eyes. They needled the surface keeping the guilt in check and it threatened to bleed.

Ariana's hand tucked into his, and just like that, the thorny ball in his chest slowly withdrew its spikes. There was a time to tell his grandmother. That because of Migs, her eldest son Pepito was killed.

But not today.

Definitely not today.

16

Ariana was helping the women prepare breakfast when Migs walked into the kitchen. He reminded her of a caged tiger, and it seemed taking a shower did nothing to chase away the thundercloud that had been hovering around his head since she'd met him at the station. He didn't sit down to eat, but simply grabbed a breakfast bun and a mug of coffee before leaving with Leon to inspect the property.

"Ari, do you know what's going on?" Bella asked her, no trace of her bubbly self in evidence. "I don't know the whole story."

"One of the trucks had cocaine," Tessa said while bouncing Gigi on her lap. "I think Leon and Migs are reviewing the security on the property."

"It's not safe here?" Cora asked.

"Of course it is," Delia said confidently, sitting beside her daughter and tucking her hair behind her ear. "It's just precautions. No one would dare harm the Alcantaras."

"But Tio Pepito was killed by the Carillo cartel, right?" her daughter persisted.

"And they were dismantled four years ago," Delia said. "That's a lesson for the narcos to learn."

"But they're back and growing stronger," Ari couldn't help saying. "What if they want revenge for what was done to them?"

For the first time since she'd met Miguel's mother, the other woman's eyes turned to ice. "Do not frighten my children, Ari."

"You cannot stick your head in the sand either," she couldn't help blurting out. "You're so far removed from the brutality of the cartels that you've forgotten what they are capable of."

"And you know this because of your brother, of course."

"Enough!" Abbi Mena slammed the cover of the pot she was tending to and rounded the kitchen counter, standing in front of the farmer's table and bracing her hands on its surface. "Things have changed, Delia. Almost a generation has passed since your *Papá* died. Many of the codes and customs people believed in have died with them. The narcos are fighting for control more than ever." She turned to Ariana, the older woman's eyes penetrating. "You have a point, but now is not the time to feed the fear.

"Look at them," the older woman continued, pointing to Miguel's sisters. "They have not experienced what you lived through. Delia moved them here to get away from it all, so I hope you understand why she wants to reassure them that their lives are not going to change."

Ariana bit her lower lip. She wanted to say that the cartel had people everywhere.

"But they will," Abbi Mena added as if reading her thoughts. "To what degree that will depend on what this family is willing to do at this time. It is a time for compromise. Not fighting." She returned her attention to Delia. "Do not blame Ariana for her past. Unlike you, she had no choice——"

"I didn't mean it——" Delia looked contrite.

Abbi Mena held up her hand. "Let me speak, *mi corazón*. I know that was said because you're afraid. Uncertain." Then she turned to Ariana. "Do not expect my daughter and grandchildren to immediately leave their comfort zones. They are fierce and they will stand by family and that family includes you now, understand?"

"Yes, Abbi Mena," she whispered.

"This is a time to contemplate your words before speaking," she continued, then her gaze pointedly rested on her grandchildren, waiting for them to respond. They nodded.

Ariana understood as well. Words said in the heat of the moment could leave wounds that never heal.

The men returned at that instant—Migs with Leon, his father and Cesar following close behind. The men must have sensed the tension in the air because their footsteps slowed upon entering the kitchen. At least Migs certainly did as his concerned gaze flew to Ariana.

"What's going on?" he barked.

"Nothing," Ariana and Delia spoke too quickly, deepening his scowl.

He stalked toward her, tense lines bracketing his mouth and he raised a hand to cup a side of her cheek. His fierce eyes searching hers. Ariana tried her best to withstand his scrutiny, she even smiled, but he wasn't convinced. His gaze lifted and swept across the table. "I hope none of you are blaming Ariana for what happened."

"Of course not," Delia said. "We were just discussing who would be stupid enough to do this to our family."

"Joaquín, for one," Tessa spoke as Cesar picked up his wife's hand and kissed the back of her fingers.

Ariana tugged Miguel's arm to draw his attention. "I told them Carillo might be regaining strength."

Migs gave a brief nod. "The cartels are so fractured right now that any one of them could be responsible, even the breakaway groups." He turned to Drew. "Anything from Joaquín?"

"He had a face-to-face with the Ponce-Neto organization."

"Is that a good idea?" Delia asked.

"They're straightforward," Drew said. "And according to Joaquín, their leadership respects the Alcantara name and gave reassurance it was not them. They're going to tap into their sources on the streets to see what they can find out."

"Why don't you all sit around the table and have a proper breakfast," Abbi Mena said. She'd gone back to the front of the stove when the men came in, returned and lowered a tureen of aromatic oatmeal on the table, before coming back with spoons and bowls. Ariana liked the Mexican version that cooked the oats in cinnamon and condensed milk. She could feel her hips expanding as she scooped a bowl for Migs.

"Where are Lettie and Pat?" Migs asked, sitting by Ariana.

"They're taking care of the *lechón* in the yard. We still have to eat, no?" Abbi Mena said and looked at her. "See, Ariana, I told you this family is fierce. The women won't let you starve. If they need to gather mushrooms in the forest to feed their menfolk, they will do it."

"Mushrooms wouldn't be enough to feed us." Migs' amusement relaxed the sharp edges of his face. "Think she can hunt a rabbit?"

"That will depend on whether Maripat is vegetarian at that time or not," Bella quipped. The three of them laughed, while Abbi Mena smiled broadly.

"There's a group whose leader goes by the name of The Whistler," Cesar continued the original thread of conversation as Cora hopped a chair over so he could sit beside Tessa. "That's all we got out of the truck driver before the DEA swooped in. Leon could've gotten more out of Ramon."

"Where's Ramon now?" Tessa asked. "I can't believe he was involved in this. He always showed pictures of his wife and kids to us."

"The DEA has him," Leon said.

"I'm worried about his family," Migs' oldest sister said.

"Joaquín is checking with them. Making sure they're not being harassed," Drew said.

"They live on the outskirts of Cayetano," Tessa said. "Might be a good idea to bring them into town."

As Cesar, Tessa, Leon, and his father discussed what to do with the family of the truck driver, Migs gave her a nudge. "Sure you're okay?" he whispered.

"I'm fine. Finish that oatmeal."

"So bossy," he muttered. "Hmm … I missed this. I don't think I've had this since I was a teenager."

"I haven't had this since before my mother died," Ariana said wistfully. Her memories of her mother were blurry, but somehow the aroma of oats cooked with the sweetened milk stayed with her.

"Didn't mean to make you sad." He stuck his spoon into the thick porridge and put the crook of a finger under her chin, lifting it up. "I don't like the shadows under your eyes either."

"I'm haggard looking?" It was the wrong time to act self-conscious, but what was a new bride to feel?

However, the way Migs' eyes softened, crinkling at the corners with amusement, took away her momentary vanity. That and the words he uttered. "You still look beautiful to me." Then just like that, his eyes hardened into onyx. "But don't think you're off the hook." He dropped his gaze from her and picked up his coffee, giving it a sip.

"What did I do?" She had an idea, but she was hoping he'd forgotten about it.

He cast her a look full of heat and rebuke. "You left the safety of the ranch without me."

"What was I supposed to do? Let my husband rot in jail?"

"Pops was on top of it."

"Can you honestly say if I hadn't called John, your stubborn ass wouldn't still be there?"

"Who's John?" Tessa asked.

Ariana resisted the urge to slap a hand to her mouth, but she froze as eight pairs of eyes zeroed in on them.

Migs had his poker face on. "A friend of Ariana's who has a finger in every law enforcement pie." He put his arm around her and gave it a squeeze. "She called in a favor."

Cesar coughed into his hand. "Very helpful...whoever he is. Thanks, Ariana."

"Yes, but—" Tessa started.

The kitchen door slammed open with Lettie and Pat stumbling in, their faces covered in soot.

"We need Miguel or Cesar in the yard." Lettie gulped in between peals of laughter. Both sisters were giggling and bent over in stitches.

"What's wrong?" Abbi Mena ran to the window just as everyone caught a whiff of something burning. "*Madre de Dios.* You're supposed to start charcoal not a bonfire."

Migs quickly finished his oatmeal and grabbed the coffee mug. Passing his grandmother, he said, "Feed their menfolk, huh?"

Ariana breathed a sigh of relief as everyone forgot her slip about John Garrison, the men emptying the table to provide their macho expertise to salvage lunch.

THE REST of the day passed with less tension. With stomachs full and with the lack of sleep taking its toll on everyone, most of them chilled out on the patio.

Drew and Delia commandeered the hammocks when the light breeze swept in during the late afternoon hours. Abbi Mena had retired to her room, saying she was done for the day and the excitement was too much for her old age.

Tessa and Cesar had left for their house.

Leon was around somewhere.

The rest of Migs' sisters were playing scrabble and Cora appeared to be winning.

"Looks like Cora is demolishing the competition," Ariana murmured sleepily against his chest.

"She's a bookish person like Lettie, and a fan of trivia games and *Jeopardy*," Migs said. They were stretched out on an outdoor swing bed and he had both arms wrapped around his wife. It fueled more than a few dirty thoughts, and he hoped like hell no emergency would come up this time and ruin his plans for the night. He was still mad at Ariana for leaving the ranch with Pops. He was antsy when he was in jail because he couldn't get hold of Garrison. The useless one phone call they allowed in jail wouldn't do shit because Garrison had to call back anyway.

Good thing, Pops was tight with the local PD and they notified him. When Migs was sprung from jail, he had a gut feeling that Ariana had contacted Garrison. He wasn't prepared for the punch in the gut upon seeing his wife, devoid of makeup and disheveled. Ariana looked too beautiful for a tattooed roughneck like Migs. His wife was too pure to be anxiously waiting at the reception area in the midst of San Diego's drunk, disorderly or low-life crowd who are hauled in during the late shift from midnight to six.

He was compelled to snatch her away and hide her, but he ended up kissing her instead.

He missed her. The idea of being away from her for a couple of hours and the uncertainty of the clusterfuck perpetuated by the DEA raid had put him on a razor's edge. Even after he was released from jail, he was consumed by the need to make her his. He was just waiting for the right time to disappear into their room.

Ah, the joy of having your family watch your every move.

As soon as this stay was over, Migs was buying a place wherever Ariana wanted to live. He'd fuck her in every corner.

His dick came to life behind his jeans. Ariana's ass was pressed against it. Good thing she was half-asleep.

"I'm making more mojitos," Pat got up from the game and walked by them. "Ari?"

"She's asleep."

"No, I'm not. None for me," she said. "I haven't recovered from our last drinking binge."

"Miguel? Beer?"

"I'll grab one later."

Pat shrugged and went into the house.

"I can feel you poking me." Even when he couldn't see her face, he could imagine her smile from her voice.

He lowered his head and whispered by her ear. "What do you say we go to our room?"

"It's early."

"Call it a delayed *siesta*."

"How about dinner?"

"Woman, how can you think about dinner when your man can't wait to sink inside you?"

Silence.

"Ari?"

"Let's get out of here."

17

THEY COULDN'T WAIT to get into their room. After giving an excuse that they were taking a nap, all eyes gave them a knowing look so that even Migs felt heat creep up his neck. Forget about Ariana. Her face was as red as a tomato, a beacon that sex was exactly what they had in mind.

Crazy energy pinged between them, and they forced themselves to walk normally through the house, waving off Pat who asked where the hell they were going. But once they got to the hallway, they hurried along like children trying to escape the school principal.

When they fell into the room, he pushed Ariana up against the wall, kissing her ferociously. His fingers slipped under the wide leg of her shorts and dug into her ass, lifting her.

"Migs." She was breathless.

He tore his mouth away. "I've been wanting to fuck you all day."

She dipped her head and inhaled him. "You smell so good."

He smirked. "I haven't showered so much in my life as I did today. After breakfast, after cooking outdoors. I wanted to be ready just in case we got a chance." He rocked into her, letting her know exactly how ready he was. "Been hard all day, babe."

"I noticed."

He canted his head as their lips teased each other, not quite touching, she was evading his kisses playfully and it was driving him mad. "Let me have those sweet lips," he commanded.

Finally, he captured them and he set her down and unfastened her shorts. He slipped his hand beneath the waistband, straight for her pussy. Drenched. He dipped a finger into her tightness, and it coated his finger with her arousal. Lifting his head again, he held her eyes captive as he sucked that finger.

"I love your taste," he growled. He dropped to his knees and he pressed his mouth against her panties before drawing them over her hips, hardly losing contact with her skin. He nipped at the flesh at the juncture of her thigh. Her back arched and her fingers held his head, pushing him lower.

Fuck yeah.

He could smell her. Her need for him. It made the caveman in him roar and he couldn't wait to fuck her, mark her as his.

Remembering how she tasted, he swiped at the sensitive bud nestled between her lips. With his tongue, he lapped up and down her slit and straight into her juices. He consumed her, ferocious like an addict in need of a fix. His self-control fractured when she moaned his name. He attacked, licking in broad strokes, his body in tune to her responses. He wanted to drive her crazy the way she'd made him come undone.

Just the taste of her. Fuck.

Migs was a goner.

After he owned her multiple orgasms, he held her up by pinning his hips to her torso. "Don't crash on me now, babe." He chuckled at her dazed expression.

"You're good at that," she murmured.

"Only because it's you," he said as he ripped a condom packet with his teeth.

He was wearing athletic shorts, so it wasn't hard to wrap up. A hand shifted to her right leg and slung it over his hip. "Last chance, Ari. Say no and I'll stop."

Her eyes flared. "Don't you dare."

He didn't need further encouragement.

He positioned his cock and drove into her.

Her moan, her eyes rolling back, unleashed the beast he was keeping on lockdown.

With one hand gripping her hair, he yanked her head back, exposing her throat. He watched the pulse fluttering beneath tender skin, watching it quicken as he thrust hard into her again and again. Her changing expressions enthralled him, and seeing that luscious mouth fall open, he couldn't help imagining it wrapped around his cock. Would its grip be as tight as her pussy?

"Open your eyes," he said harshly. His fingers tightening in her hair. "I want to watch you come again. I want you to see me fuck this tight pussy of yours, Ariana."

Her cries caught in her throat, matching his grunts as his thrusts slid her body up and down against the wall. For a fleeting second, he thought he was being too rough with her, but her nails gouging his shoulders told him otherwise.

"You're like a tight wet slide, babe." Her inner muscles clenched over him and his mind blanked. He tried to last longer, but he was so damned hard. "Come with me, Ari." He released her hair and lowered his hand between them and strummed her clit. She clawed at his neck as she muffled her scream just as he erupted inside her.

"Fuck me, fuck me," he groaned. Sensations that started at the small of his back, rippled up his spine locking his neck, his whole body shuddering with the intensity of his release. He dragged her from the wall and staggered to the bed, dropping them into it, still connected. He rolled over and continued to move, her inner muscles continued squeezing him until he finally drove deep and stayed. Migs dropped his head to her breasts, trying to catch his breath, then he fell to her side and hauled her into the crook of his arms.

No words would come because no words could describe what had just happened.

Ariana was quiet beside him, and he couldn't help trailing his fingers up and down her smooth skin. She was naked from the waist down, and all that remained was a tank top. "I'm not done with you yet."

"I would hope not," she sassed huskily. "I'm still wearing clothes and so are you."

He grinned. "Complaining already, wife?"

"Complaining? No. But I'd like to see what you so spectacularly impaled me against the wall with."

Migs barked a laugh and jackknifed to a sitting position, turning toward Ariana and grinning. "Be right back."

He quickly disposed of the condom and returned to Ariana who was about to remove the tank top she was wearing.

"Stop." He ordered as he put a knee on the bed. "I'm taking off every piece of clothing from your body tonight."

"It's barely evening."

"Quiet." He lifted her top and threw it on the floor. As he removed her bra, his temptress had her own ideas and gripped him in her hand. He pushed her back against the mattress and she started to stroke him.

And his cock cooperated and grew with each stroke.

"Wife," he growled. "You're going to be the death of me."

She arched a delicate brow. "Oh? why?"

"You're insatiable." His head lowered and he sucked a nipple. He laved her tits with his tongue, and she was squirming against him even as her hand was trapped between them. Finally, she released her hold and planted both hands on his shoulders, pushing him up and away.

Migs brows drew together. "Tell me what you want, babe."

She grinned, her mouth curving with a wicked, sensual smile that made boys into men, and made men want to sell their soul for a blow job from those lips.

Ariana got to her knees and they were face to face. Then with one hand she shoved him on his back and straddled him with her exquisitely hot core against his erection.

Her eyes were smoky with heat, and he lay mesmerized as she peeled his shirt from his chest. He grew even harder when her gaze took in his body, teeth biting her lower lip. She liked what she saw and Migs was pleased. No, he was downright fucking smug. Ariana crawled over him, gave him a wet sloppy kiss before trailing down his body while pressing kisses against his overheated skin.

His cock was already half exposed because his shorts were riding below his hips. Migs was breathing faster now as her mouth went lower. She glanced at him and smiled in triumph, and with their gazes locked, she took him in her mouth.

Migs was a goner.

Hot wet suction almost made him come. He was only saved from embarrassment because this was his second round. He gritted his teeth as pleasure rose with each pull from her mouth. Ariana held him at her mercy. Teasing him with deliberate, corkscrew twists of her mouth.

He crunched up and gripped her on either side of her head. "Ariana," he groaned. "Go faster. Take me deeper."

She released his cock and she looked so alluring with her full lips swollen and glistening. "I want you to use me."

"What?" He wasn't sure he heard her right.

"You're my big, tattooed, badass husband and yet you're treating me like glass."

His eyes narrowed. "I just fucked you hard against the wall."

"I'm talking about blow jobs. You want to shove my head down on your cock, don't you?"

God, could she talk any dirtier and get him all riled up and ready to explode?

"So do it," she said.

Migs wasn't about to disappoint his wife on what was technically their wedding night. He sat up and scooted against the headboard. "Take off my shorts."

Her eyes flashed and he was damned sure she was soaking. She did as she was told, and she slid off his clothing and his cock sprang up proudly between them.

"Now suck. If you choke, I'm going to push myself deeper."

Ariana kneeled between his spread thighs and without hesitation, swallowed him again. "Faster."

She mumbled something that sounded like *make me*.

He buried his fingers in her hair. Seeing her dark hair spread all over his crotch was the stuff of wet dreams. He'd carry the image of this for-fucking-ever. She was being a tease again, forcing him to push her head down to take more of him. They got into a rhythm, and the minx was playing with her clit as she was fucking him with her mouth.

Could Migs be any luckier?

The suction came faster, she was taking him deeper, he expected her to gag. When he tried to ease her off, her teeth scraped the skin of his cock.

"Dammit!" he growled and shoved her head down. Vibrations came from the back of her throat. Holy Fuck, she'd taken him all the way to the hilt!

"Ariana," he choked. "I'm going to come. Get off now."

Her answer was the tightest stroke up and her tongue swirling around the underside of the head of his dick.

Game over.

He exploded into her mouth, fell back helplessly against

the headboard as his body was wracked by the most incredible blow job of his life.

"You've blinded me, woman," he said hoarsely. When he managed to focus on the person responsible for the exquisite pleasure, she was still kneeling between his legs, sitting back on her ankles and eyeing him with some kind of triumphant smugness.

"You're big," she said softly. "I thought I couldn't take all of you."

"I wasn't expecting you to." He leaned forward and cupped a side of her jaw, noting her watery eyes. Shit. "Are you all right?"

"Of course," she said. "It's like I conquered Everest."

Migs chuckled. "C'mere." He drew his wife beside him, an overwhelming possessiveness had him crushing her to his side as the meaning of finally consummating their marriage dawned on him. "You exaggerate, but I'll take that as a compliment."

Her muffled laughter dislodged a muscle in his chest. There was an urge to pull away, to hide from the slew of emotions running through him, emotions he'd kept locked down to keep his secrets from his family. But the urge to stay was stronger, and the need to bask in the afterglow with Ariana was addictive, so he remained where he was.

His wife in his arms.

His heart at her mercy.

———

SOMETHING VISCERAL CHANGED BETWEEN THEM. As Ariana snuggled close to her husband's chest, her mind couldn't comprehend this utter feeling of contentment. She couldn't believe that the total uncertainty that started their day would end on a high note. Her mouth curved in satisfaction as her hand moved over Migs' taut abs down the trail of hair leading to his sizable erection that hadn't gone down yet.

"You have a beautiful cock," she murmured, tracing the veins on the smooth skin as if it were a work of art.

"Jesus, woman," Migs laughed. "Give me ten minutes."

She glanced up at him. "Ten minutes is all you need to recharge?"

He scowled at her. "You don't want me to tell you the truth, do you?"

"Ha. Men and their egos." She rested her head on his chest again. "I'm already impressed you were able to get it up so soon after you took me against the wall."

"I've been a monk since the first time I laid eyes on you."

Her brows furrowed. "That long?"

"You were hell on wheels, Ariana, not only to my job, but also to my balls," he deadpanned.

"I remember the first day you came into the clinic." She murmured, full of nostalgia. "I thought you were just one of my brothers' men."

"I was."

"You were all brusque and growly."

"And you were all sassy and shit."

She laughed. "What did you expect?"

"Miss prissy pants."

"I told my brother that I couldn't have his gang bangers show up and scare my customers. They needed to wear a uniform of khakis and black tees."

A grunt rumbled in his chest. "You got your wish. I had to shop for khakis, otherwise I'd be off your protection detail." Migs had black tees, but he detested khakis and Ariana didn't approve of those multi-pocketed versions.

"So you thought I was Raul's spoiled sister?"

"At first."

Ariana extracted herself from the furnace of his body and sat cross-legged in front of him. Migs' gaze wavered on her boobs before it lifted to her face. She rolled her eyes. "So tell me, since we're being honest, when did you think otherwise?"

"When we were at the charity drive. I saw how you genuinely cared for people." His eyes darkened. "Understand, babe, that I was fighting my own attraction to you, that's why I was as you call it 'brusque and growly'."

"I didn't really like you at first."

"I didn't notice." He chuckled. "Let me guess. You thought anyone who worked for your brother was crooked."

"Can you blame me?"

"No."

"But then you started showing your marshmallow side."

Migs groaned. "Again with the marshmallow references. Just stop."

She wouldn't. She clearly recalled the exact moment she discovered his sweet side. That time when she was curled in a ball, hiding in her room with the worst period cramps. "Remember that time I didn't come out for dinner and you knocked on my bedroom door."

"You scared the shit out of me when you moaned in pain."

"You broke down the door."

"It was locked," he muttered. "If you would've just taken a damned pain killer, but no, you had to suffer through it."

"You knew what to do when you found out it was period cramps. Now I know it's because you have five sisters." He had found a screw top bottle of wine and poured out its contents and made her a hot water bottle. And then he held her until the pain went away. Afterward, he got her a cute fluffy heating pad. She began to see him differently then.

He grunted again.

"You don't have to hide your sweet side, Migs," she whispered. "Not from me."

Her breath caught when his eyes turned fierce.

"Come here," he ordered.

"But I like talking face to face."

"And it's the first opportunity that we're both naked and I'm not wasting a second talking."

She huffed. "Men." But ended up squealing when he yanked her into him and before she knew it, she was pinned under a very aroused man. "Again?" she was surprised.

Migs chuckled. "I'm not there yet, but you are very potent for a man's libido." He frowned. "I have half a mind to hide you from the eyes of men forever, or maybe I'll have Abbi Mena make you a dress out of a flour sack."

"Are you serious?"

Instead of answering, he kissed her. It was almost like a shut-up kiss. Ariana spread her thighs and he settled between them. His hardness against her softness, a tangle of limbs and sheets, skin damp from the heat of sex, Migs worshipped her body with his tongue. This time he gave special attention to her breasts, taking his time there and then he went down on her again. And Ariana had her third multiple orgasm of the night.

By the time he flipped her on her belly and pulled her hips back against his pelvis, she was ready for more of him. He rammed inside and her breath caught in a gasp, welcoming the fullness of his shaft. He pounded into her without mercy, and she had to grip the sheets to keep from sliding. He folded over her and twisted her neck into his kiss. Then he came with a muffled grunt and they fell on the bed, exhausted.

Ariana rolled to her side, blissfully sated. She felt Migs leave the bed, moving around the room to probably get rid of the condom.

She barely registered his return, only feeling the refuge of his body engulfing her from behind. And for the first time ever, they fell asleep in each other's arms.

18

As THE DAYS passed into weeks, Migs began to see how Ariana was finding her footing in his family. It was easy to be overwhelmed by the sheer personalities of his sisters, but his wife was no shrinking violet either, and he loved her for it.

Love?

He tested the word on his tongue. He'd used it a couple of times to describe certain things about Ariana, but he'd been having a mental block with figuring out how he actually felt for her.

Bang!

The blast of a .45 echoed in the clearing and brought his thoughts back to the present. Three women were shooting cans of varying sizes off the trunk of a fallen tree.

Ariana was giving Bella and Leticia pistol shooting lessons. There were many things Raul Ortega did wrong when it came to family, but some things he got right. It was not unheard of, when your family was immersed in the narco life, that they were taught how to defend themselves. Ariana knew how to fire a gun, and she was a pretty damned good shot. In regards to self-defense, she still had more work to do in Migs' opinion and he was anxious to help her improve.

"Ah, bullseye, Lettie, good job!" Ariana and her sister Bella applauded.

"I'm not cut out for this," Bella whined. Her shot earlier had missed the mark by a mile.

"It's not your fault," Ariana said. "I think you just need a different grip on this gun."

She glanced at Migs. "Can you find something else for her? She's limp-wristing this one."

"She's anticipating the recoil," he said dryly.

"You all say that, but I don't know what that means," Bella grumbled.

Leon joined them and walked straight to Bella and handed her a different piece. "Here. Try this."

She weighed the new gun in her hand. "Hey, this feels better."

"The gun chooses its master," Lettie said solemnly.

Bella rolled her eyes.

"Remember, hold it like this." Ariana went behind his sister and guided her arms and fixed her stance. "Shoulders back, feet square. No … finger off the trigger, remember? Not until you're ready."

Leon backed away from the women and took his place beside Miguel. "Joaquín gave his statement to the DEA."

"About fucking time."

Bang!

"She almost got it," Leon murmured as the women did another assessment of Bella's shot before she went back into position.

"I've also reviewed security at the country club. All the employees' backgrounds."

Migs didn't say he'd already had Garrison do a security check, and simply nodded.

"The additional security personnel should arrive today," Leon said. "Thanks for the recommendation."

Security was a sticking point in the clan and was difficult

to coordinate because his cousins, uncles, and aunts had their own people and balked at Alcantara-Walker having autonomy. If Migs had his way, he'd scrap the celebration altogether, but Abbi Mena, who didn't want to have it in the first place, was adamant about it pushing through.

"This could be a test," she'd said. "The test of the Alcantara's mettle. If you back down now, especially after the invitations have been sent, it'll be seen as a sign of weakness."

Caught between a rock and a hard place.

He wanted Garrison's friend, security expert Kade Spear, for his grandmother's birthday celebration, but he was booked and didn't have enough resources on such short notice.

Bang!

The sound was followed by the women squealing in excitement—Bella in particular, because she finally hit a can.

"I did it! I did it!"

"Looks like your sisters are becoming ace shots."

Heaven help them.

THEIR DAYS FOLLOWED A ROUTINE. After breakfast, if Lettie or Bella were not needed at the warehouse, they would go to the clearing and practice shooting. The afternoons were reserved for practicing the entertainment for the party, and that included dancing the Tango.

Migs hated it. But it was for his grandmother, so he tolerated the endless rehearsals. Besides, it was an excuse to get his hands on Ariana. It was their foreplay and it led to many rigorous evenings of sex. A time of day he anticipated very much.

On their way back from shooting practice, Delia intercepted him. Ariana eyed him warily, but he smiled and told them to go ahead to the kitchen and eat. That was another thing that was routine. Constant cooking. Constant eating. Abbi Mena always had something simmering on the stove or baking in the oven. Having nothing else to do, especially when Migs was off fixing fences with Leon, Ariana would help his grandmother in the kitchen. They'd become very close. As for his mother, there'd been an initial coolness right after the warehouse raid, but she was slowly warming up to Ariana again.

"What's up, Mamá?"

"I need a quick word with you." Delia smiled. To Migs' relief, she extended that smile to his wife as well. Who knew tension between his mother and Ariana could occupy his headspace as much as his concerns for his family's safety? Knowing that it had resolved itself was certainly one more thing off his mind.

He followed his mother to his parents' room. She headed straight for her closet, pushing clothes aside to reveal a hidden compartment.

"I didn't know when to give this to you, but with your grandmother's celebration in ten days, I thought this would be the right time."

She went through the combination and opened the safe, extracting a metal jewelry box carved with an ornate scroll design. Delia lifted the lid, extended the accordion layers, and picked up some pieces from the bottom one and laid them on his palm.

Migs' jaw dropped, taking in the brilliance of the diamond necklace, earrings, and bracelet.

"This set belonged to your *tatarabuela*. I had it cleaned recently," Delia said. "When you were born, Mami gave it to me and said it was an heirloom from her mamá." His eyes shifted to hers and saw her smile apologetically. "I'm sorry it took me so long to give it to you. I wanted to be sure."

He knew what she meant, but he needed to hear the words. "Sure of what?"

"That Ariana loves you, because, Miguel, I can see that you love her."

He stared at the jewelry again. "I'm that obvious?"

Delia laughed lightly. "A mother's instinct tells me you are. I'm not sure if Ariana knows."

He swallowed hard and peered at his mother under guarded eyes. "I haven't told her." He sighed. "She hasn't said anything either."

"Ah, *mijo*, are you afraid to say it first?"

"It's not that. I don't want to rush her. I already rushed our marriage and it looks like I lied to her about giving her the protection of our name."

"Stop using that as an excuse. You're building a marriage here, right?"

"Yes."

"Tell her soon. If you feel it don't hold back." She picked up another piece from the box. "Tell her with this."

Nestled with the other jewelry on his palm was an antique diamond ring. "That was the engagement ring Papá gave Mamá."

"I can't take this."

"I never wore it because Drew gave me one from his mother too."

"Why didn't Abbi Mena give it to Tio Pepito or the other tios?" His mother had two other brothers.

"Honestly?" His mother leaned in conspiratorially. "I don't think she liked who they married. Too *elitista* she said. You know how your *abuela* is so connected to the land. An engagement ring is meant to go to a son's wife."

Migs chuckled. "So it's mine by default?"

"You are a good brother, a good son. Ah, Miguel, you'll make such a good husband. Ariana is lucky to have you."

"I'm lucky to have her, too," he said quietly.

"I can see that," she said. "I'm sorry if I made her uncomfortable. The situation at the warehouse spooked me a bit. I got worried and I lashed out at the person easiest to blame. You'll understand when you have children." She sighed. "I'm over that now. I see how Ari has been good for this family. I promise to be a better mother-in-law."

Migs' heart squeezed. He saw the remorse on her face and how could he blame a mother's natural reaction to circumstances.

He drew his mamá into his arms and hugged her. "Nothing to be sorry about. Ariana understands, believe me. You are both incredible women."

Leaning back, Delia raised her brow. "You're being diplomatic. I'm not forgetting you still need a church wedding. Father Tomas will lecture you that a husband's duty is to his wife first. Now put those away somewhere until you're ready to give them to Ariana."

———

WHEN MIGS RETURNED to the kitchen, he was surprised to see Lettie was the only one there.

"Where's everyone?"

His sister looked harried, mixing a pitcher of iced tea and then arranging snacks on a tray. She was muttering about surprise guests who expected to be treated like the British monarchy. "Good. You're here. Why don't you carry the iced tea with the glasses."

"Lettie." He waited until his sister gave him her full attention, which was a stretch as her eyes were unfocused when she looked at him. He would even hasten to guess she was irritated. "Where's everyone?" he repeated.

"They're in the living room—dancing," Lettie said.

"We usually do that in the afternoon."

"Oh, and Hector is here." His sister said, shoving him the tray bearing the pitcher and the glasses. "He wanted to show off his dancing skills. If you ask me, he just wants to show off to Abbi Mena. Kiss ass."

"Hector is here?"

"Yes." She walked ahead of him and he lengthened his strides to catch up with her. "He probably wants an advance on his inheritance," she added in a lower voice. "Probably gambled away all his money in Vegas, living the high-roller lifestyle. He's laying it on thick. I can tell you that."

Whatever his thoughts were about his cousin's design on their grandmother's wealth dissipated when he saw Hector dancing with Ariana.

No one danced with his wife but him.

No one.

His fingers tightened on the tray as he controlled his instinct to smash it on his cousin's head. His brain backtracked because knocking Hector unconscious wouldn't satisfy the possessive beast in Migs. Bella was dancing with Abbi Mena while his mother looked on, everyone oblivious to the simmering volcano that had entered the room.

As Hector laughingly twirled Ariana straight into a dip, both of them spotted him. Migs raised a brow as he watched his wife's upside-down face.

"Migs," she breathed.

"Ah-ah, my darling, eyes on me *por favor*," Hector clucked and brought her back to attention.

Hector was a dead man.

"Miguel!" Lettie called.

As if waking up from a trance, he scowled at his sister. "Where do you want this?"

Lettie blew out an exasperated breath. That was her version of an eye-roll. "There." She pointed to a side table.

He lowered the tray and stood at the fringes as the dancing couples swept past him. He braced his feet and crossed his arms. Was he going to claim his bride? Was he going to stalk over there, tap Hector on the shoulder, and then punch him in the face too?

Get a grip, Walker. They were just dancing. He needed to

get used to this. It was an inevitability. He wasn't going to be Ariana's only dance partner at the party.

Sure he was, his inner caveman argued.

"They are just having fun." He didn't know that his mother was beside him until she had spoken, so focused was he in imagining his cousin's untimely demise at his hands. "Wipe that dark cloud from your face, *mijo*."

He glanced at his mother and tried to smile. She shook her head. "That smile is going to scare small children."

What? Did he look like a murderous clown?

Thankfully, the music finished and, more thankfully, his cousin and Ariana didn't linger in the final position, which had her draping her leg over his hip.

"*Cabrón!*" Hector yelled as he and Ariana walked over to him. Why the hell did his cousin have a hand at the small of her back? Rather than wait for them to reach him, he moved forward and clasped Ariana's arm, giving her a tug that made her stumble into him. Without hesitation, he gave her a searing kiss, before leveling Hector with a stoic gaze. "Cuz, what are you doing here?"

"Eh, thought I could help with organizing the party."

"I'm sure my sisters have that handled."

"Careful, cuz, you sound like you don't want me here."

"Not at all, but maybe you should help your brother so he's not whining that he's doing all the farm work by himself."

"Hey, I had nothing to do with what Joaquín did," Hector protested.

"You two boys are breaking my heart," Abbi Mena stepped up to them. "Is that the way to greet each other?"

Abuelita was staring at Migs with disapproval and his balls shriveled a bit at the weight of her stare, but she was right. His own long-standing guilt mixed with jealousy, not to mention his displeasure at Hector's older brother culminated in his antagonistic behavior.

"Come here." He grabbed his cousin by the neck and

yanked him into a hug. But his inner caveman had to get in the last word. "Dance with my wife again, and I will break your legs, *cabrón*," he whispered by Hector's ear.

When he leaned back, Migs wanted to laugh at the disconcerted expression on his cousin's face and added for everyone else to hear, "Glad you're here to help."

Hector blinked before pasting on a smile so comical, Migs was certain he had thrown his cousin for a loop. That Hector wasn't sure whether to take that veiled threat as a joke or if it was a part of their history of reenacting the Han-Lando thing.

"Yes, especially since you keep on blowing off our online meetings," Lettie added.

"I was busy with the hotel, but I'm here now. My crew is at your command, ready to build the best stage for Abbi Mena."

"It's not my *quinceañera* and I'm not a bride," their grandmother reminded them. "Don't go overboard."

As Delia inquired about the Vegas holdings, the family gathered around for iced tea and snacks. Migs lowered himself to a couch and dragged Ariana on his lap.

"What's with all this possessive behavior?" she whispered by his ear.

His hand that was on top of her thigh squeezed her in answer. "Get used to it." He nipped her ear. He felt her shiver. Good.

Since Hector appeared to be staying in the house, he would be put in the room next to theirs. That meant monkey sex wouldn't be in their future, at least for the next week or so. Damn, just when they were ready to go bareback.

His eyes caught his cousin's across the room. He was watching them and gave Migs an annoying smirk and mock salute.

Maybe Migs was overreacting.

Tessa chose that moment to sweep into the living room. In

her arms were bundles of garment bags. Following her were Cesar and Drew with similar loads.

"Ladies, I have all your gowns for final fitting." Tessa turned to his wife. "Even yours, Ari."

Migs sighed as he lost the comfort of his wife on his lap as she got up to join the excitement over the dresses.

He couldn't wait until his grandmother's celebration was over. Not having absolute control over the security of the festivities was making him antsy. He was happy to see his wife blending into his family so well, but as his grandmother's birthday grew closer, a pit of unease in his gut was growing bigger and bigger.

It was like waiting for the other shoe to drop.

19

IT HAD BEEN weeks since Ariana had worn full makeup. While she waited for the bathroom to cool down after her shower, a towel wrapped her wet hair in place. She was running late but applying foundation when her face was steamed up would be an exercise in futility.

It was the day of Abbi Mena's party and everything that could go wrong did. First, the cake had a mishap, so Tessa had to scramble for another one. The favors for the event had the wrong labeling, so she and Lettie had to redo all of them.

Delia had to alter Bella's dress because she mysteriously gained five pounds from the week before. And now Ariana was staring at her own dress hanging from the bathroom door like it was about to betray her too. As of last night, it still fit, but at the rate everyone was eating, she'd be surprised if she didn't need a girdle. Her dress was a beautiful cream creation with a corset style top and a flowing chiffon skirt that hit midway between the knee and the ankle. It was perfect for dancing. Embroidered peonies studded with black beads accentuated the dress. It had enough support not to need a bra.

Returning her attention to her makeup, she went with

smoky eyes and was applying the fake eyelashes when Migs appeared in the mirror.

His eyes grew heated.

"Don't even think about it," Ariana said, positioning the lashes and doing a couple of blinks in the mirror to test the glue.

"That's all I've been thinking about all day."

"We're running late."

"We're the only ones in the house."

He was wearing the trousers to his suit but was only wearing the undershirt.

"There's a stain on your shirt."

Ariana realized her mistake when her husband discarded said clothing and exposed his magnificent musculature. Seriously, he was a work of art with his sleeve tattoos and ink on his chest. She tried to ignore the answering quiver in her lady parts, but a sheen of sweat seemed to magically appear on her upper lip.

Mierda.

"Miiiiigs ..." she warned when he straightened from the doorframe and reached for her.

"I'll be quick."

A choked laugh caught in her throat as she tried to evade him, but he caught her by the waist and spun her around, quickly divesting her of the robe, exposing her nakedness to his scorching eyes. "Don't run," he whispered. "It's exciting me even more, and I might come before I get inside you."

"That's your problem."

His breath was hot on her neck. "No, it's yours."

He boosted her up against the wall, his hand worked between them and she heard the clink of the belt buckle, the lowering of a zipper. His fingers probed her folds and she could feel how slick she was.

"Let go, Ariana," he murmured. "Scream all you want. We're alone now."

Then he impaled her against the wall, sliding her against cool tiled walls. Migs didn't hold back, his girth stretched her, filled her. He withdrew only to drive into her again. Over and over he hammered her as her fingers gripped his face. There was sheer torture on his features as if being inside her wasn't enough.

"Give me every inch of you … ahh, Miguel," Ariana screamed as his shaft hit her sweet spot, and ripples of pleasure washed over her, curling her toes, making her shiver. With her head thrown back, Migs kept his mouth on her throat, trailing fire, until he reached his own release. He stifled a roar, ending in a forceful grunt effused on her neck.

"Holy fuck," he murmured. "Fucking hell, babe." He repeated over and over. Ariana was speechless herself. Migs took her quick and dirty and it was freakishly hot.

He lowered her legs and staggered back.

"You're lucky we have to leave soon." His eyes scorched over her. "You've got this rock chick babe look going for you, begging to be fucked."

Rock chick babe?

She disengaged from the wall and pushed his hulking frame aside to look in the mirror. Her mascara and eyeliner had smeared.

"WE ARE REALLY LATE," Ariana mumbled as she slipped into her dress. She had to redo her entire face of makeup and decided for a cleaner eyeshadow look. Her husband had the talent to demolish makeup masterpieces in a few minutes of fierce fucking.

Migs was reclining on the loveseat, eyeing her lazily like a lion who was toying with his meal. He'd already put on his dress shirt and his tie was hanging loosely around his neck. Ariana tried not to think how hot he looked in starched clothes.

She walked up to him and showed him her back. He didn't need prodding, but got up and drew up the zipper, but before she managed to walk away, something cool draped around her neck. When she tried to look down, she couldn't see it so she ran to the bedroom mirror.

"Migs!" she gasped as sparkling diamonds winked at her. "Where did you get this?"

"It's a family heirloom." He gave her a brief history, that it belonged to his great great-grandmother.

"This is too much!" Emotions burned her eyes. "Now you're going to ruin my makeup again!"

He chuckled and picked up her hand and put something else on it. She stared at the matching bracelet and earrings in her palm.

"Now hurry up." Migs pressed a kiss to her forehead. "I can't wait for the family to see you in them."

TESSA WAS BLOWING up his phone when their SUV pulled into the entrance of the country club. In fact, his sister was already waiting at the driveway.

"Where have you guys been?" his sister fussed at them, and then her eyes widened at the jewelry around Ariana's neck. "Oh, never mind." She grinned. "All's good. Some of the guests are still arriving." She motioned to one of the country club employees to pick up the favors in the cargo of the Escalade.

He rounded the vehicle and gave the keys to the valet, offering one arm to Ariana and the other to his sister. "I'm escorting two beautiful women."

"Ah, Miguel, you don't need to flatter your older sister. I already forgive you for being late." She looked over to his wife. "It looks beautiful on you, Ari. Mamá told me she gave these to Migs."

As the women chatted, he shifted his arms so Ari was beside Tessa and they weren't separated by his bulk. He saw Leon by the entrance to the ballroom and they exchanged brief nods.

"Miguel!"

He turned and saw a crowd of his relatives approach. Was it weird that he wanted to grab Ariana and run away from them? His eyes lowered to Tessa's laughing face.

"Showtime, little brother."

MOMENTS LATER, he managed to maneuver Ariana past a throng of his extended family and friends. "Sorry about that," he muttered. He wiped a trace of lipstick on Ariana's cheek and she did the same on his.

"They're an enthusiastic bunch, aren't they?"

"They haven't seen me in a while." He gave her a look. "You seem to be doing okay."

"You forget, I moved in a similar crowd in LA. I try to remember names when I can, but know after the night is through, I probably won't be able to match names and faces. Besides, I think everyone is more interested in your grand-mother than our marriage."

It was because everyone was trying to get a piece of his grandmother's estate. His eyes searched for the celebrant. She was about to sit at the long table by the stage. "Abbi Mena is free now. Let's go." They hastened to his grandmother before anyone could waylay her again.

"Happy Birthday, abuelita." They'd already greeted her this morning before the craziness started.

"Ah, take me away from here, *mijo*," his abuela laughed, feigning exasperation. "I'm too old for this."

"You're pretending to be annoyed," Migs teased. "But I see you're happy to see all your grandchildren and great-grandkids."

She beamed. "Yes. It makes my heart feel like this." She separated her hands across her chest. "Good to be around family. Sometimes." Her eyes sparkled with mirth. "How are you holding up, Ariana?"

"Everyone's been great," she said.

"She's more at ease with them than I am," Migs said.

"That's because you're antisocial. Ariana is a people-person."

Delia and Drew came up beside them. "You two go circulate." Mamá's gaze landed around Ariana's neck, a satisfied smile crossing her lips and then glanced at his wife's ring finger before shifting back questioningly to him.

Migs gave a shake of his head and motioned to his suit jacket. The ring was in his pocket. His tongue couldn't find the words. He didn't know if he was overwhelmed by what he was feeling, or he was feeling that they both weren't at that point yet. He was afraid. Afraid to rock the status quo. Ariana accepted the jewelry, but the diamond ring meant so much more. He'd have to plan a more elaborate proposal that would seal their fate forever.

If his wife noticed the silent exchange between him and his mother, she didn't give any indication. She was teasing Pops about how dashing he looked in his suit.

"He takes after me." Migs winked.

Everyone laughed. Soon, Lettie joined them and shooed Migs away and scolded him, telling him to circulate with Ariana and introduce her to the family.

Just his luck, they ran into Joaquín.

His cousin was the older version of Hector. Tall, lean, and with the Spanish mestizo complexion, but that was where the similarities ended. Though their features were similar, Hector immediately exuded fun, while Joaquín was the complete opposite. Hardness and shrewdness were permanently etched into this particular cousin's face, and no amount of smiling seemed to change that first impression.

In fact, at this moment, he appeared like a shark scenting blood in the water.

"Joaquín."

"Miguel."

"Ariana, my cousin, Joaquín."

They exchanged brittle pleasantries. His wife was having trouble being civil to Joaquín after she heard Tessa spreading her displeasure at their cousin for what he'd done to Cesar.

"It's a simple misunderstanding, Miguel," Joaquín sighed. "I accept full responsibility."

"How magnanimous of you." Migs flared. He'd been doing so well keeping a lid on his temper. Being around his family did that, but apparently not with this particular one. "This simple misunderstanding could have cost Cesar and Leon their lives."

"For the last time," his cousin gritted. "I did not make the call."

"It originated from your office."

"I'm looking into it," Joaquín said. "And why were they the ones in the warehouse? Cesar always sent his supervisors for the nighttime arrivals."

"I know I'm new here," Ariana interjected. "But if you two insist on discussing the situation now, move somewhere else. People are starting to notice."

Both men glanced up and sure enough many eyes were trained on them with interest.

"I'm done here," Migs grunted.

He made to move but Joaquín grabbed his arm. Migs dropped his eyes to where his cousin was gripping his bicep before flicking it back to Joaquín, keeping them expressionless until his cousin released his hold.

"Miguel. We're family," Joaquín sighed in resignation. "What's a better time to fix this than now? It's abuelita's birthday. It will make her so happy that we all get along."

Hector sauntered over to them. "You guys are making a scene. How about taking this somewhere else, huh?"

"Perfect time for me to use the ladies' room." Ariana looked at Miguel pointedly. Talk it out, her eyes communicated. He reluctantly let his wife go and allowed his two cousins to lead him away, aware that all attention was on the Alcantara heirs.

He was doing this for his family, for Abbi Mena, and his mother.

———

ARIANA ESCAPED TO THE LADIES' room, thankful that all eyes were on the cousins. She needed a moment to regroup. It was her first public outing since Raul was killed. She wondered how many of the guests knew exactly who she was, and how many of them had been wronged by her brother. She hated to leave Migs on his own with Joaquín. Unlike Hector, it seemed that particular cousin was more sly, but she sensed there was more to the warehouse incident that had caused that rift. Migs hadn't talked about it, but Drew had mentioned Don Pepito's death. What happened to Joaquín and Hector's father? And how did it relate to Migs and his admission that he was DEA?

She checked her makeup. Still on point. She went into one of the stalls to pee. She was finishing up, when a group of women filed in.

"Did you see the cousins square off?"

"Yes, that was hot."

"Joaquín is good looking, but he seems so cold. His poor wife, Elena. I don't blame her for dallying with the foreman."

"That's gossip."

"But look at that cold fish."

"His face looks carved out of ice, you'd probably need to stick a hot iron in his ass for him to bring some heat into bed."

Ariana shook her head. Women could be vicious.

"Yes, compared to Miguel. Rawr!"

She froze and held her breath.

"Now that's one hot *papichulo.*"

"Tall, broad, and all man. Good in bed?"

The girls giggled. Ariana clenched her fists. Two of the women went to the stalls. One washed her hands. So it appeared to be three of them.

"I wouldn't mind climbing that mountain."

"Ugh, did you see who he married?"

"Are they really married? She has a ring, but no diamond."

"Ha! He got her cheap."

"Don't you know who she is?" The girl who didn't use the toilet said.

"She looks familiar—" one started.

"That's Raul Ortega's sister!"

"Yes!"

"*Madre de Dios.* Why did Miguel marry her?"

"Look at her. She's like a goddess."

"But bad family."

The sound of running water drowned their answer.

"—wouldn't last. He's just infatuated."

"Why don't you introduce me to him?"

"What? I'm not crazy enough to do that."

"Why not?"

"I don't think Miguel likes good girls. Rumor is, he has tattoos on both arms."

"Oooh, I can be a bad girl for him!"

They laughed and Ariana gritted her teeth.

To her relief, they opened the door and the rest of their words were muffled and it was silent again in the restroom.

How humiliating!

She sat there with her ass hanging on the commode while she listened to three women drool over her husband and poke at her insecurities. At least they said she looked like a goddess.

Ariana smiled bitterly. What happened when the beauty faded?

She exited the stall, washed her hands, and checked her makeup one more time.

Was Migs just infatuated? She fingered her wedding band. She never wanted a diamond. Their marriage wasn't meant to last, but these past few weeks were pure bliss. It was real.

When she emerged from the ladies' room, she was appalled to see three women standing at the mouth of the hallway. Were they the ones who were gossiping in the bathroom? Before one of them spotted her, Ariana turned the other way. She'd been in this country club when Tessa was going through the punch list with the event coordinator and knew her way around. She was about to turn into another corridor when she recognized Migs' broad back.

Maybe she'd surprise him, but a voice stopped her cold.

"Really, Miguel, let's talk about your wife," Joaquín said.

"Careful what you say, cuz."

"I'm being honest. How can you bring a gangster's sister into the family?"

"None of your fucking business."

"It *is* my fucking business, Miguel! You endanger all of us. Do you think Abbi Mena's name carries as much weight now than it did then? They're putting cocaine in our trucks! And, somehow, when I try to fix it, I'm the villain?"

"I'm done here." The voices moved further into the hallway away from her.

What was she doing eavesdropping? Nothing good was coming out of this.

"What's the matter, cuz? You're regretting it, aren't you?"

"I'm not talking to you about my marriage."

He didn't answer directly. A physical pain pierced her heart as she forced herself to move away, returning to the first hallway she'd escaped from. Thankfully, the three women weren't there anymore. The past ten minutes were excruciating, and she could feel a headache coming. She had styled her hair in a sweeping updo, but right now the pins in her hair felt like they were digging into her skull.

"There you are," Lettie hustled to her. "The speeches are about to begin. Have you seen Joaquín?"

"He went off with Migs."

"Ugh!" Lettie sounded frustrated. She was the program manager. "He's supposed to give the first speech."

"Lettie, what are you panicking about?" Hector appeared beside them.

"Where is your brother?"

He laughed and nodded to his right. "You mean that brother?"

Two men were walking around the perimeter of the ballroom, their faces both thunderous.

"Hmm, it looks like their talk did nothing," Hector said and stopped a waiter holding a tray of drinks. He grabbed a glass of wine and offered it to the women. Ariana and Lettie declined, so he shrugged and took it for himself.

"Abuelita will notice." Lettie shoved her cousin forward. "Can you tell your damned brother to smile? And you." She turned her attention to Ariana. "Do something about Migs' face."

She stalked back to the stage.

"Well, you heard the general. When did she become so bossy?" Hector took a sip from his glass and started to walk away. "I better get away from your side. Here comes your man."

Indeed, Migs was heading straight for them. The cousins nudged each other on the shoulder, on purpose, as they passed.

These two.

She was also aware of eyes on them as Migs grabbed her hand and brought her close. The doubts and heartache plaguing her eased a little. Between the two of them, their relationship was fine, but Migs wasn't an island. He loved his family, and Ariana was a complication. How long before cracks in their marriage appeared? They couldn't stay cocooned forever from the rest of the world.

"You doing okay?" Migs asked, his brows drawn together, eyes studying her face.

She was unable to withstand his scrutiny. "Yes. I was looking for you. Lettie was panicking."

"Yeah, Tessa texted me. Program is about to begin."

At the long table sat Abbi Mena's sons and daughters with their spouses. Because Joaquín's father—Don Pepito had been the eldest, Joaquín took his place at the table with his wife—a fair-skinned *mestiza* with thick, wavy hair. Ariana remembered the gossip in the ladies' room, wondering if it was true that Elena was cheating on her husband.

Migs led her to another table right behind the long one.

The emcee took to the stage and told everybody to take their seats.

"ANYONE WHO KNOWS my abuelita knows that when you visit her home, you need to be prepared to eat all day. That's why we Alacantara-Walkers are very lucky."

Laughter.

Ariana smiled as her husband spoke in front of everyone. He was the last speech before dinner, thank goodness. Joaquín gave a long, boring one that lasted over five minutes. Delia followed Joaquín and then two other cousins went. Interestingly enough, only Migs talked about food his grandmother made.

"The only time she wouldn't be cooking was when she was obsessed with a Mexican telenovela." He grinned at Abbi Mena. "Everyone would breathe a sigh of relief when the season ended because that would mean the tortillas wouldn't get burned or she wouldn't forget to put the salt in the carnitas."

Everyone cracked up and when the laughter died down, Abbi Mena interjected, "That was one time."

"Food has always been the cornerstone of our family," Migs continued. "It's not surprising that it's our business as well and that's a heritage we want to preserve. I asked Abbi Mena once why she was always in the kitchen. I was eight years old and I wanted her to fly a kite with me instead of slaving over a stove. She said it was her way of showing us love. But of course, to a boy my age that didn't make sense. It wasn't until I was a teenager and thought picking a fight with someone twice my size was a good idea, that I realized what she meant. I got my ass kicked. My mouth was swollen and it hurt to eat. And yet, abuelita painstakingly prepared food soft enough for me to handle. And the best part?" He grinned. "It tasted like dessert. And even now, anything *horchata* brings back those memories."

He gazed fondly at Abbi Mena, putting a hand over his heart. "*Te amo, abuelita.*" There were more *aws* from the crowd than in any other speech preceding his, because here was a tough-looking guy unabashed of expressing love for his grand-mother. Abbi Mena dabbed the corners of her eyes while emotions pricked Ariana's own.

It was at that moment that an overwhelming ache seized her heart—that longing to be a part of Migs' family. The purity of the love that zinged between his grandmother and him was palpable. When Migs announced dinner, the applause was deafening. He chuckled and added a quip about not knowing if that was for the beauty of his speech or the end of it.

He must have made an impression on the crowd because he was stopped by a couple of people who wanted a word with him. The waitstaff uncovered the dishes that were laid for a buffet line on both sides and some guests rushed to it while others took their time.

"You're waiting for Miguel?" Tessa asked.

"I am."

"Cesar can stay with you. Gigi is asleep anyway." She nodded to her husband and the sleeping child at the toddler chair.

"Why don't you both go? I can watch her." She glanced again at Migs. "Looks like he's going to take a while."

"Ugh, that's Tio Cris. He likes to talk and he's fond of Miguel." Tessa gave a pained smile. "He's going be a while all right."

20

MIGS TRIED his best not to show his irritation with Tio Cris. He was his godfather after all. The man had been a patient uncle and Migs had looked up to him when he was a boy. But, although he would love to catch up with him, Miguel was impatient to get back to Ariana. He glanced over his shoulder and saw her give him a small wave.

He lifted his chin and flattened his mouth.

"Ah ... impatient to get back to your *esposa*, huh?" Tio Cris waggled his brows. "Bah, newlyweds. It's still exciting, but take it from your tio, you don't want to show how crazy you are about your wife."

Apparently with age, his uncle gave the suckiest advice as well, and yet he couldn't help asking, "Why?"

"Because then they'll use it to their advantage and black-mail you into doing what they want or buying them expensive diamonds."

Migs thought of the one in his pocket. "Listen, Tio——"

"That's what your Tia did." He leaned in. "Heaven help you if she withholds sex——"

TM—fucking—I. What the fuck?

A buzz in his pocket gave him the perfect excuse to leave this nightmarish conversation. "Sorry, I'm expecting a call."

"But it's dinner—"

Migs waved him off and was already walking toward Ariana when he saw the number.

Garrison.

Why the fuck was he calling him now? "Hold a sec."

He gestured to Ariana that he had to take the call and did an about-face. His wife didn't look too pleased. "What's up? Kind of a bad time here." He pushed open one of the access doors on the divider-walls reserved for staff.

"I wouldn't be calling if it wasn't important," Garrison growled.

"What are you—"

"Shut up and listen. Carillo is in San Diego. Signal intelligence confirms this. Intel from DEA corroborates. Benito was spotted near the country club."

Migs froze. "I need to give Leon a heads up."

"I have a list of—"

A booming sound came from within the ballroom.

"What the fuck was that?" John yelled.

But Migs was already barreling back into the ballroom area. Smoke and utter chaos met his eyes.

Ariana!

People screamed and bodies littered the floor, groaning. The floor shook again, followed by another ear-splitting sound. The elaborate structure behind the stage where he'd just given his speech collapsed and slammed into the long table where Abbi Mena and his parents sat.

Nausea rose in his throat. Fighting against the surge of guests, his eyes searched frantically for his wife and family.

"Migs!" It was Tessa crying and clawing to get to him. He shoved people out of the way and yanked his sister to his side. "Where's Ari?"

"Gigi!"

"Okay, we'll find her," Migs said in a steady voice. Of course his sister would think about her daughter, but how did they get separated?

"She's with Gigi!"

Finally, he saw Ariana stagger to her feet by the table where he'd left her, and she was holding his niece.

"Gigi!" Tessa cried.

When they reached them, Migs crushed his wife in his arms, but his brain switched to his parents and he couldn't see to her comfort. He saw Pops helping his mother to her feet, completely dazed. But where was Abbi Mena?

"Is Mamá all right?" Migs shouted.

"Yes. See to your grandmother," Pops yelled.

"She's here." Joaquín fell to his knees.

Migs saw his beloved grandmother sprawled on the floor right beside what looked like scaffolding and pieces of board. His lungs seized as he vaulted over the table to get to her.

"Her arm is trapped under there," Joaquín said hoarsely. "I don't want to move her."

"Don't. Until the EMTs and the firemen arrive."

"What can I do?" Ariana rounded by his side.

At the sight of her, Joaquín rose to his feet, his face darkening with rage. Migs anticipated his reaction and blocked his path to Ariana.

"Do?" Joaquín spat. "Haven't you done enough? This is because of you!"

Migs grabbed his collar, snarling, "Shut it!" And in a low, steady voice he said, "Speak to my wife that way again, and I don't care where we are, Joaquín, I will break your fucking jaw. You don't want to fuck with me. Now, focus!"

Miguel crouched down to check his grandmother's vitals.

"Police and ambulance are on their way." Hector skidded to a stop beside them. He grabbed his head in anguish, his face pale. "*Mierda*. How could this have happened?"

"Her heartbeat is strong and she's breathing," Migs said in

relief and tried to take his own advice and to focus and assess the situation. "This might not be over." He glanced up at Ariana. "You need to get out of here." And then to Hector, he said, "Take her to Leon."

His cousin nodded. "He has the other Marias and is helping my men herd other people out."

"I'm not leaving without you!" Ariana cried.

Joaquín glared at her, but Migs shot him another scathing look. He got to his feet and clasped her shoulders. "I can't concentrate if you're here. I need you safe."

She looked about to argue but gave a slight nod. Hector took her arm.

"Mamá!" Delia screamed. Migs stopped his mother and addressed Pops. "Get them out. There may be other explosives." His other tios and tias were dazed as well but they understood the urgency to leave immediately.

"Miguel ..." his mother whispered. She was shaking uncontrollably, and he could see the conflict in her eyes.

"We'll stay with Abbi Mena until help arrives," Joaquín said. "¡Vamos!"

The people around them jolted into action and made for the exits. His eyes followed Ariana who glanced over her shoulder even as she was being rushed away by Hector.

He crouched again beside his grandmother. In a way he was relieved Abbi Mena was unconscious given that her arm was pinned. He couldn't bear the thought of her in pain.

"Funny, huh? You and I agreeing on something?" Joaquín said, dropping down beside Miguel. "Maybe until the very end."

Unbidden respect surfaced for his cousin. A man's true grit was tested in times of adversity and nothing was more adverse than this situation given there could be a ticking time bomb still in the vicinity. A pit in his stomach had him second guessing letting Ariana out of his sight, and his blood ran cold as Garrison's words sunk into him.

Carillo is in San Diego.

Fuck!

He pulled out his phone and called Leon. No answer, so he texted him to keep Ariana within his sight. He surged to his feet, eyes frantically sweeping across the ballroom. People were still staggering toward the exit, but he couldn't see Ariana or Hector. No sign of his immediate family either.

"Where are you going?" Joaquín barked when Migs walked away as his eyes continued scouring the ballroom.

He called Garrison.

ARIANA SHUFFLED ON HER HEELS, looking over her shoulder where Migs dropped down beside Abbi Mena. Anxiety choked her, making it difficult to breathe. She wanted to stay, but she couldn't distract him, not when there could be another bomb, but also because of the hate flowing off Joaquín.

He was Migs' ally in this, but not when she was around. And her husband needed all the support he could get.

Hector suddenly veered from the path the rest were taking and led her to a side access door. She stopped just inside its threshold, digging her heels in.

"Why here?" she asked.

"This is a shortcut to Leon."

The sight of an empty corridor raised the hairs on the back of her neck. She was regretting that she left her purse with her phone, but she had Gigi with her when pandemonium broke loose and forgot her things.

She resisted his pull.

"Ariana!" Hector growled. "We need to go."

"Call him," she said. "See where he is to be sure."

"My phone is dead. It got smashed."

A tendril of distrust slithered up her spine. She liked Hector. He was easy-going and carefree, but she replayed his expression when he saw his grandmother. It wasn't shock or horror.

It was guilt.

"I'm going with Delia." Just as she turned away, she heard an ominous click.

"I can't let you do that."

She faced Hector again and he had a gun trained on her.

"What are you doing?" she whispered.

"I'm sorry, Ariana," he said, eyes like ice. "But we have no time."

He stepped aside and waved the gun. "No funny moves. I know Migs has been teaching you ninja shit."

Blood left her face and, fighting the lightheadedness that swamped her, she gritted, "How could you do this? To your own *abuela!*"

"That wasn't supposed to go down that way!" he screamed. "Someone is going to pay, but first I need to settle a debt. So move! Or I swear to God, I'll kill you." And then he muttered, "It would solve all our problems."

Veins popped in his temple, and his color turned ruddy. Hector was close to losing it, and Ariana didn't want to die today.

"All right."

He pushed the gun in the small of her back, forcing her further down the corridor where the lighting grew progressively darker. When they arrived at the door to the covered parking, Hector ordered her to open it.

The door from the ballroom where they'd come from slammed open.

"Hector!" It was Leon and with him were Hector's men. "Where are you going?"

Terror gripped Ariana's heart. "Leon! Watch ..." Her warning turned into a scream as she watched Hector's men pump two bullets into Leon.

Overcome with rage, she went after Hector's gun. He

cursed and shoved her. She fell against the railing right outside the open door to the garage.

"I said not a mark on her." An unfamiliar voice spoke from that direction.

Ariana straightened and stared into the face of a stranger. Cowboy hat, dark skin, thick mustache. He wore a gingham shirt, distressed jeans, and a big-buckled belt like a Texas rancher.

"*Pendejo!*" Hector raged. "Your men fucked up the explosives. My grandmother is hurt!" Men with automatic weapons came forward and pointed their guns at Hector and his men.

The man shrugged. "Collateral damage. You were unable to pay me for the cocaine. You didn't think the price would be cheap? Now leave us. You're not a part of this."

Hector's face was ravaged by fury and distress, but Ariana felt no sympathy for his torment over Abbi Mena's injuries. Pain pierced her chest as she wondered if abuelita was okay. If she was alive. She hung on to hope that the old woman was.

"I won't repeat myself, Hector. I haven't gotten over the loss of my shipment and I have no problem killing an Alcantara."

Giving Ariana one last look, Hector retreated into the hallway.

"We finally meet, Ariana Ortega." The man opened the door of a dark Escalade. Two black Ford Explorers flanked it bumper to bumper. "Who ...?"

"Benito Carillo. You have something of mine."

"I don't have anything. Raul didn't—"

"*Jefe.*" One of his henchmen came up to him and murmured in his ear and his features morphed into granite.

"I'm afraid we cannot stay," Benito ordered. "Get in the car."

Ariana gulped. Should she scream?

As if reading her thoughts, Benito sighed heavily and jerked his chin. A man came up behind her, but she evaded him, only to be blocked by another and this one had a needle. She faked right, but someone grabbed her from behind. She screamed and cracked her head backward, her heel stomping on a foot.

Benito's man howled, and she was about to escape into the hallway when vicious fingers clawed her hair and yanked her back. Her right arm was caught in a vise and twisted high. She couldn't move without causing unbearable pain in her shoulder.

She whimpered in agony.

"*Luchadora.*" A new voice joined the mix, this one full of malice and it stopped her cold.

Benito appeared in front of her. "I didn't want to hurt you, but we're out of time."

A needle stabbed her neck and paralysis took over her system, her tongue turned thick and numb.

She was falling and then she was floating.

Her vision dimmed like she'd fallen into a tunnel, the light fading into a pin prick until finally there was nothing.

21

"Is your grandmother all right?" Garrison asked.

Migs scraped his face with his palm, then spoke into the phone, "I don't know. They're not sending anyone in until the K-9s give the all clear." He couldn't get hold of Leon, Hector, or Ariana—she left her fucking phone on the table. His father and Cesar were looking for them around the country club. The cops had sealed off all entrances and exits into the ballroom.

Migs, Joaquín, and Abbi Mena were the only ones left in the chaos of overturned chairs, broken glass, and dining debris. Each second that passed not knowing where the fuck his wife was stoked the fear that was growing in his gut. What he felt was not fear, it was terror.

Terror that Benito had her.

Terror for what he would do to her.

But his greatest fear was never seeing her again. He touched the ring in his pocket. He was a coward for not finding the words. His chest tightened and he had to force air from his lungs to fucking breathe.

"All clear!" The K-9 handler yelled.

"Fucking finally. Are you guys close?" Migs growled.

"We're a block from the country club."

"Okay, call when you get here." He ended the call as the EMTs rushed in with a gurney. Firemen followed and then the police.

Leon was in charge of overall security. He was supposed to meet the first responders. Instead, his second-in-command was the one coordinating with San Diego SWAT and PD.

Abbi Mena was regaining consciousness and her wails of pain stabbed Migs in the heart. He couldn't bear it. Even Joaquín turned away, his face mottled red from withholding tears. Whoever did this would pay.

He spotted Pops and an officer Migs recognized from the SDPD. Lieutenant Murphy was a friend of his father's.

Their grim expressions probably echoed his, but Pops looked ashen.

Migs sprinted to them. "Have you found them? Where the fuck is Leon? Where the fuck is my wife?"

At Drew's almost tearful expression, Migs was on a razor's edge from losing it.

"Tell me," he roared.

"Leon is dead," Pops said, tears tracked down his cheeks. "He was found by the SWAT in that corridor." He pointed to the far left.

"And Ariana? Hector?" he asked hoarsely.

"Hector is gone too. We couldn't find him or his men."

"Okay …" Migs took a couple of gulps of air as his mind reprocessed the information he had. "Okay. Maybe Leon sent them away."

"If there's something you know, son, now is the time to talk," Murphy said. "Do you have an idea who did this?"

"I told you," Drew said. "It was payback for the drugs." He glared at Joaquín. "You should have consulted us before you called the DEA—"

"Pops!" Migs cut in sharply. "There's something bigger at play here …"

"Lieutenant?" A cop came up to Murphy and handed him an object. "We found this in the service garage."

His lungs seized when he recognized the bracelet. "Fuck ... oh fuck." With shaking fingers, he picked it up. "It's Ariana's." He cleared his throat, voice raw. "You found it where?"

"The service garage in front of the exit door."

Migs was familiar with the layout around this quadrant. "That's the same corridor where Leon was found, right?"

"Yes."

His phone buzzed and he excused himself, walking to a spot where he watched the EMTs load his grandmother on the gurney. "Ariana is gone."

"Shit," John muttered. "We're at the back of the country club. Front is a zoo. I'm having Nadia check the traffic cams."

"Have her check the ones that are coming from the service garage of the club."

"Gotcha."

"I'm going to check on my grandmother and call you back."

"Copy that."

He approached the gurney. Abbi Mena was in a neck brace and her right arm was held in a splint. A roar inside him wanted to break free, but he had to keep it together. He did his best to force his face to relax.

"How is she?"

"She has a concussion and broken arm. Vitals are stable, but she's out of it," the EMT warned him. "We gave her a dose of fentanyl to manage the pain."

Migs stared at his grandmother with all the love he felt for her and touched her face briefly. Her eyes fluttered and she mouthed his name, a ghost of a smile on her lips.

"*Te amo, abuelita.*"

When he turned away, his father was right behind him. "Keep me posted on her condition." He passed his dad.

"Where are you going?" Drew yelled.

Migs didn't look back, but headed behind the stage opposite to where emergency personnel were streaming in. It was the exit that led straight to the back of the club. That way he was avoiding his mother and his sisters. All his lies were coming to a head, and he was too furious to talk to them or explain. He didn't have it in him to deal with that right now.

All his faculties were honed on getting Ariana back.

"POWELL IDED three SUVs entering and exiting the service garage around the time of the explosion," Garrison said.

Migs, who was in the back of the Suburban, met John's eyes briefly in the rear-view mirror. On the passenger side sat Levi who was on his laptop keeping in contact with the analyst. Bristow was sitting silent beside him.

"There's something else," John's eyes returned to traffic on West Boulevard where they'd just turned from the country club drive. "I don't think your cousin's been taken."

"He's not answering his phone."

"Could mean many things." John said. "But we tagged his vehicle in front of a traffic light not long after our suspected Benito convoy passed it. Footage is grainy, but the person sitting on the front passenger side could be one of your cousin's men."

"You have a screenshot?" Migs asked.

Levi held up the laptop.

Migs let out a deflated breath. "Yeah, that man is his." His brain was in full processing mode and it was leaning toward his younger cousin being involved in this whole clusterfuck. Otherwise, why would he run? What Migs couldn't reconcile in his head was how Hector could let Abbi Mena get hurt. He loved her just like everyone did, but Migs wasn't blind to his cousin's vices. The Alcantaras had a lot of money but being in

Vegas presented other problems with Hector. "Is there a way Nadia can look into my cousin's finances."

"She's already on it," John said. "Should we put a BOLO on Hector's vehicle?"

Either the family was going to come together over this, or relations would go from strained to downright hostile. Migs weighed his options. But only Ariana and Abbi Mena mattered. Hurt feelings could come later and he was willing to take the consequences. "Do it."

"Nadia's on the line," Levi said. "Says it's urgent."

"Put her on speaker."

"Guys, take the next exit. There is no time to waste." The analyst's voice came on and forget urgent, there was panic in her tone. She was rarely fazed.

"What's going on Powell?" John barked.

"I tracked the vehicles and I think I know where they are going ... "

Migs gritted his teeth as static filled the cabin of the SUV.

"An airfield."

Migs stopped breathing and hoped to hell he heard her wrong. "A what?"

"It's abandoned, but still functional," Nadia said. "It's not in any of our databases and I'm trying to access past satellite images, but the computer is—" there was a lot of unintelligible cursing and then, "fucking piece of shit."

"Powell, focus," John growled. "Is it operational now?"

"Moving satellite, it'll take a few minutes."

"We don't have a few fucking minutes," Migs snapped. "Take the next exit. What's the address?"

Nadia rattled off the location.

Because of the urgency of the situation, the traffic crawl appeared to have multiplied ten-fold. There was only one reason Benito was taking Ariana to an airfield.

He was taking her to Mexico.

· · ·

"ONCE HE GETS her in the air, we're screwed," Migs snarled. "Can't you drive fucking faster?" They had taken the exit but encountered another bottleneck of vehicles.

"We get pulled over then we're not just screwed, we're fucked."

He hated Garrison's calm voice and his sensible words because he was right. Migs was anything but calm. He'd left calm the moment he realized Ariana had been taken. Every time their SUV had to stop, he wanted to jump out of the vehicle and run the whole way. That might even help settle his nerves.

This unprecedented situation only highlighted why he avoided relationships when he was in Special Forces and the DEA. Migs was so emotionally compromised, he was surprised Garrison allowed him to stay on. He probably figured Migs wouldn't be willing to sit this out.

He was right.

John made an illegal swerve and rode the shoulder until they got to the intersection they needed.

"What the hell are you doing?" Migs roared.

"Shut up and let me drive," Garrison shot back. "One more word out of you, I'll have Bristow kick you out of the vehicle. Got me?"

"Just saying," he muttered.

"Heard you loud and clear, Walker." John flicked his eyes at the rear-view mirror then returned them on the road. "Powell, any update on sat images?

"Looks like a twin-engine turboprop and the SUVs are parked beside it. Hangar is lit up. Men are transferring crates into the plane from a hangar."

"How many hostiles?"

"Counting eight."

"Should we get the DEA on standby?" Levi asked.

"We can take them," Migs said confidently. "We can't get any LEOs involved. Not with Ariana as hostage."

"How's the BOLO on Hector Alcantara?" John asked instead.

"It's in flux," Levi replied.

"Guys, we have a problem," Powell's voice came from the laptop's audio. "A couple of streets opposite the airfield I see a van for surveillance with all the gizmos on its roof. Dammit!"

"What?"

"Two unmarked vans pulled in near the airfield."

"What?"

"Check the police channels," Garrison ordered. "The one for the task force."

Migs clenched his jaw to keep from yelling at Nadia to do her job faster. Somehow despite John being brusque with her, he wouldn't take kindly if Migs did the same.

"It is the task force," Powell said. "What do you want me to do?"

"Can you tell them to stand down?" Migs asked.

"That's not going to happen." John slapped his palm on the steering wheel seemingly as frustrated as Migs was.

"Well, we can't let them pull the shit they did at the warehouse," he argued. "I don't think Benito is going to take that sitting down and I'm not about to let Ariana get caught in the crossfire."

When their Suburban made the turn onto the airfield's road, they were getting flagged down by none other than Lenox. The DEA agent looked as pissed now as he did when they'd walked out of the station that morning weeks ago.

"Fuck."

"I got word to them," Powell said. "Thank me later that you all didn't cause a shootout."

"It's your job," John clipped.

"What was that again?" the analyst snapped. "Your blackmail can only go so far."

Blackmail?

Bristow snorted. He hadn't said a word on the way here,

but he sure was busy checking his gear. Migs glanced at him. "Got another one of those?" He pointed to the automatic rifle.

"Yeah," the agent handed him a long gun, twisted in his seat, and grabbed a vest from the back. "Might as well put this on."

Decelerating and then stopping, Garrison rolled down the window. Lenox ducked his head to look at the occupants, recognizing Migs. His eyes widened. "Can't say I'm surprised to see you here. I'm sorry about what happened at the country club." His tone was sincere, much to Migs' surprise. The DEA agent turned his attention to John. "Your analyst sent us your credentials, but we're about to head in. I can't let you take the lead. I hear Carillo has Ariana Ortega?"

"Walker," Migs corrected. "Don't need to remind you that's my wife with him."

Lenox nodded grimly. "We got that."

"How did you get here so fast?" John asked.

Migs wondered the same.

"Anonymous tip. That warehouse apparently has a tunnel all the way to Tijuana." Lenox leaned his hand on the roof and peered at all the men in the vehicle. "I don't need additional shit to think about and I know trying to get you guys to sit this one out is futile. So you follow us. You wear DEA flak jackets so we don't shoot you. My men are taking the lead. Got me? Gear up in first van."

"Is anyone having a bad feeling about this?" Bristow asked. "Powell, you there?"

"I'm listening and I agree. I was going to track down that tip, but I'm monitoring too many channels right now."

"Three of us are going to wear the DEA comms. Levi is going to stay with you." Garrison turned to the big guy. "Hang back, but if Powell says something doesn't look right, you signal us." He held up three fingers.

"Copy that," both Levi and Powell said.

"Anyone wonder why they're using a plane?" Bristow asked. "With no flight plan they're in danger of getting tagged by Air Patrol."

"Seems to me the Pacific Ocean would be a safer bet to move drugs," Levi added. "That's where the majority of the bigger drug shipments come in, second to the San Ysidro crossing."

"Unless they're not heading to Tijuana," Migs said grimly. "He's taking her straight to Tamaulipas."

CORN CROPS SURROUNDED the airfield on two sides while a broken chain link fence rimmed the other two. Lenox and his men didn't even need to cut through the lock on the gate. They found a gaping hole that needed a few snips with their wire cutters to allow the men and their gear through. One unit of agents approached from the fields.

John, Migs, Bristow, and Levi were with the squad assaulting from the rear of the warehouse/hangar. Benito was outnumbered. There was no sighting of the new cartel kingpin yet, but at this point all Migs wanted to see was Ariana.

Carillo's men were transferring sacks into the plane. A sick feeling in his stomach hoped that none of those were Ariana. There was no movement inside the Escalade that was parked at the entrance of the warehouse and the narcos were eerily silent while going about their business.

Migs covered his mic. Seeing him do this, Garrison did the same. "You get a feeling …"

"That something smells fishy?" John finished.

He nodded.

"It might be a trap."

Lenox made a roll call on the three-unit leaders. When everyone was in position, he asked them to standby.

"Garrison." It was Lenox. "Any idea from your analyst where Benito is? We're drawing a blank."

John looked at Levi. "Anything from Powell?"

Their teammate shook his head. "She's not liking the situation."

"My analyst agrees this could be a trap."

"We're picking up two heat signatures from within the Escalade though," Lenox said. "But they're unusually faint."

Migs couldn't breathe as a sense of déjà vu hit him. Not nine months ago, Ariana witnessed her brother's death when his Escalade exploded and landed on him. But it was another cartel responsible. But would it matter? The whole incident was on the news for weeks.

His breathing came fast and furious. "Ariana," he whispered harshly, his limbs itching to spring into action. "We need to do something!"

Bristow was fiddling with one of his toys. "I'm not isolating any signal of a transmitter on the Escalade. Remember the one Nadia picked up when Ortega's vehicle exploded?"

Levi interjected. "She thinks the place is clean too."

"I'm not risking my men," Lenox said. "Steer clear of the warehouse. We'll have to get Explosives out here after we round everyone up. Okay, teams, you know your quadrants. On three, two, one."

"Freeze. DEA!"

All teams swooped in. Carillo's men who were transporting the sacks into the plane, dumped their loads, and the ones holding weapons threw them away as everyone dropped to the ground.

"Goddammit," Migs growled when several DEA agents including Lenox approached the Escalade with weapons drawn.

"Benito Carillo, we have a warrant for your arrest. Come out of the vehicle with your hands up."

Even before the raid commenced, Migs had a sinking feeling that they'd been tricked. Everything was too easy and from what he'd been learning about Benito, he didn't make many mistakes. Bristow and Nadia's assessments were good enough for him because the not knowing was killing him and he'd reached his limit. He started for the Escalade.

"Walker," Garrison grabbed his arm, but he yanked it away.

Lenox dipped his head as if giving him permission to check the vehicle. Migs was deaf to anything else, blind to everything except the vehicle that either held his wife captive or would be the beginning of a nightmare.

Standing by the door behind the passenger one, he clenched his jaw and exhaled what could be his final breath.

He yanked open the door.

A despairing howl pierced through the night.

Migs dropped to his knees and lost it.

22

WHAT FOLLOWED NEXT WAS A BLUR. Finding the dead bodies in the Escalade shattered whatever was left of his control.

The first thought that hit him was that none of those life-less bodies were Ariana's. And the second? That Carillo had already taken his wife to Mexico. The proximity of the country club to the border, and not discounting Benito's resources, sneaking Ariana out of San Diego was not a farfetched conclusion. Or maybe that was what the cartel boss wanted them to think. Did he take Ariana back to Los Angeles? Had Raul hidden something Benito wanted?

They wasted precious time chasing the wrong lead.

Fuck.

They were on their way to the hospital to drop Migs off to check on Abbi Mena. No one spoke a word to him once they were on the road because there were no words. No paltry sentiments asking him if he was okay. Because Migs clearly wasn't. Nobody swore to get Ariana back because at this point, that would be more of a hollow promise than a vow. They had nothing to go on.

That wasn't entirely true. The dead bodies in the Escalade belonged to two country club employees. Their vehicles were not in the staff parking, but they were found later in another parking garage.

Benito had swapped vehicles again.

What would have been a lead was yet another dead end.

Their Suburban pulled in front of the emergency room of the San Diego Sacred Heart hospital. Migs was functioning like an automaton, and it wasn't until he registered Bristow calling his name that he realized he was still in a ballistic vest. He zipped it off and laid it in the back seat.

"I'm sending Bristow back with a vehicle," John informed him.

Migs nodded.

Garrison hesitated. His colleague wasn't his usual sarcastic self and somehow that made the situation worse. "We'll call you when we find out anything."

Again, he nodded.

"Hope your gram is fine."

"Thanks."

When the Suburban rolled away, Migs stared at the emergency room doors, watching them slide open and slide close. A few hours replaced a beautiful memory with one filled with horror. He swallowed hard and forced his feet to move. One step in front of the other.

This feeling of helplessness was not him. Ariana wouldn't want him to mope while his family needed him. And why the hell was he thinking as if she was already dead?

Self-loathing pumped blood into his veins and quickened his strides. He entered the emergency waiting room and was immediately greeted by the sight of his family sprawled on chairs and couches.

Most of them rose when he entered the area, but the expressions on their faces were lead in his gut.

His mother didn't rise with the others to greet him. Instead, she looked away, but not before he witnessed the anguish on her face. His sisters' expressions were sad, and none of them could meet his eyes either. Though they wouldn't look at him, Migs felt their collective condemnation.

It was Pops and Tessa who stopped him from advancing further.

Fear made his stomach clench as the possibilities messed with his mind. "Is abuelita okay?" The EMTs said she was fine, but head injuries could be treacherous, especially given his grandmother's age.

"She's fine. They're doing an MRI," Drew said, quickly grabbing his arm and leading him back to the exit. "Listen. I don't think you should be here."

"Pops? What the fuck?" His eyes cut to Tessa.

"Ariana?" she asked, her voice quavering.

Words lodged in his throat. All he could do was shake his head, but his inability to speak partly stemmed from his growing anger that everyone was blaming his wife again. He cleared his throat. "Thanks, sis." His voice started rising with each word. "At least someone in my fucking family is concerned that my wife is missing!" He spat the last word in controlled fury.

"You have some nerve showing up here," a steely voice said beside them.

Joaquín.

It was his cousin like he'd never seen him before. Fury evident in every line of his face, which had shown nothing but stoicism for as long as Migs had known him.

"Choose your words carefully, cuz," he warned. One word against Ariana and Joaquín would be checking himself into this hospital.

"I don't need to choose words. Pictures explain everything."

Joaquín whipped out his phone and shoved it under his nose.

Blood drained from Miguel's face and, having been riled up right before this second, he learned the true meaning of having the rug pulled out from under him. "Where did you get this?"

His cousin barked a bitter laugh. "Does it even matter, Miguel?" Joaquín jutted out his chin, his eyes doing nothing to hide his disgust. "Why don't you explain why there's a picture of you and *mi Papá* on the day he died, huh?"

His cousin poked at his chest and all Migs could do was take a step back.

"He was wearing that shirt when he was killed. Why the fuck were you there?"

How the tables had turned. At that moment, it was Migs who couldn't meet anyone's eyes, not even Mamá's when she gave her full attention to their confrontation.

Another poke on his chest.

Another step back.

"Look at me, Miguel!" Joaquín growled, snapping his gaze back to his cousin's accusing stare. "But more is the question …" his cousin broke off, mouth pressing into a thin line, face turning red as tears brimmed his eyes. "Where …" he cut off again with a ragged breath and the effort to push the words out.

Tears stung his own eyes and Miguel's voice cracked. "Joaquín—"

"Where were you when they pumped him full of bullets?!" he roared.

Migs saw the fist coming but refused to dodge, welcoming the pain that cracked on his jaw, and felt not only the physical power behind the punch, but the rage behind it. A shoulder into his gut sent them crashing into the floor. Screaming and mayhem ensued.

Joaquín punched him again and again, but Migs didn't fight him back. He deserved this.

Hospital security and Cesar pulled his cousin away, still sputtering and cursing at Miguel and wanting to have a go at him again.

Migs picked himself up from the floor and didn't fight it when Tessa and his father led him out of the emergency room.

He sniffed and touched his nose, his hand coming away with blood. Somehow his sister magically produced a towel and dabbed at it.

"Smells like baby powder," Migs said.

"Shut up, you idiot," Tessa said. "Cesar told me who you worked for."

He gave her a look.

Tessa shrugged. "He can't hide anything from me."

"Why am I not surprised?"

"We're worried about Ariana," Drew said.

"Are you? Really?"

"Don't be sarcastic," Tessa scolded. "And the only reason I'm not punching you is because I know you're trying to keep it together."

"Don't be all understanding and shit," Migs hissed. "I fucked this up. I thought I gave Ariana protection, but I ended up offering her up on a silver platter."

"See, I don't get it. She left with Hector," Pops said then paused. "Where the hell is Hector?"

"I didn't see him …" At his expression, her sister broke off. "No!" She shook her head, her hand flying to her chest. "Is he feeling guilty because it was his men who built the structure that fell on abuelita?"

Migs couldn't answer her, but it was a good thing his phone buzzed, just as he saw the Suburban pull up beside the emergency room. The windows rolled down, revealing Bristow.

"I gotta go."

Pops grabbed his arm. "Go where?"

He leveled his father with a determined stare. "Get my wife back."

"I DON'T CARE what you do. Get me a damned plane," Migs growled. He was on the phone with Garrison. The spook and Levi were on their way to Los Angeles to gather resources.

"I can't just pull one outta my ass," Garrison said dryly. "I requisitioned one, but it might take a couple of days."

"My wife doesn't have a couple of days."

John fell to silence where Migs could almost hear him thinking. Finally, the other man said, "You'll have to help Nadia narrow down possible landing sites."

His fingers tightened on the phone. "I'll get you a damned location, you get me that plane ASAP. I don't care if you have to make a deal with the devil."

"Roger that," Garrison muttered and ended the call.

He and Bristow arrived at a house near the San Ysidro crossing and pulled into its garage. Migs noticed there was no other vehicle except a motorcycle he recognized as his. He realized he hadn't thought of his Harley in all that time he'd been with Ariana. He wasn't into the biker life, but knew enough to use it as a cover, and he loved the freedom of the road. An urge to ride it now hit him hard. The need to clear his thoughts and find perspective in the swirling storm raging inside him.

Bristow slammed out of the vehicle and rounded it to where Migs was inspecting his former ride. He'd left it in his garage in Los Angeles.

"John broke into my house?" Why wasn't he surprised.

"He thought you would miss it, so he brought it over."

He turned to the ex-SEAL. "You and I know John isn't the sentimental type. He's hoping I go undercover again in a motorcycle gang, get into Mexico." He shook his head. "That cover is blown. Benito knows about my role in shutting down the Carillos four years ago."

"Shit."

"Yeah. And no way am I leaving Ariana again." But she left him ... No, she was taken. "Any news on Hector?"

They entered the house. It had no clutter and the bare minimum of furniture. He imagined the bedrooms were the same, just enough to use for a transient stop.

"BOLO is out on him as a person of interest in the bombing at the country club," Bristow said, slinging his backpack on the table and extracting his laptop.

"He wouldn't go back to Vegas," Migs said. "Think he hightailed it to Mexico?"

"Possible," Bristow said. "But given his connections, he could be anywhere, in any vehicle, which is why Garrison wants us to concentrate on Carillo's strongholds in Tamaulipas." He fired up his computer. "Nadia gathered intel from combined DEA and CIA databases. She needs your help finding a lab."

"A lab?" Migs brows furrowed. "That's Nadia's assessment? Carillo has taken Ariana to a lab?"

"There's recent chatter on the dark web that a cartel has a virus and is putting out feelers in the arms dealing circuit," Bristow said, instead of confirming. "We're not talking about small time dealers. We're talking Russian and North Korean. The meet is not happening in the US, it's happening south of the border."

Bristow turned the screen to him, showing him a map of southeast Mexico, with red markers. "Garrison didn't say much. After we dropped you off, he got a call and instead of heading here, he had us drop him at a private hangar at San Diego airport. You want to find Ariana? We need to figure out what Benito has, what he wants with her. Oh, by the way, it's our belief it was Benito who tipped off the DEA."

"I thought we'd already established that," Migs frowned.

"Not tonight. The raid on your avocado warehouse, the one where you and your brother-in-law got arrested."

"But why would he sacrifice three million dollars in cocaine?"

"Once it reached your warehouse, it was Hector's problem."

Fuck. Pieces of the puzzle were falling into place. Hector had more than just a small gambling problem. "My cousin was using our trucks to move coke into LA and Vegas?"

"It's millions of dollars in business, but you probably already know of your cousin's other vices."

Gambling, expensive cars, high society parties. Migs shook his head. Joaquín was innocent in this after all. "That means Benito has someone working inside their Michoacán plantation."

"Sure looks that way," the ginger-haired operator replied, then nodded to the screen.

They went to work, pouring over satellite images of the area, planning a recon route of possible locations.

"Does John have informants on the ground?" Migs asked. "These satellite images tell us nothing. It's better to have local assets get close and inform on activities. That's a sure way to tell if people are coming or going."

"He does." Bristow enlarged the area of Tampico. "How about here?"

"This was shut down a long time ago." It was the location of the compound where the cartel kept the young girls they kidnapped and held special auctions to the sick fucks who bought them. Another location came to mind. "They had a backup compound in Venustiano Carranza."

"That sounds familiar." The other man cross-referenced a separate file. "Yes, there's increased activity. Satellite images are showing trucks heading into the area."

"I have contacts there," Migs said.

Before Bristow could reply, Migs' phone pinged with a message. It was from Tessa. He rose from the seat.

"Where are you going?"

"Got something I need to do. Give Nadia this info." He scrolled through his contacts. "He's my asset closest to Venustiano. Money is not a problem. Tell Nadia I'm willing to pay them anything they want. Got me?"

Bristow eyed him solemnly. "Roger that."

MIGS TOOK the Harley to see Abbi Mena. The text he got from Tessa said most of their relatives had left, and the hospital was keeping their grandmother overnight. Lettie and Delia were staying in the suite. There was a San Diego PD officer posted outside the door, and Migs recognized some of Pop's and Joaquín's men loitering in the hallway. His family wasn't taking any chances. He could explain that the threat was over, that all Carillo wanted was Ariana, but he was having trouble trusting his judgment these days.

The men merely nodded when they saw him. No one was keeping him from his grandmother anyway. He probably shouldn't have left earlier, but he didn't want to waste time in the waiting room while he was able to do something productive to find the people responsible for this clusterfuck.

He opened the door and was surprised to see Abbi Mena sitting up, taking a sip of water, with Lettie beside her.

"My prodigal grandson shows up."

Lettie leaned in and kissed their grandmother's forehead. "I'll leave you two alone." She looked at Migs. "Mamá went to get coffee." His sister walked into him and gave him a tight hug, whispering in his ear. "She doesn't know Ari is missing." Lettie gave his arm a squeeze, letting him know that she cared. Then stepping back, she said loudly. "Don't leave until Mamá comes back. She wants to talk to you."

"Miguelito, where is your wife?" Abbi Mena asked.

Scrambling for something to say, he said, "She wasn't sure she should come here."

A resigned look crossed her face. "I am sad she feels that way. If anyone in our family blames her, send them to me."

Migs had to smile at this. "Oh, and what would you say?"

"I'd threaten to disinherit them." She said, her eyes drooping.

"You need your rest, abuelita." Migs bent over to kiss her temple.

"*Mijo.*" Her eyes widened a fraction. "Let go of your guilt."

Startled, he didn't know what to say.

"I know everyone is expecting you to take charge of the hacienda, but Joaquín is happy doing it. Don't stay away again. Okay …?" Her eyes fluttered closed again.

He let out a sigh of relief because he'd kill his cousin if he burdened their grandmother with the pictures on his phone.

"Bring Ariana next time," she mumbled. "And look for Hector …"

He backed away slowly, glad he was able to talk to his grandmother before he embarked on the most important mission of his life. The next time he saw abuelita, Ariana would definitely be right beside him. He just wasn't sure what mental or physical state she would be in. Migs viciously squashed those despairing thoughts. That was not what he needed right now. That poison of negativity.

The door opened and he turned. It was Mamá.

She motioned for him to come out and Lettie went in to stay with their grandmother.

They walked the hallway in awkward silence. Migs didn't know what to say, and it appeared his mother was at a loss for words for how to start too.

When they reached a window at the end of the hallway, Delia sat at the bench below it and motioned for him to sit beside her.

"I don't know how to start this conversation, Miguel," she said softly, canting her head to look at him. Her eyes were rife with sorrow and he was angry at himself for causing it. "Drew and I had a fight. He said you had to do what you had to do."

"I'm sorry."

Her eyes filled with tears. "I just want to know why my brother was killed. And how my son could keep the truth from me for four years. You were there when Pepito died. That's why you avoided the family. Drew assured me you weren't cartel, but that would mean ... were you with the government?"

"How much are you ready to hear?"

Garrison had told him what he could say to his family when he was ready to unburden his role in his uncle's death.

"Everything."

"I can't tell you everything and the reason I didn't want to tell you any is ... I didn't want to taint your memory of Tio Pepito."

"He was killed in Tamaulipas during the time the Carillo cartel fell. That's all I know. He was there for a town fiesta."

"Tell me, Mamá, why would Tio Pepito go to a fiesta in a place that's a stronghold of a cartel not friendly to the Alcantaras?"

"That's what the family never understood!"

Migs exhaled in frustration. "Because he was doing business with Carillo. At that time, they were dealing heroin and not cocaine."

"But why? The farms were doing so well."

"Gambling debts. And he found it was easy to launder money for the Carillos in addition to offering routes a few times a year."

"I still don't understand ..."

He put a hand on her shoulder. "Mamá, I'll explain more, okay? Just know in the end, Tio Pepito did the right thing, but it cost him his life." The words backed up in his throat, but he pushed them through. "He gave us information that took down the Carillo cartel."

"Us? So, you are federal? DEA?"

He kissed the top of his mother's head. "I am anyone who would want to keep the Alcantaras safe."

Migs stood and left his mother to mull over his words and hopefully accept that he did what was best for the family.

AFTER LEAVING the hospital Migs went straight home to gather his things. Thankfully no one was there. His footfalls were like lead on the wooden floors, echoing in the empty house. He thought of Leon, how he was a casualty in all this. There would be a time to mourn his friend, and he still couldn't wrap his mind around how Hector got involved in this.

Did Hector know that Migs caused his father's death?

An eye for an eye.

He kept his eyes averted from the bed he'd shared with Ariana. Finally getting a grip on his emotions, any reminder of the happiness of the past few weeks would send him spiraling into a useless mess again. So he called upon his training as a CIA operative because the person who would save his wife was the soldier, not the husband. It was the killer, not the man who'd fallen in love with her.

Emotions had no place in dealing with men like Benito Carillo.

Migs changed into jeans, a black tee, and biker boots. He slipped the ring out from the suit jacket pocket and carefully hid it in a compartment in his duffle. The second he got Ariana back, that ring was going on her finger.

Ariana was his and he was getting her back.

And with renewed determination, he left the Alcantara-Walker ranch.

23

HER BODY WAS PARALYZED, her mind numb. Bright light in a haze of orange flickered behind her eyelids, but they were stuck together, refusing to open. Ariana floated in and out of consciousness. Every time she thought she could drag herself out of the quicksand of her darkest dreams, she'd get sucked in again.

She would always hear music, whistling, and it would be followed by a prick on her neck.

And she was helpless to stop it.

She didn't know how long she'd been under, but the voices talking around her were no longer muffled.

"We should wake her up," a female voice said.

"When are you going to give it to her?" said a voice that she knew belonged to Benito.

"I'm still establishing a baseline."

The malicious laugh curled her gut. "Oh, come now, doctor, my men are looking to have fun with this one."

"Rein in your men. No one is touching her."

Silence, and then there was a scuffle, metal things clattering to the floor. What followed was a woman's strangled cry.

"*Perra.* You don't give me any orders!"

"Let me go!" the woman choked.

There was a shuffling of footsteps, a straightening of furniture.

"Your buyers would want to have data. What if you're wrong and she doesn't have the antibodies?" The woman wheezed. "The virus will kill her."

"You think I care?" There was a grunt of displeasure. "You have three days. My buyers are impatient."

Footfalls faded and Ariana breathed a sigh of relief.

"I know you're awake," the woman said.

Ariana opened her eyes, astonished to see a female in full medical protection gear including a face-shield. The walls looked strange, uneven.

"Where am I?"

"In the lion's den," the woman said. "In Venustiano."

"I'm … I'm in Mexico?"

"I'm Charly. Or you can call me Doc."

"You work for Benito?"

"*Work for* is a stretch. You can say I'm here under duress."

"Wait. Are you the virologist who escaped with my brother?" Ariana struggled to get the words out clearly, her tongue felt alien in her mouth.

Charly's mouth tightened.

Her mind was hazy, but all she could remember was this person also created another version of the virus. "How could you?"

The virologist turned away. "How could I what? Study the virus? I'm a scientist."

"Science shouldn't mess with nature."

Charly scoffed. "And you mess with the natural selection when you infuse your clients with much needed nutrients that their bodies couldn't digest. So, how are we different?"

Ariana's head was throbbing. She was at a disadvantage in

this argument. "I don't weaponize viruses that could kill people … sell it to the highest bidder."

"I'm not the one selling anything. And you're jumping to conclusions that I created this virus, but you can be sure I'm finding a cure. Which is exactly what I'm doing now." She held up a syringe.

Ariana tried to move, but realized she was secured to the bedrail of a hospital bed. "Let me go. Don't do this."

The other woman lowered her head by Ariana's ear. "You have to play along. I'm injecting you with a placebo." She paused. "Not the real virus."

"Why does Benito think I have the antibodies in the first place?"

Charly straightened and spoke in a normal voice. "Because when your brother escaped the CDC, he stole my work, and gave it to your nurse."

"Connie?"

"Yes."

"So how can I have the antibodies?"

Charly exhaled an irritated breath. "I checked and you do have the antibodies. You're full of them. Connie must have given them to you with a shot of your vitamin infusion."

Ariana thought back to the last time she'd had the infusions. She'd had them twice since Raul's death. Twice administered by Connie.

"Well, then Connie must have taken them for herself."

"She didn't."

"How can you be sure?"

"Because I've tested her blood. She's negative for antibodies. She said she wanted to be sure it worked on you and carried no side effects, before injecting herself with a drug that had no trials." Charly's mouth twisted. "Except when they threatened her daughter to get to you, she knew she picked the wrong side."

Ariana eyed the needle in Charly's hand. It was a very large needle.

The virologist's gaze slid to her briefly. "The sooner you cooperate, the sooner Benito will let you go."

Even though she knew the virologist said it for the surveillance camera's benefit, Ariana laughed sarcastically. "You believe that? And I heard my brother suffered badly."

"Then better hope the antibodies work."

"DIDN'T John say he was coming in this morning?" Migs asked. "We've wasted an entire day waiting for him."

"He's left LA. Flying in. Should be here any minute." Bristow was cleaning his weapons. Migs probably should be doing the same.

Ariana had been gone for forty-eight hours and it felt like a lifetime. Nadia had been keeping them busy with data from NSA's satellite feed in addition to intel from the ground. The compound in Venustiano Carranza was fully functional. His asset fed them enough recon details to decide infiltration and exit points. Nadia also sent them a brief dossier on Benito's trusted men—his *sicarios*. At the top of the list of hitmen was The Whistler. Not much was known about him except for several grainy photographs and that Benito called him "Silba."

They were landing in an area controlled by the Ponce-Neto Organization, next to Tampico. It made his stomach turn having to negotiate with the narcos, but the agency had historically been known to do this in the name of the greater good. A sneer wanted to form at the corners of his mouth. Sometimes 'the greater good' was in the interest of the lobbyists in Washington. But John was one of the good guys, he didn't give a shit about who was pulling the strings in DC. He was concerned for the greater good of the country and not the benefit of the few. Which was probably why his handler was frequently demoted and reinstated because although he excelled at his job, John didn't care who he pissed off.

Migs hadn't heard much about what the Carillo cartel was after, but it wasn't hard to deduce that the weaponized Ebola virus had reared its ugly head. The original Z-91 had been manufactured unknowingly in one of Antonio Andrade's labs and had been self-injected by Raul in a whole elaborate scheme to create a deadlier strain. This was completed inside the CDC when a rogue virologist used the mutated virus in Raul's system to sequence its DNA and the Z-92 was born.

But why Ariana? He thought about the vials and the buccal swabs in the house in the Valley where she went in exchange for Connie's daughter. Did they need a close DNA match to duplicate the success of the strain that was in Raul? Carillo went to a lot of trouble to get to her.

He'd been itching to ride his motorcycle again to burn off the agitation of waiting when he heard a vehicle pull up the driveway. He stalked to the window and took a peek.

A Jeep Gladiator was idling before it shut off and Levi got out from the driver's seat. Garrison slammed out from the passenger side. Migs frowned when the door behind the driver opened. More reinforcements? They could use more men.

What he wasn't prepared for—or rather who—was Antonio Andrade.

What the fuck?

It was a miracle Migs didn't rip the hinges from the door when he stormed out to meet the newcomers.

He glared at Andrade. "What the fuck is he doing here?"

"Worried I might steal Ariana?" Andrade raised a brow. "You married her to protect her. How's that working for you?"

Migs barely heard the shouting when, with a roar, he tackled the other man to the ground. He hammered him left and then right, but the Brazilian got one hard hit in. It felt like a wallop from a bat. Migs, being fueled with rage, didn't care.

They rolled on the ground until several arms restrained him, and he struggled to break free. The behemoth that was Levi finally managed an armlock around Migs, and with palms pressed against the back of his neck, immobilized him.

John got in his face. "Get a grip, Walker, or we're leaving you behind."

"The fuck you are! Just try, just fucking try."

Bristow gave Andrade a hand up. The Brazilian dusted off his stupid suit, got a handkerchief from the breast pocket and patted the blood from his nose, his cut lip. "I believe you have to direct that challenge to me."

John spun on Andrade and stabbed a finger in his direction. "Shut up."

Andrade raised a brow. "It's my plane."

"And we can get another," Garrison pointed out.

"Are you sure? The reason you came to me was because I can make it happen quickly. You're lucky I was still in LA."

"What the fuck, John?" Migs growled.

The spook gave him a look. "You said I could make a deal with the devil."

"That's not very flattering," Andrade deadpanned.

"Why are you helping?" Migs snarled, fighting to get out of the armlock. Finally, Levi let him go. Migs shook off his frustration before he launched himself at Andrade again. "You think you can get Ariana back for yourself?"

"I may be many things, but I do respect the sanctity of marriage." Antonio's blue eyes gleamed. "Even though Ariana was supposed to be my bride and you gave her a quickie Vegas wedding." He flicked an imaginary lint off his suit. "I would have given her a wedding fit for a queen.

"Stop goading him," John censured. "Can we take this inside?"

"CONNIE DID WHAT?" Migs said incredulously.

"We have Andrade to thank for this lead and we finally got Connie to confess," John said. "He was able to track down one of Benito's associates who was a member of Águila."

"Ariana was given a test vaccine for Z-92? Why did Raul give her this?" He paused. "Was he planning on releasing the virus in LA?"

"Probably," Andrade said. "He still had his delusions about terrorizing the city to show his superiority. But in the end, he still cared for his sister."

Despite Ariana's estrangement from Raul over the years, Migs knew she loved her brother, and apparently, Raul loved her too in his own twisted way. He did everything to draw his sister back into his orbit, even fake a cancer diagnosis.

"So what does Carillo want with Ariana?" Migs asked.

"Give her the virus," Garrison said. "Test the efficacy."

"But why Ariana? Benito doesn't have any other test samples of this vaccine?"

"There were two missing vials from what were retrieved from Raul's property. Connie said she'd dosed Ariana with one. She was keeping the other one for her daughter, but Carillo took it from her."

So Carillo was hanging on to that one vaccine, probably didn't have the facility to produce it and would need a partner, but to do that he had to prove its efficacy. Migs surged to his feet and began to pace. "This is fucked up." Then he glared at Andrade. "When did you suspect she'd been inoculated?"

Andrade's own eyes gleamed dangerously. "I hope you're not suggesting that I wanted Ariana because of what her blood could offer."

Migs glanced at Garrison and noticed that John was staring at the billionaire thoughtfully and knew it wasn't his own jealousy that had arrived at the same conclusion.

"What then?" John asked quietly.

"My interest is what has become of the virologist,"

Andrade said. "He is the link to the traitor in our organization."

"Charles Bennett," Migs said and noticed John give a start, but settled down and compressed his mouth in a thin line. "Right?"

"Yes," John clipped.

"You're not thinking of handing him over, are you?" Bristow asked their handler.

He seemed to consider his answer carefully. "Mr. Andrade is fully cooperating with the CIA and we agreed it will be done under the agency's supervision."

"On U.S. soil?" Bristow pressed.

"Yes."

"Because we can't let someone as dangerous as Charles Bennett fall into the hands of a megalomaniac arms dealer." Migs was looking at Andrade.

"I might cop to being a megalomaniac but I take issue with being labeled an arms dealer," Andrade said mildly.

Migs sighed. "I wasn't referring to you. But we know South America is a hotbed for arms dealers right now given the situation in Venezuela. All I'm saying is you have an interest in seeing stability in the region. I'll admit it's even altruistic. So we call a truce and let's roll."

Silence.

He was the soldier, not the husband. He could overlook his competition with Andrade with regards to Ariana for the greater good.

Even John was surprised given his brows had shot to his hairline, his jaw slackening.

Andrade regarded him with disbelief as well, but he extended his arm. "Truce."

Their handshake was firm.

No ego.

No jealousy.

As for Migs, hope in getting Ariana back was kindled.

24

"JUST ONE MORE."

Ariana watched the top of Charly's head as the doctor drew blood from her veins, hopefully for the last time. Then her gaze lifted to a mystery man standing in the shadows against a sheeting of plastic. He had on protective gear, so his features were not distinct. She'd finally figured out her surroundings this morning. She was in a makeshift structure made of several layers of plastic. Operating theater-like lights hung from above her. She certainly hoped they wouldn't cut her open and do an autopsy on her body if she died.

"What day is it?" she asked Charly when the virologist turned away to make notations in a chart.

"You asked me that this morning."

"I feel like I've been here for days."

"Three."

The man against the wall moved forward, but Charly stopped him. "Enough with that. It's interfering with my tests."

"You're the one who kept dosing me," Ariana accused the stranger. Her stomach lurched. "I feel nauseated."

"It's the sedative." Charly turned to Mystery Man again.

He retreated several steps and took position against the opaque wall.

"I don't need you here, Silba. Can you leave us alone?"

"Benito wants me to make sure that you are working 'round the clock on this."

"I've hardly slept in the past twenty-four hours," Charly retorted. "He shouldn't have made promises to his buyers. I get nervous when you watch me and it's delaying my work."

Silba crossed his arms and squared his stance.

"I'm serious," Charly snapped. "I'll stop working and you can dose me with Etorphine. Then we'll see how pleased your boss will be."

Ariana wanted to clap, but her hands were still cuffed to the hospital bed, but she held her breath as a wave of violence poured from the man.

He turned around and ducked between the sheets. Then Ariana thought she heard whistling before something sounding like rain on sheets drowned out the melody.

"Was he whistling the whole time I was unconscious?"

Charly grinned. "Yes. Why? Did you like it?"

"No, it's like an annoying tune in your head that you can't get rid of."

Ariana didn't know why she shared a laugh with Charly. It was hard not to like her. She appeared to hate Benito and Silba, but maybe this was a ploy to win her cooperation, to get Ariana relaxed and trusting before she stabbed her in the neck and cut her open in the name of science.

Ugh, her thoughts had turned morbid.

It was this place. It reeked of the dead.

"What will they do to me when you're done?" she asked. Or pretend to be done. Charly whispered to her that she'd been using her blood to run through a virus simulator to fib the results. But the virologist could only delay for so long before Benito would have both their heads.

Charly looked at the vials in front of her and shook her head. "I don't know."

"I see."

"You're very calm about this." The virologist looked at her.

"I always wondered if I deserved to be happy," Ariana whispered.

"What? What are you talking about?"

"Raul destroyed so many lives and he didn't get a chance to atone for them."

Understanding dawned in the other woman's eyes and they hardened in rebuke. "You're not blaming yourself for what your brother did, right?"

"No, not anymore. I think I've paid more than enough," she replied. Her feelings about Raul were at peace. Because of her brother she'd been shunned, kidnapped, poked, and prodded. She'd more than atoned for her brother's sins. But the missing piece was wondering whether her brother loved her at all, and now she knew. In his own twisted way, he'd been protecting her in the end. Ariana would take that as a sign of love. Her heart was free to trust the emotion again. "I may still have a chance at happiness. I found people who are willing to accept me even being the sister of the most notorious crime lord who ever lived." Her thoughts strayed to Migs and Abbi Mena. "But I need you to help me. Give me this chance."

"I'm not sure what you mean?"

A vehicle screeched in the distance.

Then the ground shook as a thunderous boom sounded like a train smashed into a wall.

Faint pops of rifles followed, growing louder and louder until a full-blown firefight erupted in the background.

Ariana smiled. "You asked me why I was calm about this? Because I knew my husband would come for me."

"EAST WALL," Nadia said over comms.

"I'm over the fucking east wall," Migs growled. "There's no fucking window." His eyes scanned the walls of the Carillo mansion. It was built in the golden age of the roaring twenties but had obviously fallen behind in its upkeep. The grass was tall and jungle-like vines hung from the trees.

"The blueprint says you should be staring at a wall with a window."

"There's no window, Powell." Bristow replied more calmly than Miguel. Their team deplaned in Poza Rica, thirty miles from their target in Venustiano Carranza. They were met by a team of Special Activities Division forces operating in the area against the cartels. Ponce-Neto had provided some intel on the ground, but it was the first time anyone had infiltrated the mansion.

Satellite images couldn't see past the thick growth of trees.

But as Migs studied the length of the wall, he saw exactly what had happened. "They filled the windows with cinder blocks so no one could see in. In its place, there's an exhaust fan."

"Does it look recent?"

"No, they restored it pretty good. Couldn't tell." Narcos were experts at concealment. "How many guards are circulating in this section?"

"You've got two outside that wall."

"And you're certain Ariana is in this wing?"

"I'm showing constant heat signatures in the middle of a big room, could have been the drawing room. There's some movement, maybe three to four people at a time, but there is always one."

Nadia had already told Migs it looked like she was elevated on a bed. As much as he wanted to rush in and grab his wife, going all Rambo wasn't going to work. They needed a coordinated attack so no one could get to her before they grabbed her.

Migs and Bristow dropped to the ground and lowered their night vision goggles. He immediately saw the two guards Nadia pointed out. They crouch-walked through the shrubs and lush trees, careful to step lightly and not snap dried branches.

"Don't act yet," John warned through comms. He was leading a team of special ops on the other side of the mansion to retrieve the virus samples that—according to their intel— were stored in the basement. In what form, no one knew.

Levi and another team were providing the distraction.

"Wasn't going to."

"Just reminding you about the last time."

Migs grunted. It wasn't anyone's fault, really, but now they were aware that the criminal underbelly was using high technology as well. The last time Migs slit the throat of a hostile, that person was hooked up to biometric sensors that alerted of death. So now, any approach needed to be coordinated, the assault simultaneous.

"I'm in position," Levi said. "You guys ready?"

The teams checked in, and all were set to go.

A screaming of tires pierced the darkness. The guards in front of them started running toward the gate until a military personnel carrier smashed through the barrier and judging from the inhuman screams, it took down some cartel thugs too.

Migs and Bristow sprung out of their concealment and sprinted toward the mansion. Bristow unloaded a personal battering ram and did quick work of splintering the door. He gave it a kick until it crashed open.

"Two tangoes coming at you, East team," Nadia called them by their mission call signs. Migs was East One, Bristow was East Two. "West One," she addressed Garrison. "Six coming your way."

If indeed Nadia's assumptions were correct, most of the hostiles were congregated in an area on the opposite side of where Ariana was being kept. Because of the packed heat signatures, it was difficult to tell how many men Carillo had on premises.

Migs quickly fired off a shot. Bristow took down another.

"Watch out!" Nadia said.

Miguel managed to duck, and went under the hostile, getting in behind the man and breaking his neck.

"Damn, where did that guy come from?" Nadia muttered. "They're swarming back into the house," she said urgently. Static noises filled the airwaves and when her voice came on, she said, "They know you're after Ariana."

"Shit."

Migs and Bristow ran in the direction of the drawing room and stopped at the sight of sheets of plastic hanging from the ceiling forming a containment in the middle of the room. There was a tube leading into the room with pipes overhead. A decontamination chamber, if he were to guess.

He looked at Bristow, who nodded, and they pulled up their respirator masks. Migs led with the barrel of his rifle, finding and splitting the slit where the plastic sheets met. A spray activated and rained down on them. It smelled of bleach and antiseptic.

When they made it through, a woman in PPE already had her arms up, but it was the sight of Ariana, sitting up and thrilled to see him that captivated his attention. It was a split second before fury took over and he saw her wrist cuffed to the bed rails.

He stalked into the room, keeping his weapon trained on the lab woman. "Name."

"Charly Bennett."

"Charles Bennett?" Migs did a double take.

"I guess."

"What do you mean you guess?" Bristow barked and gestured to Migs that he had the other woman. He rushed to

Ariana's side and knocked off the cuff with the butt of his rifle. "Are you okay?"

Her lips tipped up. "I am now."

He bent over to lift but she twisted away. "Don't!"

"What the fuck," he growled.

Ariana's eyes frantically sought the other woman's. "You're certain I'm not contagious?"

"Yes," Doctor Bennett said as Bristow patted her down. "I didn't lie when I said I was giving you a placebo."

Migs didn't wait for another second and yanked his respirator down and gave his wife a brief, but fierce kiss. He helped her down, noting she was wearing scrubs and there were slippers at the bottom of the bed.

"We're in the basement!" Garrison barked through their comm channel. "The virus containment chamber has a code."

"What's the code?" Migs snapped at the virologist.

The doctor hesitated.

"Now!" he pressed.

The doctor rattled off an alpha-numeric code. Migs repeated it to Garrison.

"Got it. We're in," John said.

Turning to Ariana, he said. "Can you walk?"

"Yes."

Hitching his rifle over his right shoulder, he took her hand.

"Hostiles are almost on you! Find cover!" Nadia said.

He split the plastic sheets with his rifle and looked back at Bristow, patiently waiting for the doctor to pack up shit in a pelican case.

"Sure that's safe?" Migs called to Doctor Bennett.

"I'm not an idiot," she snapped.

Bristow shot him a long-suffering look. "Garrison ordered we pack everything possible."

Of course he did. Andrade would probably be ecstatic, too.

He pulled Ariana forward and hesitated before the sterilization tube.

"She doesn't need it and you can cover her," Charly said. "But if it would make everyone feel better"—she nodded to a stack of towels—"just dry her afterward."

"Just get me out of here," Ariana said.

He lifted Ariana and ran quickly through the tube, rushing with her behind the nearest wall and quickly toweled her dry. Then he leaned forward to take a peek around the wall, and quickly retracted when a bullet splintered its wooden frame.

Benito Carillo.

His cowboy hat was a dead giveaway.

He and a group of men were barricaded behind a sweeping staircase and the massive pedestal table at the center of the foyer. Cartel bosses were usually in the thick of the fight with their men which explained the loyalties they had for their leader. Benito obviously was no different.

And they were standing between Migs and his group and freedom.

"Where the hell is Garrison?"

"Three minutes," the spook muttered. "Taking heavy fire."

"What's the matter?" Benito screamed. "Scared to come out? Come on, *puta*. Let's see what you're made of."

Migs looked at Bristow. Did they have three minutes?

"Come on, you cowards." A barrage of automatic fire sprayed the wall they were hiding behind. Ariana cowered against Migs. What protected them was the lower portion of the structure that was made of concrete or marble, but the wood paneling above them was disintegrating with the gunfire.

"Where the fuck are you, John?"

"Pinned down." Was the response.

"Walker," Bristow nodded to the chandelier above the

heavy foyer table that was the lone source of light for Benito and his men. Migs nodded.

His partner aimed and shot at the fixture, instantly plunging the room in darkness followed in a split second by the shattering of glass. Migs lowered his NVGs and swept into the room, a burn ripped through his side, but he capped two hostiles in the head. Others fell from Bristow's shots. Head on a swivel, he swung his scope right and left and picked off another man behind the stairwell. That man screamed and fired blindly. A force slammed into Mig's chest, knocking him on his back, but adrenaline fueled his muscles and he managed to lever up on his side, and, balancing on an elbow, pumped two successive rounds into the hostile's body.

The almighty searing in his chest finally stole his strength and he found himself staring at the ceiling.

Silence.

"Migs!" Ariana screamed.

"I'm okay," he forced out. "Stand back."

Bristow rushed to his side. "You okay, man?"

Migs, unable to speak another word, waved him forward to check the last man he shot.

"None of these are Benito."

What?

Migs needed to see it for himself. Taking superhuman effort to rise to his feet, he staggered over, every pull from his lungs an effort as a bullet most likely bruised his ribs. He just prayed none of them were broken. Thank God for the SAPI plates.

A cowboy hat sat a few feet away, but the body beside it wasn't the cartel boss.

A pained cry had him swinging around and he saw Ariana frozen near the table. Migs cursed as he stalked back to her, ignoring the protest in his ribs. "There's broken glass!" he growled as he sank to his knees and inspected her foot. Big shards of glass had pierced through her thin slipper.

"I wasn't thinking, and I couldn't see," Ariana whispered. "I was worried."

"I have first aid in my case," Doctor Bennett said.

"We're good," Bristow countered. "I have one in mine too."

With two medical personnel on their team, he felt better. It was just a cut, but Migs was more concerned with what was done to Ariana in that makeshift lab.

Movement at the door had them tensing and raising their weapons.

"Looks like we're late to the party," Garrison announced, but his eyes were on Doctor Bennett. Before he could say anything, a blast rocked the courtyard.

"What the ... ?" Migs sprung to his feet and instinctively tucked Ariana closer to him.

"It came from the hillside," Nadia said. "Hit our vehicle. Levi, are you okay?"

No answer.

"James, do you copy?" Garrison yelled, hurrying back outside with a few of the special ops team.

"Guys, we've got another problem," their analyst announced. "Jeeps are rolling in. Looks like Mexican Army."

"Goddammit," Migs growled. "This just keeps getting better." He was about to lift Ariana when she resisted. "I'm okay."

"Your foot is bleeding."

"I can hop," she insisted. "If I slow you down, then you can carry me."

"Wait for my signal to come out," he ordered.

Just as he and Bristow cleared the door, renewed heavy arms fire erupted in the courtyard. The truck that Levi used to plow the gates was in front of them. Migs gestured for the women to come out. Ariana and the doctor darted past the team to hunker down behind the truck's engine block and giant tire. Garrison rounded the front of the vehicle, dragging an unconscious Levi with him.

"Mexican Army," Garrison informed them through the din of artillery blasts.

"Think you could bargain with them?" Migs shouted back.

John shook his head. "Carillo has them on payroll. At least in this part of town."

"The entrance is blocked." Nadia said.

"Roger that," Garrison gritted. "How about from where Migs and Bristow came in?"

"It's clear."

John grabbed his arm. "Take the women and get back to base."

Migs eyes narrowed. "What about you guys?"

"We'll hold them off. It's imperative the women and this get out of here." John handed him a backpack, which contained the virus.

At Migs' hesitation, the spook added, "This will all be for nothing if we get caught. I can get the men out of this if we're captured. Trust me."

John was right. The mission couldn't fail, and he couldn't concentrate with Ariana in mortal danger.

He gave a brief nod

"I can carry you," Migs told Ariana.

She shook her head. "I can run. The bleeding has stopped."

Migs knew she was lying, but there was not a second to waste. With his NVG shield down, he checked to see if there were hostiles lurking in front of them or behind the cover of the overgrown shrubbery and ancient trees. There was no movement. All the action was behind him in front of the truck. Taking hold of Ariana's hand once more and nodding to Doctor Bennett who returned an acknowledgment of her own, they ran.

Bullets struck the ground around them, kicking up divots of earth but they didn't slow down and continued running.

Migs ignored the urge to check if Ariana was in pain because they would be in a bigger world of hurt if they were captured.

So, even as bullets flew past them, they didn't stop.

Even when another explosion rocked the night, they didn't slow.

With the rear exit finally in sight, his lungs expanded and contracted in measured breathing. Slamming against the wall beside the red metal door, he yanked it open. It was hidden by creeping vines on the side facing the street. Whether it was deliberate or not, Migs didn't know. It concealed their exit point and that was good enough for him. Without asking her, Migs swept Ariana off her feet and hurried to the nondescript sedan parked on the side of the road.

Ten feet away from the car, a whistling sound streaked by his ear, and a flash blinded him just as a booming blast deafened him. For the second time that night Migs was flat on his back. For the second time that night, his helmet protected his skull, but the weight of Ariana motionless on top of him had him choking in fear. He shoved up his NVGs and sat up carefully, a dizzying relief hitting him when she groaned and bitched at the explosion that shocked them.

"Mierda! Seriously? We can't catch a break."

"Are you okay?" Migs yelled behind him at Doctor Bennett.

"Okay," she mumbled.

An SUV screeched in front of them.

"Get in."

Andrade.

Without hesitating, he gestured for Doctor Bennett to get into the front seat while he packed into the middle row with Ariana.

Before he got the door fully closed, Andrade was spinning wheels to get out of there.

"Antonio Andrade. You are?" Migs heard the Brazilian's curt address to the doctor.

"Charly Bennett."

Migs would have loved to have heard Andrade's reaction, but a jumble of voices broke out in his earpiece, he finally heard John's. "Are you guys all right?"

"Yeah!"

"Nadia said your vehicle caught an RPG."

"Yup. Toast."

"Bristow nailed that motherfucker."

"No shit?" Thank fuck.

"Motherfucker," Andrade cursed and Migs was flung into the door when the other man swerved the vehicle to the right. "Road block."

"What?"

"They're blocking our exit back to base."

"Who?"

"Mexican Army," Andrade growled, flicking his eyes to the rear-view mirror and Migs was sure he was checking for a tail. "Carillo must have called in a huge favor. They crossed into PNO territory, but their scouts were able to sound the alarm, so I told my plane to take off."

"Your plane is gone?"

"I had it divert to Mexico City."

"That's where we're heading?"

"That's the plan."

"I'm surprised you didn't leave us there," Migs said.

Andrade barked a short laugh, but it wasn't amused. "I wouldn't abandon Ariana." His eyes and Migs' met in the rear-view mirror. Although it wasn't very good lighting, he could see the challenge in the other man's eyes. "Are you okay, sweetheart?"

"She's not your sweetheart," Migs snarled.

"Cool it, Walker. No need for jealous husband bullshit. Besides," Andrade glanced over to the quiet doctor. "I've got another prize catch in mind."

"I'm not a fish," Doctor Bennett snapped.

"No, you're a poor excuse of a human with no conscience. Creating a weapon in the name of science—" Andrade broke off in a sound of disgust.

"And how about you?" the doctor challenged. "Don't tell me you're a Boy's Scout."

Migs should be enjoying this sparring, but it was giving him a headache. Ariana's fingers gripped his, and he stared down at her. "Is your foot in pain?"

"What's wrong with her foot?" Andrade asked.

Ignoring his question, Migs addressed the doctor. "First moment we get, I need you to look her over."

"What was done to her?" the other man asked softly.

"Stop it," Ariana said. "Doctor Bennett just drew blood. It was that Silba person who made me sick." She froze. "Abbi Mena! How is she?"

"She's fine. Broken arm and concussion. She had to stay overnight at the hospital."

"I'm so sorry she got hurt because of me."

"It wasn't because of you, babe. Stop thinking like that."

When she didn't answer, he gave her arm a squeeze.

"I'm trying to stop blaming myself. I think I need to do it slowly, but I'm not feeling guilty about Raul's sins anymore."

"Good."

"I'm worthy of having a family."

"You are."

"Sorry to interrupt the heart-to-heart"—Andrade stated grimly—"but we've got company."

25

"SEATBELTS," Andrade ordered, but he was looking at Charly.

"Need me as shooter?" Migs asked, getting his wife upright and pulling the seatbelt across her body. "Any chance this SUV is bulletproof?"

"You wish," the other man muttered.

Migs had to hand it to Andrade— for a stuffed shirt, he sure had skills behind the wheel. Ariana was white knuckling his fingers and he wouldn't be surprised if he had nail marks embedded in his skin. They had passed a group of small homes before entering a commercial area. That was when the bullets started flying.

It was muffled at first. Then the rounds started hitting their vehicle like a tin can being pelted by pebbles.

"Hang on," Andrade yelled, and everyone slammed to the left when he veered sharply onto a side street.

Migs got a clear outline of the vehicle behind them when it followed the turn. It was an open jeep with a mounted machine gun. The men were bad shots, it was surprising they hadn't—

The rear windshield shattered.

Well, fuck!

"Engaging," Migs clipped and lowered a second-row seat.

"Be careful!" Ariana said.

He didn't answer her but gave her arm a squeeze before lumbering into the third row and landing on his back. Rifle in hand, he checked his mag, shoving it back into position, and rolled to his knees. He shouldered his weapon, lined his target, and started shooting. His shot went wide when Andrade took another turn. "Keep it steady!"

"You want us to be lame ducks?" the Brazilian scoffed.

"That's *sitting duck*, you idiot," Migs snarled back. He wasn't as experienced a sniper as Bristow. He was more an in-the-gunfight type of guy.

The jeep tailing them did a serpentine pattern, swerving left and then right, but that also messed with their assailant's aim. Migs shook his head. Another group of guys who'd watched Peter Falk and Alan Arkin in *The In-Laws*.

"What the hell are they doing?" Andrade said.

"Don't ask. You just hold the fuck steady." He fired two rounds in succession. On the third one, he hit the right tire.

The jeep lost control and crashed into a building.

"Good shot," came from the driver.

Migs raised a brow. "Thanks."

His earpiece crackled. Finally, some reception. "Walker, you there?" That was Nadia's voice.

"Yeah. Where's Garrison?"

"They managed to get away, but they're on foot."

"Shit. How's Levi?"

"Functional. Last I heard they were dodging around houses in the neighborhood."

"How long ago was that?"

"Not long. Garrison asked me to check on you."

"Andrade? Are we going to Mexico City?"

"For now."

"Get that, Nadia?"

"Copy that. I'll tell Garrison."

Migs jumped back onto the second row. Ariana's hand gripped his.

"You okay?" he asked, noting the clamminess of her palm.

She sighed. "Adrenaline crash, I think. I need to get used to you being an action hero."

The man in the driver's seat snorted.

Ignoring Andrade, because obviously the fucker was a sore loser, he kissed Ariana on the temple.

THEY MADE it to the next town when Andrade pulled over behind a twenty-four-hour convenience store. Migs switched places with Charly so she could tend to Ariana's foot. He held the flashlight for additional illumination.

Andrade stepped outside to keep watch, but Migs saw him make a call.

"Can you keep the light angled here?" Charly said.

He did as he was told. He hated watching his wife flinch every time the doctor poked and removed pieces of glass. "Didn't think you would go all Bruce Willis and *Die Hard*, babe." He attempted to keep her attention off Charly's ministrations.

"I'm never going to live that down, am I?" Ariana sighed.

"Nope." Migs squeezed her hand. "Stubborn. Told you not to move. You couldn't even see where I was."

"But I heard you cry."

Just his luck, Andrade took that time to return.

"Walker cried?"

"I did not cry," Migs muttered, "I grunted."

"I'm sure Nadia has a recording of it."

Migs flipped him off. Ariana patted him on the arm. "Doesn't matter. You swooped in like my knight in shining armor. I knew you would come."

"You did?" This warmed his heart. No, it made his chest puff up with pride.

"I knew I had to hang on as much as possible. Not give up."

There was so much Migs wanted to confess. His despair when she went missing, almost losing hope. But he didn't fancy Andrade giving commentary every time he was sweet to his wife.

Charly leaned back and started wrapping Ariana's foot in bandage. "You're lucky, none of these need stitches. If you can stay off your feet for a couple of days, that would be great. We need to get you better shoes too."

"Usually, I'd make a remark about women and shoes, but in this case, I agree," Andrade drawled.

The doctor shot him an irritated look, just as the other man frowned as he slid out his phone to take another call.

Migs could hear the Brazilian cussing.

"They're going to pay for this," he seethed. "How dare they block my plane from landing? What the hell do they mean terrorist activities?"

"Looks like Mexico City is a no-go," Charly said dryly.

Migs got out of the passenger side and exchanged positions with the doctor. There was one place they could go, but he wasn't looking forward to asking for a favor.

Andrade stalked back to the vehicle. "Bunch of extortionists. My pilot hasn't been allowed to land. The air traffic controller said we do not have a flight plan, but I usually can get past those."

"So what happened to your friends with Ponce-Neto? Couldn't they help us?"

"We're in Carillo territory and apparently the Mexican military had been bought. Not all. Only the ones in the area of Venustiano, but I suspect Mexico City too."

"So what's the plan?"

Andrade was pacing the length of the SUV. But Migs had to give it to the billionaire—even getting shot at, he managed to remain calm and didn't panic. Made Migs wonder just how

rough his life had been before he'd been adopted into the
influential Andrade family. Rumor was he never went to
college and was given an honorary degree by the University
of São Paolo.

When he stopped pacing, he said, "You have a cousin in
Michoacán."

"You know I do."

"How much do you trust him?"

"I trust him. Doesn't mean we like each other."

Andrade smiled. "Look at us. We don't like each other but
we managed to survive."

"You have a point," Migs sighed. "I'll give him a call."

THEY STOLE AN OLD STATION WAGON—A Volvo from the early
nineties before all the computerized shit made it difficult to
steal a car. He was impressed with how deftly Andrade lifted
the locks and got the engine started. Migs could have done it
himself, being a mechanic was in his cover after all, but he had
a conscience about stealing that the other man didn't.

At Migs' raised brow, Andrade shrugged. "I'll track them
down by the license plate and buy them a new one."

Of course he would.

They drove for a few hours and made a stop at a roadside
market. The ones where their owners slept in the stalls. But
with the rising sun, some of them were already humming with
activity, preparing breakfast and brewing coffee. Andrade still
did the driving, because Migs was the lookout and the billionaire admitted he wasn't as good of a shot as Migs. Their
vehicle pulled into a dirt parking lot, shaped by the repeated
uses of cars whose occupants wanted to buy refreshments
from the makeshift shops. As Andrade offered to buy them
food, Migs went off to make the calls.

First, to his cousin Joaquín who was not surprised by his

call. News travelled fast when a cartel boss was almost assassinated and needed to bribe the Mexican Army to intervene. His cousin was barely starting his day, and either he was pissed at being woken up so early in the morning or he wasn't pleased at being bothered by Migs. Probably both. But with the Alcantara plantation also being a part of Miguel's legacy, his cousin had no choice when he called and asked for sanctuary.

He kept the call brief and moved to the next on his list—John. He and his team managed to steal some vehicles as well and were currently laying low in a town not too far from Tampico. They were dealing with a myriad of injuries including Levi's concussion and it was lucky Bristow had stayed behind.

"You can make a break for the American Embassy in Mexico City," Migs said.

"That's the plan," John replied. "But, according to our last transmission from Nadia, there's some chatter that the Mexican Army has set up covert checkpoints on all arteries leading into the city."

"Verified?"

"Nope. And we couldn't raise her at all. Spotty reception," John said. "Also left a message for the CIA station chief. Waiting to hear back from him."

So they were cut off too.

Because the op against Benito was clandestine, and the Mexican Government wasn't informed, John was avoiding regular channels of communication since Mexican intelligence was notorious for wiretapping. Hell, the cartels pioneered phone tapping in the country. It was how they got the dirt on high-ranking government officials then gave them two choices: take the bribe and be rich or suffer the consequences of an indiscretion and possible assassination.

"I'm figuring the next time I see you it'll be stateside," Garrison said.

"Yes. Andrade redirected his plane to our family's private airfield."

"You could also try for the American Embassy."

"I thought of that, but Andrade would be left on his own."

"He's a survivor."

"Seriously, John, would you leave a man behind after he rescued your ass?" He paused. "No matter how much you disliked him."

"No. I get where you're coming from," John said. "Might be a good idea to hide the virus from our ambassador, though. Not sure he'd like to get caught up in that mess."

"Fucking State Department. He'd probably return our haul back to the Mexican government."

There was an extended silence on John's end, and he thought they'd been cut off. "When you see your cousin, remember the sensitivity of the information regarding your uncle's death."

"They have pictures, John. I need to explain that."

"All I'm saying—"

"I get what you're saying."

After finishing the call, he walked back to the station wagon parked under overreaching boughs of a big tree. Andrade brought back two bags of food and was handing bottled water to the women together with a couple of wraps.

"They only had *huevos rancheros,*" Andrade told the women, but they didn't seem to hear him as they grabbed the offering and scarfed it down in silence.

Guess they were starving.

Andrade looked at him. "Did Garrison get out?"

"Yeah, they're laying low in some town." He didn't need to be specific. As much as Migs appreciated the man rescuing their asses, he was still on a need-to-know basis.

"They're going to make a run for the American Embassy in the city," Andrade said. "That makes the most sense."

Migs shrugged.

The other man continued looking at him. "You three could do it too."

He met Andrade's stare. "You want me to leave you behind?"

"It's not the first time that's happened. Besides, I can fend for myself. But the virus, the last vaccine, and the doctor's laptop stays with me."

Migs grabbed the bag of food from Andrade and took his time unwrapping the item. Then he took a couple of bites, swallowed, and chased it with water. "Not gonna happen."

"Why not? That's the least the CIA can offer for ditching me." Andrade rested an elbow on the roof of the vehicle, leaning in.

Migs finished his breakfast in a couple of bites and pointed the tip of the bottle toward the Brazilian. "It's not gonna happen because I don't make it a habit of leaving a man behind." Considering the matter closed, he opened the door and got into the vehicle beside Ariana.

There was no movement from Andrade for a while. He probably expected Migs to jump at the chance of making a go for the Embassy. Lucky for Andrade, Migs wasn't built that way.

Besides, the man was growing on him.

"Two cars behind us." They were six miles from Cayetano when Migs spotted the tail. They were in a section where there was farmland for miles. The road was busy with trucks and smaller farm vehicles, but there were also regular ones like their Volvo—well, not exactly. No luxury car except theirs.

Two vehicles—a jeep with a mounted gun and a smaller version of an Army personnel carrier appeared out of nowhere.

They just passed the town of Zirimbo, and if Migs were to guess that town had spotters on the roof. Frequently they were street kids who aspired to be a narco one day. People like Benito exploited that dream by giving them a sense of belonging when they were not wanted at home.

The mood of the traffic changed. Regular cars behind them fell back as the military vehicles picked up speed.

"Buckle up," Migs muttered.

"I see them," Andrade said.

If he'd have to engage, it would be from the passenger window this time. He handed his phone to Ariana. "Call Joaquín. Tell them we're five miles out."

Ariana called his cousin.

"Put him on speaker."

"Miguel?" Joaquín's voice came on.

"Yeah, cuz, we're almost there. We're on *Uruapan - El Copetiro* highway. Unexpected guests on our tail."

"Situation?"

"Two vehicles. Military type. Not sure how many men on the carrier. Other is a jeep with a machine gun."

"Okay. Mobilizing Yetis."

His cousin ended the call.

"Yetis?" Andrade chuckled.

"Are you seriously laughing at a time like this?" Doctor Bennett snapped.

"Oh, she speaks."

Come to think of it, the doctor had been quiet since their last rest stop. Migs wondered if she didn't take too kindly to Andrade saying he was going to take ownership of her work should he be left behind. Whatever. They could resume their weird vibe when they arrived in Michoacán.

"Your cousin's private army?" Andrade asked.

"Watch the fucking road."

He was thankful they weren't passing through another town, waiting for an ambush. The only way they could've found Migs was that Benito knew he was going to go to Michoacán.

"They better be good," the other man muttered.

Their tail was almost on them and was within firing distance.

Migs glanced briefly at Ariana. Tense lines bracketed her mouth, but determination gleamed in her eyes. He reached down and slipped out his semi-automatic plus two loaded magazines and handed them to his wife. "Here. Just in case."

"Migs ..."

"It's going to be fine," he stated resolutely, keeping his eyes on the road. Deep in his gut, he knew this to be so, but he didn't know fuck all where that confidence was coming from.

The gunner on the jeep took position. Migs rolled down the window on his side. "Brace."

The word barely left his lips when their pursuer riddled their car with a barrage of bullets.

Andrade cursed and their vehicle swerved.

"Hold it steady," Migs yelled. The last thing he wanted was to catapult out of the Volvo as he assumed his shooting stance. Anchoring his leg between the seats, he hung out the window and returned fire, setting his rifle on fully automatic.

His bullet struck the driver's windshield and the jeep spun out of control, throwing the men in the back. The army carrier behind them clipped the jeep, but barely slowed down. The passenger stuck out a rifle and started shooting.

The women screamed.

"Are you hurt?" Andrade yelled at someone. "Charly! Ariana! Dammit."

Migs ducked back into the car and the headrests had bullet holes. If the women weren't hunkering down, they would have been shot through the head.

"I'm okay. The bullet hit the windshield," Charly said.

"I'm fine," Ariana gritted. "Go." She was looking at Migs.

Resuming shooting position, he aimed at the driver again, but hit the side mirror. Taking out the driver frequently ended in a more disastrous crash for a vehicle but the outcome of shooting out the tire wasn't as predictable. Swearing, he went for the bigger target and pumped a couple of rounds at the tire. A few of them ricocheted off the asphalt and the tire itself until one seemed to have penetrated enough to damage the threads.

The pursuing vehicle listed and was slowing down.

"Miguel!" Ariana screamed.

A force jolted him. Migs hit his head on a hard edge and the whole world spun, sending his body bouncing around in the steel death trap. The crunch of metal was deafening, the beating his body took was a bitch and he tried to hang on to Ariana's voice calling his name in horror, over and over.

26

"MIGUEL!"

Ariana watched in horror as her husband got tossed around in the Volvo when another vehicle rammed them from the side. When their car stopped spinning, Antonio ordered them out. There was no time to even catch a breath. Barely able to move her shaky limbs, Ariana went around to Miguel's door and opened it. Antonio shoved her aside and dragged her husband's unconscious form out.

"I smell gasoline," Antonio said, and she clamped her mouth shut. Anything was better than being trapped in a burning vehicle. "He's stubborn. He'll be fine." He hefted Miguel on his shoulder and grabbed the rifle.

Ariana wasn't too confident in that statement. She recalled seeing Migs cracked his head really hard on the edge where the window met the roof of the car.

"Go! Get behind those rocks." Antonio turned to Charly and snarled, "Leave those and—fuck! Leave it, dammit!"

Ariana realized Antonio's urgency when men appeared at the edge of the road up the embankment. Men with guns pointed at them.

"Run!" Antonio roared. "I've got him, Ariana."

She shook out of her hesitation and ran for her life, trusting the man to carry her husband—and she hoped, not use him as a shield. Her chaotic thoughts swirled as rapidly as the bullets that chased them, but they seemed to be locked on Antonio.

When they finally reached the rock formations, Antonio lowered Migs to the ground and checked his rifle. "He doesn't have a full mag. How about you?"

She showed him the gun and the two magazines Miguel gave her.

"I'm their target," Antonio told them. "They don't want to kill you or Charly. We'll fight as long as we can, but if they kill me and Walker, do not fight them. You hear me?"

"I can't go back," she whispered.

"Yes, you can," he told her. "Garrison found you once. He will find you again."

"I can't do it without Miguel."

Antonio was about to say something when a voice below her said, "Yes, you can."

"Migs!" she cried, sinking to the ground beside her husband.

"Guys, they've left the roadside," Charly warned. "You've got to hold them off now."

"I'm okay," Migs told her. "Help Andrade. Let me shake this off."

Heart pounding, she pressed a hard kiss on his lips and gripped the gun.

A line of men approached stealthily as one would when circling a wounded and feral animal. They were using the Volvo as a shield. But as they moved closer, they shot against their rock.

"I'm going to draw their fire," Antonio said. "Hope you hit a couple of them." Before Ariana could ask what he meant, he popped up, aimed, and fired before running off toward a cluster of rocks to their left.

A rattle of artillery followed him.

Heart in her throat, Ariana emerged from hiding and started shooting at the men who were all turned toward Antonio. She managed to hit one in the leg and caught another in the back, but she didn't let up.

Bang! Bang! Bang!

Guns swung back in her direction and bullets kicked up rock fragments. Ariana dove to the ground.

"Oh my God! Oh my God!" Maybe she should draw their fire away too. She inhaled a series of ragged breaths and waited for strikes on their location to veer back to where Antonio ran off to. Bullets pelting their craggy shield appeared to be ebbing and the billionaire was drawing their fire again. Ariana steeled her spine to shoot back, but hands closed over hers. She didn't notice that Migs had crawled over to her.

"I've got this."

"But Migs—"

"But nothing. I'm good." He split a look between Charly and her. "Both of you withdraw further—to that boulder when I draw their attention. Okay?"

"But—" Charly started.

"Okay?" he repeated firmly.

Without waiting for their answer, he ran the opposite direction Antonio had taken and started shooting.

"Come on," Ariana shouted over the din of the fiery exchange. They belly-crawled to another section of brush and jagged rocks where a bigger boulder sat, and she realized why Migs asked them to move. A tree line was behind it and if things got desperate, Ariana and Charly could run and hide in the forest. It was a better chance. But for whom?

She couldn't bear to think of life without Migs. Her heart was feeling this strongly now.

The shooting was relentless and more men in army

uniforms joined the fray. Minutes passed and the left corner became silent.

Antonio was out of ammo. Their attackers realized this and rose up from their cover of shallow rocks. Migs tried valiantly to draw them away from Antonio, but he ran out of bullets too.

"Now what?" Charly whispered.

One of the army guys ransacked the Volvo and came away with the pelican case and the backpack with the virus.

"Oh hell no." The doctor rose, but Ariana yanked her back down.

"Wait."

"Wait … what?" Charly snarled. "It's over. Andrade and Miguel are going to die if we don't surrender."

There were nine men left standing and they split into threes. One line went toward Antonio, another went toward Miguel, and the last three men headed for them.

"Migs has something planned," Ariana said. Her husband wasn't stupid enough to let the enemy know he'd run out of bullets.

It took all her effort to stay where she was, to trust her husband. She'd dug half-moon circles into her palm to keep still and just when she was ready to break out of her skin, Migs sprung up from nowhere and plugged three successive rounds and took down the men after him.

An altercation exploded where Antonio was holed up.

When she saw Migs go down, struck by a bullet, she started running.

"Noooo! I'm here. Don't shoot him!"

"Ariana," Migs roared. "Run, goddammit! Run away."

"No. No. I won't." She skidded to the ground beside him. "I'm not leaving you. Never."

She looked at the men closing in on them. "I'll not fight you. Just swear that you won't kill him. Otherwise, just shoot me too."

Ariana got on her knees, ignoring the sharp rocks piercing into them. "Just me."

"And me." Charly said from behind her. "I'll go. Benito wants me. Just spare the lives of these idiots." She glanced over to where Antonio was being held down by two men, a third one ready to pump a bullet into his head.

The men who held them prisoner smiled, but it wasn't a benevolent one. It was a smile that froze the blood in her veins.

"No," she whispered.

The de-facto leader of the remaining army guys ordered his two cohorts to grab Ariana and Charly.

She fell on Migs in a panic. "No."

Before she knew what was happening, Migs had switched their positions and covered her body.

Renewed gunfire erupted and when the frenetic noise stopped and the smoke cleared, men in blue camouflage and red berets approached.

Leading them was Joaquín.

ARIANA WAS FUMING. She really shouldn't be because Joaquín saved their asses. When she thought she was going to witness Migs die before her eyes, fear gripped her entire being. It hadn't released her from its haunting grasp since.

"I didn't know how to clue you in," Migs murmured beside her, their fingers clasped tight as they were led into the Hummer.

"I thought they were going to shoot you in front of me," she whispered, a tear trickling down her face.

"Hey." He wiped her tears with the pad of his thumb. "I'm not that easy to kill."

She had many things to say to that, but she didn't know how to phrase her words. Luckily, Joaquín got into the vehicle.

"We'll get you settled in, cleaned, and fed," His cousin angled his head toward Miguel. "Then you can tell me all about the mess you're in."

Ariana's hackles rose at the scathing tone in Joaquín's voice, as if this was all Migs' fault, but they smoothened a little with his next words.

"Then you can let me know how I can help." After throwing that bit out, Joaquín faced forward and told his driver, "*Vámonos.*"

She still longed to rant at her husband, but knowing they had an audience, she decided to look out the window at the Mexico she had left all those years ago. Twenty to be exact. All through this, Migs played with her fingers, kissing the back of them while giving them a squeeze. She was thankful for the contact. She needed it.

She was in a weird place, but maybe this was a form of post-traumatic stress she was experiencing. This constant agitation. Why couldn't she settle down when they were so protected?

"We're almost there," Migs said. "You'll be safe, Ari."

So many times she thought she was safe, and every time this was proven wrong. But still, she nodded. Her faith in Migs hadn't diminished. She just had to come to terms with her fears.

When they arrived at the hacienda, it was like one of those places that Ariana both admired and loathed as a child. She never thought she would see what was on the other side of the wall, and yet here she was. The Hummer drove through a fortified gate and armed men patrolled the area.

"Is security always this heightened?" Migs asked his cousin.

"No," Joaquín replied. "Ever since the attack at Abbi Mena's party, I've upped patrols. But we're on high alert now since you tried to assassinate Benito Carillo."

"That wasn't the objective. There are so many things you don't know."

"And I expect to have the answers, like why is Carillo so interested in your wife?"

Migs didn't answer.

"I've heard rumors, but …" Joaquín looked pointedly at his driver. "I hope you'll enlighten me on certain things."

The Hummer pulled in front of the sweeping staircase of a two-story Spanish-style villa. "I can't tell you everything, Joaquín."

"*Entiendo*," he replied. "I understand this. But in saving your life, I deserve to know exactly what I'm getting into."

"Does saving your cousin's life come at a price?" Ariana cut in. "Shouldn't you be doing this because you're family?"

"Respectfully—and that's because Migs already warned me what will happen if I talk to you in any other way—your husband owes me an explanation regarding my father's death."

Joaquín shoved open his door and opened Ariana's. She stepped down but was immediately swept up by her husband. "We'll talk later. My wife needs attention."

"Miguel, your ribs!" she exclaimed.

But all her husband did was grunt and proceeded up the staircase. Ariana recognized Elena waiting for them at the top of the steps.

As *señora de la hacienda* she certainly looked put together in a poofy up-do and a face that appeared sculpted from porcelain.

Ariana was aware of her own hospital scrubs and torn slippers and admired the other woman's silk sheath dress. When did silk dresses become the attire for the hacienda?

Old insecurities reared their ugly heads.

"I have rooms ready." Elena looked past them, her blood red lips parting when she saw their other companion. "Is that Antonio Andrade?"

Ariana resisted the urge to roll her eyes, and she felt a

rumble in Migs chest. Although he didn't acknowledge Elena's question, he did mutter her name in greeting as he passed her.

There was an urgency to his footsteps as he followed the majordomo who led them down the grand hallways of the villa. The bedroom they were put in had ornate walls of stenciled damask plaster. Ariana doubted they were wallpaper as venetian plaster was more suitable to this weather. Renaissance furnishings included a king-size four-poster bed complete with velvety drapes.

When he lowered her to the parquet flooring, her gaze took in the room, and felt like she was transported to a different era. "Wow."

Migs grunted as he started stripping off her clothes.

"Migs!" She stilled his fingers. "I want to look at you first."

"I'm fine," he growled.

"No, you're not! You got hit twice."

He tapped his chest. "SAPI plate."

"Well that's good, but I still want to see," she said. "Strip."

"For a minute I forgot how bossy you are," he mumbled as he obliged, taking off his shirt. She noted his effort not to wince.

"Stop pretending it doesn't hurt," she said.

He glared at her but pulled at his thin vest. Ariana's eyes widened at the dents. "You were hit five times?" she shrilled.

"Yeah."

"Oh my God, Miguel," she cried.

"Hey." He gripped her shoulders and drew her close. "These are high-performance vests. I had one for you in the truck that got destroyed. I would have given you mine, but it would fall off you."

"And why would you think to give it to me?" She scowled. "I wasn't the one in the line of fire. I was cowering."

"Don't say that! You helped me a lot, Ari, by staying calm." He frowned. "Although we need to be on the same page on some things."

Ariana barely heard him. Her eyes filled with tears, the fear exponentially rising. Black and blue color shaded his entire front. "Oh, Miguel."

She started to trace his chest, but he gripped her wrist. "Don't. Let's get you cleaned up before I end up taking you down to the floor."

He was horny?

"Adrenaline, Ari."

Something in his voice made her glance up and, indeed, his eyes were smoldering. Sex had been the furthest thing from her mind, but just one look from her husband and it awakened an answering need in her. All her soreness was forgotten.

Seeing her response, he gathered her close. "After the heat of battle," he murmured. "It makes me want to fuck."

Her breath hissed.

"Let me fuck you in the shower." His mouth was very close to hers, but he didn't kiss her. He was vibrating with controlled aggression and this time it was focused on her.

"Okay."

He didn't wait a second longer but backed her into the en suite. Her mind briefly registered that it was as luxurious as the bedroom—white and gold Italian tiles. Migs stripped her naked, eyes darkening at the bruises on her skin where Bennett had drawn blood.

"They don't hurt."

"Doesn't lessen the urge to kill someone."

"Not Charly, please. I think she's good."

His hands came up and cupped her breasts. "You've lost weight."

"I haven't."

A palm cupped the back of her head, tilting it to receive his kiss. It was gentle at first, then demanding. They were swaying from side to side in the wide bathroom, and before Ariana knew it, water rained down on them from the center of the shower.

Migs turned her around to face the tiles and soaped her back, spun her around again and kissed her, before soaping her front, taking the time to wash her secret places, slowly and gently. He shampooed her hair, massaged it. She tried to return the favor, but the water stung his bruises.

No words were said. None were needed. He boosted her up against the tiles and thrust into her. The shower drowned her moans as she came, and he roared as he reached his climax. Temporarily sated, they came down from their high, only to stare at each other, water sluicing in between them, washing away the brutal events of the past few days, at least for a moment.

27

"I was so fucking scared, Ari." Migs' arms wrapped securely around his wife. They were lying in bed after cleaning up. If they stayed cocooned like this for the next few days, he wouldn't mind at all. He'd missed Ariana so damned much.

"Don't blame yourself—"

He tipped her chin up so he could stare into her eyes. "But the worst thing in all this was I thought I would never see you again." He exhaled heavily and strengthened his resolve. There was no time to waste. He was going to tell her how he felt. He didn't care if it was too soon. "And I was frustrated along the drive from Venustiano, I wanted a moment—the right damned moment—for a chance to tell you I love you."

Her eyes widened, and for a fleeting second, he thought she was going to pull away, but then a watery smile curved her lips, her face visibly brightening. Encouraged, he angled toward the nightstand and opened its drawer where he'd stashed the ring when she wasn't looking. Thank God, he'd kept it on him this whole time.

He slid it on her finger. "I'm fucking in love with you, Ariana Walker."

Lips parting, her eyes went to the ring, then to his eyes

then back to the ring again. He loved how her breath caught. "How? When?"

"That belonged to abuelita," he said softly. "I was going to give it to you after the party, but you were kidnapped." He bent over and kissed her long and sweet. Pulling back, he continued, "I lost my damned mind when we lost your trail. We thought we'd cornered Benito only to realize he'd changed vehicles.

"I vowed to raze the earth to find you. I knew I might find you broken, but I was prepared to be with you every step of the way and nurse you back to health. I'll never leave you. Ever."

He brushed a stray tendril from her face. "There is so much to tell you."

She was still staring at her ring. "What?"

He laughed. "Hey, have I become chopped liver now? Did you even hear my undying vow of devotion?"

"Of course." A tear streamed down her cheek. "I'm just so overwhelmed."

He brushed that tear away and with apprehension, he asked, "Do you like it?"

"Like it?" she gushed. "I'm mesmerized. The jeweler took special care carving the band." She glanced at him. "It's beautiful, Miguel. Thank you. You must know I—"

A voice from the outside cut off what she was about to say, and Migs couldn't hide his irritation when the majordomo called out, "Do you need anything Señor Walker? El Señor Alcantara was wondering if you want to join him for lunch in an hour."

He didn't want to leave this bedroom, but knew he had to face his cousin who, after all, saved their necks.

"We have to show up, Migs," his wife said.

"We can just sleep," he offered. "We haven't slept a wink since last night."

"There'll be time for a siesta."

"Señor?"

"Yes!" Migs called in a slightly irritated voice so that his wife pinched his side. It actually stung. He grunted.

"Oh my God, I'm sorry," Ariana gasped. "I forgot you were hurt all over."

He fell back on the bed, folding his arms under his head.

"I know how you can make me feel better."

"Oh?" His devilish siren shifted to her knees and was on all fours. A delectable view, and his cock approved, but he wanted desperately to hear something else.

"Tell me what you were going to say before we got interrupted."

Her naughty expression morphed into a tenderness that nearly dislodged the organ in his chest.

She crawled closer. "I'm in love with you, Miguel Alcantara Walker."

And just like that, all the hits and bruises he'd sustained today became a worthy price for this moment.

He reached for her and sealed their declarations with a kiss.

"THIS IS A LOVELY MEAL, my compliments to your staff, Elena, Joaquín," Andrade said.

"May I suggest a stroll in our avocado grove before *la siesta*?" The lady of the hacienda suggested before turning to Ariana. "Oh, I'm sorry. Can you walk?"

She forced a smile. "I'd rather not."

"I've advised her to stay off her feet," Charly said sharply, causing Ariana to glance her way, but she was scowling at Elena and for some weird reason, Antonio was smirking.

Migs patted her hand. "And there's something we need to discuss with Joaquín."

Startled, she met her husband's gaze. "You want me in that discussion?"

"What discussion?" Elena frowned.

"I don't think our wives need to concern themselves with our issues," Joaquín said.

"I don't want to hide anything from Ari. If anything, this concerns her too."

"Well ..." Elena started, but glanced at Antonio who stood from the table and offered his hand to Joaquín's wife. She preened and stood up. "Why don't you show me around your avocado plantation."

Ariana glanced at Joaquín who had his usual expressionless face on.

"We can talk some other time, cuz," Migs said. "I'd just as well retire with Ari. It has been a long night. You can show Andrade around if you want."

"Nonsense," his cousin replied. "We can talk at the veranda. *Mi amor*," he addressed Elena. "Before you show Mr. Andrade around, can you tell Consuelo to serve dessert and coffee on the veranda?"

Elena's eyes flashed with what looked like defiance, before accepting the Brazilian's proffered arm. But Andrade wasn't finished with whatever he had in mind.

"Doctor?" Andrade said. "Care to join us? It looks like a family matter and you'll only be in the way."

Ariana was offended for Charly, but she needn't have worried, because the cool doctor apparently had her own comeback.

"Are you sure I won't be in *your* way, Mr. Andrade?" Charly yawned. "I'd rather take a nap after that lovely lunch. Dessert will have to wait anyway." She stood and thanked their hosts and headed the opposite direction from where Antonio and Elena were going.

Apparently, the billionaire wasn't the type of man to be

thwarted. She watched Antonio let go of Elena and stalk after Charly. When he caught up with her, he gripped her upper arm, stopping her in her tracks. "Oh, but I *insist*, Doctor Bennett." He lowered his head and whispered something in her ear.

Charly reeled back and glared at him but allowed herself to be led out the door for their avocado grove tour.

The three of them were left at the table and she didn't know what to say.

"Something strange is going on between those two," Migs observed, but Ariana wasn't sure which two he meant.

"Yes," Joaquín clipped. "It's surprising my wife is intent on making a fool of herself. I'll meet you both at the veranda. I have some calls to make."

"What just happened?" Ariana asked.

"Long story short? Joaquín married Elena for her connections in society. I can't speak for their marriage, but you can see for yourself."

Ariana felt sad for the couple. They weren't happy. When Migs helped her get up from her seat, she stared at him. "I couldn't bear it if you looked at me with such coldness."

"I didn't marry you for your connections."

"You married me to protect me."

His face was pained. "I lied about that."

"You knew differently then." She put a hand to his cheek. "We're past that now, don't you think?"

He looked at her, his expression grave. "Repeat that to me after my talk with Joaquín."

A feeling of trepidation gripped her heart. "Is it bad?"

"It's in the past. It's something I had to do, but it might make you think twice about spending the rest of your life with a man like me."

"Cigarette?"

Migs declined the offer for a smoke and Ariana shook her head as well when Joaquín held the golden case out to her.

Shrugging, he leaned back against a chair, gaze in the distance, studying the endless rows of avocado trees. "This is the Alcantara legacy. The land. We grew limes before, and now we cater to America's love of avocado. And no one can grow it better than the people of Michoacán. As the eldest son, it fell to me to take care of this, but many didn't agree, did they, Miguel?"

"I had nothing to do with it."

"No. The people loved Don Amado's eldest daughter— Delia. Today is Leon's funeral, by the way."

That caught Migs off-guard and he admitted to himself that he didn't think of his old friend because of the speed at which events unfolded, but he had hoped to attend the funeral.

"You knew he always loved your mother?" Joaquín looked at the end of his cigarette.

"Of course he loved her. They were childhood friends." Migs tensed. He'd heard malicious rumors all his life, but they were absurd. He was witness to their friendship and that was all there was to it. He didn't see unrequited love at all. "But if you're implying that he was in love with her, I'm shutting that shit down right now."

"Why would a man stay single and devote himself to the security of the Alcantara-Walker family?"

"See, that's where you're wrong," Migs said. "He said he was not the family type." And he didn't want to add that Leon was quite the womanizer in the day.

"Because he already has family."

That was it. Migs rose slowly from his seat. "If you're implying my mother cheated with Leon, I'm outta here and to hell with the truth about Tio Pepito."

Joaquín surged from his seat as well and rounded the table and met him nose to nose. "No. I'm not implying that Tia Delia cheated or that any of you are bastards—"

"Migs!" Ariana pushed back from her chair and touched his arm when he'd gripped his cousin by the neck.

"But it was Leon"—Joaquín choked—"That the people of Cayetano looked up to. When he rose in the ranks with the Mexican police, everyone was proud of their Cayetano son. Then he quit to be the Alcantara-Walker head of security. When Abbi Mena wanted to live with the Walkers, it cemented the myth that Delia's children deserved to be head of the Alcantara holdings. Not us."

For fuck's sake. His cousin was a smart businessman but Migs wondered how he managed his people. "Because you don't care for the workers or the town the way *el abuelo* and *abuelita* did. It has nothing to do with my mother, Leon, or Abbi Mena. You need to show them that you care. Relax some of that stiff upper lip."

Ariana gasped, but when Migs looked at her she had a hand over her mouth as if stifling a laugh, but the crinkle at the corners of her eyes was a dead giveaway that she found it funny.

Migs had to fight back his own smile.

"I'm trying." The corner of Joaquín's mouth tried to lift, but his cousin really needed to work on that stick in his ass. "Their perception is changing," he reasoned hesitantly. "But it's not enough. It's an uphill battle. Elena is not helping either, preferring to socialize with her high society friends than to see to the well-being of our workers. And Hector—"

"Yes, let's talk about Hector," Migs jumped in.

"You wanted to have my brother arrested!"

"Wait, you don't know?" Migs blew out a breath. "Shit. I didn't tell anyone, did I?" He was so focused on getting Ariana back and trying to come to terms that he needed to come clean about his uncle's death that he subconsciously tried to spare his family the truth about Hector's betrayal.

"Tell anyone what?" his cousin asked.

"Hector was the one who turned me over to Carillo," Ariana said.

"That's a lie!"

"It was his men who killed Leon," she said. "I saw it with my own eyes."

"We don't know if they worked for Benito," Migs corrected.

"But why would he do …?" Joaquín closed his eyes. "It was Hector who was using our trucks for cocaine."

"Yes. Do you know where Hector is now?"

Joaquín's face lost its composure, cracking with disbelief. "He left a message for me the other day, but I was busy trying to find out who tipped off the DEA from our office. I never returned his call."

"Did he say where he was?"

"No. Just that the police were after him and he was lying low. I think he wants to come here."

"Shit."

"I wonder if he's in Mexico," Migs muttered, then he backtracked to his cousin's statements. "Did you find the man who called the DEA?"

"Woman," Joaquín corrected. "One of my temp-assistants didn't show up for work after the warehouse incident. I have since hired an investigator to go through all my personnel files. At least the ones who have access to my office and computers."

"It could be Hector who sent you those pictures."

"What pictures?" Ariana asked.

Joaquín looked at her. "You didn't know?"

"I haven't had the opportunity to tell her anything." Migs eyed his cousin steadily and decided to rip off the Band-Aid.

"I work for the government, but you probably already know that based on our latest escapade into Carillo territory."

His cousin's face slackened as he turned eyes on an unsurprised Ariana, and, in true Joaquín fashion, he was able to regain his composure, that stoic mask. "I guess I can believe it. I shouldn't be surprised. I've turned this over and over in my head." He pointed between them. "Are you two married because of the job too? Did you recruit Ariana as an informant? Is that why Carillo wanted her?"

Migs puffed a laugh. "No. Ariana and I are married because I thought the Alcantara name would protect her. And unfortunately, I can't tell you why Carillo wants her."

His cousin gave him a look. "Classified, huh? You're CIA, aren't you?"

He shrugged, and when Joaquín turned to Ariana, she lifted her shoulders in the same gesture.

Joaquín turned away and stared off at the avocado grove once again. He was quiet for a while and then gave a shake of his head. Still not looking at them, he asked, voice hoarse. "What did my father do? Why was he in those pictures?"

Migs repeated what he'd told his mother—about the gambling debts, about how he'd laundered money for the cartel. That it was Migs who recruited Tio Pepito as an asset, told him that the CIA was aware of his money laundering scheme and there was only so much Miguel could do before the agency would make it difficult for the Alcantaras to do business.

"You blackmailed him," Joaquín accused.

"I offered him a way to make things right," Migs replied evenly. "I was the only one standing in between the agency and them shutting down the Alcantara business for drug trafficking."

"You were not doing this for us—the Alcantaras, but your own family."

"Tell me, cuz, what's the difference? How am I different

from you? You protect the entire Alacantara legacy by running the business side of things, and I choose to get into the nitty gritty of its security because that's how I want to operate."

"You got my father killed!"

"Did Migs pull the trigger?" Ariana challenged.

"Stay out of it." Joaquín jabbed a finger at his wife which Migs knocked away. Ariana had stepped between him and his cousin and Migs was trying to keep her from getting into his face.

"No, I won't," she spat. "Don't you see? The cartel has a way of destroying lives, but we shouldn't let it destroy ours. Our relationships. My own brother destroyed so many people and I had to live with that guilt, but not anymore. I refuse. Don't take it out on Miguel. He didn't pull the trigger. He was trying to save your uncle from a bigger mistake."

"He was shot twenty times," Joaquín said hoarsely, face ravaged in a way Migs had never seen. And the image of watching his uncle gunned down as Migs was held back by the rest of the CIA team replayed like a nightmare in his head. He'd punched a few of his own men, trying to get to his uncle but they jumped on him, sat on him, so he wouldn't get himself killed.

"I was there," Migs whispered. "I saw him go down and I was helpless because my team held me back." Ariana gripped his hand, and he drew strength from her to go on. "But that's no excuse. I should have been with him."

His cousin stared at him for a long time. "And have yourself killed as well?"

"It felt that way for the longest time," Migs said raggedly. "I would have willingly taken the bullets for Tio Pepito. Please know that."

"Your guilt makes sense," Joaquín said quietly. "The destruction of the Carillo cartel soon after his death only solidified the code that it was forbidden to harm an Alcantara. I guess it worked in perpetuating the myth?"

Migs stared at the floor.

"So my father gave up the cartel's inner circle," his cousin asked after a length of time.

"Yes."

"*La Tia* Delia knows this."

"I've told her, but as far as my family is concerned, I'm DEA."

Joaquín smiled faintly. "They probably suspect more by now."

"What?" Migs growled.

"The incident in Venustiano has probably reached their ears."

"Shit." Migs scrubbed his face. "I have to let them know we're okay."

"Already done. I told them you got Ariana back when you were cleaning up. I should have told you to call them back."

Migs exhaled deeply. "Thanks, cuz."

"They have questions."

Fuck.

Before Joaquín could say anything else, Elena burst into the veranda, her usual polished self nowhere in sight.

"Joaquín?" she said nervously.

"What happened?"

"They left."

Migs stilled. "What do you mean they left?"

"Antonio used the excuse to see the plantation to get to the airfield. He left with Doctor Bennett. He pulled a gun on our driver."

"Where the fuck did he get a gun?" Migs growled. "Unbelievable. I can't believe that fucker left us here." He vented his frustration by kicking a chair.

"Wait, what about the vi- ... Doctor Bennett's stuff?" Ariana asked. "She wouldn't leave without them?"

"You mean the things those Army guys were looting?" Joaquín scoffed. "Mr. Andrade had them transferred to his plane immediately. He said he doesn't trust our security. Why, what's in it? Money?"

"Important intel," Migs clipped.

"Look at you, such a *gringo* agent," Joaquín smiled. "Don't worry, I have a plane. I can have you flown to the U.S."

Migs thought about Garrison. He wasn't going to like this. "I need to make some calls."

28

"WHAT DO you mean you can't get hold of Garrison?"

Migs was on the phone with Nadia. The spook and the entire spec ops team was last heard from entering Mexico City, dodging the corrupt Army soldiers and trying to get to the American Embassy.

"That's what I'm saying," Nadia snapped. "They went radio silent, probably to avoid getting caught."

"Fuck," Migs said. "Okay. I've left him messages. He'll call me back when he's clear."

"I'm trying to get through to one of his contacts in the Mexican police. We're trying to keep this on the down low without letting the government know this is happening."

"Too late," Migs said. His eyes lifted to see Joaquín who was giving him the signal that they were about to take off. "Listen, I'm getting on a plane."

"Still can't believe you let Andrade get away," Nadia said.

"I didn't think he was going to pull a runner."

"He kidnapped an American citizen. Did he think about that?"

"Fuck knows what he was thinking," Migs grumbled, but he also wondered if the virus was now out of Benito's grasp, would he stop pursuing them? "Listen. I've got to go. I'm heading to San Diego and I don't want to make my family here take any heat from the Mexican Army."

"I thought they had their own private defense."

"They do, but no telling how desperate Benito is or what he will do once he finds out the virus is gone. Contact me immediately when you hear from Garrison." Migs ended the call and headed up the clam shell steps of his cousin's private plane. Joaquín was talking to the pilot, leaving instructions before turning to Migs. "I hope to see you again under better circumstances, cuz."

"Yes. I'm sorry if trouble is heading your way."

"Don't worry. They can't force their way into town. I've already called their commandant."

"Heard he's incorruptible."

"One of the few," Joaquín nodded. "Carillo should have known better than to mess with the Alcantaras."

His cousin glanced over to where Ariana was already buckled into a seat. "So you see, your husband didn't lie. You have the protection of the Alcantara name. Our armor has a few dents, but we're going to hammer those out."

"Thank you."

The two cousins faced each other and gripped each other's shoulders in a parting gesture.

"*Cuídate.*"

"*Gracias*, Joaquín."

Migs took his seat beside Ariana who snuggled up to him after takeoff. And as their plane rose higher, he felt the shackles of his guilt falling away. He still needed to come clean with Abbi Mena, but Joaquín was the biggest hurdle. As for Hector, he probably already knew because Migs suspected his younger cousin was the one who sent those pictures to his brother.

He pressed a kiss on top of Ariana's head and couldn't wait to get her back Stateside.

ARIANA GLANCED out the window in trepidation. Their plane taxied into a private hangar at San Diego International Airport. Migs was on the phone with his father and, from what she could glean from his side of the conversation, they were waiting at the hangar. How would they react when they saw her? Everything bad that had happened to them was because of her. Abbi Mena was hurt, and Leon was dead. Granted, Hector had a hand in things. He was running cocaine through their avocado trucks, and from what her husband had told her, Benito manipulated the events so the younger Alcantara would owe him. Carillo used the pictures of Migs and his uncle to further tip Hector into betraying his family.

"You ready?" Migs asked.

She tried her best to put on a brave smile despite the uncertainties spinning inside her. Ariana was no stranger to rejection, but there was a difference between her situation before and what it was now. Miguel. This kidnapping had shown how devoted he was to her. She could feel his anguish when he saw her on the hospital bed being used as a specimen.

"Ready when you are." This time her smile was more natural. The door opened and the clam shell steps unfolded. Faces of the Alcantara-Walker family greeted her—Drew, Delia, Bella, and Tessa who had Gigi in her arms. Faces that erased doubt of her place in their family. Smiles and tears mingled, but as she and Migs emerged from the plane, they rushed toward them, embracing her first with welcoming arms.

Acceptance.

"Ariana, mija" Delia cried. "I'm so glad you're okay!"

Emotions and garbled words were exchanged. Tessa and Bella called her *querida hermana* over and over. Their beloved sister.

Migs reclaimed her from them and said they needed to pass through customs. Which would have been a problem because they didn't have their passports, but Nadia worked her magic and sent the paperwork over and all was well.

As soon as she got into the familiar SUV of the Alcantaras, Ariana's body gave into exhaustion and she fell asleep.

"LET HER SLEEP. Don't wake her." It was Abbi Mena's voice.

"Abuelita, should you be up?" Miguel asked.

"She's been stubborn," Lettie's irritated tone had her smiling.

"Quiet. Ariana is tired," Abbi Mena said. "All your talking is disturbing her."

"I'm taking her to our room," her husband said.

"I'm glad you gave her the ring, Miguel," his grandmother whispered. "It was time."

THERE WAS light streaming through the windows when Ariana woke up to the familiar surroundings of their bedroom. They arrived in San Diego late the night before. Or was that in the early hours of the morning?

She blinked and noticed that Miguel's side had been slept in. A smile touched her lips.

They were home.

She stretched, wincing slightly at the odd aches and pains due to a long journey. The sluggishness.

She sat up and the blanket fell away, revealing her own clothes. Soft pajamas, not the scratchy hospital scrubs or the ill-fitting clothes she wore at the hacienda and during their trip home.

Her own clothes. She gingerly swung her legs to the floor. And right there were her slippers.

Her own footwear.

Home.

Ariana checked the clock and was surprised it was already eight in the morning. The ranch should be awake ...well, except for Bella. She remembered her first morning in this house. She could use some coffee, and, boy, was she starving.

Looking forward to having breakfast with Miguel's family, she quickly showered and changed into thin sweats, and decided to wear her slides that had air-cushion soles. That would be easy on her poor feet. She followed the aroma of coffee and toasted bread, strolling through the portico that joined the wings of the house. Abbi Mena's garden was in full bloom and she felt bad that the older woman would not enjoy her fields of vegetables this summer.

The strange atmosphere hit her before she entered the kitchen.

She heard crying.

Ariana paused at the entrance to the heart of the home and took in the heartbreaking tableau.

Migs was standing, head bowed, hands gripping the back of a chair. Abbi Mena was sitting at the center of the table which was unlike the usual dynamo she was in the kitchen but, given her injury, that was understandable. No, it was seeing the indomitable matriarch of the Alcantara family looking so broken, sobbing and dabbing at her eyes furiously with a paper towel.

Migs' sisters sat stunned—Tessa, Lettie, and Bella, who was surprisingly already awake at this time. Pat and Cora were nowhere in sight. Ariana had an idea what Migs had told them. Drew and Delia were at one corner of the table, staring blankly at their plates—her husband's mother was quietly crying.

He'd told them about Don Pepito.

More than one pair of eyes flew in her direction and she froze, unsure whether to proceed into the kitchen or not. Migs turned to her, smiled sadly, but held out his hand. "Come, babe."

"I'll get you coffee," Delia rose, but Ariana waved her off. "I can get it, you all continue to talk." She asked if anyone needed a refill, but she was met with a shaking of heads.

There also wasn't much talking, just sobbing.

Finally, Abbi Mena said, "I always wondered what happened to Pepito. I suspected he was in trouble. A mother knows these things."

"I'm sorry, abuelita," Migs said. Ariana had her back to them, and she took her time pouring herself coffee as tears stung her eyes. How difficult this must be for Migs. To unburden his guilt over and over.

She composed herself; her husband needed her. Making her way back to the table, she took her seat and tried to pull him down in the one next to her, but he gave one shake of his head. Did he feel he wasn't worthy of his family any longer? If her heart was breaking, his must be shattered.

Abbi Mena got to her feet. "I'm not angry at you, Miguelito. But here"—she clutched her chest with her good hand—"I feel your pain. But I cannot say it doesn't hurt to look at you. I need to be alone." She pushed back from her chair and shuffled around the table. Lettie rose to aid her, but she waved the help away. "I can manage." A couple of steps away she glanced over her shoulder. "Don't waste the food. Doesn't mean because I cannot eat, you shouldn't either. *Ustedes coman.* Eat."

Ariana stared at her plate, her mouth twitching with the odd desire to giggle at this very inappropriate time. She glanced up and saw Lettie and Bella doing the same, fighting back laughter. Their eyes met and they all couldn't help the puff of laughter that escaped their lips.

"Your abuelita will be fine," Delia told her son. "She just needs to be alone."

She glanced up at Migs. His head was still bowed, a

muscle working his jaw overtime. Then he walked away from them and exited the kitchen into the patio, moving to its far edge and stared out into the field of corn.

She rose from her chair to go to him.

"Leave him," Delia said. "He needs his space to think."

"No," Ariana told his mother. "I'm his wife. He needs me."

Her mother-in-law smiled faintly and gave a brief nod. "You're right. Go to him."

ARIANA APPROACHED her husband and put a hand on his shoulder. "Migs." He twisted toward her and snagged her into his arms, clutching her tight as if she was a lifeline. He buried his nose in her hair and breathed her name. "Ari ..."

The way her name caught at his throat, the way his body shuddered against hers, threatened to spill emotions from her eyes, but she held them back. That was all she could do, be his anchor in his storm.

"The way Abbi Mena looked at me," he said hoarsely. "It was as if I shot her through the heart."

"Oh Miguel." She drew back and cupped his jaw. His eyes were red, and she wanted to erase the anguish etched into his features. "She was surprised. She didn't know how to react, but I did not see condemnation on her face. She knows you're hurting, and I think that's why she said she couldn't look at you."

"You're trying to make me feel better, babe, and I appreciate that—"

"That's not true. Don't be condescending when I'm telling you the truth of what I saw." She squeezed his jaw to make a point.

"I thought it would be easier to tell her."

"Than Joaquín?"

He nodded.

"I think because he already had time to stew over the pictures," Ariana said. "With Abbi Mena, it was a total surprise. She had to relive the pain of your uncle's death."

"At least she's not left wondering anymore," Lettie said from their sides. Ariana lowered her arms and they both turned to see his three sisters standing there.

Drew stood behind his daughters. "Your Mamá went to check on Abbi Mena."

"I catch her sometimes," Lettie continued. "Staring into space and on her lap is Tio Pepito's picture. I remember that one time she said the hardest part was not knowing why he was senselessly killed. *What did he do?* She asked. She suspected Joaquín was keeping something from her, to protect her. She knew Tio Pepito wasn't all on the straight and narrow." At Migs' face, his sister added, "No, I'm not trying to make you feel better either."

"Were you three eavesdropping?" he asked, but there was a smile to his voice.

"Maybe," Bella said and took a step forward. "So, what, bro? You never admitted it, but are you CIA?"

"Don't be ridiculous, Bella," Lettie scolded. "You think Migs would tell us if he were?"

Bella looked at Ariana. "I bet she knows."

Ariana laughed.

"See, that laugh is an admission," Bella persisted.

Migs lowered his mouth by her ear and whispered, "You'd make a terrible agent."

She pulled back and pushed him forward. "Go. They need to hug their brother."

Her husband took two steps forward and opened his arms. Bella stepped into him first and then Lettie. Tessa was teary eyed, and with Gigi in her arms, she joined the huddle and somehow Migs was able to embrace them all.

Delia quietly joined Ariana at her side. "Mami is okay. Everything will be fine." Drew picked up his wife's hand and she leaned into his chest as they watched their children. His mother glanced at her. "I told you this the first day Migs brought you here and I will say it again. Thank you for bringing my son home."

MIGS STRAIGHTENED the fencing along the west side of the ranch. Strong winds had knocked them down and they hadn't been repaired.

It had always been Leon's job.

A sadness twisted a muscle in his chest as he remembered their family friend and security chief. Although Leon's responsibility was mainly the warehouse, he was on top of what the ranch needed from fencing to surveillance to personnel. Right now, Cesar was double-timing at security and was going to interview Leon's replacement soon.

The man at the guardhouse and the few who were patrolling the ranch were not familiar to him. He tossed the broken fence board to the ground and observed his handiwork. How ironic that he was mending fences as the ones in his own life were splintering.

A scraping of footsteps on the ground had him squaring his shoulders. He recognized the gait and waited for the person to speak.

"It's strange to see you fixing that and not Leon," Abbi Mena said behind him.

Migs rose to his feet and grabbed the Stetson from his head to flick the dirt from his jeans before turning to his grandmother. He kept his eyes on the hat, rimming it with his fingers. "I've helped him before." He cleared his throat and lifted his gaze, reluctant to see the look in her eyes. There was a sadness in them, but he was relieved the pain wasn't as stark as it had been this morning.

"You know what I mean, *mijo*." She exhaled heavily and

looked at her cornfields, lit in a beautiful golden cast over green fields by the setting sun. "The past few days have been trying. Ariana's kidnapping, Leon's death and now … what will the family do about Hector?"

"He has a lot of explaining to do," Migs said, jaw hardening.

"I understand, but is Ariana sure he gave the order to have Leon killed?"

Migs shook his head. "What exactly do you want to happen here, Abbi Mena? He's guilty no matter how you look at it. A man is dead. And not just any man—a man closer to this family than Hector ever was."

"It didn't used to be that way. You and Hector used to be tight like brothers."

"We grew up." Or grew apart. "Are you trying to justify what he did because of Tio Pepito?"

"I'm trying to understand. Leon is dead and nothing can bring him back. I don't want Hector's life ruined because of a mistake he might be regretting. Done in the heat of the moment."

"That was no heat of the moment." He was having a hard time keeping hold of his temper. "It was premeditated. The explosives in the stage. Ariana's kidnapping. Let's not forget about that. I nearly lost my wife!" He ended on a roar. He spun away and stared at his boots and sighed heavily. "I didn't mean to yell at you. I'm sorry."

"See what I mean," she said. "You regret immediately. For Hector, he is blinded by his anger that you played a part in Pepito's death." Her voice cracked and it was tearing him up inside again. "But I don't want to believe my children and grandchildren are totally evil. That they are not capable of remorse."

Footsteps snapped a branch, causing Migs to swivel and reach for the gun he had behind his back.

It was Crispin, one of the new guards. "I'm sorry, *Señor*

Walker, there is a man at the gate, and he wants to speak to you."

He frowned. A man? Garrison? "Who?"

"He said his name is Hector Alcantara."

His eyes snapped to his grandmother's, but she looked on defiantly.

"Did he call you?" he clipped.

"Hear him out," she said softly.

"What bullshit did he feed you?"

Abbi Mena's nostrils flared and her face turned cold. "We may not agree on things, Miguel, but you will show me respect."

Her tone would have made him instantly contrite, but he was too pissed at the whole situation to apologize. He stalked back toward the house and into the kitchen with Abbi Mena following behind. "He's not going to be anywhere near my family."

"Your father stopped him at the gates." The guard kept pace with him.

Migs stopped and turned to Crispin. "Don't let anyone out this door, understand?" He looked pointedly at his grandmother, who stoically took a seat at the table.

Lettie, Bella, and his mother were in the kitchen. The three of them rounded the counter.

"What's going on?" Lettie asked.

"Hector is at the gates."

Mamá's face darkened. "How dare he show up here? After what he had done to this family and Leon."

"Apparently Abbi Mena invited him."

"Abuelita!" Bella exclaimed.

"He deserves to be heard."

"He doesn't deserve anything," Mamá said. "Leon is dead because of him. He handed Ariana to the Carillos! He's selling drugs just like Pepito."

Their grandmother's expression remained mulish.

"Where's Ariana?" Migs asked.

"She's in the living room with Tessa and Gigi, looking at pictures … should I—" Lettie started.

"No, don't tell them anything," Migs headed out the kitchen, through the portico and then into the main foyer. The door opened, revealing Cesar who looked ready to kill someone. "Drew sent me to get you. Hector is here."

"I know. Stay here. Don't let anyone out." He passed his brother-in-law and skipped the steps. Cesar's Bronco was idling in front of the house and Migs got in to drive to the gates.

MIGS DROVE the pickup through the gates and parked beside a black Escalade. It appeared his cousin wasn't hovering at the poverty line yet.

He shoved out of the Bronco.

"Migs!" Hector broke from his heated discussion with his father and rushed toward him, but his cousin's forward momentum stalled when Migs advanced on him.

"Take it easy, cuz," Hector held out a palm and backed a step.

"Take. It. Easy?" Migs snarled, grabbing him by the collar and slamming him against the Escalade. He brought his face close. "You traded my wife because you lost a drug shipment. You had Leon killed—"

"That was not the plan," Hector sputtered. "The old man shouldn't have followed us."

"He was onto you, wasn't he?"

"I did not start this, and you know it!"

Migs released his cousin and stepped back. "This is about Tio Pepito."

"Yes." His younger cousin spat. "Don't you think I'm justified? No one was supposed to die or get hurt. I swear. Benito said he would release Ariana once he was done with her. Unharmed."

"And you believed him?"

Hector started pacing, gesturing wildly. "I panicked, all right? I believed what I wanted to believe. I owed him three million dollars and I didn't know where to get it. When he said he wanted Ariana ..." he glanced at Migs whose face must have been a thundercloud because his cousin chewed on his words before stuttering. "You just met her. How did I know that you'd get pussy-whipped? You never stick to one woman anyway—"

"So you're saying my wife is disposable?"

Hector looked at him warily. "Is that a trick question?"

Migs gave him the answer he'd been itching to give the moment he saw his cousin again. He punched him across the face. Hector wasn't a fighter and Migs' easy jab allowed him to feel cartilage smash and bone break, blood spattering everywhere.

Drew yanked him back. "Miguel. Enough!"

"Motherfucker," he growled at his cousin. "I should kill you."

"Leave something for the cops," his father said.

"I shouldn't even be here," Hector said. "I know—"

Two unmarked vehicles and a dark blue Suburban converged on them simultaneously.

"What the fuck?" Migs growled, drawing his weapon and dragging Pops behind him.

But the new arrivals were cops—DEA to be exact.

Lenox stepped out of the Suburban, armed to the teeth. All this for Hector?

"Sorry, I couldn't let you kill my informant."

"Informant?" Migs said incredulously. "Since when?"

"Hey, I never agreed to anything," Hector protested. "And what the fuck are you guys doing, showing up here?"

Lenox looked at Migs. "You're not DEA. You're something else, and whoever you're working for has created headaches for the State Department."

He didn't say anything. Lenox could be fishing because last he talked to Nadia, there was still no contact from Garrison yet.

"I'm going to need to bring you in," Lenox started pulling his cousin away, and then glanced at Migs. "I have a few questions for you too, if you would oblige."

"I can't right now."

Hector yanked his arm away and glared at Migs, grabbing him by his shirt. "Fuck! You made me forget what I came to tell you."

"What? That you're sorry you kidnapped my wife? Killed Leon?"

"Shut up for a minute and listen," Hector gritted out. "I did something stupid. I nearly forgot that I gave it to him."

Migs stilled. His blood turning cold. "What did you do?"

"There's a way into the ranch from the tree line. I was with Leon when he was checking—"

"You didn't ..." he whispered.

"I thought ..." But his words were cut short.

Gunshots exploded from the house.

29

ARIANA DECIDED to give her husband some space. When he said he was going to mend fences, she thought she could take up Tessa's offer to show her the family album. Abbi Mena was still in her room—processing.

What a mess, but she was sure they would find a way to live with this truth.

This family loved hard, and Ariana had every faith in them to get through this. She sighed.

"Hey, did you hear me?" Tessa asked.

"What? Yes, I'm sorry." She looked at the picture Tessa was showing her. Miguel in a Batman costume.

"That's his first trick-or-treat. All little boys want to be Batman. I went as Princess Jasmine. Aladdin was big that year." Migs' sister looked at her again. "You're distracted."

"I'm sorry," she replied. "I thought I needed the distraction."

"We probably should go help the girls with dinner," Tessa said. "I'll check on—"

A scream tore through the house.

Tessa frowned. "Bella probably broke a nail."

But Ariana was tense. Hyper-vigilance was what Migs

called it, maybe even PTSD. The other woman glanced at her. "We better—"

More screams and yelling.

And voices of men that were not familiar in this household but were familiar to Ariana. Her heart raced and her breathing came in fast.

"What the hell?" Tessa muttered.

Two successive gunshots rang out.

"Oh my God, oh my God," Tessa whispered, all color leaving her face. "What's going on?"

Ariana sprang into action, dragging Tessa who had Gigi in her arms into the hobby room that adjoined the living room. She opened and closed closets rapidly until she found one with different quilts and crocheted blankets hanging in columns. "Stay here. And *por el amor de Dios*, keep Gigi quiet."

"Where are you—"

She shut the door on Tessa and hustled back to the living room and when she peeked into the hallway, a shadow in the darkness moved and grabbed her around the waist, spinning her so an arm was behind her back and another was pressed against her throat.

"Hola, *mamacita*, we meet again."

Silba.

The Whistler hauled her across the house like she was a rag doll. She was powerless against the cartel's most dangerous hitman. Her mind froze in horror when she saw a man face down on the portico. It was too dark to discern the color of the pool of liquid beneath the body, but it could only be blood.

Silba shoved her into the kitchen and she stumbled, falling on her knees where Cesar was prone on the floor, a map of red on his back. No sooner than a blink, fingers grabbed her hair and she was spun around, facing the women in the kitchen.

"You and your husband have cost me a lot of money,"

Benito's menacing voice said in her ear. She could smell the stench of his breath—coffee, cigarettes, and pungent food. "For payback, and for fun, we're going to make it hurt. And they"—he pointed to abuelita and Delia, who were tied to chairs and silently crying—"are going to blame him for this nightmare for the rest of his miserable life."

"*Jefe*," one of his goons hurried into the kitchen. "*Están viniendo.*"

Migs!

"*Vámonos!*" Benito shoved her back to Silba and grabbed Bella from one of his men. "I'm going to start with you."

She, Lettie, and Bella were dragged out the kitchen door, the older women looking on helplessly.

Benito had four men with him.

Ariana was tossed over a shoulder and their abductors started running. Benito was laughing and sounded as high as a kite. That could work to their advantage. Unfortunately, Silba appeared stone-cold sober and had his wits about him. She listened to the cartel boss rage about how he was going to rape them, and they would spend the rest of their lives in one of his brothels because they were too old to sell to his human trafficking clients.

"Too bad the twins aren't around," Benito said. "They might make me some money. I have customers who would pay a fortune for twins even if they're not sixteen."

Sick bastard.

Her ribs were in agony as she continued to bounce on Silba's shoulder. Finally, the *sicario* lowered her and she recognized the stream that Migs took her to for their first picnic. Under the bough of the ancient tree were several ATVs. Was this how they came in? A sick feeling sunk to her gut.

Three women against five men, and one of them was a known *sicario*. *How are they going to get away?*

"Ariana!" Migs' furious roar ripped through the night.

"Bella!"

"Lettie!"

A knife appeared by her throat. "Scream and I cut out your tongue. Now get on the ATV."

"No!" It was Bella who screamed, fighting Benito. "I'm not going. Just kill me here."

Shit, Bella. Ariana glanced frantically around for a weapon to use. Anything. She'd seen Silba's gun behind his jeans, but he was fast.

"Do you have her, *Jefe*?" Silba asked warily. It was subtle, but Ariana caught the unease in his tone. Far from the calculating cartel capo he was, it seemed this last blow the CIA dealt Benito made him a loose cannon. His own hitman wasn't trusting his boss's judgment.

"I have her, *estúpido*," Benito spat and drew his gun, pointing it at Bella's head. "I will put a bullet through your head, and I will fuck you even when you're dead! Now, get up."

A commotion broke out between Lettie and her captor. One of the goons went to help him, laughing at his narco buddy for not being able to handle a tiny woman.

Benito continued pacing in front of a stubborn Bella, his hands in his hair, gripping them in frustration as he spewed threats against her.

Silba cursed and stalked toward his boss to settle the matter, and that was when Ariana stuck out her foot, tripping the *sicario* who landed hard on his knees. As Silba tried to get up, Ariana dove for the rock she'd seen and swung it toward his head, ending with a sickening thud. He fell forward, groaning, and she took that opportunity to steal his gun, managing to evade his blind attempts to grab her.

When the fifth man rushed over to help Silba, several things happened simultaneously.

A gun went off.

Lettie screamed for everyone to run.

Bella shrieked.

Benito went down.

The fifth man got distracted and that was when Ariana shot him.

"Run!" Lettie screamed again just as another shot was fired.

The three women converged on the incline. She heard voices of men in front of her. Their freedom only seconds away.

Lettie scrambled up first.

Bella kept sliding, unable to get purchase.

Ariana's injured foot couldn't gain traction, pressure on it sending a jolt of pain up her leg.

A hand gripped her ankle and dragged her whole body with it.

She was flipped on her back, and she caught a flash of steel heading straight for her heart.

This was it.

Her life flashed before her as Silba's silhouette was the last thing she'd see in this world before he killed her.

MIGS FLOORED THE GAS, the Bronco barely gaining maximum speed before he braked in front of the house and jumped out the vehicle. The urge to burst into the house was strong, but he fell back into his training and waited for Lenox and his men to catch up.

He flattened against the wall beside the door. Lenox took position on the other side and tossed him an earpiece.

"Wear this," the DEA agent ordered. "You know the drill." The man knew like the last time it would be useless to tell him to stand down.

Migs stepped back and kicked the door, and their team stormed in.

They split up to search the house. Lenox and two other

agents went with Migs toward the kitchen, alternating between leading and providing cover as they hit each corner. His jaw clenched as he recognized Crispin sprawled on the portico.

"Check him," Lenox told one of his men. They had called for an ambulance when they first heard the gunshots.

No matter how many times he'd been on this road before, the fear of losing Ariana was a struggle to contain. He had to call on the soldier and not the husband once again, as he took his first step into the kitchen.

And almost lost it.

Blood, so much blood.

Tessa, valiantly keeping pressure on Cesar's bloody back, raised tear-streaked and anguished eyes to him. His eyes went to his mother who was carrying Gigi and turned away from the carnage in the kitchen.

"Miguel," his sister whispered.

"Help's coming," he said grimly. "Which way?"

With her good arm, Abbi Mena pointed to the fields. "They took Ariana and your sisters. Get them back, Miguel. Please."

Migs was already sprinting out to the patio and into the fields.

"Ariana!"

"Bella!"

"Lettie!"

He had to give them hope that help was not far away. Lenox and his men stopped beside him and listened.

"No!"

It was faint, but he knew where it was coming from.

"There!" He pointed. They were at the stream.

Migs ran ahead of everyone, thankful for the last rays of the setting sun.

A gunshot echoed in the clearing and his legs broke into a dead run.

His familiarity with the land had him flying over the terrain as the others struggled to keep up. By the time he reached the embankment, his pulse was pounding in his ears and his lungs were about to burst, not from the effort of the run, but from the effort to restrain his fears. Movement in his peripheral vision had him swiveling his neck to the right.

"Help them!" Lettie cried.

And that was when he saw, the glint of the blade getting ready to plunge into the woman he loved.

Gun raised, sprinting forward, he plugged the motherfucker with successive rounds until the man fell on his back.

He slid to his ass beside Ariana, weapon aimed at Benito Carillo.

"Don't!" Lenox shouted. "Walker. Don't shoot!"

Breathing hard, his finger tightened on the trigger.

"We need him!"

He glanced down at Ariana. "How many were there?"

"Five," she whispered, lying on her back and breathing just as heavily as he was.

"We have three either wounded or dead." An agent shouted further from the hill where they sat.

"You have all of them," Migs told Lenox. "Ariana said there were five men."

Lenox cuffed Benito, who was hunkered down in a weird way.

Bella stomped over to the cartel lord and slapped him across the face.

"Here's the last one!" She screamed and kicked him in the nuts.

The once feared Benito Carillo crumbled like a pile of bricks, leaving Lenox speechless, if not a bit amused.

"I have to say, Walker. Your women are vicious."

Lettie ran down the incline and the sisters hugged.

"Fierce," he corrected, pushing to his feet and helping Ariana up. He hugged her tightly as all the tension and the fear he'd kept inside leaked out like he'd been shot a hundred times. His hand, that had been steady holding his weapon, was now trembling as he brushed away strands of hair from her face. "You know," he said as emotion clogged his throat. "I don't know if I can ever let you out of my sight again."

"I know," she whispered. "I seem to get into trouble when you're not around."

"Ariana ..." he said achingly and lowered his head to kiss her.

But as usual, his sisters thwarted his plans.

"Miguel! Miguel!" He turned and caught Bella and Lettie in the security of his arms. And after quick hugs amidst sobs of relief, the four of them hurried home to check on their injured.

30

THREE DAYS later

"No. Move him this way."

"Ouch."

"Fix the pillows on his back."

"Ouch."

"Cesar, are you okay?" Tessa asked.

"I will be, once you all stop fussing over me," Cesar grumbled, wincing as he tried to get comfortable against the pillows.

Migs bit back a smile, standing back to let his sister take over. Tessa and Cesar were moving in temporarily with the rest of the Alcantara-Walker family while his brother-in-law recuperated from his gunshot wounds. Their injured security guy, Crispin, was in the other room. Pops and Ariana helped settle him in at what was now known as the infirmary section because their rooms were across from Abbi Mena's. Tactically, it made it easier to handle their needs and, his abuelita, despite the cast on her arm, still ruled with an iron fist.

"Stop complaining," Abbi Mena said, standing by the

door and looking into the room with satisfaction. "You scared the crap out of us, bleeding out in my kitchen."

Everyone laughed except Cesar.

He was trying not to because any movement originating from his upper torso hurt. "Don't make me laugh," Cesar grimaced. "And thanks for your concern. Though I'm not sure whether your concern is for the floor or me."

Abbi Mena's brow rose. "Don't be a smart ass."

Tessa's jaw dropped and Migs snorted a chuckle.

"What?" their grandmother said. "Surprised I can curse like the rest of you? After what this family has been through, I earned it. We've earned it."

Everyone's faces turned solemn. It had been a challenging few days. Cesar and Crispin each had to undergo two surgeries for their wounds that hit their shoulders and torsos in fairly identical spots. Migs figured it was Silba who'd done it—it was his MO. Well, that motherfucker was dead. The two men Lettie shot survived and even if Migs wished they'd ended up with Silba's fate, he didn't wish that burden on his sister. As for the man Ariana shot and killed, his wife seemed to be handling the onus on that well. In some ways he and Ariana were the same. Though Migs grew up in a loving family, he chose to mix into the dregs of the cartel. As for his wife, she had no choice. She was born into it, and now, he was glad he could share his family with her.

"Yes, we did," Migs said.

His grandmother slid her gaze to him. "Still shouldn't use the Lord's name in vain."

"Understood, Abbi Mena," he responded instantly.

Her eyes narrowed. "You and I know you can't help it."

He walked toward her and kissed the top of her head. "That's right, but you'll forgive me anyway."

"*Sí, mijo*," his grandmother sighed. "Now go check if Delia and the rest of the girls have dinner ready. We need to feed the invalids."

Cesar groaned. "Please let there be carnitas. I'm tired of jello."

Migs left the room, chuckling as he ducked into Crispin's room, and rapped on the open door. Ariana was fixing the pillows behind his back just like Tessa was doing for Cesar. "Everything all right in here? The general asked me to check on the sick."

Ariana gave him a smile and a salute.

"Where's Pops?"

"He got a call. I think a visitor."

Migs frowned and backed away from the room.

His phone buzzed and he slid it out to look at the screen. Recognizing the number from Nadia, he walked the opposite direction to get to a French door that led to the flower fields of Abbie Mena's garden.

"Walker."

"Patching you through," came Nadia's clipped response.

He held his breath. Garrison. His handler and the entire team had arrived at the American Embassy two days before. The news wasn't making the headlines, but from what Migs had gathered, this was causing a big headache for the State Department.

"Walker?" John's tired voice came over the line.

"Motherfucker," Migs murmured. "Fucking glad to hear from you."

"Missed me?"

"More like worried. You guys out?"

"About to board the plane for the fucking USA," John said.

"Everyone okay?"

"A bit worse for wear, but we'll survive." There was a pregnant pause and then. "So Carillo went for you guys, huh?"

"Yeah."

"Benito was desperate. He messed with the wrong arms dealers. Maybe Andrade made a good move."

"He kidnapped an American citizen," Migs reminded him.

"We'll sort that out when I return. Just wanted to let you know we're on our way back."

"You in trouble?"

John chuckled. "You mean we? Don't worry. I doubt they'll banish you to Antarctica. Not when you handed Benito to the DEA."

They ended the call soon after. Neither of them were fond of using phone conversations or text messages to exchange sensitive information despite the full encryption on their devices.

Remembering that Pops had a visitor, he headed to the foyer and was shocked at what he saw.

Or who.

What the hell was Hector doing here?

He and his father were arguing in hushed tones.

"You have some nerve showing up here," Migs growled as he stalked toward his cousin. "What the fuck do you want? And how the hell are you walking around scott-free?"

"Hardly scott-free." Hector raised a pant leg to reveal a device around his ankle. "And a DEA agent drove me here."

"You're under house arrest?" Migs scoffed.

"I deserve more than that," Hector said quietly. "No. I'm helping the DEA with a few things." His mouth turned down slightly. "History repeating itself, huh?"

At the reminder of Tio Pepito, Miguel's initial anger lessened, but he refused to let the guilt weigh him down anymore.

"You haven't answered why you're here."

"I've never apologized to Abbi Mena and Ariana."

Migs' situation with Tio Pepito was different. He didn't want his cousin anywhere near his wife after what he'd done, but who was he to deny forgiveness to his cousin. It wasn't his to give.

"Hector?"

Migs clenched his jaw at the sound of his grandmother's voice.

"Abuelita," Hector said quietly, his eyes glazing. "*Lo siento*, Abbi Mena."

Their grandmother passed Migs and, after Hector cast him a brief glance, he moved forward to embrace her.

Drew walked over to Migs and gave his shoulder a brief squeeze.

Abbi Mena and Hector went to the sitting room, his cousin openly crying now as he continued to ask for his grandmother's forgiveness.

Would he even doubt Abbi Mena would forgive Hector?

No. Because she forgave Migs for Tio Pepito.

There was no bringing back his uncle or Leon, but Migs sure hoped Hector would make up for what he'd done.

"What the …?" Ariana appeared beside him and clutched his hand. "What's he doing here?"

"He wants to apologize to you and Abbi Mena." He eyed her warily. "You okay with that?"

Emotions played on his wife's face. "Honestly? It's too soon." She glanced up at Migs. "You okay with that?"

Migs smiled, relieved. The last thing he wanted was to force his wife to simply get over being kidnapped to appease his family. Honesty was what was needed.

He hugged her close. "Totally fine with that, babe."

———

HECTOR DIDN'T STAY LONG. For one thing, he was under DEA custody still and that didn't allow him to behave as a free man. His one condition to help the federal agency was to see his grandmother. It was evident that it tore him up inside that his abuelita was hurt because of his greed and idiocy. As for Ariana, her answer was clear. She left Migs at the foyer and made her way to the kitchen without talking to Hector.

Ariana was busy sorting the herbs and vegetables from the garden when Abbi Mena walked into the kitchen with Migs and Drew. The men's faces were neutral, and it was hard to tell what transpired, but the older woman's peaceful countenance gave Ariana her own gratification. That was further solidified when Abbi Mena walked up to her, took her hand and gave it a squeeze.

No words.

Just a squeeze.

Delia and Migs' sisters looked at them questioningly.

"What's going on?" Miguel's mother asked.

"Hector came by," Abbi Mena said, her gaze sweeping across the curious faces among them. "He wanted to apologize."

Those curious faces turned to ones of anger, and then their eyes flew to Ariana.

"You okay with this?" Bella gritted out.

"His apology was to your grandmother," Ariana said. "I wasn't ready."

"Neither are we," Delia said furiously. "What he did to Leon—"

"Benito had him on a tight leash," Migs interjected. "Those men came from Carillo and acted independently. That's according to him. I have yet to confirm."

"And that makes it better?" Lettie put in her two cents. "Let's not forget he handed that asshole the keys to our backyard."

Abbi Mena held up her good arm. "Enough. Hector isn't expecting instant forgiveness. I see his remorse, but he will pay for it. Will it be enough to satisfy our outrage?" She shrugged. "Only time will tell. I've lost one son already to the narcos, I'm just glad I won't be losing a grandson as well." She exhaled heavily. "Hector will not be getting off lightly. If he did, I'll find a way to put him in jail myself. Now"—her eyes took on a steely gaze

—"We've got two patients in need of care. Is their food ready?"

And just like that, Abbi Mena turned everyone's attention back to the immediate priority. Outraged feelings were set on the back burner and the Alacantara-Walker family worked together to care for their patients. Lettie offered to take over Crispin's care for the night. Bella was babysitting Gigi while Tessa looked after Cesar.

After dinner, Abbi Mena and Delia shooed Ariana and Migs away from the kitchen, telling them that everything was being handled.

When they arrived at the wing of their bedroom, Ariana looked up at her husband. "Have you noticed they've been constantly pushing us to go to bed early?"

Migs chuckled. "The same way abuelita keeps on asking us when we're giving her a great grandbaby?"

Heat crept up her cheeks and Ariana glanced away. "That too."

She could feel his gaze scorching the top of her head, but she didn't say anything even when they went inside the room. Did she want a baby? Did he?

Migs pushed her up against the wall beside the threshold, arms caging her in. "Look at me, Ari."

She raised her chin.

"What do you say? Should we go for it?"

Ariana didn't even pretend to misunderstand him. "Have a baby together?"

"Yes."

She bit her bottom lip, thinking, and after a few seconds, she said, "Are we ready?"

Migs laughed. "Looks like the family is ready."

"But aren't we moving back to LA? What about your job?" And her own. After spending time with Abbi Mena, she was rethinking the business model for a new clinic.

"We'll work something out." A muffled noise of doors

opening and closing reached them through the thick walls and Migs winced. "We'll need to find a place of our own and soon."

Ariana raised her arms and wrapped them around his neck. "But I will miss your family."

"Hmm ...sometimes I wonder if you love me because of my family or just me."

She laughed. "Oh, are you fishing for compliments?"

"No. Now, tell me again," he murmured, his lips a hair's breadth away, and the effect on her girly parts was immediate. Yet it was her heart that beat with what he needed to hear.

"So needy and bossy," she whispered, and he rocked his hips against her, and his hardness made her more eager to let him have the words.

"I love you, Miguel Alcantara Walker."

His eyes smoldered and his fingers shifted under her butt and boosted her up. "Now let's get you pregnant, Mrs. Walker."

And he proceeded to show her how.

EPILOGUE

Two Months later

"Oh no."

Ariana rushed to the bathroom and hugged the porcelain bowl. It was the third time that morning. Of all the days to get sick, why did it have to be today?

She could blame the party Migs' sisters threw for her the night before.

A soothing hand rubbed her back.

"I told Bella those oysters looked suspect," Delia said.

"Yes, it's not as if Ari and Migs need them," Lettie added.

"*Mi amor*," Delia chided. "Not helping."

"But Migs thought it was a great idea," Bella defended. "He said Ari loves them."

"Ari loves oysters probably because our brother convinced her that she did." Tessa's voice joined the conversation. "Remember he convinced her to go to a taqueria on the first date? Is she feeling better?"

"She doesn't look any better to me," Lettie said.

"I think her color is better," Delia contradicted her daughter.

"Maybe she needs something bubbly," Pat announced.

Dios mio. Can't someone have some privacy while she's dying in front of the toilet, Ariana thought.

"Oooh, what's in all those glasses?" Bella asked.

"Peach mimosa." The self-appointed bartender of the family announced with flare. "It's one of my best ones yet. Right, Cora?"

"It's yummy," her twin said. "Yes, the fruitiness and bubbly might help with your nausea, Ari."

Ariana dry-heaved again as Migs' family devolved into a multi-pronged discussion of her predicament as though she was an intriguing science experiment.

"Uhm, should we tell Migs and Father Tomas that we're going to be late?" Tessa asked. "I know Cesar said they're on their way to the chapel."

"Maybe postpone until eleven," Bella said. "Why didn't we just have it in the evening? The reception is at night anyway."

"Something about schedules," Lettie said. "Everyone seemed to want this particular Saturday, and it's not like it was such short notice."

"I think," Delia said. "This nausea is temporary."

Her stomach begged to disagree, but Ariana was coming to the same conclusion herself.

And it appeared from the sudden silence, so did everyone else.

"You don't mean—" Lettie started.

"Oh my God." Pat.

"Oh, wow." Cora.

"Way to go, *hermano*." Bella.

"When was your last period, Ari?" Tessa asked.

Kill me now, Ariana groaned.

"Everyone out," Abbi Mena's voice was a welcome one in

the suddenly crowded bathroom. "None of you are making this any easier. Cora, open the windows in the bedroom, it's stuffy in here. Bella, call Cesar and explain that we're going to be an hour late and have Father Tomas move the schedule to eleven. That's still an available time, we'll just have to push lunch an hour later."

Ariana sat back on her haunches and accepted the wet towel from Miguel's mother and wiped her face. "I think I'm pregnant."

Delia and Abbi Mena nodded solemnly; their smile serene.

"That's why I made you ginger tea," Abbi Mena said. "Come on, don't want to keep your husband waiting."

———————

"I'm glad you and Ariana decided to receive God's blessing," Father Tomas told Migs. They were standing in front of the San Lazaro Chapel located in a small park near the ranch. It was frequently used for weddings because of the adjoining botanical gardens and the Spanish-Mexican architecture of the surrounding buildings. As the *padre* continued lecturing him about the sanctity of marriage, which he would probably hear again in the sermon, his gaze narrowed at Cesar. His brother-in-law had taken a call from Bella during which he had to walk away.

It didn't help his suspicion when Cesar cast Migs surreptitious glances. It further didn't lessen his anxiety when Cesar caught his stare, winced, and looked away.

What the hell was Migs worried about? Ariana was already his wife. This was a mere formality to appease his family.

But more than anything, he wanted to give her a proper wedding. But after what happened at Abbi Mena's birthday, and even if Benito Carillo was rotting in jail somewhere, everyone was still understandably wary of holding a big celebration.

That suited Migs and Ariana perfectly.

In the end, the celebration this evening consisted of the Alcantara-Walker family and a few friends. The only family visiting was Joaquín who would be arriving via a convoy of three SUVs. His cousin told him Elena wasn't coming, but he was bringing with him more security guys.

Cesar had ended his call and was walking back to them.

"What's going on?" Migs asked.

His brother-in-law turned to the priest. "Bella asked to push the ceremony to eleven."

Father Tomas frowned. "That's fine, but is everything all right?"

"Yes, Cesar," Migs gritted. "Why didn't they call me?"

"Ariana is running late, and Bella didn't want to call you because you would want to talk to your wife and delay her further."

"That wasn't Bella's decision," Migs growled.

"No, it was a directive from Abbi Mena."

Migs swore under his breath, whipped out his phone and called Ariana while he paced the chapel's entrance.

It was Bella who answered.

"She's fine," his sister said.

"What happened?"

"Period cramps," Bella chirped.

"Fuck," Migs muttered. "She has terrible ones. She doesn't like meds."

"Duh, we know. Abbi Mena already made her ginger tea. She's feeling better."

"Make her a hot water bottle. Shit. Maybe I should come home."

"Don't you dare!" Bella screeched. "We have this handled."

"Miguel," Tessa's stern voice came over the line. "We've

got this. She's showered and we're all getting her ready for you. Why don't you stroll in the botanical garden?"

"I don't want to take a stroll in the botanical garden."

"Well, you need to chill."

The line went dead.

Migs would have uttered a crisp expletive if he hadn't remembered he was at a chapel in the presence of the man who'd given him his first communion.

"Ah, Miguelito," Father Tomas said with a knowing look. "I believe you have this marriage thing well in hand. I doubt you will need my sermon. I've known you since you were a boy." He gave a pleased smile. "Now I see a man who loves his wife very much. You were always in Abbi Mena's prayers, her intentions. She always lit a candle for you and Pepito."

At the mention of his uncle, his chest twitched. It wasn't guilt, but a feeling of bittersweet acceptance.

Father Tomas sighed. "She told me she was at peace with Pepito. Now there's Hector she's praying for."

Migs caught the muscle jumping at Cesar's jaw. With the exception of Abbi Mena, the Alcantara-Walkers had not forgiven Hector yet. It was going to take a while.

"Come, maybe we can wait at the administrative office," Father Tomas offered.

"If you don't mind, maybe I will take their advice and walk." He turned to Cesar. "Stay here and wait for Pops. I know he's on his way, too."

MIGS WAS thankful that the botanical garden was a short distance from the chapel. The daytime temperatures were in the low seventies and he took off his jacket. It was a new suit. His last one didn't survive the wreckage of the country club. There were no matching entourage clothes, thank fuck. He doubted the men of the household would be tolerating fittings as they had for Abbi Mena's party. But Ariana insisted on new clothes and all the women were enthusiastic about them, especially Bella who immediately suggested several designers.

For Migs, he didn't care what he wore, because his vows came from his heart and not the way he looked in a suit. He thought back to when they first got married. Deep down he admitted the vows had been real for him. When he offered Ariana the protection of the Alcantara name, his word had been absolute, unwavering. Migs wasn't surprised he'd been ready to stay married to Ariana forever.

Only Ariana.

His One.

A bird warbled overhead, and Migs checked the time on the phone impatiently. Not ten minutes had gone by and he resisted the urge to call his wife. Sighing, he walked further ahead until he came onto a wooden arched bridge. Below him were water lilies and ducks floating along a man-made pond. He leaned against the railing and stared at his distorted reflection in the water.

They were moving back to LA in a few days. Actually, they'd been back and forth in the past two months with Migs diving back into the fray of terrorism threats, and Ari scouting locations for her new clinic. She and Connie had worked out their differences and remained friends, but it was Connie herself who said it was better if she didn't work for Ariana anymore.

Migs couldn't agree more with that assessment. Once that kind of trust was lost, it was hard to regain.

This last trip though was about closing on their first house together and Ariana finally putting hers on the market.

His fingers moved to his phone again, but he lowered his arm and bent forward, arms resting on the rail of the bridge. He decided to occupy his mind with steps to wean them from his family. He could see how Ariana loved them, but he also knew she was eager to start a life with him away from his meddlesome family.

A smile kicked up the corners of his mouth. Meddlesome, yes, but they showed his wife what it meant to belong to a family who loved fiercely. He could never thank them enough for opening Ari's heart to trust people again despite her past. He recalled her talking to Abbi Mena about her plans once she returned to LA.

Migs didn't know how long he'd been lost in his thoughts when a flash of movement on his right made him turn his head.

Ariana appeared, and he damned near swallowed his tongue. He hadn't seen the dress. The women had hidden it from him. All Bella told him was that it was a tea-length gown … whatever that meant.

Seeing her now, gorgeous in a bare-shouldered number that emphasized her tiny waist and flared out in voluminous layers of mesh fabric, Migs could only blink. And blink again.

"Hi," Ariana's husky voice jolted him out of his trance.

He strode forward, checking his phone to see if he had missed a call or a text. He hadn't.

"You're here." His voice was hoarse. He was confused why she wasn't waiting in the car and he had a sinking feeling in his gut that he had fucked up his purpose of making this wedding day better than their original one.

However, the expression on her face, her lips that had shaped into a smile on a face full of tenderness and adoration, told him he was missing a piece of the puzzle.

Migs swallowed the ball of emotion lodged in his throat. "You could have texted me. You didn't have to walk."

They were face to face, toe to toe, gazes searching deep within each other.

"Miguel, you were always the one coming for me. The one always saving me," she said. Her eyes shimmering with love. "It was time I came for you, too. I love you, Miguel Alcantara Walker."

She tipped her chin up for his kiss.

He didn't disappoint.

IT WAS WELL past midnight when they made it into the bridal suite at the Westin hotel. After Ariana's unsettled morning, the rest of the day went off without a hitch. Close family were at hand when she and Miguel exchanged their vows at the San Lazaro chapel. It was followed by a family lunch at a restaurant before the guests started arriving at the ranch. There was excellent food and Abbi Mena finally got the entertainment she wanted for her birthday. Ariana and Miguel started off the dancing with the Tango and the rest of the grandchildren followed. In a way, they ended up combining the two affairs and, for Ariana, it became more meaningful. That after the challenges of the past few months they came out on top with these blessings.

And hopefully there would be one more.

Ariana was glad her wooziness was confined to the morning, which gave her renewed anticipation for their wedding night for more than one reason.

For good measure, she avoided alcohol.

The send-off from the Alcantara-Walker family was boisterous, although as Migs drove them away in the Audi, there was a bit of poignancy as she watched the ranch lights fade in the distance. They would be seeing the family again for breakfast the next morning, but the ranch had been her home for almost three months.

"Ah, alone at last," Migs said as he dumped his keys on the bureau and wheeled in their suitcase for the night—mostly Ariana's stuff. Thankfully, her husband was already used to her propensity of not traveling lightly and barely raised a brow when she insisted on using the biggest suitcase for their overnight stay.

As the door to their suite swung shut, he gathered her into

his arms, and Ariana rested her head on his chest. "You okay?" he asked.

"Yes. Today went well, didn't it? Despite the delay this morning."

Migs leaned away and tipped her chin up. "Usually you're down for the day when that happens. I guess Abbi Mena's tea worked well."

She smiled. "Bella lied, Migs."

His brows cinched together as his hands moved to her shoulders, gripping them. "What do you mean? Is something else wrong with you?"

"I wouldn't say something is wrong with me." She gently extracted herself from his arms and walked over to her purse, extracting a brown bag. And from that paper bag, she lifted an elongated box.

Turning to face her husband, Ariana almost laughed at the expression on his face. Jaw slackened, brows drawn deeper, eyes focused on what she had in her hands.

"Is that ..." he started, visibly swallowing as his gaze captured hers. "You're pregnant?"

Ariana shrugged. "I don't know for sure yet. The Marias and Mamá wanted to find out, but I knew I wanted to do this with you."

He reeled her into his embrace. "Ariana," he rasped. "Thank you."

"What? We don't know yet."

Migs' eyes searched her face. She could feel his heart pounding where she had her palm on his chest. "It doesn't matter what the result is," he said. "You know that, right? But this ... the act of doing this together ... it's strangely exciting and ... terrifying."

Ariana laughed because she was feeling exactly the same way. "Let's do this then." It was a wonder she was functional at the reception when her mind had been straying to what might or might not be growing in her belly.

Five minutes later, they were standing at the door leading to the bathroom, staring at a stick—several actually—that were laying on the counter beside the sink. Delia must have purchased all the pregnancy tests that were in the pharmacy.

She realized she was gripping Migs' fingers tightly, probably cutting off circulation to them, but her man didn't complain. He never did.

"Well," he said, staring at his watch. "It's over five minutes. We should know, right?"

"Yes," she whispered. Ariana didn't realize how much she wanted the test to be positive until this moment. This day had been surreal. So many things had gone wrong in her life she was almost afraid to take a step. Migs must have sensed her trepidation and urged her forward.

They looked.

Ariana exhaled a tremulous breath.

Two pink lines. All of them.

She puffed a breathless laugh. Her husband had already swept her into his arms and was carrying her into the bedroom. He laid her gently on the mattress and followed, looming above her, bracing his arms on either side of her.

"Miguel …"

He stole her breath with a ferocious kiss. Migs pulled back and stared down at her, his eyes flaring with emotions Ariana couldn't describe. Love, adoration, and passion.

"We're pregnant," he growled with an absolute fierceness that made her quiver. His hands worked between them and somehow she lost her panties and he was sliding inside her. "We're celebrating."

She rounded him with her limbs, but she could tell he was holding back. Smiling, she whispered, "You're not going to hurt the baby if you pump harder."

"Fuck," he groaned, and he sank into her in slow, deliberate thrusts that somehow felt deeper than ever. Exhilaration swept straight to her core. He started kissing her again, not abating, receiving her cries of orgasm in a way that he let her know that those unequivocally belonged to him and him alone.

When Migs reached his peak, he tore his mouth away and grunted into her neck. He slowly rocked into her kissing her ear, her jaw, and then her lips before looking into her eyes.

Ariana spoke first, "That was some celebration."

"Yeah?" he answered. "You just made me the happiest man alive."

She beamed at him. "You make me happy, too."

"I love you, Ari."

*** THE END***

Thank you for reading! If you liked this book, please consider leaving a review. It's much appreciated!

Antonio and Charly's story is next in THE BOSS ASSIGNMENT.

If you want more Gabby and Declan, download this short story, Second Chance Baby !

AFTERWORD

One of the challenges of Protector of Convenience was considering which foreign words to italicize and which ones to accent. I've agonized over this during the proofreading stage, but I finally decided to err on the side of readability. Italics and accents make the eyes weary, so although there were words that could have used the accent marks or italics, I left them out. There were no hard and fast rules on this and a book on copyediting suggested not italicizing when it's Spanglish.

The town of Cayetano is fictitious, but it was based on the town of Tancítaro which is a municipality in Michoacán. It really did rise up against the cartels and formed its own paramilitary force. Another article about green gold causing war and violence in Mexico was featured in the LA Times and provided a springboard for the plot. All the cartels in this book are fictitious.

This was one of the fastest books I've ever written. I wrote the first draft in six weeks. The bulk of that happened in May when I decided to shake off the lockdown blues and get my writing mojo back into gear. But as usual, it did take me some time to clean up the draft and prepare the manuscript for publishing.

The final polish of this manuscript wouldn't be possible without my wonderful book tribe.

A big thanks to my developmental editor, Geri. As always,

you're a great sounding board for my ideas by helping me expand on its possibilities. I love that you encourage me to overwrite since I'm technically a sparse writer while promising to ground me if I ever do get on the crazy train. A few books in and we've hit our stride. I look forward to all our brainstorming sessions and enjoy our impromptu book chats.

Special thanks to my editor Kristan Roetker. I love how you "get" me and my writing. I'm always confident that whenever I send you my work it'll be in great hands. I also love our random daily chats about books, life, and everything in between.

To Sue, thank you for your continued support over the years. I look forward to sending you my manuscript each time for your fabulous feedback and suggestions. I'm constantly impressed by your command of the English language and I know whenever I would massacre an idiom or slang, you would always set me straight. ;)

Thank you to Dana Curtlett-Dunphy of A Book Nerd Edits for your excellent proofreading skills and turning this around quickly for me.

Thank you to Penelope Croci for finding time in your busy schedule to give my manuscript a critical eye and double-check my Spanish. I appreciate the great suggestions or alternatives you've given that enhance the authenticity in certain scenes that called for them.

To Debra of Buoni Amici Press. Thank you for being on top of author-related stuff so I can spend most of my time writing.

I absolutely love my readers! Special mention to my **Very Important Paige** readers and book bloggers/bookstagrammers who continue to read/review my work. Thank you for letting me write what I want as long as I promise that HEA.

And lastly, thanks to the hubby for understanding the importance of my writing time, and Loki for his snuggles whenever mom needs a break and a hug. Both of you are everything that this author needs to thrive and I love you endlessly for it.

CONNECT WITH THE AUTHOR

Find me at:

Facebook: Victoria Paige Books
Website: victoriapaigebooks.com
Email: victoriapaigebooks@gmail.com
FB Reader Group: Very Important Paige readers

facebook.com/victoriapaigebooks

tiktok.com/@vpaigebooks

twitter.com/vpaigebooks

instagram.com/victoriapaigebooks

ALSO BY VICTORIA PAIGE

Rogue Protectors
The Ex Assignment

Protector of Convenience

The Boss Assignment

Her Covert Protector

The Wife Assignment

Guardians
Fire and Ice

Beneath the Fire (novella)

Silver Fire

Smoke and Shadows

Susan Stoker Special Forces World
Reclaiming Izabel (novella)

Guarding Cindy (novella)

Protecting Stella (novella)

Always
It's Always Been You

Always Been Mine

A Love For Always

Misty Grove
Fighting Chance

Saving Grace

Unexpected Vows

Standalone

De Lucci's Obsession

Deadly Obsession

Captive Lies

The Princess and the Mercenary

* All series books can be read as standalone

Made in the USA
Las Vegas, NV
27 July 2023

75299910R00204